D1197955

"Macomber is a master at pulling heartstrings, and readers will delight in this heartwarming story of friendship, love, and second chances. Leanne, Nichole, Rocco, and Nikolai will renew your faith in love and hope. The perfect read curled up in front of the fire or on a beach, it's as satisfying as a slice of freshly baked bread—wholesome, pleasantly filling, and delicious."

—KAREN WHITE, *New York Times* bestselling author of *Flight Patterns*

"Beloved author Debbie Macomber reaches new heights in this wise and beautiful novel. It's the kind of reading experience that comes along only rarely, bearing the hallmarks of a classic. The timeless wisdom in these pages will stay with you long after the book is closed."

—SUSAN WIGGS, #1 *New York Times* bestselling author of *Starlight on Willow Lake*

"Debbie dazzles! A wonderful story of friendship, forgiveness, and the power of love. I devoured every page!"

—SUSAN MALLERY, #1 *New York Times* bestselling author of *The Friends We Keep*

## Last One Home

"Fans of bestselling author Macomber will not be disappointed by this compelling stand-alone novel." —*Library Journal*

"Family, forgiveness and second chances are the themes in Macomber's latest stand-alone novel. No one writes better women's contemporary fiction, and *Last One Home* is another wonderful example. Always inspiring and heartwarming, this is a read you will cherish." —*RT Book Reviews*

"Tender, real, and full of hope."
—*Heroes and Heartbreakers*

"Once again, Ms. Macomber has woven a charming tale dealing with facing life's hard knocks, begging forgiveness, and gaining self-confidence."
—*Reader to Reader*

"Macomber never disappoints me. . . . She always manages to leave me with a warming of the soul and fuzzy feelings that stay for days."
—*Fresh Fiction*

"A very heartwarming novel of healing and reconciliation . . . that touches on life's more serious moments and [will leave readers] hoping to revisit these flawed but lovable characters in the future."
—*Book Reviews & More by Kathy*

# Rose Harbor

## *Silver Linings*

"A heartwarming, feel-good story from beginning to end . . . No one writes stories of love and forgiveness like Macomber." —*RT Book Reviews*

"Macomber's homespun storytelling style makes reading an easy venture. . . . She also tosses in some hidden twists and turns that will delight her many longtime fans." —*Bookreporter*

"Reading Macomber's novels is like being with good friends, talking and sharing joys and sorrows." —*New York Journal of Books*

## *Love Letters*

"[Debbie] Macomber's mastery of women's fiction is evident in her latest. . . . [She] breathes life into each plotline, carefully intertwining her characters' stories to ensure that none of them overshadow the others. Yet it is her ability to capture different facets of emotion which will entrance fans and newcomers alike." —*Publishers Weekly*

"Romance and a little mystery abound in this third installment of Macomber's series set at Cedar Cove's Rose Harbor Inn. . . . Readers of Robyn Carr and Sherryl Woods will enjoy Macomber's latest, which will have them flipping pages until the end and eagerly anticipating the next installment."
        —*Library Journal* (starred review)

"Uplifting . . . a cliffhanger ending for Jo Marie begs for a swift resolution in the next book."
        —*Kirkus Reviews*

"Mending a broken heart is not always easy to do, but Macomber succeeds at this beautifully in *Love Letters*. . . . Quite simply, this is a refreshing take on most love stories—there are twists and turns in the plot that keep readers on their toes—and the author shares up slices of realism, allowing her audience to feel right at home as they follow a cast of familiar characters living in the small coastal town of Cedar Cove, where life is interesting, to say the least." —*Bookreporter*

"*Love Letters* is another wonderful story in the Rose Harbor series. Genuine life struggles with heartwarming endings for the three couples in this book make it special. Readers won't be able to get enough of Macomber's gentle storytelling. Fans already know what a charming place Rose Harbor is and new readers will love discovering it as well."
        —*RT Book Reviews* (4½ stars)

# Rose Harbor in Bloom

"[Debbie] Macomber uses warmth, humor and superb storytelling skills to deliver a tale that charms and entertains." —*BookPage*

"A wonderful reading experience . . . as [the characters'] stories unfold, you almost feel they have become friends."
—Wichita Falls *Times Record News*

"[Debbie Macomber] draws in threads of her earlier book in this series, *The Inn at Rose Harbor,* in what is likely to be just as comfortable a place for Macomber fans as for Jo Marie's guests at the inn."
—*The Seattle Times*

"Macomber's legions of fans will embrace this cozy, heartwarming read." —*Booklist*

"Readers will find the emotionally impactful storylines and sweet, redemptive character arcs for which the author is famous. Classic Macomber, which will please fans and keep them coming back for more." —*Kirkus Reviews*

"Macomber is an institution in women's fiction. Her principal talent lies in creating characters with a humble, familiar charm. They possess complex personalities, but it is their kinder qualities that are emphasized in the warm world of her novels—a world much like Rose Harbor Inn, in which one wants to curl up and stay." —*Shelf Awareness*

"The storybook scenery of lighthouses, cozy bed and breakfast inns dotting the coastline, and seagulls flying above takes readers on personal journeys of first love, lost love and recaptured love [presenting] love in its purest and most personal forms." —*Bookreporter*

"Just the right blend of emotional turmoil and satisfying resolutions . . . For a feel-good indulgence, this book delivers." —*RT Book Reviews* (4 stars)

## The Inn at Rose Harbor

"Debbie Macomber's Cedar Cove romance novels have a warm, comfy feel to them. Perhaps that's why they've sold millions." —*USA Today*

"No one tugs at readers' heartstrings quite as effectively as Macomber." —*Chicago Tribune*

"The characters and their various entanglements are sure to resonate with Macomber fans. . . . The book sets up an appealing milieu of townspeople and visitors that sets the stage for what will doubtless be many further adventures at the Inn at Rose Harbor." —*The Seattle Times*

"Debbie Macomber is the reigning queen of women's fiction." —*The Sacramento Bee*

"The prolific Macomber introduces a spin-off of sorts from her popular Cedar Cove series, still set in that fictional small town but centered on Jo Marie Rose, a youngish widow who buys and operates the bed and breakfast of the title. This clever premise allows Macomber to craft stories around the B&B's guests, Abby and Josh in this inaugural effort, while using Jo Marie and her ongoing recovery from the death of her husband Paul in Afghanistan as the series' anchor. . . . With her characteristic optimism, Macomber provides fresh starts for both." —*Booklist*

"Emotionally charged romance."
                    —*Kirkus Reviews*

## Blossom Street

### Blossom Street Brides

"[An] enjoyable read that pulls you right in from page one." —*Fresh Fiction*

"A master at writing stories that embrace both romance and friendship, [Debbie] Macomber can always be counted on for an enjoyable page-turner, and this Blossom Street installment is no exception." —*RT Book Reviews*

"A wonderful, love-affirming novel . . . an engaging, emotionally fulfilling story that clearly shows why [Macomber] is a peerless storyteller."
—*Examiner.com*

"Rewarding . . . Macomber amply delivers her signature engrossing relationship tales, wrapping her readers in warmth as fuzzy and soft as a hand-knitted creation from everyone's favorite yarn shop." —*Bookreporter*

"Fans will happily return to the warm, welcoming sanctuary of Macomber's Blossom Street, catching up with old friends from past Blossom Street books and meeting new ones being welcomed into the fold." —*Kirkus Reviews*

"Macomber's nondenominational-inspirational women's novel, with its large cast of characters, will resonate with fans of the popular series."
—*Booklist*

"*Blossom Street Brides* gives Macomber fans sympathetic characters who strive to make the right choices as they cope with issues that face many of today's women. Readers will thoroughly enjoy spending time on Blossom Street once again and watching as Lydia, Bethanne and Lauren struggle to solve their problems, deal with family crises, fall in love and reach their own happy endings."
—*BookPage*

## Starting Now

"Macomber has a masterful gift of creating tales that are both mesmerizing and inspiring, and her talent is at its peak with *Starting Now*. Her Blossom Street characters seem as warm and caring as beloved friends, and the new characters ease into the series smoothly. The storyline moves along at a lovely pace, and it is a joy to sit down and savor the world of Blossom Street once again."
—Wichita Falls *Times Record News*

"Macomber understands the often complex nature of a woman's friendships, as well as the emotional language women use with their friends."
—*NY Journal of Books*

"There is a reason that legions of Macomber fans ask for more Blossom Street books. They fully engage her readers as her characters discover happiness, purpose, and meaning in life. . . . Macomber's feel-good novel, emphasizing interpersonal relationships and putting people above status and objects, is truly satisfying."
—*Booklist* (starred review)

"Macomber's writing and storytelling deliver what she's famous for—a smooth, satisfying tale with characters her fans will cheer for and an arc that is cozy, heartwarming and ends with the expected happily-ever-after." —*Kirkus Reviews*

"Macomber's many fans are going to be over the moon with her latest Blossom Street novel. *Starting Now* combines Macomber's winning elements of romance and friendship, along with a search for one woman's life's meaning—all cozily bundled into a warmly satisfying story that is the very definition of 'comfort reading.'" —*Bookreporter*

"Macomber's latest Blossom Street novel is a sweet story that tugs on the heartstrings and hits on the joy of family, friends and knitting, as readers have come to expect." —*RT Book Reviews* (4½ stars)

"The return to Blossom Street is an engaging visit for longtime readers as old friends play secondary roles while newcomers take the lead. . . . Fans will enjoy the mixing of friends and knitting with many kinds of loving relationships."
—*Genre Go Round Reviews*

## Christmas Novels

### *Dashing Through the Snow*

"Wonderful and heartwarming . . . full of fun, laughter, and love." —*Romance Reviews Today*

"This Christmas romance from [Debbie] Macomber is both sweet and sincere."
—*Library Journal*

"There's just the right amount of holiday cheer. . . . This road-trip romance is full of high jinks and the kooky characters Macomber does so well."
—*RT Book Reviews*

## *Mr. Miracle*

"Macomber's Christmas novels are always something to cherish. *Mr. Miracle* is a sweet and innocent story that will lift your spirits during the holidays and throughout the year. Celebrating the comforts of home, family traditions, forgiveness and love, this is the perfect, quick Christmas read."
—*RT Book Reviews*

"[Macomber] writes about romance, family and friendship with a gentle, humorous touch."
—*Tampa Bay Times*

"Macomber spins another sweet, warmhearted holiday tale that will be as comforting to her fans as hot chocolate on Christmas morning."
—*Kirkus Reviews*

"This gentle, inspiring romance will be a sought-after read." —*Library Journal*

"Macomber cheerfully presents a holiday story that combines the winsomeness of a visiting angel (similar to Clarence from *It's a Wonderful Life*) with the more poignant soulfulness of *A Christmas Carol* to bring to life a memorable reading experience." —*Bookreporter*

"Macomber's name is almost as closely linked to Christmas reading as that of Charles Dickens. . . . [*Mr. Miracle*] has enough sweetness, charm, and seasonal sentiment to make Macomber fans happy." —*The Romance Dish*

## Starry Night

"Contemporary romance queen Macomber (*Rose Harbor in Bloom*) hits the sweet spot with this tender tale of impractical love. . . . A delicious Christmas miracle well worth waiting for."
—*Publishers Weekly* (starred review)

"[A] holiday confection . . . as much a part of the season for some readers as cookies and candy canes." —*Kirkus Reviews*

"A sweet contemporary Christmas romance . . . [that] the best-selling author's many fans will enjoy." —*Library Journal*

"Macomber can be depended on for an excellent story. . . . Readers will remain firmly planted in the beginnings of a beautiful love story between two of the most unlikely characters."
—*RT Book Reviews* (Top Pick, 4½ stars)

"Macomber, the prolific and beloved author of countless bestsellers, has penned a romantic story that will pull at your heartstrings with its holiday theme and emphasis on love and finding that special someone." —*Bookreporter*

"Magical . . . Macomber has given us another delightful romantic story to cherish. This one will touch your heart just as much as her other Christmas stories. Don't miss it!" —*Fresh Fiction*

## Angels at the Table

"This delightful mix of romance, humor, hope and happenstance is the perfect recipe for holiday cheer." —*Examiner.com*

"Rings in Christmas in tried-and-true Macomber style, with romance and a touch of heavenly magic." —*Kirkus Reviews*

"The angels' antics are a hugely hilarious and entertaining bonus to a warm love story."
—*Bookreporter*

"[A] sweetly charming holiday romance."
—*Library Journal*

Dear Friends,

As an author with a long publishing history, I'm often asked if there's a favorite book I've written. Certainly some stories are stronger than others. That said, I'm proud of every single published book. Perhaps the best way to explain this is to say that behind the words on the page beats the heart of the writer. My love of story is right there ready to link with your love of reading.

I want you to know *A Girl's Guide to Moving On* is a special book. I couldn't wait to get to my computer each morning, and the chapters poured out of me in such a rush that I could barely get the words on the page fast enough. My hope is that you feel that same enjoyment when you read Nichole's and Leanne's stories. When I read a good book the story will often linger in my mind. It's hard to let go of the characters. I had a hard time letting go of Rocco and Nikolai. Treat them with care and fall in love with them the way I did.

Hearing from my readers is a huge bonus to me as an author. I'd love to hear from you. Contacting me is easy. You can leave me a message on my webpage at debbiemacomber.com or on Facebook or Twitter. If you'd prefer to write a letter, my mailing address is P.O. Box 1458, Port Orchard, WA 98366. I look forward to reading your comments.

Warmest regards,

Debbie Macomber

# A Girl's Guide to Moving On

## BALLANTINE BOOKS BY DEBBIE MACOMBER

For a complete list of books by Debbie Macomber, visit her website at debbiemacomber.com.

# DEBBIE MACOMBER

# A Girl's Guide to Moving On

*A Novel*

BALLANTINE BOOKS · NEW YORK

2016 Ballantine Books Mass Market Edition

Copyright © 2016 by Debbie Macomber
Excerpt from *If Not For You* by Debbie Macomber copyright © 2016 by Debbie Macomber

Published in the United States by Ballantine Books, an imprint of Random House, a division of Penguin Random House LLC, New York.

BALLANTINE and the HOUSE colophon are registered trademarks of Penguin Random House LLC.

Originally published in hardcover in the United States by Ballantine Books, an imprint of Random House, a division of Penguin Random House LLC, in 2016.

ISBN 978-0-553-39194-7
ebook ISBN 978-0-553-39193-0

Cover design: Belina Huey
Cover photo-illustration: Debra Lill

Printed in the United States of America

randomhousebooks.com

9 8 7 6 5 4 3 2 1

Ballantine Books mass market edition: September 2016

To
Jim and Dolores Habberstad
in appreciation for the joy and
friendship they bring to
Wayne and me

# A Girl's Guide to
# Moving On

# PROLOGUE

# Nichole

Not so long ago I assumed I had the perfect life. Because my husband made a substantial income, I was a stay-at-home mom for our toddler son, Owen. My husband loved and cherished me. We lived in an upscale community outside of Portland, Oregon. Jake and I were members of one of the area's most prestigious country clubs. My in-laws lived close by and adored their grandson, especially my mother-in-law, Leanne.

Then, in a single afternoon, my entire world imploded. I learned that my husband had been having an affair, possibly multiple affairs, and had gotten his latest conquest pregnant. Leanne was the one who told me.

It was common knowledge that over the course of their marriage my father-in-law had been less than faithful. I often wondered if Leanne knew or if she turned a blind eye.

She knew.

When Leanne learned that Jake had followed in his father's footsteps she couldn't bear seeing me go through the humiliation and crippling low self-esteem she'd endured through the years. Her fear was that Owen would grow up to be like his father and grandfather, disrespecting his wedding vows, tearing apart his wife's self-worth.

I wasn't like Leanne. I refused to look the other way and I couldn't pretend all was well in my marriage. That said, I was afraid to walk away from Jake. I feared being alone, facing all the struggles of being a single parent and so much else. A divorce would mean a complete upheaval in my and Owen's lives, not to mention our finances. I needed encouragement and support.

My parents were gone, having died within a short time of each other. My two sisters lived in another state, and while they were supportive and wonderful, I needed someone close who would walk with me through this valley of tears.

That person, to my surprise, was Leanne. When I filed for divorce, she followed suit and filed at the same time, walking away from her thirty-five-year marriage. She'd had enough.

This was how we ended up living in apartments across the hall from each other in downtown Portland. We became our own support group, encouraging each other. She helped me wade through the emotional mire that went hand in hand with the death of a marriage. Together we faced each day of our new independent lives. I don't think I would have survived without her, and she said the same of me. We'd been close before, but we were even closer now.

Soon after we moved into our apartments, Leanne and I made up a list of ways in which we would get through this pain. We called it *A Guide to Moving On*.

The first item on that list was: **Don't allow yourself to wallow in your pain. Reach out. Volunteer. Do something you love or something to help others.**

That was easier said than done. I often found myself weepy and struggling against this desperate loneliness. I missed Jake and all the little things he used to do, like gassing up my car or changing batteries and fixing things. It added up to a thousand annoying tasks I was forced to do myself now. Plus, being a single mother is no cakewalk, either. I'd always lived with others, first at home with my family, then in college with roommates, and from there Jake and I married. For the first time in my life I was basically alone, and that took some getting used to.

Leanne was the one to suggest we each take on a volunteer project. One that would get us out of the house and force us to stop dwelling on our own loss. She opted to teach English as a second language two nights a week. And me . . . I love fashion and keeping track of the latest styles. One of my favorite things to do was read magazines while Owen napped. That was a luxury now. When it came to being a volunteer, I found an agency that helped dress women going into the workforce for the first time. To my delight, I discovered I enjoyed it immensely.

The second item on our list: **Cultivate new friendships.**

We've both lived the country-club life, our social lives revolving around our friends from the club. I thought I had good friends in Lake Oswego, but all of a sudden I was a third wheel. As soon as I filed for divorce my social life dried up. That didn't bother me as much as it could have. What bothered me was how eager my so-called friends were to talk about Jake. They were looking for gossip. A few well-meaning ones couldn't wait to let me know that they'd been aware of Jake's indiscretions for years and just hadn't known how to tell me. Yes, it was definitely time to find new friends, which was one reason Leanne and I chose to move to the thriving downtown area of Portland.

The third item and possibly the hardest, for me, anyway: **Let go in order to receive.** This one came from Leanne, who felt it was important that we not get caught up in a quagmire of resentment and bitterness. She seemed to have a better handle on this than I did. To be fair, she'd separated herself emotionally from Sean years earlier.

This divorce business (emotional separation) was new to me and I struggled to have a positive attitude. (Even now our divorce isn't final, almost two years into this mess. Jake has done everything humanly possible to delay the proceedings.)

This was by far the hardest because it was a mental game. There wasn't a checklist I could mark off. The goal was to think positively. That was a joke, right? Leanne assured me that once I let go of my bitterness my heart and my life would then be open to receive.

I've had two years to practice and I admit I have been getting better. I don't hate Jake. We have a son together and my soon-to-be ex-husband would always be part of Owen's life. Leanne was right, but this step demanded effort. Real effort.

Leanne is emotionally stronger than me. She is older and has the advantage of life experiences. I appreciate her insight and wisdom. I was also the one who came up with the last item on our list simply because I felt it was that important: **Love yourself.**

Again, this isn't as easy as it sounds. When I learned Jake had been having affairs, I immediately felt that there was something lacking in *me*. Okay, not immediately, but a close second to the consuming anger that attacked first. This is really about separating ourselves from the weaknesses in our husbands. I lost fifteen pounds the first month after I filed for divorce. My skinny jeans fit again, and while that was great, I was depressed and miserable. It'd been a low point. Loving myself meant eating, sleeping, and exercising—taking care of myself emotionally and physically. (I was so much better off making a list, and I could do that with this step.)

It meant taking care of myself spiritually, too. After Owen was born I'd gotten slack about attending church services, so after filing for divorce I went back, needing the positive messages and the fellowship. Leanne did, too. And Owen loves his kids' club class.

The church offered a divorce support group, and Leanne and I both attended the classes. They were wonderful and many of the items we discussed were part of the list we've compiled. The pastor made a funny comment. He said that when he taught marriage classes most of those attending took naps. It was the divorce classes where everyone took notes. I could understand this. I certainly hadn't gone into my marriage thinking Jake and I would be divorced one day. To me, marriage was forever.

So this is it. Our guide to moving on. Our guide to letting go and taking the next step to whatever the future might hold.

# CHAPTER 1

# Nichole

The first step in our *Guide to Moving On* was also the most enjoyable. Every other Saturday I spent the entire day at Dress for Success, a gently-used-clothing boutique. I loved dressing these ladies, whose courage inspired and stirred me. Many had come out of abusive relationships or were looking to get off welfare and find their place in the workforce. It was a joy to fit them with a wardrobe that gave them confidence and the hope that they could succeed.

"Would you look at me?" Shawntelle Maynor said, as she studied her reflection in the mirror. She turned around and glanced over her shoulder, nodding, apparently liking what she saw. "This hides my butt good."

Shawntelle was a good five inches taller than my own five-foot-three frame. Her hair was an untamed mass of tight black curls raining down upon her shoulders. She critically studied herself in the outfit I'd put together for her first job interview.

I found it hard to believe the difference clothes made. Shawntelle had arrived in baggy sweatpants and an oversize T-shirt. Now, dressed in black slacks and a pink Misook jacket, she looked like a million bucks.

"Wowza." I stepped back and reviewed my handiwork. The transformation was stunning.

"I need help with this hair," she said, frowning as she shoved it away from her face. "I should have known better than to let Charise cut it. She was all confident she could do it after watching a YouTube video. I was crazy to let her anywhere close to my hair with a pair of scissors." Her fingers reached up and touched the uneven ends of her bangs, or what I assumed must be her bangs. "I thought it'd grow out, and it did, but now it looks even worse."

"I've already made you an appointment next door." The hairstylist in the shop next to Dress for Success volunteered to give each woman at the boutique a wash and cut before her job interview.

Shawntelle's eyes nearly popped out of her head. "Get out of here. Really?"

"Really. When's your interview?"

"Monday afternoon."

"Your hair appointment is set for ten. Does that time work for you?"

Her smile was answer enough. Shawntelle had recently graduated from an accounting class and was looking for her first job. She had five children and her husband had deserted the family. The agency had gotten her an interview with a local car dealership. She'd gone through several practice interviews, which had given her a boost of confidence. Now, with the proper outfit, she beamed with self-assurance.

"I never thought I'd make it without LeRoy," she whispered. "But I am and I refuse to let that cheatin' scumbag back. He's screwed me over for the last time."

I smiled at the vehemence in her voice. I was walking this same rock-strewn path. In addition to my volunteer work, I was a substitute teacher for the Portland School District. My degree was in French literature with a minor in education, which qualified me for a teaching position. Unfortunately, no full-time positions were available, so I filled in as needed.

Thankfully, Leanne was available to watch Owen for me and as a backup there was a drop-in daycare center down the street from our apartment building. I eked by financially, in stark contrast to the lavish lifestyle I'd become accustomed to while married.

I had to remind myself I was still technically married. The final papers had yet to be drawn up to Jake's satisfaction. My husband had made this divorce as difficult as possible, thinking he could change my mind. He'd been persistently begging me to reconsider. When he finally realized my determination to see this through, he'd set up every roadblock he could, dragging out the settlement hearings, arguing each point. Our attorney fees had skyrocketed.

Divorce is hard—so much harder than I'd ever imagined it would be.

"You'll call after the interview?" I asked Shawntelle, determinedly pushing thoughts of Jake out of my mind.

"You got it."

"You're going to do so well." I gave her arm a gentle squeeze.

Shawntelle turned and wrapped me in a hug. "Them Kardashian chicks ain't got nothin' on me."

"You're beautiful." And I meant it.

By five I'd finished for the day and I was eager to get back to my son. Leanne had taken Owen to the park. At nearly four my little man was a ball of explosive energy. I imagined my mother-in-law was more than ready for a break.

I got in my car and was starting the engine when my phone rang. I drove a ten-year-old Toyota while my soon-to-be ex-husband was in a nearly new BMW, a car I'd bought him with the inheritance I'd gotten after my parents died. That was another story entirely, and one I had to repeatedly push out of my mind. Rule number three: **Let go in order to receive.**

I frantically searched through my purse until I located my phone. Checking caller ID, I saw that it was Jake. No surprise. It seemed he found an excuse to call me just about every day. I was able to remain civil, but I resented his efforts to keep me tied to him. Friends had been all too eager to tell me he hadn't changed his womanizing ways. Now that I was out of the house my husband didn't bother to hide the fact he was a player.

This was supposed to have been his weekend with Owen, but he had a business trip. Or so he claimed. Because of what I knew, I'd become suspicious of everything he said.

"Yes," I said, making sure I didn't sound overly

friendly. It was difficult to maintain an emotional distance from him, especially when he worked overtime to make it hard. Jake knew all the right buttons to push with me. Through the negotiations for the divorce he'd played me like a grand piano.

"Hi, sweetheart."

"You have the wrong number," I said forcefully. Every time he used an endearment I wondered how many other women he called "sweetheart."

"Come on, honey, there's no need to be bitter. I'm calling with good news."

Sure he was. "Which is?"

He hesitated and his voice sank lower, laced with regret. "I've signed off on the final negotiations. You want a share in the house, then fine, it's yours, but only when I choose to sell it. That's what you asked for, right?"

"Right." Which meant this bitter struggle was over and the divorce could go through. Twenty-five months after I'd filed we could sign the final papers.

"You signed off?" If that was the case I'd be hearing from my attorney shortly, probably Monday morning.

"It's killing us both to drag this out any longer than it already has."

From the minute I'd moved out of the house Jake had believed he could change my mind. I'd gladly given up living in the house despite the fact that my attorney had advised me to stay put. All I asked for was my fair share of the proceeds when he chose to sell it.

I wasn't interested in living in that plush home any longer. My life there with all the expensive furnishings and designer details had been a sham. The memories were too much for me. Sleeping in our bed was torture, knowing Jake had defiled it. For all I knew he may even have made love to another woman in that very bed. Besides, holding on to the house would be a financial struggle. I needed to break away completely and start over. Jake had been surprised when I agreed to move out. I'd used the house along with the country-club membership as bargaining chips in the settlement agreement.

"Aren't you going to say anything?" Jake asked.

I wasn't sure what to say. "I guess this is it, then," I whispered, staggering against a wall of emotion. My attorney assured me that eventually Jake would cave. It was either that or we would be headed to a meeting with a court-appointed negotiator. I was willing, but Jake had balked. Neither one of us wanted this to go to trial. The attorneys and the divorce proceedings were expensive enough.

"Yeah. It'll be final soon," Jake said, his voice so low it was almost a whisper. His words were filled with regret.

"Final," I repeated, and bit into my lower lip.

"You okay?" Jake asked.

"Yeah, of course." But I wasn't. After all this time one would think I'd be glad this bickering and madness were about to end. I should be over the moon, eager to put my marriage behind me. I was more than ready to move on. Instead my heart felt like it was going to melt and a huge knot blocked my throat.

"I thought you'd want to know," Jake said, sounding as sad and miserable as I was.

"Thanks. I've got to go."

"Nichole . . . Nichole . . ."

I didn't want to hear anything more that he had to say, so I ended the call. With tears blurring my eyes, I tossed my phone back inside my expensive Michael Kors purse. A purse I'd purchased because Jake insisted I deserved beautiful things. Now I understood he'd wanted me to have it because he'd felt guilty. As best I could figure, I'd bought the purse shortly after he learned Chrissy was pregnant with his child.

Wiping the moisture from my cheek, I put the car in reverse, stepped on the accelerator, and immediately backed into a ditch.

# CHAPTER 2

# Nichole

I don't know how long I sat in my car with my forehead resting against the steering wheel. I was embarrassed and shaken, and it wasn't only from the accident. My marriage was over. I thought I was ready, more than ready. The reality of it hit me full force; a deep sense of loss and unreality swamped my senses.

"Nichole, are you all right?"

A disembodied voice came at me. When I lifted my head I found Alicia, the hairstylist, standing alongside my upended car. When I didn't answer right away she knocked against the driver's-side window.

"Nichole. Nichole."

I lifted my head and nodded. "I am such an idiot."

"Are you hurt?"

I assured her I wasn't.

"You're going to need a tow truck to pull you out of here."

I figured as much.

"Do you have Triple A?"

I shook my head. It was an added expense I couldn't afford.

"Do you want me to call someone for you?"

"Please." Still I remained in the car, praying I hadn't done any damage to my vehicle.

Alicia hesitated. "Are you sure you're all right? You didn't hit your head or anything, did you?"

"No, no, I'm fine." I wasn't. I wasn't anywhere close to okay, but that wasn't due to the fact my car was head up in a ditch.

Alicia hesitated and then left me. Breathless, she returned a few minutes later. I remained seated in the car, clenching the steering wheel. She opened the driver's-side door. "Potter Towing will be here within thirty minutes."

I nodded. "Thanks."

"You need help getting out?" She studied me as if unconvinced I hadn't suffered a head injury.

I sniffled, ran my hand beneath my nose, and shook my head. "I'm not hurt, just a little shook up."

"Listen, I'd wait with you, but I'm giving Mrs. Fountaine a perm and I don't want to leave the solution on too long. Denise has gone for the day, so I'm all alone."

"Don't worry; go take care of Mrs. Fountaine. I'll be okay." I wanted to blame Jake for this but I was the one who hadn't looked where I was going.

Just as Alicia promised, a tow truck pulled into the parking lot about twenty-five minutes later. By then I had climbed out, had collected my purse, and was pacing anxiously, waiting. I'd called Leanne and told her what happened.

"You're sure you're okay?" Leanne asked, and I could hear the concern in her voice.

"No, no, I'm perfectly all right. I just wanted you to know I'll be later than usual. Look, I need to go, the tow truck just pulled up."

"Don't worry about Owen. He's doing great. Take your time."

I disconnected just as a hulk of a man jumped out of the tow truck. He had on greasy overalls and a sleeveless shirt. Both arms revealed bulging muscles and full-sleeve tattoos. His eyes were a piercing shade of blue as his gaze skidded past me to my car.

"How'd that happen?" he asked, studying the position of the car.

"I wasn't drinking, if that is what you think."

He shook his head and grinned. "You mean to say you did that sober?"

For the first time since I'd ended the conversation with Jake, I smiled. "I guess it does look like I was on something."

His smile was friendly, lighting up his eyes.

I wrapped my arms around my waist. "How much is this going to set me back?" I asked.

He named a figure that caused me to swallow a gasp. "I'll need to put it on my credit card." I had one I used only for emergencies. I'd once been free and easy with money. I could afford to be then, but no longer.

"I can give you a discount for cash," he told me as he pulled out a thick wire cord and hooked it onto the car's bumper.

"How much of a discount?"

"Ten percent."

I did a quick calculation in my head. "What about my debit card?"

"Still got to pay the bank fees with that. Cash only."

"Will you take a check?" I had a checkbook in my purse.

He paused and glanced over his shoulder. "Is it good?"

I was pissed that he'd ask. "Yes, it's good."

"Then I'll take your check."

Big of him.

"I know Alicia," he said as he walked back to his truck. "She said you work at that used-clothing place." He motioned with his head toward the shop.

"It's a volunteer position, so it isn't like a job."

"Yeah, that's what she said. She said it's a shop that dresses women looking for work. Guess you must have a good eye for that sort of thing."

He didn't expect an answer and I didn't give him one.

Once the car was connected to the tow truck, it took only a few minutes to bring it out of the ditch. He waited to make sure the engine started and I hadn't done any further damage.

I set my purse on the hood of the car and pulled out my checkbook. He took the check, folded it in half. He looked at me and then paused before slipping it into his pocket. It seemed like he had something he wanted to say. I waited and then realized he was probably worried about the check.

"It's good," I assured him again, annoyed that he seemed to think I'd stiff him. Maybe he'd gotten stiffed before.

"Anything more I can do for you?" he asked.

"Nothing. Thanks. I need to get home."

He gave me a salute and said, "It was nice doing business with you, Ms. Patterson."

"You, too, Mr. . . . ?"

"Nyquist. Call me Rocco."

"Rocco," I repeated with a smile. "Thank you for your help, Rocco," I said, eager now to be on my way.


As soon as Leanne answered the door, Owen dropped his toy and raced into my waiting arms. I got down on one knee and my son hugged my neck, squeezing tightly.

"Did you have fun at the park?" I asked.

"Grandma took me on the slide."

"Was it scary?"

He nodded and then, typically, the first question he wanted to ask was about dinner. "Can we have hot dogs for dinner?"

"Sure." Wieners were his all-time favorite meal, along with macaroni and cheese. Good thing, because with what I'd been forced to pay for the tow, we were going to need to cut back on groceries.

"Did you have a good day?" Leanne asked.

I nodded. "It was great." And it had been until the call from Jake.

I didn't tell her about our discussion. I would later. Her divorce had been finalized eighteen months ago. Sean had made it as easy as possible, giving her whatever she wanted. He seemed almost glad to be out of the marriage. I was envious Leanne hadn't been dragged into this emotional minefield Jake seemed intent on putting me through.

That was until I found Leanne crying nearly hysterically one afternoon, shortly after she'd signed the papers. It hadn't been kindness or guilt that had prompted Sean's actions, she'd told me. Sean said he was simply glad to have her out of his life. According to him, she'd gone to seed and he'd lost all desire for her years ago.

If I hadn't disliked my father-in-law before, then I detested him now. How a man could be so thoughtless and cruel to a woman who had shared his life all those years was beyond me. Leanne was a beautiful woman. Yes, she was a few pounds overweight, but it didn't distract from her overall appearance or beauty. She was kind and thoughtful, loving and generous. I admired her more than any other woman I'd ever known.

Owen collected his things and we walked across the hall to our two-bedroom apartment. It was about a third of the size of our home near Lake Oswego. I missed my garden and the flower beds. Gardening had become a passion of mine. When Owen and I could manage it, I'd buy a house and plant another garden.

Happy to be in his own home, Owen raced around the living room, his chubby legs pumping as he ran circles around me. I hoped it would tire him out enough that he'd go down for the night without a problem. I read to him each night, and the stack of books grew as he wanted to listen to all his favorite stories. I knew Jake didn't read to him, because Owen complained that he didn't.

We ate wieners for dinner along with green beans that Owen lined up on the tabletop in an arch above his plate. I managed to bribe him to eat two of the green beans. Getting him to eat his vegetables was an ongoing battle.

After I read him his ten favorite books, he settled down for the night. It'd been quiet all evening, which was unusual. I hadn't gotten a single call, which made me wonder if I'd let my battery run down. I probably needed to charge my phone. But when I dug through my purse I couldn't find it.

Immediately a sense of panic filled me. I needed my phone. Thinking I must have somehow missed it, I emptied the entire contents of my large purse and sorted through each and every item.

No phone.

I stood with my hand over my heart when the doorbell chimed. From the peephole I saw it was Rocco, the tow truck driver, standing on the other side. He must have known I was checking because he held up my phone as if to explain the reason for his visit.

Unlatching the door, I heaved a sigh. "Where did you find it?" I asked, with a deep sense of relief.

"After you drove off I saw it lying there on the blacktop and realized it must be yours. I got your address off the check you wrote."

"Of course. Come in."

He stepped into the apartment and his bulk seemed to fill the entire room. His size was intimidating. I figured he had to be at least six-four. He'd cleaned up and changed out of his coveralls. Now he wore a T-shirt and faded blue jeans that emphasized his long legs.

"I just realized I didn't have my phone and was

going into panic mode. Thank you." I clenched the cell to my chest.

"No problem." He stuffed his hands into his pockets. His sleeves bulged with his muscles. I wanted to examine his tattoos but didn't want to be obvious about it. It made me curious if he had more tattoos elsewhere on his body.

"Daddy?" Owen said, racing out of his bedroom. The doorbell must have woken him. Either that or he hadn't been entirely asleep. He came to a screeching stop when he realized the large man standing just inside the apartment wasn't Jake.

Owen's eyes grew huge as he tilted his head back and gazed up with wide-eyed wonder at Rocco.

Rocco squatted down and held out his hand. "How about giving me a high five, little man?"

Owen hesitated for only a moment before swinging his arm into a big circle, slamming it down on Rocco's open palm.

"That's quite a hit for such a little guy."

Owen smiled proudly.

I placed my hands on Owen's shoulders, steering him back toward his bedroom. "Okay, young man, back to bed."

"When will I see Daddy?" he asked, his big brown eyes pleading with me.

"He'll come for you next weekend, buddy," I assured my son. I glanced toward Rocco. "I need to put him back to bed."

He surprised me by asking, "Do you mind if I wait?"

Although I was taken aback, I gestured to the sofa. "Make yourself at home. This shouldn't take more than a few minutes."

Maybe Rocco was looking for a reward for return-ing my phone. My mind raced with what I could pos-sibly give him. Maybe I didn't want to know. It probably hadn't been the smartest idea inviting him into the apartment. I was a woman alone, and I needed to be more aware of dangers. Funny, really. As big as he was, I didn't feel the least bit threatened. I'd learned to listen to my instincts and they said I was safe.

Getting Owen down a second time wasn't as easy as I would have liked. A good ten minutes passed.

When I returned, Rocco had turned on the televi-sion and had made himself comfortable. He sat with his ankle balanced on his knee and his arm stretched out across the sofa, looking completely relaxed.

"You have coffee?" he asked.

I blinked before I found the ability to answer. "I do." I hesitated.

"Make yourself one while you're at it," he sug-gested.

This man had nerve. Nevertheless, I brewed us each a cup. He helped himself to milk, digging the carton out of the refrigerator and then putting it back.

Apparently he had an agenda other than deliver-ing my phone. We stood in the middle of my small kitchen, facing each other, each holding a mug of cof-fee. If he could be direct, then so could I.

"What can I do for you, Rocco?"

He reached inside his pocket and removed the check I had written him earlier. "I have a proposition for you."

Seeing the check sitting on the kitchen counter, I wasn't sure I was going to like what he was about to suggest. "What kind of proposition?" I asked, frowning up at him.

The edges of his mouth curved upward as if he'd read my mind. "Whatever you're thinking isn't it. I have a fifteen-year-old daughter. Her name is Kaylene and, well, she's a typical teenager. That girl has a mouth on her . . ."

"Most teenagers do."

He didn't agree or disagree.

"I substitute teach at the high school. I hear the way they talk."

He arched his thick brows. "Must be hard to tell the difference between you and the students."

I wasn't sure that was a compliment, so I let it go. "What about your daughter?"

Rocco sipped his coffee. "She wants to attend this dance, which, according to her, is a big deal."

"And . . ."

"And I am not letting her out of the house with the dress she bought with her friends."

"And . . ."

"And so I thought we might strike a deal. If you help Kaylene dress for this dance in something I can approve of, then I'd be willing to tear up this check and call us even."

That sounded almost too good to be true. "What will your boss have to say about that?" I asked.

"I am the boss. I own Potter Towing."

"Oh." Then I paused. "I thought you said your name was Nyquist."

"Good memory. I got the business from a man named Potter. Do we have a deal?"

I didn't need to think twice. "Sure." So that was

why he'd been so curious about my work with Dress for Success.

Rocco thrust out his hand and I did, too. His huge hand swallowed my much smaller one. As far as I was concerned, I was getting the much better end of this transaction.

# CHAPTER 3

# Leanne

I never expected to be living in an apartment at this time of my life. I held it in my mind that after Sean retired our relationship would improve. I thought that we'd travel and spend time together, and, optimist that I am, I hoped we'd make a go of it. I quickly learned that I'd been living a fantasy, believing that with effort we might be able to rekindle the love that had brought us together all those years ago.

Even in the early years of our marriage Sean had been a generous husband. Hardly a week went by when he didn't bring home a gift of some sort. To anyone looking in on our marriage we were the perfect couple and my husband was crazy in love with me. In public, Sean was openly affectionate and I was the envy of my friends. He was a good provider and I'd never had to work outside the home.

We'd been married about five years when I first learned that Sean was involved in an affair. I was devastated, shocked, and unbelievably hurt. If I'd been in my right mind I would have confronted him then and there. Although I wanted to scream and cry and demand to know why he would do such a thing, I didn't. Instead I swallowed my pride for fear of where it would lead, afraid of what would happen.

How foolish I'd been, but I loved my husband and Jake was a toddler. The thought of tearing our son away from his father, whom he adored, was more than I could bear. My parents loved Sean, and while it might sound foolish to say this now, there'd never been a divorce in my family. I didn't want to be the first. In retrospect, that makes absolutely no sense. All these years later I can see that I had been emotionally wounded to the point that I couldn't think clearly.

I became pregnant just a few weeks after we were married and Sean wanted me to be a stay-at-home mother for our son. He assured me that he needed me to be his emotional support and he didn't want to entrust our child's upbringing to a daycare worker. As his career advanced he seemed to rely on me more and more, as did Jake. I became involved as a school volunteer and chauffeured our son to sports and Scouts, church activities and tennis lessons, and never did take a job outside the home.

Over the years I discovered Sean's involvement in a number of affairs. It didn't take long before I was able to pick up on the signs that there was another woman in his life. The late nights, the extra care he took in his grooming, the unexplained charges on our credit cards. All the while I was praying desperately for a second child. Foolishly, I believed that if I was able to give my husband more children he would love me and wouldn't crave other women's affections.

When I look back on those years I want to slap myself. I did everything within my power to hold our lives together, to perpetuate the lie that we had a strong marriage. It was a fluke when I learned that Sean had a vasectomy, making it impossible for us to have more children. He'd had it done without me knowing, after a close call when he thought he'd gotten one of his women pregnant. All those years I'd been living in a dream world.

It wasn't until Jake entered college that I gathered the courage to threaten divorce. I was serious and even filed. Sean knew that I'd reached my limit, and he begged me to reconsider. He swore on the life of our son that he would never cheat on me again. Fool that I was, I took him at his word. For six months I believe he made a sincere effort to remain faithful.

Six months was all it took. Then it started up again and I knew. And Sean knew that I knew. I moved out of our bedroom and into the spare room, and emotionally distanced myself from him. To the outside world I pretended all was well. It wasn't. My self-esteem was shredded and my pride was eaten up with the acid of my husband's infidelity. For ten years before the divorce we'd basically lived separate lives, but to our country-club friends we were the same happy couple.

The brightest spot in those years was when Jake married Nichole. She became a daughter to me. As far as I was concerned, Jake couldn't have married a better woman. Her own mother was gone and Nichole often looked to me for advice. I came to love her, and after Owen was born my grandson became the center of my world.

It wasn't until I happened to overhear a conversation between my husband and Jake that I learned that my son had followed in his father's shadow.

"Dad, I have a little problem I need your help with," Jake had said, keeping his voice low, barely above a whisper. I was in the hallway outside our bedroom, putting away towels in the linen cabinet. Funny how little details like that stick in one's mind.

I assumed what Jake wanted to discuss had to do with finances. In the early years of our marriage, Sean's parents had helped us out a couple times. I thought this little heart-to-heart was about money.

I was wrong, so very wrong.

Our son had gotten another woman pregnant. I stood frozen in place, sick at heart, hardly able to breathe, while Sean gave our son the contact information for a doctor friend of his who would perform an abortion.

For days I pretended to have the flu while I confined myself to the bedroom. My mind raced with what to do. I couldn't tell Nichole. This news would devastate my daughter-in-law. At the same time I couldn't keep quiet, either. I was consumed with guilt, knowing that by looking the other way, ignoring Sean's affairs, I'd given our son tacit permission to cheat on his own wife. This had to end, and it had to end with Jake because I refused to let this behavior continue into the next generation.

I knew that Nichole wasn't as naïve as I'd been. It would only be a matter of time before she'd figure out Jake was cheating. I didn't want to be the one to tell her, but in the end that is what I did. The price of pretending to not know, of looking away, was far, far too high. For her and for me.

Seeing that Jake had followed in his father's footsteps, I had to believe that when the time came Owen would as well. My grandson would grow up and think fidelity and marriage vows were mere suggestions rather than heartfelt, meaningful commitments.

The hardest thing I've ever done was tell Nichole about Jake's affair. I had to admire my daughter-in-law for the way she took the news. Like I'd been all those years earlier, she was shocked and broken. I watched her crumble right before my eyes. But unlike me, she regrouped quickly.

That same afternoon she'd looked at me and said there was only one thing to do.

Her strength and courage caught me by surprise. How I wish I'd had the foresight to take hold of my life when I first learned of Sean's affairs. It was then that I realized I wasn't dead. It wasn't too late. All that was left of our marriage was a thin shell. If Nichole could take action, then so could I, and I did.

Because of Sean's repeated offenses, Nichole had no reason to believe Jake could be any more faithful than my husband had been to me. Unlike me, Nichole wasn't willing to give Jake a second chance. As far as she was concerned, her husband had shattered her trust and there was no going back.

My divorce was smooth sailing. Sean seemed to be expecting me to file. It was almost as if he'd mentally prepared himself for the dissolution of our marriage. He made it as painless as possible, giving me half of everything. I would have no financial worries; he'd been the one to insist I remain at home with our son, and he paid dearly for that. My attorney saw to a fair and even distribution of our assets.

What I hadn't been prepared for was the vindictive attitude that followed just before we signed the final papers. Sean made sure to let me know he saw me as unattractive and old. He took pleasure in telling me that my sagging breasts and body were a complete turnoff. He'd gone so far as to say I'd gone to seed. Although I no longer loved my husband—he'd destroyed that love when I'd learned about the vasectomy—his words hit their mark. I'd been crushed by his cruelty and found it hard to look at myself. I felt old, dumpy, and past my prime.

Jake didn't take Nichole's decision nearly as easily. I had to give my son credit. He didn't want to lose his wife and son, and had gone to great lengths and expense to delay the divorce. I wanted to believe Jake was sincere and that he would change this need he seemed to have to seek out other women. Sadly, I had no way of knowing if he could. Evidence and experience said otherwise.

At one point, Sean had tried and been unable to change. I had to accept that Jake could take after his father in more ways than appearance.

Nichole and I moved into downtown Portland. The first few weeks we muddled through each day, depressed and uncertain.

One afternoon, in those early dark days when we were floundering in our misery, we wrote up a list . . . a list to help us move on and make a new, better life for us individually and for Owen. We listed only four items because we didn't want to overwhelm ourselves.

It was one step at a time. One day at a time. It helped tremendously that we were in this together.

The first item on that list was to ease the pain with a distraction, by giving to others. With me, that was teaching.

I'd graduated from college with a master's in education, but I'd never taught. I wasn't looking for a full-time position, so I found a volunteer job, an evening class two times a week, where I taught English as a second language.

It proved to be a good choice. I enjoyed my students and admired their determination to tackle the complicated idioms and slang of the English language. I had ten students that had immigrated from all around the world.

More and more I found myself looking forward to teaching my class. A large part of the satisfaction I derived came from one of my students named Nikolai Janchenko. At my best estimate Nikolai was close to my own age and from Ukraine. By far he was my most enthusiastic student. What I enjoyed about him most was his ability to make me laugh.

Monday night I parked in the Community Center parking lot. As soon as I pulled into the designated slot, I noticed Nikolai standing outside the center's front door. He was a fine-looking man with a thick head of salt-and-pepper hair. From our conversations I knew he worked in a deli as a baker. His shoulders were broad from all the upper-body work he must do. He wasn't a large man by any means, average height with strong but blunt Eastern European features.

From what his school file told me, he'd been living in the States for five years and had recently acquired citizenship.

Nikolai must have recognized my car because he hurried across the street to meet me. By the time I'd reached for my purse and books, he had the driver's door open and offered me a hand to help me out. I enjoyed how much of a gentleman he was.

"Good night, Teacher."

"It's evening, Nikolai. We would say 'good evening,' versus 'good night.'"

"Good evening, Teacher."

"Good evening, Nikolai. It's good to see you."

"It's very good to see you," he said. His eyes sparkled with warmth as he proudly handed me a loaf of bread. "I bake for you."

The loaf was still warm from the oven and the aroma was heavenly. I raised it to my nose, closed my eyes, and inhaled the scent of yeast and flour.

"This is bread made with potato."

"It smells delicious." I would enjoy toasting a slice for my breakfast and planned to share the loaf with Nichole and Owen.

"I make it special for you." He walked alongside me, his head turned toward me, watching me closely.

"I'm over the moon."

He stopped abruptly and frowned. "Over the moon? What does this mean?"

"That's an idiom, Nikolai, and what we're going to be discussing in class this evening."

"You explain this moon. You jump over it like cow in school rhyme?"

"No." I had to smile. I found myself doing that a

good deal whenever I spoke to Nikolai. His mind was eager to soak up everything I had to teach. All my students were keen learners, which made these two classes the highlight of my week.

It wasn't a surprise to see Nikolai take a seat at the table at the front of the class. He chose the spot front and center each time and hung on my every word.

I put my purse and books down on my desk. Moving to the front, I leaned back and placed my hands against the edge as I looked out over my students.

"Good evening," I said.

The class returned my greeting in a mingling of different accents.

"Tonight I want to talk about idioms." Knowing that some of my students needed to see the word written, I walked over to the board and wrote *idiom* in large letters for them to see and copy down.

"Idioms are part of every language," I said. "They are a word or phrase that isn't meant to be taken literally. For example, if I say I am over the moon, that means I'm thrilled or happy."

José raised a timid hand. "Then why not say you're happy?"

"I did. Only I said it in another way. Here's a second example. Perhaps you've heard the phrase 'It's raining cats and dogs.' It doesn't mean cats and dogs are literally falling from the sky."

Titus raised his hand. If I remembered correctly, he'd come from South Africa. "We have a similar saying in Africa. We say it's raining old women with clubs."

The discussion turned lively after that, as the other students shared idioms from their own cultures. Some

I found hilarious, and soon we were all laughing and sharing.

It always surprised me how quickly the class time passed. Before I realized it was even possible, our session was up. As had become his habit, Nikolai was the last to leave. He waited so he could walk me to the parking lot.

"Do you understand now what I meant when I said I was over the moon?" I asked as I collected my purse and books.

"Yes, Teacher. You say you are happy I bake bread."

I felt a little silly having him call me Teacher all the time. "Nikolai, you can use my name if you prefer."

His eyes widened slightly.

"My name is Leanne."

"Leanne," he repeated, pronouncing it as if it were foreign on his tongue, which it probably was. At the same time, he said it as if he were speaking in church or a library, slowly, with a low voice, like a prayer. "*Leanne* is a beautiful name."

"Thank you," I said as we walked out of the classroom.

"A beautiful name for beautiful woman."

I must have given him a startled look. After the ugly things Sean had said to me, I didn't think of myself as beautiful.

"You no believe?" Nikolai asked, shocked. "You no believe you beautiful?"

Embarrassed, I looked away, unable to answer.

He frowned and, reaching up, he ran his finger slowly, deliberately down the side of my face, easing it over my chin and down my neck in a gentle caress. I inhaled sharply at the electric shock that went straight through me. It'd been so long since a man had touched me that my body reacted instantly. Nikolai locked his gaze with mine and spoke softly in Ukrainian. I didn't understand a word. Whatever the meaning, it sent a series of chills racing down my arms.

With effort I pulled my eyes away and picked up the pace, walking toward the parking lot, my steps hurried. Nikolai followed and he, too, seemed eager to move beyond whatever had transpired between us.

"Thank you again for the bread," I told him, unlocking my car door.

"I am raining-cats-and-dogs glad to make it for you."

I smiled, unwilling to correct him. "Did you get it from the bakery?" I asked, knowing he rose in the wee hours of the morning to bake for the deli.

"No, no," he said emphatically, shaking his head. "That bread comes from machine. I make with my own hands this bread to show you thanks. As I knead dough I think of you, think of you eating my bread, enjoying the taste of my bread. I think of you smiling when I give you my bread."

"I'm sure I'll enjoy it," I told him.

His smile was wide and warm. "I bake you more."

"Nikolai, I am only one person. It will take me several days to eat all this bread."

"Still I bake you more. I bake you bread every class. You will eat and enjoy my bread and I will remember your smile. Your smile make me smile here." He tucked his hand over his heart.

I hated to squelch his enthusiasm by explaining I couldn't possibly eat that much bread living alone; I would need to share it. I set my purse on the passenger seat and was ready to slide into the car. "You know the class is going to think you're the teacher's pet."

A shocked look came over him as he stepped away from me. "You treat me like dog?"

"No, no," I said, unable to hold back a smile. "It means you're my favorite student."

Immediately his look softened. "This is another idiom you say."

"Yes, another idiom."

His smile blossomed. "I see you Wednesday, Leanne."

He stepped back from the car and raised his hand in farewell. As I backed out of the parking space, he walked alongside my car. Before I pulled away he knocked on my window. I rolled it down and he looked at me, his eyes dark and serious.

"I come again on Wednesday with more bread."

# CHAPTER 4

# Nichole

"You must be Kaylene," I said. Rocco had arranged for me to meet him and his daughter Tuesday afternoon at the Lloyd Center. His daughter was tall, thin, and straight as a toothpick. I remember being fifteen and wanting so badly to be as beautiful as my sisters. It was an awkward age before I started to develop. One look told me Kaylene was on the cusp. She was a lovely girl who'd inherited her father's height and bone structure. It wouldn't be long before she blossomed into a woman. I understood her need to be noticed, and her father's fears that she would be.

The dance was the first one of the school year and was set for that Friday night.

Kaylene stood with her arms folded across her chest; her feet were braced apart and her face held a hard look of defiance. She didn't respond until her father nudged her with his hand. She stumbled forward a couple of steps. "Yeah, I'm Kaylene."

"I'm Nichole. I understand you're looking for a dress for the school dance."

She squinted her eyes up at her father. "I already have a dress, but my father thinks it shows too much skin. In his words, it makes me look sleazy."

I met Rocco's gaze. He might have been a bit more diplomatic. No wonder Kaylene was upset.

"My friends and I spent a lot of time picking out that dress. It isn't like I've got a date or anything. It's just a bunch of us girls going, so I don't see what his problem is."

"Are boys going to be at that dance?" Rocco asked.

"You know they are."

"Then you're not wearing that dress."

I could see this was fast disintegrating into an argument between father and daughter, and I had best put an end to it now. "Why don't we check out a few of the stores and see if we can find something more to both of your liking?"

"I like the one I have."

"You mean the one you're not wearing?" Rocco returned.

"It doesn't hurt to look, Kaylene," I said, hoping to be the voice of reason.

Her shoulders sagged, accepting defeat.

"Then let's get started," Rocco said.

"Just a minute," Kaylene cried out, and came to an abrupt halt. "No way are you coming with us." She glared at her father.

"How else am I going to approve your dress?"

"Dad. It's not happening." Her horrified look intensified.

"Listen here, Kayl—"

I cleared my throat in an effort to get their attention. I didn't intend to stand between a father and daughter, or to get caught in the middle of this exchange, but clearly someone had to say something.

"Rocco," I said before their argument escalated further. To help him to look my way I laid my hand over his forearm.

His gaze jerked toward me and then down at my hand on his arm as if my touch had burned him. I dropped my hand and stepped back.

"Do you realize how awful it would be for me if one of my friends found out *my father* went shopping with me?"

His gaze reverted back to Kaylene. "I don't care what your friends think. If you want to go to that dance, then . . ."

"Rocco," I said again, louder than before. This time I placed my hand in the middle of his chest before he turned to look at me.

"What?" he snapped, diverting his eyes away from his daughter.

"Do you trust me to find an appropriate dress for your daughter?" I asked, because if he didn't, he shouldn't have asked for my help. Otherwise, all I'd be doing was mediating between father and daughter.

He didn't answer.

"Do you?" I asked forcefully.

"I guess." His lack of confidence was almost comical.

"Leave," I said.

At first I thought he was going to make a fuss, but then he snapped his mouth closed and slowly nodded. "How long do you think this will take?"

"Give us a couple of hours."

He glanced at his watch. "Okay, fine," he said, none too graciously. "I'll meet you back here at six-thirty."

I checked my own watch. "We'll call if we're going to be any later than that."

"Later? You might need *more* than two hours?" He all but rolled his eyes as if he thought I was being ridiculous.

I gently patted his forearm. "These matters take time. Relax, Kaylene's in good hands."

Rocco plowed his fingers through his hair as if he was second-guessing his decision to ask for my help. I gestured with my head for Kaylene to follow me. We'd gone only a few steps when she whispered a heartfelt "Thanks."

"No problem. I would have hated it if my father went shopping with me."

"He wants me to dress like someone's grand-mother."

I remember thinking the same thing when I was her age, only it'd been my mother. It took me a moment to recall my conversation with Rocco over coffee when he'd dropped off my cell and asked for my help.

"Where would you like to start?" I asked.

"I get to choose?" Kaylene sounded surprised. "You're not going to drag me into any of those old-lady stores?"

I hated to think of which stores she considered "old lady" stores. I probably should have asked, but I was afraid she might mention the very department stores I frequented.

For the next hour and a half we flitted from one dressing room to another until we found an outfit we both felt was perfect. I was confident it would make Rocco happy, and Kaylene looked lovely in it. To sweeten the deal, the dress was on sale, marked down fifty percent. That gave us enough left over in the budget to find matching shoes.

"We have one more stop," I said, glancing at my watch, noticing it was six-twenty-five.

"Dad doesn't like to wait."

"Tough. This is important."

Kaylene looked confused. "I thought we had everything."

"We're going to Victoria's Secret."

Surprise showed on her face, followed by a huge smile. "Are you going to tell my dad?"

I shrugged. "Why should I? You can if you want. He gave us a budget and we stayed within that amount. The proper underwear is all part of the outfit."

"Let's go," she said, giggling like the schoolgirl she was.

"Give me your phone and I'll text your father and tell him to give us an extra fifteen." She handed it to me and I did a quick text. When I finished, I found Kaylene inside the store, sorting through bras, searching out ones that were far too big for her. I looked at her and raised my eyebrows.

"A girl can dream, can't she?"

We both laughed. We hadn't gotten off to a great start. Kaylene resented the fact that I'd been asked to help. I can't say I blamed her. When we first started shopping, she didn't want me picking out the dresses. I gave her free rein, letting her make her own selections. I could quickly see that her father had a point.

My chance came while she was in the dressing room.

I removed the rejects and brought in fresh outfits I felt were a good compromise. Once she saw that my choices were relatively close to her own, the first barrier went down. She quickly lost the attitude, and for the rest of the time it'd been fun.

With a bit of power shopping, we found what we needed at Victoria's Secret: lace panties and a matching bra. Kaylene had to add a few dollars of her own money, but she did so willingly. We buried the recognizable bag in the one for the shoes and then rushed to the meeting spot. At that we were still five minutes late.

Rocco was there, pacing impatiently when we strolled up to him.

"So," he said, looking between Kaylene and me. "How'd it go?"

"We found a compromise dress," I said, not wanting to appear overly pleased. Kaylene had her pride and I was determined not to stomp over it.

"Nichole did a good job, Dad. I wouldn't mind shopping with her again."

Now, that was high praise.

Rocco caught my eye and arched his brows. "I have the final say."

"Dad."

I cocked my head to one side and eyed him steadily, as if to remind him he had put his trust in me and needed to keep it there.

Rocco must have read me, because he quickly changed the subject. "I bet you're hungry."

"Starving," Kaylene said. "Are you going to treat us to dinner?"

Rocco looked to me. "Care to join us?"

I hesitated. The offer was tempting, but I'd left Owen with Leanne and I hated to take advantage of her.

"Come with us," Kaylene said, her eyes wide and appealing.

"Let me make a call first." I felt guilty even asking, but Leanne was fine with keeping Owen.

"Go. Enjoy," my mother-in-law insisted. "Owen and I will cook together. He loves helping me in the kitchen, you know."

I did. My preschooler was a budding chef.

Both Kaylene and Rocco looked toward me as I disconnected. "No problem."

"Great."

Rocco let Kaylene choose and she wanted pizza. Not the best choice for me, calorie-wise, but I wasn't going to complain. Besides, it'd been months since I'd last indulged myself with something other than frozen pizza.

We headed out in separate cars and met up at the restaurant, which was only a few blocks away. I couldn't help wondering what Jake would think if he saw me with Rocco. No two men could be any more different.

Rocco looked as if he'd walked out of the Alaskan woods. He had the physique of a lumberjack and the tattoos of a biker. By contrast, Jake was a suave businessman who dressed like he'd stepped off the pages of *GQ*. The contrast had me smiling.

I met up with them at the pizza parlor. By the time I got inside, they were sitting in a booth. Within minutes we ordered. A meat lover's pizza for Rocco and a veggie pizza for Kaylene and me to share. Rocco asked for a beer and I had a glass of New Zealand sauvignon blanc.

"Dad, one of the kids from my school is here. Give me some quarters, okay?"

Rocco dug in his pockets for spare change and gave what he had to his daughter. Within minutes Kaylene disappeared into the arcade. I felt a little weird sitting in the booth with Rocco like the two of us were on a date.

"Kaylene said it went well and that you were supercool."

"She's a great kid, Rocco. You're doing a good job with her."

"I try. She doesn't make it easy."

"No teen does."

Our drinks were delivered and I took a sip of wine. It was crisp, cold, and refreshing. I leaned back against the booth and looked down at the wine.

"She can be difficult," Rocco said, continuing our conversation. "That girl finds the stupidest stuff to argue about. I want her to be smart and strong, but I'm not a good example, and her mother, God knows, wasn't, either."

"You're a man, Rocco, and Kaylene's a teenager. What do you expect? Give her time."

"The thing is, I gave my parents hell, so I expect my daughter will do the same to me." He drank down a third of his beer and set the mug aside. "So what's your story?" he asked.

"My story?"

"I take it you're divorced."

I lowered my head. "Soon to be. We've been nitpicking over the details for the last two years. I got word on Saturday that Jake has agreed to the settlement offer. We're ready to sign the final papers."

"The day you backed into the ditch."

"Yeah." My fingers curled around the wineglass stem. "I was so sure I'd made the right decision to leave Jake. In the beginning I was strong. I mean, it hurt like crazy, but I refused to stay in a marriage when my husband's brains and sense of honor shifted below his belt."

"He cheated? On you? Is the man blind?"

His words were good for my ego. Rather than go through the gory details, something I preferred not to discuss, I turned the question around to him. "What about you? What's your story?"

"It isn't pretty," he said, focusing on his beer. "I knocked a woman up one night when I was too drunk and horny to care about using the proper protection."

Rocco was nothing if not blunt. "Kaylene was the result?" I asked, seeing what he meant when he said it wasn't pretty.

"I didn't believe the baby was mine until Kaylene was tested. It shook me up, being a father and all. It wasn't the way I saw myself. Up until then I'd pretty much done as I wanted, but this kid was a responsibility I couldn't ignore. Her mother wasn't much of a mother, and so I took her as much as Tina would let me. By the time Kaylene was three, she was living with me about seventy-five percent of the time. I worked for old man Potter, and we got along good. Then Tina got herself killed in a car crash, so Kaylene came to me full-time."

"Potter sold you the business?"

"No, I couldn't afford it. He never had a family, so

when he got cancer, I helped him as much as I could, taking him in for treatments and doctor appointments. I lived with him for a while there toward the end, caring for him. When he passed, he left the company to me. That's the reason I never changed the name." He took another big swallow of his beer. "Told you my life wasn't pretty."

I appreciated his honesty. "You're a good father and a good person."

He shrugged. "I try. Don't think Kaylene will sing my praises, though. I don't want her making the same mistakes her mother and I made."

The server delivered the pizza, and as if she had pizza radar, Kaylene immediately appeared. I reached for my fork and knife, and spread the paper napkin on my lap. Rocco held a thick slice dripping with cheese halfway to his mouth and then he paused. He set the slice down and stared at me aghast. "You don't eat pizza with your hands?"

I hadn't realized using a fork would make him uncomfortable. "Not generally, but I can, if it bothers you," I said, and set the utensils aside. Reaching inside my purse, I pulled out a small bottle of hand sanitizer and gave it a little squirt, then rubbed the liquid into my hands. When I finished I took a slice of vegetarian pizza.

"Do what makes you most comfortable," he said.

"Okay." I reached for my fork and knife. It was the way I always ate my pizza.

Rocco grinned and I had to say his whole face brightened. "I don't think I've ever met anyone as classy as you, Nichole."

I smiled back at him. "I'll take that as a compliment."

"I meant it as one."

I ate two slices of pizza and it tasted like heaven. Rocco consumed his entire pie.

Kaylene was up and down for most of the meal and complained when it was time to go.

Rocco walked me to where I'd parked my car and leaned over the top of the door after I slid inside. "Thanks for everything."

"Any time," I said, and to my surprise I meant it. I liked Rocco and I liked Kaylene.

Rocco stepped back, and I was prepared to close the door when he said, "If you don't mind me saying so, I think your husband is an idiot."

I smiled, soaking in the balm of his words. "I don't mind in the least." The truth was, I agreed with him. Jake and I could have had a good life together.

# CHAPTER 5

# Leanne

"Come golf with me," Kacey Woodward, my best friend, encouraged me.

"I can't," I told her, pressing the phone to my ear as I wiped down the kitchen countertops. Owen and I had enjoyed our evening together, but we'd made a mess.

"Why not?" Kacey pressed.

"Golf and the country club aren't part of my life anymore." I'd gladly given that up. Sean was the one who yearned for the country-club life. That had never been me. Rule number two applied. New friends. For the most part, I avoided the women I'd once considered friends except for Kacey. We'd been close, and she knew me better than just about anyone.

"You aren't afraid of running into Sean, are you? That man is such a sleaze. I don't know how you stayed married to him all those years."

Kacey had never been a fan of Sean's, which may have been the very reason she'd remained my best friend. I'd never know how many women at the club Sean had slept with, and frankly I preferred it that way. The one woman I trusted not to fall under my ex-husband's charismatic spell was Kacey.

"I'm teaching tonight and I need to prepare for class," I explained.

"You're seriously enjoying that, aren't you?"

"I am." More than Kacey would ever know. I loved my students' eagerness to learn and how freely they shared during class time. They told me about their lives and how much they appreciated the opportunities available to them in America. It wasn't unusual for them to bring me gifts to show their gratitude. Just that morning I'd made toast from the bread Nikolai had given me and it'd been delicious.

"Okay, then we're going out to lunch," Kacey said.

"At the club?" I'd prefer we didn't. The women there were more Sean's friends than mine. It would be awkward and uncomfortable for everyone.

"Any place you say," Kacey clarified.

"We can decide that later. Come into the city."

"Okay."

After agreeing, Kacey hesitated, which could mean only one thing. Something else was on her mind, something she was reluctant to say over the phone. I waited, weighing if I wanted to know what she had to tell me. No doubt it was a matter involving Sean. Sensing her hesitation, I said, "I know you called about more than golf or lunch. Just tell me." She'd be uncomfortable until she did.

"Tell you what?" she said with a hint of defensiveness.

"About Sean's latest flavor of the month." I knew

Kacey all too well. "You aren't going to rest until you do, so spill it."

"Oh Leanne, that man has everyone talking. He's got this woman living with him and I swear she can't be a day over thirty-five. He's parading her around the club, and I'd be shocked if her brain was any bigger than that of a hummingbird."

I smiled because when it came to beautiful women, I was convinced Sean's brain wasn't much larger. But actually, when it came to cheating, he was a Mensa member with the clever lies he told.

"We'll do lunch and you can tell me more." We set a date and I disconnected.

I finished wiping down the counters, turned on the dishwasher, and checked the time. Nichole got a substitute-teaching job for the day and I was scheduled to pick up Owen from his preschool class at two. I didn't have nearly as much time to dedicate to my lesson as I wanted.

The dishwasher went into the washing cycle when my phone rang. Thinking it was Kacey again, I reached for it and held it to my ear. "Now what?" I asked cheerfully.

"Leanne."

It was Sean.

This was the first time I'd talked to my ex since the divorce was final nearly a year and a half earlier. My pulse raced and my hand automatically went to my throat. "Hello, Sean," I said as evenly as I could manage.

"How are you doing?" he asked in that caring, sincere way of his. At times he could be charming and gracious, which was what had made it so hard to leave him. His ability to be tender and loving was equal to his capacity to be deceptive and underhanded. He could rip out my heart and then be the first one to pick it up and hand it back to me.

"I'm doing well." With effort I resisted the urge to add that he appeared to be doing all right himself. "What can I do for you?" I asked, wanting to send the message that I had no intention of wasting time on idle chitchat.

"Could we meet?" he asked.

"Meet? Why?"

"I need to talk to you about Jake. I'm worried about him and could use your advice."

That he would reach out to me couldn't have been easy. Still, I hesitated.

"It would be just the two of us. Let me take you to dinner."

My hand moved from my throat to my forehead. "When?"

"Tonight, if you're available."

"I'm not." That seemed to surprise him, and so I added, "I have class."

"You're taking a class. Leanne, that's wonderful. I'm glad to hear you're looking for ways to expand your education."

"Actually, I'm teaching a class." I smiled, gratified to have surprised him further.

"Oh, okay. Tonight works best for me. How about after your class, say around nine-thirty? Or is that too late?"

"No, that should work."

He picked a popular bar not far from my apartment. If he hadn't mentioned our son I wouldn't have agreed. I wasn't uneasy about meeting Sean—well, maybe on some level I was, and really, who could blame me? We shared a long history and a child. I couldn't ignore either. I assumed when we divorced that there would naturally be some contact between us.

"See you then," Sean said, and we disconnected.

Nikolai met me in the parking lot the same way he had on Monday evening, and true to his word, he had baked me another loaf of bread. I thanked him and he walked me into class, taking the same prominent seat he had before. Everything about him spoke of eagerness. When I'd told him he was my star student, I hadn't been exaggerating.

We continued the lesson on idioms. With each one we discussed, Nikolai took notes in a small pad he tucked in his shirt pocket as if to keep it close. He also had a list of idioms he didn't understand that he brought to class for us to discuss.

Again, once class was dismissed, he waited until I was ready to leave and then walked with me to the parking lot.

I was beginning to feel mildly guilty that he stayed because of me. "Nikolai," I said softly, not wanting to hurt his feelings, "I appreciate your thoughtfulness, but you don't need to escort me to and from the parking lot every class."

As I feared, his face fell. "You no like?"

"It's thoughtful of you, but it isn't necessary."

"I keep you safe."

I didn't need a bodyguard. The neighborhood was

decent and I hadn't heard of any crimes taking place close to the Community Center.

"It is my honor, but if you no want . . ."

I didn't mean to offend him, and from his expression I could see that I had. "Nikolai," I said, starting again. "I know your job requires you to be at the deli early in the morning. I hate the thought of you losing sleep when you could be heading home instead of waiting for me." There'd been a couple times that it was close to nine-thirty before I was able to leave class.

"I sleep like tree every night. No worries."

*Like tree,* I thought, confused, until I remembered this had been an idiom we'd discussed in class. "Oh, you mean you sleep like a log."

"Yes, yes. Like log, not tree. I can still walk with you, okay?" His face was full of hope.

"If you want," I said.

His smile became huge, as if I'd just announced he'd won a million dollars in the state lottery.

He stepped back when I opened my car door.

"Teacher . . ."

"Leanne," I reminded him.

"Yes, Leanne. You look . . ." He paused and searched for the right word and then shook his head at a loss.

Knowing I would be meeting Sean, I'd taken extra care, dressing and applying makeup. "Pretty," I suggested.

Again he flashed me one of his big smiles. "Yes."

I was far too old to blush, but I felt the heat seep into my cheeks as I accepted his compliment even though I'd given him the suggested word. The appreciation in his eyes stayed with me as I hurried to meet Sean.

By the time I had parked and walked to the lounge it was a few minutes past nine-thirty. Sean had chosen well. I was afraid the bar would be busy and loud. Instead the atmosphere was subdued and low-key. While the room was crowded the noise level was held to a minimum.

Sean stood when I entered and then walked around the table to greet me, holding out his hands.

"Leanne," he said, eyeing me appreciatively. "You look stunning."

I smiled and took my seat. Compliments rolled off his tongue with practiced ease and I was never sure how sincere they were.

"You've lost weight."

I had, but I doubted that he would notice the five pounds. However, I wouldn't keep that weight off if I continued to eat Nikolai's delicious bread.

Sean already had his drink—a dirty martini. He held up his glass for the waiter, who immediately stepped over to our table. I ordered a glass of white wine, which was more to my liking. Sean had never approved of the fact that I didn't appreciate hard liquor. He would have preferred if I drank martinis or some fruity cocktail. I imagine his latest conquest slurped those down with no problem.

We made small talk until our drinks arrived.

Sean's easy smile disappeared, replaced with a troubled look. "I asked to see you because I'm worried about Jake."

"How do you mean?" I leaned forward, holding on to the wineglass by the stem, concerned for our son.

"He isn't doing well, Leanne. I found him drunk earlier in the week. You know that isn't like Jake. He was angry when I confronted him and then he broke into sobs. I don't believe I've ever seen him like this."

"I know that recently he and Nichole have reached a final settlement agreement," I supplied. My heart ached for Jake; I knew he didn't want this divorce. As much as possible I had stayed out of it, refusing to take sides. I wished with all my heart that I could believe Jake would remain faithful from here on out, but I had my doubts, not that I shared those with Nichole.

Sean nodded. "That must have been what set it off. Jake is a broken man. He doesn't want this divorce. He'll do anything to get his wife and son back, and it's breaking his heart."

"What about his . . . little friend?" I asked, carefully choosing the term for the woman he'd been involved with.

Sean answered with a shake of his head. "Jake was never serious about that woman. She meant nothing to him."

"He got her pregnant," I reminded him, stiffening.

Sean signed. "He took care of that, and the girl. She's out of his life. Jake knows he made a mistake."

"A doozy," I said, and sipped my wine. "The fact that he got rid of 'the mistake' doesn't matter to Nichole. Jake was unfaithful and she doesn't think she can ever trust him again." I knew from experience this was a key issue in any possibility of a reconciliation.

Sean hung his head, as if the weight of his own failings fell heavily upon his shoulders. "I blame my-self . . ."

"It doesn't do any good to cast blame now." I carried my own fair share. If I could help our son I would. "What would you like me to do?" Although I asked, I knew.

He raised his head, sighed, and said, "Will you talk to Nichole?"

Just as I thought, but I felt at a loss as to what I could possibly say. "What do you suggest?"

"Just what I've told you. Jake wants his family back and he's willing to do whatever it takes to make that happen. Nichole will listen to you."

He made it sound as if this decision rested with me instead of with Nichole. "It isn't as cut-and-dried as it seems."

"Nichole admires and respects you. You've been like a mother to her," he argued. "If anyone can get through to her, it's you."

I'd always wanted a daughter, hungered for a second child. At one point I'd suggested we adopt, but Sean refused. I'd gone so far as to contact a couple agencies, thinking if my husband understood how badly I wanted another baby, he'd give in. I'd been wrong.

Sean must have seen the pain in my eyes because he leaned forward and placed his hand on my knee. "Leanne, I know that I've hurt you, and, God help me, I couldn't be more sorry. What I'm asking isn't for me. This is for our son." His eyes searched mine and I could see the sincerity in him. "Will you talk to Nichole?"

I knew it hadn't been easy for Sean to reach out to me. He never would have if not for our son's sake. I didn't like the thought of Jake agonizing over his divorce any more than Sean did.

"Will you?" he repeated.

Slowly, I nodded.

His relief was instantaneous and his shoulders sagged as if he'd been holding in his breath. "Thank you," he whispered.

"I'm not making any promises."

"I know."

"I'll talk to Nichole, and if she's willing to hear him out one last time then it's up to her to get in touch with Jake and arrange something."

"That's all I ask."

I set my half-full glass of wine aside.

"It's good to see you, Leanne," Sean said, and as far as I could judge, he meant it.

"You, too."

He relaxed. "So you're teaching?"

"English as a second language at the Community Center. It's not far from here."

"I bet your students love you."

I smiled. "They're wonderful." My mind immediately went to Nikolai and the caring way he looked after me. His appreciation was huge. He couldn't seem to do enough for me.

We finished our drinks, and then Sean paid the waiter. We left together and stood outside for a couple of minutes.

"Where are you parked?" Sean asked.

"Around the corner." I'd been fortunate to find a spot relatively close.

"I'm across the street," he said, and leaning forward, he kissed my cheek.

I walked alone to my car as Sean looked both ways and then jogged to the other side of the road. We took off in different directions as we had most of the years of our marriage.

# CHAPTER 6

# Nichole

My attorney mailed the final divorce papers and all that was left to do was sign my name. I read them over, even though I knew my lawyer had already scrutinized every detail. I set the thick manila envelope aside.

When I married Jake I thought it would be forever, until death do us part. I believed with every fiber of my being that we would grow old together. I took my vows seriously. In the five years we'd been married I never once looked at another man. Oh, I admired a few—who doesn't?—but never with any intention of doing anything more. My appreciation was more cursory glances than actual interest. My faith and trust in my husband were total.

I could remember once shortly after our wedding, Jake and I talked about his father and the fact that Sean had often strayed. Jake had seemed appalled and embarrassed by his father's behavior. Yet it seemed that barely five years into our marriage Jake had fallen into the same pattern of cheating on his wife. Cheating on me.

With a heavy heart I collected Owen before leaving for work at the Portland High School. I'd been fortunate enough to have gotten a three-month substitute job teaching a sophomore English class for a teacher who'd broken her leg and required surgery. Mrs. Miller had taken a three-month leave of absence.

I was happy to get the job, particularly for the extra income. I needed a new car, but wanted to save for a substantial down payment before I seriously started looking.

I hadn't been at the school more than a few days when I discovered Kaylene Nyquist was a freshman there. We passed each other in the hallway one day and I immediately recognized her. Not wanting to embarrass Rocco's daughter by singling her out, I smiled. She did a double take and moved on. The second time we happened upon each other she waved. I smiled and waved back. I wanted to ask her about the dance, but waited for her to approach me.

When school was released for the day I checked my text messages and saw that I had one from Shawntelle Maynor.

*I didn't get the job.*

I sighed with regret. I'd connected with Shawntelle. I loved her wit and the way she viewed life. That girl called a spade a spade and didn't hold back. I wanted to hear every single detail, so I pressed the button to connect us. Shawntelle answered after the first ring.

"What happened?" I asked. She'd told me how prepared she'd felt after the practice interviews.

"I thought I was going to blow them away, too."

"Oh Shawntelle, I'm so sorry. Don't let this discourage you, you hear me?" I hated the thought of her getting down on herself because the employer didn't appreciate her potential. All she needed was a chance to prove herself.

"Those suckers are losing out," Shawntelle insisted.

"Yes, they are. How about I take you to lunch on Saturday and you can tell me all about it?"

"You're treating?"

"That's what I said."

"Okay, sounds good."

"Great. I'll see you Saturday." We set up a time and place. Going out would mean that Leanne would need to watch Owen. She'd do it because I'd let her talk me into going out to dinner with Jake. I'd hesitated, unsure seeing Jake was the right thing to do, but in the end I'd agreed. I knew he was hurting, but then so was I. Leanne was in a difficult position, wanting the best for both of us. The only reason I decided to go was because Leanne had asked.

Shawntelle and I chatted for a few minutes longer. I'd started toward the teacher's parking lot when I heard someone call my name. I turned around and saw that it was Kaylene Nyquist.

I held up until she joined me. "Hey," I said.

"Hey." She clenched her hand around the strap of her backpack and drew in a deep breath.

"I've wanted to ask you about the dance. How was it?"

Her eyes brightened. "Fun. I had a blast, and Dad didn't go all hyper on me."

"Did he like the dress?"

"I guess. I showed it to him and he didn't tell me to

take it to the trash barrel and burn it. We don't actually have a trash barrel, but he says that when he hates whatever I'm wearing." She paused and then added, "He says that a lot. If he chose my clothes, I'd look like a nun."

"So if he doesn't want you to burn something, that's his stamp of approval?"

"Yeah."

I grinned. That sounded like Rocco.

Kaylene looked down at her feet. "Do you have a minute?"

"Sure." I needed to collect Owen from the daycare center, but I could talk.

Once more Kaylene hesitated. "I've got a problem with my dad," she said, "and I don't know what to do."

"Oh, is he being a dad again?" I meant it as a joke, but she took me seriously.

"I'm in this group of girls around my age that my dad wanted me to join. It's part of Boys and Girls Club and it's for daughters being raised by single fathers. We go over things that mothers would normally tell their daughters, and other stuff, too. I've made a lot of friends in the group."

"Cool," I said. It sounded like a great program.

"The leader decided it would be a good bonding experience to have a dance for fathers and daughters. All of us are excited about it. I have my dress from the school dance, so Dad wouldn't need to buy me anything new."

If she told me Rocco wasn't willing to take his daughter to the dance I would be terribly disappointed in him. "Your dad doesn't want to go?"

Kaylene's face tightened and for a moment it looked as if she was struggling to hold back tears. "Dad said he'd go if he had to."

Such enthusiasm.

"But he said no way was he going to dance."

"What?"

"Dad says he doesn't dance."

"Oh Kaylene, I'm so sorry. What would you like me to do?" I'd try to help her, but I wasn't sure there was anything I could say that would change Rocco's mind.

"Would you talk to him?" She folded her hands as if praying. "Please, Nichole, you're my only hope. Dad thinks you're classy. He said he never knew a woman who ate pizza with a knife and fork."

I struggled to hide a smile.

"Will you?"

I hesitated, but not because I wasn't willing to help; I didn't know what to say other than that this dance and this group of friends were important to his daughter and he should reconsider.

"I'll do my best, but I don't know what I can do other than talk to your dad."

"You have to, you have to convince him," she said. "It'd be horrifying if my dad sat through the whole night while all the other girls were dancing with their dads."

I agreed. Kaylene would be embarrassed in front of her friends and the group leader.

"I don't know that your father will listen to me," I told her, "and I don't know that he'd appreciate me butting into your family business."

"I'll tell him I asked you to talk to him, so if he gets

mad it'll be on me." Her eyes were wide with appeal and hope.

I could see how important this was to her. "All I can do is try," I said. "I'm not making any promises, but I'll do my best."

She smiled and then, catching me by surprise, she tossed her arms around me and gave me a hug. "Thank you, thank you. I knew you'd help. Dad will listen to you."

I wasn't nearly as convinced. "Tell your father I'll be at the dress shop on Saturday and ask him to stop by before four. He knows where it is."

"Okay," she said, walking backward. "You don't want to call him?"

Strategizing, I bit down on the corner of my lip. "It'll work best if I talked to him in person."

"Thanks again, Nichole. This means the world to me."

All I could do was hope that confronting Rocco would make a difference.

Saturday afternoon Shawntelle met me at the shop and we left for lunch. "Tell me about the interview," I said, once we were seated and had placed our orders.

"The interview went good, I thought," she said, fiddling with the paper napkin. "That woman from human resources asked every single question I'd practiced. I nearly stopped her to say I could ask and answer the questions if she wanted, but thought better of it. I didn't want to intimidate her with how smart I am."

I silently agreed. My biggest fear was that Shawntelle wouldn't be able to keep her mouth shut. "Alicia styled your hair?" Although it'd been several days, Shawntelle's hair still looked great. What a difference a decent haircut made.

Shawntelle gave me a limp-wristed wave. "My hair has never looked better. With my wild curls she had to use enough hair product to sink an oil freighter. I told that woman from HR that she shouldn't expect me to look this gorgeous every day because I'd had it done up special for the interview."

I couldn't help it; I laughed out loud. "Did you really?"

"Sure I did. And look at these fingernails, girlfriend. They are a thing of beauty." She held out her hands for me to examine. Shawntelle was right. They were painted a bright, bold shade of red with tiny white daisies in the corners.

"Alicia?"

"Naw, it was a friend of hers who's training. She used me to practice on."

I'd thank Alicia later.

"I walked in that car dealership like I owned the place." Shawntelle slapped her hand on her hip and raised her chin, giving me a demonstration.

I was beginning to get the picture and it wasn't necessarily a good one.

"I told the sales manager I'd take that showroom Mercedes." Illustrating, she stretched out her arm and pointed across the restaurant. "And another in red, if available. And he could add a black BMW to the list. He didn't appear amused. Guess I shoulda quit while I was ahead."

"Maybe," I said.

Shawntelle's smile was gone by now. "That HR woman had her mind made up about me even before I went in for the interview. I could tell she didn't think I was their type. Well, la-di-da."

"Do you have another interview lined up?" I asked.

"Nope." Her face fell. "Finding a good job ain't gonna be easy for someone like me, is it?"

"Now, don't you go losing faith," I insisted. "There's a great job for you out there. Be patient."

"I'm gonna try. Next time I'll do better at keeping my trap closed. Maybe I should bake cookies and bring them in with me. I make a wicked batch of peanut-butter cookies."

"I bet you do."

We ate lunch, and although Shawntelle put on a good face I knew she was discouraged. We walked back to the shop, and just after we entered I caught sight of a patch of blue pulling into the parking lot: Rocco's tow truck.

It seemed Kaylene had convinced him to come see me. I'd half expected Rocco to refuse. I almost wished he had. While I wanted to help the teenager, there was no reason Rocco would listen to me, especially if he hadn't with his own daughter.

"I need to talk to someone briefly," I told Shawntelle. "This won't take long."

"Sure thing, Sugar Pie." She sifted through the rack of clothes and peered through the window.

By the time I was out the door, Rocco had climbed out of his truck. He met me in front of the shop.

"Kaylene said you wanted to talk to me." He crossed his arms over his massive chest and braced his feet apart. He resembled the Jolly Green Giant, except he wasn't smiling. And he wasn't green.

"It's good to see you, Rocco," I said, using a gentle tone.

He blinked and cautiously glanced toward me. "I know Kaylene told you about that father-daughter dance. I don't care what you say, I'm not changing my mind."

This wasn't starting off well. "It means a lot to your daughter."

He held firm. "I don't dance."

"You don't really have to dance dance," I assured him. "It isn't like it is on television, where you're going to be judged or asked to do complicated steps. This is just you and your daughter."

"And about twenty others watching me make an ass of myself. It's not happening."

"Rocco, every other father there feels the same as you."

He stiffened. "I don't think you heard me. I. Don't. Dance."

My head went back at the vehemence in his voice. "Did you have a traumatic experience as a teenager?" I asked, half joking.

"No."

He was an impregnable force, unwilling to move.

"Rocco, listen, Kaylene came to me because she wants to do something special with you. I promise it won't be as bad as you think."

He snickered.

I was growing desperate. "Tell you what. You and Kaylene stop by my apartment one night and I'll teach you."

He blinked, cocked his head to one side as if he didn't believe me, and frowned.

"Are you willing to do that much?"

He hesitated. "You throwing in dinner with that invitation?"

"No."

His mouth quirked and his frown deepened.

"Oh all right, dinner." I didn't like it, but he gave me no options.

"When?"

"Monday. Come at six."

He cracked a smile and his eyes brightened. "You got it. See ya then."

"You drive a hard bargain, Rocco Nyquist." Grumbling under my breath, I shook my head and returned to the store, none too pleased. I'd gotten roped into this and I wasn't happy about it.

Shawntelle was standing in front of the picture window with a keen eye watching me. "Who was that?" she asked, hands on her hips. "Girl, you been holding out on me."

"Rocco's a friend," I said simply. I didn't want her thinking otherwise.

"Sweetie Pie, that is one fine-looking man. My panties got wet the minute I saw him."

"Shawntelle!"

"You say he's just a friend. What's wrong with you? You don't friend-zone a man like that. You hog-tie him down and give him a piece of whatever he's missing."

Amused, I shook my head and explained, "It isn't like that with us. I'm helping him and his daughter."

"He married?"

"No."

"I'll tell you what. You don't want him, then you throw him my way. I'll be more than happy to show that man a little bit of heaven."

# CHAPTER 7

# Nichole

By the time I got back to the apartment it was late Saturday afternoon. The first thing I did was check in with Leanne. I knew how tiring Owen could be, and I wanted to be sure she was up to the task of keeping him longer. The truth was I would have welcomed an excuse to put off dinner with Jake.

"Mommy, Mommy," my son cried, racing toward me. "Grammy let me make cookies."

Owen didn't seem the least bit disappointed to remain with his grandmother while I left again. We hugged and he settled down to a Disney movie while Leanne cooked his favorite dinner.

My mother-in-law didn't ask about my dinner with Jake, and I was relieved. She hadn't shared her thoughts or given me advice. Leanne couldn't, and I appreciated her position. I knew it was difficult for her to see Jake in this kind of emotional pain. At the same time she couldn't bear for me to endure the soul-sucking degradation she'd suffered because she'd made the choice to stay in her marriage.

It was times like these that I needed my mother, only my mother was dead. Karen, my oldest sister, lived in Spokane and Cassie was in the Seattle area. I'd reconnected with Cassie two years earlier, after nearly fourteen years of estrangement. She'd been trapped in an unbearably abusive marriage and had finally escaped. Not knowing if I'd be able to reach either of them, I got my phone and dialed Karen first.

Karen's life was busy with family responsibilities. Her kids, Lily and Buddy, were involved in a number of activities, so to catch her and have a decent conversation was almost impossible. Nevertheless, I felt I had to try. To my relief, she answered almost right away.

"Nichole, what's up?"

"You in a rush?" I asked.

"I'm always in a rush. What's happening?"

"Hold on. I'm going to see if I can catch Cassie." I put her on hold and punched the key that would connect me with my middle sister.

"Hey, Nichole," Cassie answered.

"Do you have a minute?" I asked.

My voice must have revealed my mood because Cassie said, "Everything okay?"

"Hold on. I'm going to connect with Karen."

With the click of a button I had both my sisters on the phone. "I'm having dinner with Jake tonight," I said, thinking that would be explanation enough.

"Why?" Cassie asked, point-blank. Having been through a divorce herself, she had a better understanding of what my feelings were, although our circumstances were vastly different.

"Are you having second thoughts?" Karen asked. "The last I heard Jake had agreed to a settlement and all you had to do was sign the papers and the divorce was a done deal."

"Sean asked Leanne to convince me to meet with Jake."

"Your in-laws, right?" Cassie asked.

"Yeah. Sean told her Jake is having a hard time and doesn't want to lose his family."

"Tough," Cassie cried. "He's the one who couldn't keep his zipper closed."

"Cassie," Karen admonished. "Give Nichole a chance. Do you want a reconciliation?" she asked gently.

That was the crux of the issue. "I don't know. None of this has been easy."

"But you've made it on your own for over two years," Cassie reminded me. "You proved you can do it. It's just like Jake to decide he wants you back as soon as he realizes you're strong enough to stand on your own two feet."

"Do you still love him?" Karen asked, diverting my attention away from Cassie's comment.

"I do," I whispered. "I've always loved Jake, but I don't know if I can ever trust him again." I didn't mention the rumors I'd heard.

"You can't trust him," Cassie insisted. "It's a pattern. Look at his father and that's all you need to know. Like father like son."

"That's unfair," Karen cut in.

"But Cassie's right," I said. "When I first told Jake I

wanted out of the marriage he was incredulous. He didn't think I was serious."

"But you showed him." Cassie again.

"Yes, I proved to him I was serious, but it took time. For the last year I think Jake's been in denial. He seemed convinced I would eventually give in and change my mind. And to be truthful, I've wavered more than once."

"Of course you did," Karen said soothingly. "You love your husband and you took your vows seriously."

"Unfortunately, Jake didn't," Cassie reminded me.

"Divorce is so much harder than I ever imagined. Forget the financial and property settlement. That is nothing compared to what it's done to me emotionally. I feel like my heart is being ripped out of my chest."

"How's Owen doing?" Karen asked.

Our son was another consideration. "He misses his daddy." Involving a child in this divorce made the legal process all the more complicated. Owen needed his father and shuffling him from house to house every weekend had confused and upset my boy.

"Have dinner with Jake and listen to what he has to say," Karen advised.

"Cassie?" I asked. Although I knew what she thought, I still wanted to hear it.

My sister was silent for a moment, and when she spoke her voice was low, as if she didn't want anyone to overhear what she had to say. "I don't know if I ever told you, but Duke reached out to me a couple of years back."

I'd had no clue.

"He's in prison, which is exactly where he belongs,

and you know for one insane second I actually considered reconnecting with him. The man used me as a punching bag for years. Even knowing the violence he was capable of, there's an emotional connection that nearly sucked me in. Unbelievable." She paused and exhaled a deep breath. "All I can advise is this: Your gut will tell you the right thing to do, Nichole. Listen to your gut."

"Thank you both." I knew I was holding them both up and they had their families and busy lives. I appreciated their advice. Basically my sisters were reminding me of the very steps Leanne and I had compiled. I needed to let go of the past and at the same time love myself enough to do what I knew was right for Owen and for me.

"Listen," Cassie said before we ended the conversation, "while I have you both on the phone, Steve and I are seriously talking about taking the next step in our relationship."

"Marriage?" Karen asked.

"That's what we're discussing. I'll give you details once I have them."

"I'll wait to hear," I said. I deeply admired my middle sister and was grateful she'd been given a second chance at love and happiness. Steve was a widower, and I fully expected that if they did go ahead with wedding plans they'd want to start a family of their own fairly soon.

"Let us know," Karen said. "Gotta scoot."

"Talk soon," Cassie promised, and she, too, cut the connection.

I sat on the end of my bed for a long moment, holding on to my cell, grateful for the chance to connect with my sisters.

Following the conversation with Karen and Cassie, I showered and changed my clothes. Despite talking to my two siblings, my stomach remained in knots over this dinner with Jake. I returned to sit on my bed and pressed my hand over my tummy. Other than a few stilted conversations when Jake came to collect Owen or drop him off, it'd been more than two years since we'd spent more than a few minutes together.

My gaze automatically went to the divorce papers that rested on top of the small desk I had managed to fit in the bedroom. They sat next to my lesson plans for the following week. I stared at them for a long time, closed my eyes, and asked God to guide me.

I told Jake I'd meet him at the restaurant. It seemed simpler that way. It wasn't what Jake wanted, but he'd agreed, albeit reluctantly. He'd made reservations at the best steak house in town. I dressed in a sleek sleeveless black dress that fit my hips like a second skin. I wore the pearls he'd given me for Christmas and the diamond earrings he'd presented to me after Owen was born. I took a clutch and a featherlight lace shawl and headed out the door.

When I arrived, I found Jake sitting at the bar. He slid off the stool as soon as he saw me and kissed my cheek. Leaning back, his intense dark eyes held mine. "You take my breath away," he whispered. "You always have."

I lowered my gaze, but he placed his finger beneath my chin and lifted my eyes to his.

"I still remember the first time I saw you," he said, his voice low. "I felt like I'd been sucker punched. You're everything I've ever wanted, Nichole."

I forced a smile. I'd expected he would use flattery, but I was past the point of believing what he said, no matter how much I wanted to believe it. Flattery whispered in my ear wasn't going to change my mind.

He tucked his arm around my waist and led me to the hostess desk. The young woman smiled warmly and assured us our table was ready. We were escorted into the dining room and seated in an intimate booth. As soon as we were comfortable we were handed menus.

Within minutes our waiter appeared and took our drink orders. The server went into great detail outlining each of the specials, and then he left us to make our decision. If only this issue of a reconciliation were as easy to make as our dinner choices.

Jake barely glanced at the menu. He set it down on the table and reached for my hand, lacing our fingers together.

"Thank you for this," he whispered, and then brought my hand to his mouth for a lingering kiss.

I gently pulled my hand back. I didn't have anything to say. Although I had agreed to dinner, I hadn't decided on anything else. Jake's eyes rounded as if I'd disparaged him. I wasn't intentionally being reserved; I simply didn't know what to expect or what to read from his actions. Yes, I knew what he wanted, but he didn't seriously believe all it would take was a few words and buying me an expensive dinner, did he?

Within minutes the waiter returned with a high-end bottle of champagne. Surprised, I looked to Jake. We hadn't ordered it. It seemed Jake had earlier. If he assumed tonight was a celebration, then he was premature. My look must have said so, because he gently squeezed my hand.

The waiter poured us each a glass and Jake made the toast. "To love that lasts a lifetime," he whispered, and clicked his glass with mine.

I started to protest, but he gently pressed his finger against my lips.

"I don't mean to be presumptuous, Nichole. My heart is full of hope and that is all this is. Hope. I'm celebrating that you're here with me, nothing more."

I sipped the champagne and had to admit it was the best I'd ever tasted. After a discreet moment the waiter returned for our dinner orders.

Jake waited until the man had left and then he reached again for my hand, holding it in both of his. "I don't mind telling you, I haven't done well without you and Owen," he said, and his voice cracked just enough for me to notice that he was struggling with emotion.

I squeezed his hand. "This divorce hasn't been easy on either of us. Or Owen."

Jake kept his head lowered. "I miss my family. I can't sleep. I can't eat. I know I don't deserve a second chance, but, Nichole, I'm begging you not to sign those divorce papers."

I bit into my lower lip. "We haven't lived together in two years, Jake."

"I know, and those have been the hardest years of my life. When you first moved out I was sure you'd eventually change your mind and come back to me, but you didn't. And then the attorneys got involved and I did everything I could to hold up the proceedings. I thought that in time we'd be able to work this out."

I'd caught on early to his tactics and resisted every ploy he'd used.

"At first I couldn't believe you were serious," Jake admitted. "And then I was angry. It's only been in the last few weeks that I've realized my life wouldn't be worth anything without you and Owen. I need you both so badly."

I needed my husband, too, and Owen needed his father, which was what made this decision so difficult.

"Coming home to an empty house is killing me because I know I'm the one who drove you away. Tell me you'll give me another chance, Nichole. Give me hope that I haven't destroyed our lives by my stupidity."

The waiter arrived with our dinner salads and Jake eased back. "Let's enjoy this wonderful meal," he said. "Let's make it a true celebration."

I hesitated for only a half-second before I nodded.

Jake smiled and it seemed as if the tension eased from his shoulders. "I love you, Nichole, more than you will ever know."

After we finished our salads our steaks were served. Jake had ordered four side dishes, far more than we could ever eat. He dug in, and then, turning to me, he said, "I've missed your cooking so much."

That was a surprise, knowing that he often ate out at what he claimed were client dinners. Only later did I realize the majority of his so-called meetings had nothing to do with his job as the head of sales for a large wine company.

It was almost as if he knew what I was thinking. "I've learned my lesson, Nichole. With God as my witness, I will never give you cause to doubt me again."

A knot formed in my throat. How badly I wanted to believe that was true.

We declined dessert. Jake ordered a glass of port, but all I wanted was a cup of coffee. I excused myself and visited the ladies' room. When I returned I noticed the hostess at our table, chatting with Jake.

Jake slid out of the booth and stood when I returned. His manners had always been impeccable. As soon as I sat back down I doctored my coffee. Jake was smiling, jubilant. "I'll arrange for a moving van to come and collect your things. I know you have a lease, but I'll pay that off."

My head shot up. "I haven't agreed to any such thing, Jake. Before I make a decision I'm going to need to carefully think this through."

He looked as if I'd slugged him.

"This is an important decision and I want to be sure I'm making the right one."

For just a moment it looked as if he was about to break down. "What more can I say?" he asked. "What more can I do to convince you I'm a changed man?"

"Be patient," I whispered.

"How long are you going to make me wait? Nichole, this is killing me. Please. I want my family back."

"I'll let you know in a few days."

"Three? Four?"

"As soon as I've made my decision, you'll be the first to know."

He paid our bill and we left together. I paused at the hostess desk and waited while the woman called for the valet to bring around his car. I watched as the hostess returned the valet slip ticket and how Jake's fingers *accidently* brushed against hers.

I swallowed tightly and looked away.

Owen slept over with Leanne. I couldn't sleep. I was up half the night. I tried to read, but my thoughts drifted back to my dinner with Jake. I knew he was sincere. I knew he had every intention of remaining faithful and he would for as long as he was able. Still, I couldn't get the picture out of my mind of how Jake's hand had touched the hostess's. Anyone looking would say it was accidental, and perhaps it was. I would never know. He must have sent off some vibe for her to have approached the table while I was away, and I noticed how his eyes had briefly followed her as she'd crossed the room.

The crux was I couldn't trust Jake. I would spend the rest of our married life doubting him, questioning him every time he was late coming home or taking a weekend trip for business. The lies flowed so easily from his lips I would never be able to tell if he spoke the truth or not.

Cassie had told me to listen to my gut and my gut told me the marriage was over. As badly as I wanted to believe Jake would never stray again, my gut said he would.

With tears streaming down my face, I reached for my cell and sent him a text.

A part of me will always love you, but I feel it's best for Owen and for me to proceed with the divorce. I wish it could be different.

Once I pushed the send button, I went to my desk, took the divorce papers out of the manila envelope, reached for a pen, and signed my name.

# CHAPTER 8

# Leanne

I looked forward to lunch with Kacey Woodward, who had been my best friend through the years. Knowing how much she enjoyed tuna fish, I made tuna sandwiches with Nikolai's latest offering of bread. I cut thick slices, savoring the aroma of the dill weed and something else I couldn't name. Along with the sandwiches, I put together a fresh fruit salad from the berries I'd purchased Saturday morning at the farmers' market.

Owen had been with Jake for the weekend. My son hadn't taken the news that Nichole had decided to sign the divorce papers very well. When I gently inquired how he was doing, he'd burst into a tirade against his now ex-wife, bitterness and anger spilling out of him.

"I was willing to do anything if she'd take me back. Well, screw her. If this is what she wanted, then fine, I don't need her." He'd gone on for several minutes, blaming Nichole, claiming she was an unreasonable shrew, and casting blame on me, accusing me of siding with her against him. I tried to explain this wasn't a matter of taking sides, but Jake clearly didn't want to hear it. The decision had been hard for Nichole, and when she told me she'd planned to go ahead with the divorce she'd been in tears.

I closed my eyes as Jake continued to rant. I did my best to encourage him to move on. He didn't want to hear it and considered me a traitor both to him and to his father, claiming I'd had the power to persuade her to reconsider. To Jake's way of thinking I could have done a lot more to help him and I hadn't. To put it mildly, it wasn't a pleasant conversation and I felt emotionally and physically shaken afterward.

Because Kacey was notoriously late I gave myself an extra fifteen minutes before I set the table. Predictably, Kacey showed up at twelve-fifteen, bursting with life, enthusiasm, and the latest gossip from the club she was certain I would want to hear.

I led her into the kitchen and poured us each a tall glass of sweetened iced tea.

"I so love this apartment," Kacey gushed as she looked around. She'd been to my place before but never for any extended period of time, which was one reason I'd decided we should eat in.

I had another reason, too; I was rather proud of my decorating efforts. In the divorce settlement with Sean, I'd basically left everything in the house to him and purchased all new furnishings for my apartment. I'd placed three short lime-green sofas in a U shape around a large square white coffee table in front of the fireplace. Both sides of the fireplace had mahogany bookshelves bursting with books, many of which were autographed. This was a thirty-year collection I treasured; my books were one of the few things I'd brought from the house.

My kitchen was a bright, cheerful shade of yellow. I'd painted it myself shortly after moving in. I'd arranged white ceramic accent pieces across the counter. The second bedroom was where I chose to place the television. I had two chairs with an end table between. The closet was full of Owen's toys and he knew right where to go when he came to visit.

"You've decorated it so beautifully," Kacey said once she'd arrived. "You could have gone into home decorating if you'd wanted to," she added, and then grew thoughtful. "Actually, you still could. Have you ever thought of that? Because you're a natural. I always liked the way you did your house, but you've excelled with the apartment. If this is something that interests you . . ."

"It isn't," I admitted, reveling in Kacey's praise. "I enjoy doing my own, but wouldn't presume to know anyone else's tastes."

"Staging, then. I know this great real estate agent who . . ."

"Kacey," I said, smiling, holding up my hand. "I don't need anything to fill my time. I'm perfectly content with my life as it is. Now, come eat before our sandwiches get soggy. I made tuna fish, your favorite."

"You're happy? Really?" Kacey took her place at the table and removed the soft orange-colored napkin from its holder and spread it across her lap.

I considered the question and then nodded. "Yes. When Nichole and I first moved out we made a list of ways to help each other move on in life. The first thing on our list was to refuse to wallow in our pain."

"How could you not—especially you?" Kacey asked, and seemed genuine. "You were with Sean for thirty-five years."

It would be impossible for Kacey to understand. "I had enough pain being married to Sean. Still, there was a grieving process because divorce is a death in its own way. Nichole and I talked about how best to deal with that deep sense of loss and failure. We were each letting go of a dream, of our expectations of what it meant to be a wife, and striking out on our own for the first time. Both of us married right out of college. Neither one of us had ever lived on our own. The truth of it is I don't know if I could have ever found the courage to divorce Sean if not for Nichole." I carefully spread my own napkin across my lap. I knew Kacey found that difficult to understand.

The few friends I had kept all seemed to want to keep me updated on Sean's exploits. It was as if they were now free to tell me what I'd known all along but had refused to face. It was after such a lunch that Nichole and I decided on Rule #2, **Cultivate New Friendships.** I didn't want to abandon longtime friendships, but the longer I was out of the marriage the less I found in common with those from the club.

"Didn't you tell me you're volunteering at the Community Center?"

Just thinking about my English-as-a-second-language class brought a smile to my face. "Yes, and I'm really enjoying it."

"That's what you said." Kacey took the first bite of her sandwich, chewed slowly, and then looked up.

"My goodness, this is great." She eyed the sandwich, turned it over, and studied both sides. "This bread is homemade, isn't it? Don't tell me you've become a gourmet chef now, too."

"Not me. One of my students bakes me a loaf twice a week. It's actually very sweet of him, although I have repeatedly told him I can't possibly eat all this bread myself."

"It's delicious."

I agreed. Nikolai's bread was by far the tastiest bread I'd ever eaten.

Kacey finished off her sandwich in record time, hardly talking while she savored her meal. "I'm dying to tell you the news, but I can't stop eating. I don't think I've ever tasted bread this good."

"Nikolai is a talented bread maker." Whatever news Kacey was dying to tell me was sure to involve Sean, and frankly I wasn't interested. The key was moving on, and as best as I could, I had. Looking back stalled the progress I'd made.

"Sean—"

I held up a hand, stopping Kacey. "I don't want to hear it."

Kacey's mouth sagged open. "But it's a juicy piece of gossip." She shook her head. "I don't care if you want to hear it or not, I'm telling you. Sean took that woman, you know, another one of his 'flavors,' to dinner at the club Saturday night and—"

"He's had several through the years."

"Don't we know it. Anyway, he brought her to the club. You know how the club is on Saturday nights. Formal jackets required and all that nonsense. Anyway, this woman he had living at the house apparently found out that he'd been chasing another skirt and was outraged. She made this huge scene right in the dining room. Sean did his best to calm her down, not that it did any good. Then she stood up, took her cosmopolitan, and emptied it in his face before she stalked out."

I could imagine how mortified Sean must have been. Appearances were everything to him.

"I'm telling you, Leanne, it was all I could do not to stand up and applaud that woman, 'flavor' or not."

"She had more courage than I ever did," I said, although there'd been many a time I would have enjoyed embarrassing my husband for the way he'd humiliated me.

"Apparently, she moved out on Sunday."

I knew Sean had another woman in the house and wondered how long it would last. He seemed to grow bored with his conquests in short order.

Kacey studied me. "Don't you have anything to say?"

"Not really." Having finished my sandwich, I reached for the fresh berries. The blueberries were ripe and fat this year and had long been my favorites. "I don't wish Sean ill," I explained, meeting Kacey's eyes. "I'm not a vengeful person. We had a few good years. At one time I loved him with everything I had, but no longer. He isn't part of my life now and I'm fine with that."

Kacey continued to stare at me. "Sometimes I don't understand you, Leanne. You should be gloating."

"Why?"

"Because Sean will never be able to find anyone as wonderful as you."

I wanted to believe that, but refused to allow myself to dwell on anything having to do with my ex. "I'm not looking for revenge or justification or anything else. I have a new life and I'm just beginning to explore what all that means. I'm happier now than I've been in years."

"You know what they say, don't you?" Kacey asked, and then answered her own question. "Happiness is the best revenge."

"I am happy."

"You need a man in your life, though," Kacey insisted. "That would really tie Sean's tail in a knot and piss him off. I don't think he'd be able to stand it."

Laughing, I calmly shook my head. "I don't need a man. In fact, a romantic relationship is at the very bottom of my list of wants. If I've learned anything in the last two years it's that my life now is good exactly as it is."

"But having a relationship helps."

"I disagree," I said, although I didn't want to argue with my friend. "I'm just learning who I am and what brings me joy," I explained. Teaching, I discovered, gave me a sense of pride and accomplishment; I looked forward to every class. "Another relationship at this point would cloud my focus." While married, my life had revolved around Sean; I kept our home, entertained on his behalf, and managed our social calendar. Basically I'd seen to him and the needs of his career to the point that I'd lost my own identity. I found pleasure in discovering the things I enjoyed.

"There are dating sites that specialize in people our age. You should check them out."

"Why would I?"

"Do you want to be alone the rest of your life?"

I carefully considered the question. "I'm not really alone. I have my son and of course there's Nichole and Owen, you, and other friends." Making friends was another benefit I'd recently discovered. While married to Sean I'd avoided close friendships. I hadn't realized it until recently, and now I understood why. Friends were a risk when I was married.

Eventually, one would feel obligated to tell me about Sean's affairs. Those who didn't treated me differently after learning I had an unfaithful husband. They avoided me or were extra-sensitive or sympathetic without saying why. Friendships became awkward and weighty, and so it was best to keep only two or three women I knew were true friends.

Kacey looked so surprised by my lack of interest in a new relationship that the room went silent for several long moments.

"You really mean that, don't you." It was a statement and not a question.

"I do," I assured her.

"You're not interested in finding someone on the Internet? It's all the rage, you know."

"Kacey, not interested."

"A blind date?"

"No."

"Not interested?"

"Not interested," I echoed, amused by how insistent she was. "I'm perfectly happy."

Kacey grew serious. "You're not still hung up on Sean, are you?"

"Not at all. I wish him well. I wasn't able to make

him happy, and my hope is that he'll find a woman who will."

"You actually want him to be happy after the way he treated you?" Kacey wore a shocked, disbelieving look.

"You mean the way I allowed him to treat me?" I asked. "I could have walked out at any time. I'm the one who turned a blind eye. I'm the one who chose to die a little with every one of his affairs, so no, bottom line: I choose not to hate Sean. If I have any anger, it's directed at myself. I don't know why I waited so long to take care of myself emotionally and spiritually."

Kacey slowly shook her head. "You're the most amazing woman I've ever met."

My face relaxed into a smile. "Thank you, but I don't know if that's true. I'm being very selfish with myself right now. Taking care of me, feeding my own soul."

Kacey studied me as if she didn't know what to say.

Seeing that we'd both finished our lunches, I stood and carried our plates and bowls to the sink.

"That bread," Kacey said, repeating herself, "is amazing."

"It is," I agreed. "I'll be happy to give you a loaf." As it was, my freezer was full of bread. Despite my polite protests, Nikolai insisted on baking me bread for every class.

"Where does this talented student of yours work?"

"Koreski's Deli. From what I understand, Nikolai bakes all their bread."

Kacey wandered into the living room and looked at the bookshelves as if she'd never seen my collection before. "You have to take me there so I can buy my own."

Actually, I'd never been to the deli. "I'm not sure they sell full loaves."

"Then we should find out," Kacey insisted, reaching for her purse. "Let's go."

This was just like Kacey. Once she had her mind set on something she became an unstoppable force, forging ahead.

"Now?"

"I'm here. I can't think of a better time, can you?"

I tried to think of an excuse, but knew even if I did Kacey would veto it. Amused, I grabbed my purse and out the door we went.

Koreski's Deli was less than a mile from my apartment. Finding a parking space was almost impossible. I would rather have walked, but Kacey had insisted on driving.

Seeing that it was the lunch hour, customers formed a long line, waiting to place their sandwich orders. As best as I could see, the deli didn't sell the bread. That didn't stop Kacey, however. She got in line as I wandered around the deli, looking over the specialty items. At one point I thought I saw Nikolai in the back, but I couldn't be sure. The kitchen was visible through a small window in the door and there appeared to be several workers purposefully moving about.

I picked up a jar of garlic-stuffed olives when the door from the kitchen burst open.

"Teacher." Naturally, it was Nikolai.

Turning at the sound of his voice, I saw that he was

dressed completely in white. I smiled, letting him know I saw him.

"Everyone, please, you must see my teacher." Nikolai came around the counter and reached for my elbow, urging me toward the counter. "Mr. Koreski, this is my teacher. She knows all about English."

"Nikolai," I protested under my breath as he nearly dragged me to the front of the line to meet the owner.

"Leanne," I said, extending my hand.

Mr. Koreski wore a large white apron and was well into his sixties. A huge smile broke out across his face as he took my hand. "Nikolai talks about you all the time."

I feared that might be happening. He'd mentioned Koreski's Deli so often I knew working there was a big part of his life.

"I bake her bread," Nikolai continued proudly. "Show her appreciate."

"Appreciation," I corrected under my breath.

"Yes, yes, appreciation." Taking hold of my elbow, he led me to another employee and introduced me again. This process was completed until I felt I must have met everyone in the entire deli, including several of the customers. By this time I was convinced my face was pink with embarrassment.

"Nikolai," I said, stopping him before he dragged me onto the sidewalk so I could meet passersby. I didn't want to dampen his enthusiasm, but this was too much. "My friend is here," I said, hoping to distract him. "I made us lunch with your bread and now she wants to buy her own."

Right away he shook his head. "Not possible. I only make bread for you."

"I know, you explained you don't bake the bread here." I wanted to be sure Mr. Koreski didn't think Nikolai was stealing from the deli.

He looked at me and blinked. "Here bread is mixed by machine. At home I make with my hands."

"The deli doesn't sell your bread . . . I mean, other than just for sandwiches?"

"Not the same."

"So Kacey can't buy your bread?" I asked again, for clarity.

"No," he said again, his eyes holding mine prisoner. "I only bake bread for you, my teacher." And then he added something I didn't quite make out, but it sounded as if he said "my Leanne."

# CHAPTER 9

# Nichole

Monday afternoon, I checked my phone for text messages as I walked across the school parking lot. Sure enough, Shawntelle had sent no fewer than six messages. Each one mentioned Rocco. The last one made me smile.

Shawntelle: You lasso in that man because if you don't want him, I do.

Rocco and I were friends. I wasn't even sure you'd call us that. We were more acquaintances than real friends. I knew Kaylene better than I did him, and this dancing lesson was for her benefit, not Rocco's or mine.

Me: Rocco and I are just friends.
Shawntelle: I can have him?
Me: You might want to ask him first.
Shawntelle: I knew there was a catch.

Me: U want me to give him UR contact info?
Shawntelle: Do bears poop in the woods?
Me: U got it.

I was still smiling when I picked up Owen from daycare, and I had just walked into my apartment when my phone rang. Owen charged into the apartment as I pressed the cell to my ear.

"We still on for tonight?" Rocco asked, sounding none too happy.

"Yeah. You're not canceling, are you?"

He snickered. "Do you seriously think Kaylene would let me?"

I smiled, knowing that if he backed out now he'd never hear the end of it. "You're right. Do you like wieners and homemade macaroni and cheese? If you don't, bring your own dinner, because that's what I'm serving."

"I'll eat anything I don't have to cook myself," he assured me. "I feel bad. I shouldn't have asked you to make dinner when you're the one doing Kaylene and me a favor."

"Hey, a deal's a deal. I agreed, so come around six with an appetite and then be prepared to work it off."

Background noise filtered over the phone and I didn't hear what Rocco said next. "Sorry, I didn't get that."

"Probably better you didn't," he grumbled.

"Okay, see you and Kaylene at six." I was about to disconnect when I remembered Shawntelle's avid interest in hooking up with Rocco. "Rocco," I said hurriedly.

"Yeah?"

"One of the women at Dress for Success saw you and is interested. Do you want me to pass along your contact info?"

He chuckled. "This is a joke, right?"

"No, I'm serious. Her name's Shawntelle. She's a whole lot of woman and has got the personality to match."

He didn't answer, and at first I didn't think he'd heard me. "Rocco? Did you get that?"

"Got it."

"And?" I didn't want to pressure him, but I knew Shawntelle would bug me until she had an answer.

"No thanks."

"Okay, I'll tell her. See you later."

His response was unintelligible, but he sounded gruff, as if he was annoyed. I guessed this whole dance-lesson business had put him in a bad mood. When we first spoke he sounded like he was in good spirits, and then he'd gone all quiet and pensive on me. He might not have appreciated me trying to set him up.

By six I had dinner nearly ready. The cheese sauce was simmering on the stove and the pasta water was at the boiling point. I had brussels sprouts that I'd boiled and then sautéed in butter and garlic.

Owen was full of energy. My son got down on his knees and was driving his trucks across the living room floor and making loud noises when the doorbell rang.

It could only be Rocco and Kaylene. I greeted them and saw that Rocco wasn't in any better mood than he had been earlier. He carried a six-pack of beer in one hand and a bottle of white wine in the other.

"You ready for this?" I asked, enjoying myself. Rocco looked like a complete grump.

"I'm ready," Kaylene answered enthusiastically.

Owen jumped up and ran to greet our guests, tilting his head back as far as he could go without falling backward in order to look up at Rocco.

"Owen, you remember my friend Rocco, don't you?"

Owen nodded and Rocco stuck out his hand for Owen to bump. My son grinned and they bumped fists.

"This is Rocco's daughter, Kaylene."

Owen immediately grabbed hold of Kaylene's hand. "Come see my twucks." His lisp was becoming more pronounced lately. I was concerned, but Jake felt sure he'd grow out of it.

Looking at Rocco with fresh eyes, I had to agree Shawntelle was right; he really was a gorgeous man, something I hadn't appreciated until now. "You ready to boogie?" I joked.

He scowled at me. "Whatever."

"Dad," Kaylene growled. "Attitude check."

"Attitude check?" I repeated.

"Yeah, Dad says that to me all the time." She was down on the floor with Owen.

"What happened to put you in such a sour mood?" I asked.

Rocco followed me into the kitchen, set down the six-pack, and opened up one for himself. He held one out to me, but I declined.

"Nothing's wrong with me," he countered after taking a deep drink of the beer. "I wasn't excited about this dance lesson earlier; why should I be any more so now?"

"It'll be fun, I promise."

He'd set the wine bottle on the counter next to the beer. I knew a few high-end wines because Jake worked as the head of sales for one of the more prestigious wine companies in Oregon. This bottle wasn't one of the cheaper brands.

"This is a great bottle of wine," I said, a little surprised that he was familiar with wine.

"I figured anyone who ate pizza with a fork and knife wouldn't be interested in beer."

For whatever reason, my pizza-eating habits bugged him. "I sometimes drink beer." Not often, it was true. He had me pegged when it came to preferring wine.

"Are you telling me I wasted fifty bucks?"

"Not at all, I'll enjoy the wine." The water on the stove had gone to a gentle boil so I added the pasta, stirred it, and then set the timer for nine minutes.

Rocco lifted the lid and inspected the brussels sprouts.

"I hope you like brussels sprouts." I'd taken a risk, but they were one of my favorite vegetables.

He shrugged.

"They're Dad's favorite," Kaylene called from the living room.

I looked at Rocco and saw that he was frowning again. Reaching up, I cupped the side of his face, pulling his attention to me. "Rocco, I promise you I'll make dancing as painless as possible."

His gaze held mine for the longest moment before he exhaled and nodded. Abruptly he turned away. "Anything I can do?" he asked with his back to me.

"No, I've got everything under control."

He placed the rest of the beer in the refrigerator and then went into the living room and sat down on the sofa. Owen walked over to him and simply stared at him as if he couldn't believe how big he was. Rocco gave him a high five.

"How you doin', buddy?" he asked.

"I like twucks."

"Me, too."

Kaylene walked over to Owen. "Dad drives a truck like this," she said, pointing to Owen's toy tow truck.

Owen's eyes doubled in size. "Weally?"

For the first time since he arrived, Rocco grinned. "Really. You want me to take you for a ride one day, little man?"

Owen nodded so enthusiastically I was afraid he might topple over.

"Great. We'll figure out a time with your mom and I'll take you out."

"Weally, weally?" Owen asked again as if he couldn't believe his good luck. "Pwomise?"

"Promise, as long as your mother agrees."

Both Owen and Rocco looked to me. I smiled. "As you can see, Owen would be beside himself. Thanks, Rocco. That's really nice of you."

The timer dinged and I tested the noodles. I was about to empty the pot into the strainer when Rocco stepped behind me. "Let me do that," he insisted.

I handed him the pot holders while I got out my largest ceramic bowl. The cheese sauce tasted great. I cheated and made it with Velveeta instead of real cheese and then made it even creamier by adding a half-cup of sour cream.

He drained the noodles, added them to the bowl, and then poured the sauce over the mixture. Licking his finger appreciatively, he said, "This doesn't taste like it came out of a box."

"It didn't. I made it from scratch."

"You did?" Kaylene sounded more than impressed. "I've never had macaroni and cheese that didn't come in a box."

"This dinner might make this dance lesson worth the hassle," Rocco muttered.

Kaylene walked over to the table. "Wow, this is a real dinner."

"Wieners are my favorite." Owen climbed into his chair and eagerly reached for his fork.

"Weally?" Kaylene joked with the same lisp as Owen. We all smiled, even Owen.


I'll admit the dinner was good and my mac and cheese couldn't have turned out better. Rocco's mood improved after we ate, and I had to assume he'd been grouchy because he was hungry. Both Rocco and Kaylene helped themselves to seconds. It seemed a home-cooked meal was a rarity for them. From bits and pieces of the conversation I learned that most of their meals were thrown together or takeout.

After the dishes had been done, Kaylene was eager to get dancing. I'd chosen several songs I thought would ease Rocco into some dance moves. My hope was that he'd become more comfortable as we progressed down the playlist.

"I'm not interested in learning to tango. Just a few basic steps." He stood in his Jolly Green Giant pose again, arms crossed, glowering at me from across the room.

The music started up and it had a fast-paced beat. Kaylene leaped into the middle of the living room and gyrated her hips. She jerked her arms above her head, involving every part of her body as she proudly showed her dad her practiced moves.

Rocco's eyes rounded. "And I'm definitely not doing that."

"Come on, Dad," Kaylene called out, thrusting both arms toward him, wanting to get him moving.

Rocco shook his head. "No. Way."

"Come on, Rocco," I said, reaching for his hand. Getting him to move was like trying to uproot the Statue of Liberty. He wasn't budging. I figured the only way to encourage him was to join Kaylene and demonstrate less-frantic moves. I moved into the middle of the floor and swayed my hips while shuffling my feet back and forth.

Owen leaped in and started jumping up and down like he was on a trampoline. "Wike this. Wike this," he shouted to Rocco.

"Great, now I'm taking dancing lessons from a three-year-old."

I hid a smile. "Just move your body a little," I told him in what I hoped was encouragement. "That's all that's necessary. Don't you feel the beat?"

"What I feel is . . ." He bit off whatever he intended to say, and from the look on his face I was grateful.

Another song played. Kaylene bent over at the waist, catching her breath. Owen mimicked her, bracing the top of his head against the carpet.

"You honestly danced like that at the school dance?" Rocco asked, scowling at his daughter.

"It's how kids dance," I assured Rocco. I reached for his hand and this time Rocco moved, stumbling forward a couple uneasy steps. "Just move your feet like this." I did a simple shuffle, moving my feet from side to side. Rocco awkwardly followed my example, watching his feet as if he expected them to curl up and fly away.

"I feel like an idiot," he muttered.

Kaylene and Owen danced circles around him, laughing as if they were having great fun.

"You're doing good."

Rocco looked up and his eyes held mine. He looked completely miserable.

"Let me show you what to do with your arms," I said, seeing that he was getting more uncomfortable by the minute and needed a distraction. I scrunched my elbows against my sides and moved my fingers along an imaginary keyboard.

"That's it?" He sounded shocked. "That's all I need to do?"

"For now," I assured him, confident that once he loosened up he'd enjoy himself and be more inclined to find his own moves.

"Dad, you look great." Kaylene paused long enough to beam him a smile.

"Do not."

"Don't argue," I said, smiling at him.

He focused his attention on me and returned with a half-smile of his own. "This isn't so bad."

"See, I told you."

"So you're one of those told-you-so women."

"Guess I am," I said, but we were both smiling and enjoying ourselves.

After another two or three dances, just as I thought, Rocco played those imaginary keys like he was Elton John. Soon his shoulders got into the rhythm of the beat and he moved those along with this fingers.

"Would you like me to show you how to dance to a slow song?" I asked.

He stopped moving. "You mean like a waltz?"

"Sort of. I took ballroom dancing classes—"

"Of course you did," he said cutting me off.

"I promise it's easy."

He closed his eyes and shook his head. "I can't believe I'm doing this."

The next song was a slower one, and I held my arms out to him. He hesitated for the briefest moment before pulling me into his embrace and wrapping both his arms around my waist, clasping them at the small of my back. He stood stock-still, staring down at me.

I sucked in a breath. For a moment all I could do was stare back. My heart started to race and it wasn't due to any exercise I'd gotten from teaching Rocco to dance. For the life of me, I couldn't stop staring up at him.

"This okay?" he asked, frowning again.

"Yeah, great." Thankfully, he didn't seem to notice anything different about me.

"What do I do next?" he asked, and when I didn't answer, he said my name. "Nichole?"

I shook myself out of this trance I was in. Had I really just stood there gawking up at him like he was a Greek god? How humiliating. I quickly broke eye contact and said, "It's really no different than what I showed you earlier. Just move your feet, but at a slower pace, while holding your partner."

"Like this?" he asked, resting his cheek on the top of my head while he held me close enough to hear his heart. Perhaps what I heard was my own, hammering at a staccato pace. It'd been nearly two years since I'd been in a man's arms. My head and my heart were swamped with feelings I was grossly unprepared to experience. I didn't make an effort to move. He was so much taller than my five feet three inches that when I closed my eyes and leaned against him my head reached only as far as his chest. His scent was distinctly male. He smelled of the forest, woodsy, with the slightest hint of diesel, which might sound unappealing, but on him it was enticing, romantic. I didn't know how to explain it. I wanted to inhale that scent and log the memory of it into my brain.

"How am I doing?" he asked in a whisper.

"Great." My own voice sounded low and slightly odd. I cleared my throat. "Actually, you're doing really good."

"Try slow-dancing with me, Dad," Kaylene said.

Reluctantly I dropped my arms and stepped back. I didn't dare look up at Rocco for fear of what he might read in me. Something had just happened between us and I wasn't sure what . . . wasn't sure I even wanted to know.

Kaylene replaced me as I stepped back. I made a determined effort to avoid making eye contact with Rocco. Picking up Owen, I pretended to be dancing with him. My three-year-old was exhausted, and within a few minutes was asleep on my shoulder.

I motioned to Rocco and Kaylene that I was putting

him down for the night and waltzed down the hallway to his bedroom. The kid was zonked-out and didn't stir when I changed him into his pajamas.

By the time I returned, Kaylene had turned off the music and they were ready to go.

"Thanks," Kaylene said, and impulsively threw her arms around my neck for a thank-you hug.

I looked at Rocco. He didn't say anything, and if I read him right, and with men it was hard to know, he looked confused. "I'll catch you later," he said.

"Dad did great."

"He did," I said. "Who woulda thunk he'd turn into another Baryshnikov."

"Who?" Kaylene asked.

"Never mind," Rocco muttered.

"You don't know, either, do you?" his daughter taunted.

Kaylene laughed and Rocco frowned, but he held my look for the longest moment and seemed to see straight into me.

Uncomfortable under his scrutiny, I walked them to the door and closed it, leaning against the wooden frame as I pondered what unspoken thing had just happened between Rocco and me.

# CHAPTER 10

# Leanne

Nikolai was absent Monday night and I was worried. He'd never missed class and I was convinced something must have happened to keep him away. This wasn't like him. He was my most dedicated student, the first one to arrive and the last to leave.

Right away my mind ran the gamut of possibilities. My first thought was that he could be sick or, worse, that he'd been injured, perhaps a job-related incident. My mind filled with possibilities, all of which distressed me. Throughout class I was distracted. It didn't feel right without Nikolai sitting in the front row, contributing to the discussion. I hadn't realized how much he added to the class or how much his fellow students relied upon and liked him. The two hours of class fell flat; the evening dragged.

By the time I walked to the parking lot I couldn't bear not knowing what had happened. If he needed medicine or help I'd be willing to do what I could. I had his contact information in the records that were given to me, which included his cell number.

Sitting in my car in the Community Center parking lot, I debated whether calling him was the thing to do. The decision came when I realized I wouldn't rest easy until I talked to him.

I punched in his number. Nerves caused my finger to tremble and I held my breath when the phone connected. After four rings I was prepared to disconnect when he answered. He sounded groggy, as if I'd woken him from a sound sleep.

"Hello," he said in that deeply accented voice I had come to enjoy.

"Nikolai?"

"Teacher?" Right away he brightened and I could imagine him tossing aside the covers and bolting upright.

"Did I wake you?" Clearly I had, but I asked anyway.

"You okay?" he asked, fully alert now.

"Of course I am. I'm calling about you. You weren't in class tonight." I probably sounded like a dunce telling him something he already knew.

"No." His voice dropped to that of a whisper.

"Are you sick?"

"No."

"Were you injured on the job?"

"No, no hurt, no pain."

"Then you must be overly tired and then I woke you. I apologize . . ."

"I stay home."

"But why?"

He hesitated. "You know Milligan's?"

"Milligan's?" I didn't know why he was asking or what that had to do with him not being in class. Perhaps he'd taken on a second job. "You mean the bar close to the school?"

"Yes, bar. You meet me, have beer."

"Now?"

"You no want beer with me?" He sounded deflated, as if I'd insulted him.

"No . . . I mean yes, I would be happy to have a beer with you." I pressed my hand to my forehead, unable to believe I'd agreed to this. I'd assumed I'd drive back to my apartment the way I always did.

"I be there soon. I get table, order you Ukrainian beer. You like?"

To my surprise, I found myself smiling. "I've never had Ukrainian beer, Nikolai. Is it like American beer?"

"No, no, much better. You judge."

"Okay, I'll judge."

We disconnected and I had the strongest urge to press my hand over my mouth and laugh. I couldn't believe I was actually meeting Nikolai for a beer. Even more of a surprise was how much I was looking forward to it.


As he promised, by the time I arrived, he had gotten a table in the popular Milligan's Bar. When I walked inside, Nikolai leaped to his feet and waved, his face bright with eagerness. He pulled out a chair for me and then hurried around to his side of the table.

"I didn't know Ukraine produced beer," I said, but then I was ignorant when it came to most everything about Ukraine. Well, ignorant of anything other than the current troubles the country and the people had experienced with Russia.

"You not know about Chernihivske?"

"Say that again?" The noise level was high with music and lively talk. I strained to hear the unfamiliar name he mentioned.

"Chernihivske? A popular beer in Ukraine."

"No, sorry, I've never heard of it." I couldn't seem to stop smiling.

Nikolai's eyes were intense, focused solely on me. "You must taste. You like."

Apparently he'd already placed the order, because a server delivered two chilled mugs and two bottles of beer.

Nikolai poured my beer first, tilting the glass at an angle. "Key to good beer is lots of foam. Taste better with foam." When he finished he placed the glass in front of me, waiting for me to take a taste before he poured his own.

Because I wasn't much of a beer drinker, I was uncertain how to respond. I didn't know what I'd say if I found the taste not to my liking. Hesitantly, I lifted the glass to my lips and took a small sip.

Nikolai studied my face, patiently waiting for my reaction.

Truthfully, it was good, although not unlike other beer I'd tasted. But then I am no beer connoisseur.

As soon as I made my pronouncement, Nikolai's face broke into a huge smile. "I know you like." He poured his own glass and took a deep swallow, his Adam's apple moving up and down in his throat.

"I like."

As if he'd forgotten, he reached down and set a loaf

of bread on the table. "I make you brown bread. You eat with beer, okay?"

I smiled and nodded. My mouth hurt from smiling so much. This wasn't like me. My heart felt light and carefree, sitting in this loud bar with this man I barely knew, drinking Ukrainian beer.

We chatted for a good thirty minutes while I discussed with him a few of the slang words and idioms we'd talked about during class that evening. His mind was quick, and we laughed and joked with each other.

"We missed you tonight," I said when conversation lagged.

Nikolai instantly dropped his gaze, avoiding eye contact with me.

"You're not only my favorite student, but it seems everyone else thinks highly of you, too."

"I am your dog?"

"Teacher's pet," I corrected.

"Oh right, I your teacher pet." A hint of a smile showed, but he still didn't look up.

"Nikolai, can you tell me why you skipped class?" He seemed to be in good spirits and he wasn't ill.

He exhaled and his shoulders rose and sank when I pressed the question. "I didn't think you like me no more."

I blinked, finding that hard to understand. "Why would you think such a thing?"

"I embarrass you."

"When?" I couldn't remember anything he might have done to embarrass me, especially lately.

"At my work," Nikolai said, keeping his head lowered. "When I introduce you to my friends as my teacher."

"That was a week ago." He'd been to class that night and the following Wednesday.

"Mr. Koreski ask this afternoon. He ask if you'd forgive me for embarrassing you. Until then I not think. I not know. I feel bad in here." He pressed his hand to his heart. "I feel embarrassed."

"Are you saying you didn't come to class because of that silly offhanded comment?"

"What is offhanded?"

"Mr. Koreski was making a joke. He wasn't serious."

"But it is true. I remember look on your face when I showed you my friends. You get red face."

"I was embarrassed," I admitted, "but only because I'm not accustomed to being the center of attention." Thinking he might not understand, I elaborated. "It's uncomfortable for me to have people looking at me."

"Ah. I no mean to embarrass you. I am proud you my teacher."

"And I'm proud to be your teacher."

He looked up and his eyes held mine. He grinned and it seemed as if a weight had been taken from his shoulders. "We good?"

"We're good," I assured him. "But, Nikolai, the next time you have any doubts I want you to ask. Don't make assumptions." He might not understand that, so I added a bit more. "Ask and let me explain. Don't decide what you think I feel. Ask me instead. Okay?"

"Okay, I ask."

"You missed an important lesson tonight."

He laughed. "I'm happy I miss class."

"You're happy?" That didn't make sense.

"You call me. You miss me."

He had me there. "Yes, I did miss you. We all did."

"But you more?" His face was bright with hope.

My admitting this seemed important to Nikolai. A tingling sensation went down my arms and suddenly I was nervous. Uneasy. In that moment I realized he was right. I had missed him more than I would have any other student.

Right then I knew my heart was tender toward this man. It startled me how quickly he'd become important to me. I suppose it was understandable. I was single for the first time in thirty-five years and here was this attractive man full of respect and appreciation for me. I hadn't felt that in a very long time. I soaked up his words like a parched garden in the heat of a summer drought.

I made a show of looking at my watch. "It's time for me to go."

"You no finish beer?"

"Please, Nikolai, it's late and I should go."

His forehead compressed into a frown. "What I do? What I say? You not smile now."

"Oh Nikolai, you did nothing. You're sweet and caring and I . . . need to get home. It's late and I . . . I have things to do in the morning."

"You tell me to ask and I ask," he said, serious now. "What I say that make you run like frightened hamster?"

"Rabbit."

"You go pale and say you must go. I embarrass you again?"

I shook my head and stood, grabbing hold of my purse. "I'm sorry. Really sorry. I'll see you Wednesday in class." Reaching for the bread in the middle of the table, I rushed out of Milligan's Bar as if the building was on fire. I felt foolish and ridiculous and wanted to place my hands on my cheeks for behaving like a schoolgirl on her first date.

I'd gone only about half a block when I heard Nikolai call my name from behind me. I refused to stop and picked up the pace.

Nikolai followed me.

I was horrified by my behavior. My insides were shaking, and for just an instant I was afraid I was about to throw up on the sidewalk. God help me, I continued walking so fast I was nearly trotting.

I should have guessed my rushing away wouldn't stop Nikolai. He followed me to where I'd parked my car on a side street. I wasn't sure what I would tell him.

"Leanne?"

His voice was soft and so caring that I nearly dissolved into tears.

He stood on the street beside me and my car, his eyes full of questions as he searched my face. "Why you run from me?"

I shook my head, unable to answer. "I shouldn't have called you."

"Why? You make me happy when you call. So happy."

I couldn't look at him, afraid if I did he'd see the longing in me. It pooled in the pit of my stomach, so unfamiliar I didn't know what to make of it. "It's not appropriate that I see you."

"What this appropriate?" He raised his hands in question.

"I'm your teacher . . . it's not seemly," I said.

"I quit class, then it be this . . . what that word? Appropriate?"

"Oh Nikolai . . ." I looked up and raised my hand to cup his strongly defined chin.

His hand joined mine, and he turned his face and kissed the inside of my palm.

The sensation that shot through me was so strong my knees nearly buckled. "I don't know what I'm doing," I whispered, looking away.

"I'm glad you call," he whispered, inching his hand around the side of my neck. "All day I think about you. I want to say how I feel, but I don't know right words." His dark eyes grew more intense as he looked down at me. "I give you bread to say what I not able to say with words."

My whole being hungered to hear those words. His eyes held mine, bright and unblinking, filled with longing.

With pressure at the base of my neck he eased my head forward and settled his lips over mine. I am at a loss to describe what his kiss did to me. I felt that single kiss in every part of my body. My response was immediate. I opened to him like a desert flower after a cloudburst that flooded the arid soil. My heart beat so hard I was afraid it might injure one of my ribs.

Nikolai's fingers wove through my hair, and when he broke off the kiss, he buried his face in my neck.

I was speechless, unable to utter a single word, shocked at my unbridled response to him. It frightened me that I could feel such overwhelming emotion from a single kiss.

This came less than a week after my conversation

with Kacey. I'd insisted that I didn't need a man in my life. What I found shocking was that I wanted a man. Not any man. I wanted Nikolai. With effort, I eased myself from his arms.

He leaned his forehead against mine. "You give me chilly bumps."

I smiled gently and softly pressed my lips to his. "Goosebumps."

"See. Look at my arms." He stretched out his arm for me to examine. "You do that. You make my heart loud. Feel." He captured my hand and pressed it against his chest. "See what you do?"

His face was open and warm as he studied me. He saw me as beautiful, as if I were a woman to be worshipped and cherished. His eyes were so tender I was unable to keep the tears at bay.

The first teardrops made wet trails down my cheeks. Nikolai used the pads of his thumbs to smear them away. "Why you cry?" he asked, frowning. "I hurt you with my kiss?"

"No, never."

"But you cry?"

"I don't know why." I did, but telling him would only encourage him to kiss me again.

"I come to class on Wednesday," he promised.

I nodded.

"We talk then. Have more Ukrainian beer."

I couldn't help myself. I smiled.

"You even more beautiful when you smile." He opened the car door and I slid inside. He closed it and stepped back. I drove off, my head muddled, my thoughts confused.

It was after ten by the time I arrived back at the

apartment. Knowing Kacey was a night owl, I sat on the sofa in front of the fireplace and called her, pressing the cell hard against my ear.

"Leanne, has something happened? Are you all right?"

I wasn't sure how to answer her. "I'm wonderful."

"If that's the case, then why are you phoning me this late? This isn't like you."

She was right. In all our acquaintance I'd never phoned past nine. "I was thinking about what you said last week when we had lunch."

"I said a lot of things."

"I know. I'm talking about your suggestion that I log on to one of those dating websites."

"You're gonna do it?" She sounded surprised.

I closed my eyes and bit into my lower lip. "Yes," I whispered. "I'm ready to date again."

Nikolai had shown me exactly how ready I was.

## CHAPTER 11

# Nichole

The final divorce papers, signed and recorded, arrived in the mail on Tuesday afternoon. Neither Jake nor I were required to be in court. The entire cut-and-dried process had been handled by our attorneys. I didn't read the papers, didn't even open the envelope until after Owen was down for the night. As soon as my son was asleep, I took them out of the envelope and stared at the legal jargon for several minutes. My heart pounded like the judge's gavel, securing the nails in the coffin of my marriage.

Two hours later I sat in the dark, sipping the expensive wine Rocco had brought with him the week before in appreciation for the dinner and dance lesson. I didn't know when the tears started. They came unbidden, unwelcome. I thought I'd shed all the tears I had in me over the failure of this marriage. But I was wrong.

Within an hour I'd emptied nearly an entire box of

tissues and blown my nose so often I was sure it would be as red and swollen as my eyes come morning.

When my cell rang I almost didn't answer until I saw that it was Jake. I knew he had to be hurting as much as me.

"Hey," I whispered, not wanting him to know I was crying.

"Hey." He paused. "You okay?"

"Yeah. What about you?"

Again, the hesitation. "I'll survive. You got the final papers today?"

"Yeah. You, too?"

"Yeah." We didn't have that much to say to each other.

"It's my weekend for Owen," he reminded me. "I'll pick him up from daycare Friday afternoon."

"Okay."

We both went silent, our aching hearts beating in unison.

Jake spoke first. "I don't know what more I could have done, Nichole. I didn't want this."

I didn't, either, but I couldn't go back into a relationship and constantly be afraid, wary of trusting him again. I couldn't constantly be looking over my shoulder, wondering where Jake was or who he was with every time he was late. I wasn't his mother. I couldn't live the way she had all those years.

"I loved you," Jake whispered, and his voice was hoarse with pain.

Yes, Jake had loved me, but not enough to remain faithful. "I loved you, too."

"You'll never find anyone like me."

I tilted my head back and stared at the ceiling. "Isn't that the point, Jake?"

"I treated you like a princess," he continued, ignoring my comment.

What he said was true. He had spoiled me; he'd given in to my every whim, constantly buying me gifts, pampering me. I wondered again if those presents were given out of love or because he felt guilty after sleeping with other women. I guess I would never know. It wasn't important now, and I pushed the thought aside.

"I'll make sure Owen has enough clothes with him to last the weekend," I said, because really there wasn't anything more for us to discuss.

"Yeah, do that."

"Good-bye, Jake."

"Yeah, whatever." He abruptly cut off the connection.

I returned to crying, and reached for another tissue when my cell rang again. "Ye-s-s," I said, my voice wobbling on the tail end of a sob.

Silence followed.

I was about to hang up when I heard Rocco's voice. "That you, Nichole?"

"It's m-e." I paused and blew my nose.

"Are you . . . crying?"

"Ye-s-s."

"I'll call back another time?"

"O-k-ay." My emotions were too much for him to handle. I can't say I faulted him. "Did you . . . n-e-e-d some-t-h-i-n-g?" I asked, doing my best to sound normal and failing miserably.

"I'll text it, okay?"

"O-kay."

We disconnected and I set the phone aside, waiting for his text. After ten minutes I gave up. It seemed having to deal with me sobbing into the phone was enough to send him running for the hills, not surprisingly.

I'd been around enough men to know they were uncomfortable with women's tears. Although I didn't know Rocco well, I suspected he'd do just about anything to avoid a crying female. Since he hadn't sent me a text, I had to believe whatever he'd wanted couldn't have been important. More likely, it was something he could ask me later.

After fifteen minutes my doorbell chimed. It could only be Leanne. I hadn't mentioned I'd gotten the final papers and I wasn't sure I was up to one of our pep talks or a review of our guide to moving on. The lights were off and she'd probably assumed I was down for the night, even if it was only a little after nine.

"Open up, Nichole," Rocco called from the other side of the door. "The ice cream is melting."

*Ice cream?* I frowned and turned the dead bolt and opened the door.

He stood on the other side of the threshold holding a pint of Ben & Jerry's Cherry Garcia ice cream.

"It's dark in here," he commented, looking past me.

"The light hurts my eyes."

"Are you going to let me in?" He held up the container, as if I hadn't already seen it.

I stepped aside and he came inside the apartment.

"Sit down and I'll bring you a spoon," he said.

I returned to my spot on the sofa. "Bring two.

Otherwise, I'll eat the whole thing myself," I said and sniffled.

I heard a crash in the kitchen followed by a swear word. "Can I turn a light on?" he asked.

"I guess."

"I'll turn it off once I find the spoons," he promised.

"Leave it on." I didn't much care.

Rocco kept the light on and joined me in the living room. He handed me a spoon and then sat down next to me. He stared at me and shook his head. "You look awful."

"Thanks."

"Why all the tears?"

I dipped the spoon in the carton and took out a large mouthful of ice cream, which by this point had gone soft. "The final papers for my divorce arrived."

"I thought it was already final."

"It is now."

Rocco took his first bite. "Do you still love him?"

I hiccupped a sob and nodded. "Stupid, isn't it? I divorced him and I still love the jerk."

"I'd think less of you if you didn't love him," Rocco said, helping himself to more of the Ben & Jerry's. "He fathered your son and at some point he deeply loved you."

"Just not enough to keep his pants zipped."

"He regrets that now. Hopefully it's a lesson well learned."

I swallowed against the cold ice cream and closed my eyes. "Then why am I the one hurting like this? Why am I the one crying my eyes out?" It was an unfair question because I knew Jake was hurting, too.

"Because you loved him."

I grabbed a tissue as fresh tears rolled down my face. "You do this often?"

"Do what?"

"Bring women with broken hearts ice cream?"

He chuckled. "No. Whatever you do, don't tell anyone. My friends hear about this they'll think I've grown a vagina."

At first his words shocked me and then I sucked in a deep breath as the amusement rolled up inside me, coming from deep within my stomach. His words had caught me by surprise. I couldn't breathe, and when I could, I doubled over with laughter.

"Nichole?" Rocco said, sounding concerned. "You okay?"

I laughed so hard I nearly choked.

"Are you laughing or crying?"

"Laughing," I said when I could.

"You think that's funny? I'm serious. Kaylene's forced me to watch enough chick flicks through the years. I know that's what women do when they're brokenhearted. I figured you could use a little Ben and Jerry's therapy."

"I promise not to let your secret out."

He frowned and set his spoon aside. "I knew this was a terrible idea." He was off the sofa and pacing.

I stretched out my arm. "Come on, Rocco, who am I going to tell? I don't know any of your friends. Cross my heart." I made a huge *X* over my chest.

He visibly relaxed.

"You called earlier. You need something?"

He looked uncertain and pinched his mouth as if debating whether or not he should ask.

I patted the empty space besides me. "I promise not to laugh."

"I'm more afraid of your bite."

I didn't know how I could go from the depths of despair to laughing hysterically in just a matter of minutes, but Rocco had managed to achieve the impossible. "When did I bite you?" I demanded.

"You talked me into that ridiculous dancing lesson."

I wasn't going to let him off easy. "Which you enjoyed. Admit it!"

He sighed. "Okay, it wasn't as bad as I thought it'd be."

"A girl could swoon with the compliments you give." I placed my hand over my heart and fell sideways on the sofa and then released a loud sigh.

He cracked a smile. "I got a deal for you."

"A deal?"

"You know. I-tow-you-out-of-the-ditch-and-you-shop-with-Kaylene kind of deal."

I wasn't sure I liked the sound of this. "Okay, I'm curious enough to find out what it is."

He started walking again, pacing in front of the coffee table. "Kaylene got this bug up her butt about getting pictures for this father-daughter shindig before the dance. She wants you to take them."

That didn't sound like such a big deal.

"She says you're the only one she trusts to do it right."

"And what do I get in exchange?"

"What do you want?" He backed up a couple steps, as if he expected me to demand the outrageous.

I pressed my index finger against my chin as if deep

in thought. "You did promise to give Owen a ride in your tow truck. He mentioned it this afternoon. I told him I'd ask you about it."

"Deal." He leaned forward and thrust out his hand.

I held mine back. "I'm not done yet."

"I should have known," he grumbled, narrowing his eyes.

"Let's be fair. You'd basically already told Owen you'd give him that ride, so you're not really doing anything beyond what you've already promised. Right?" It was important he understand.

"Right," he agreed, although begrudgingly. "What else do you want?"

"I don't know. One future favor at my discretion."

"And mine," he added.

"Fair enough." I held out my hand for us to shake.

This time it was Rocco who pulled his hand back. "That's two favors I'm giving you with me only getting one."

"Yes. So?"

"So I should get two."

I arched my brows.

He cocked his head to one side. "Fair is fair."

"All right, what do you want?"

He shook his head. "Don't know yet. One future favor at my discretion."

"And mine," I said and smiled.

"Deal?"

"Deal."

Rocco held out his hand and we shook.

He joined me on the sofa. "The dance is Saturday night."

"What time?"

"Seven, so you should come to the house around six-thirty."

The man was a dreamer. "I'll be there no later than six."

"What? I'm not asking you to film *Gone With the Wind*. It's just a couple of photos. Nothing big."

"Now I know why Kaylene wants me to take the photos."

"All right, whatever."

"See you then." I got off the sofa, took the lid for the Ben & Jerry's, snapped it back on, and stuck it in the freezer.

When I finished I saw that Rocco was standing by the door. He had his hand on the knob. "This woman friend of yours. Shawn something."

"Shawntelle."

"She still interested in meeting me?"

"Oh yes. She asked about you again. You want me to text you her contact information?"

He hesitated and then nodded. "Yeah. It might be a good idea."

"You got it, but be warned, she's a whole lot of woman."

His smile was off-centered. "I consider myself duly warned." With that he left the apartment.

I turned the door lock and pressed my forehead against the wood panel as an uneasy feeling settled over me. It surprised me Rocco wanted to meet Shawntelle, but then why not? She'd certainly let me know she was interested. Normally I enjoyed matching up friends, but not this time, and I wasn't entirely sure why.

# CHAPTER 12

# Leanne

Sean contacted me Tuesday afternoon, suggesting we get together. He implied it was a matter of some importance.

"If this is about the divorce settlement—"

"It isn't," he said, cutting me off.

"Then what's it about?"

"You okay?" Sean asked, ignoring my question. "You don't sound like yourself."

"I'm great," I rushed to say, although I could feel the heat warming my cheeks. It was beyond understanding why I should feel any guilt over what had happened between Nikolai and me. My life was my own now and I could date or kiss anyone I wanted. As ridiculous as it sounded, I felt like I had a large red A painted across my forehead.

I didn't have much of a social life after Sean and I separated. It didn't feel right to date when I was still legally married, although that had never stopped Sean. Since the divorce, I hadn't felt the need. I wanted time for my heart to heal and for my head to wrap it-self around these major life changes.

His call came out of the blue. It was almost as if he sensed that I was finally and truly moving on. Perhaps he'd gotten word that I'd contacted an online dating service.

Earlier in the week I'd found a website I liked and signed up. I answered countless questions and looked forward to taking the leap back into the dating world. A connection came so quickly, it took me by storm. Earl Pepper would be my first date, and we were set to meet that Friday night. Okay, it wasn't an actual date. I couldn't think of it that way. It was a meeting to see if we were interested in dating.

"So what's this about?" I pressed.

He hesitated. "It's Jake."

"Again?" I asked. "Is this something you can't tell me over the phone?"

"I'd rather not. Will you see me or not?" His words had an edge to them, which was rare for him. "Let's have lunch."

I paused. Not at his suggestion we meet for lunch, which was unusual in itself. His voice betrayed him, and while I couldn't detect what it was right then, I knew him well enough that it would come to me later, once I'd had a chance to think about it.

"Sean, is something wrong?"

"No," he flared. "Why would you think that?" he asked, his composure back.

"I don't know that it's a good idea for us to go out."

"Would you be more comfortable eating in? I could come to your apartment. I'll let you fix me some-thing," he said as if joking, although I knew he wasn't.

Still, I hesitated. Something was wrong, something Sean wasn't keen to share with me over the phone. I hadn't lived thirty-five years with this man to not pick up on the subtleties of the conversation, the unspoken message.

"Can I see you or not?" he demanded.

"Okay," I agreed, and we set a time for Saturday.

On Wednesday I was nervous about seeing Nikolai again. I hadn't stopped thinking about the kisses we'd shared. They lingered in my mind, wrapping me in unfamiliar warmth I couldn't forget, no matter how hard I tried. I wanted to shove the memory of his embrace aside, but found my head and my heart returning to that night again and again, reliving each moment. I savored each word we'd exchanged; the taste and feel of him remained with me. While I tried to forget, I struggled with equal determination to remember.

When I arrived at the Community Center, despite my resolve not to, I automatically looked for Nikolai. Sure enough, he was waiting, and my gaze shot straight to him. The instant he saw my car pull into the lot a huge smile lit up his face. Even before I'd parked, he started walking toward me. As he had from the beginning, he brought me a loaf of his wonderful home-baked bread. I'd dreaded this evening and looked forward to it in equal measures.

As soon as I turned off the engine, Nikolai opened the car door for me. His expression was filled with such adoration that it made me want to throw open my arms and whirl around like Julie Andrews in the opening scene of *The Sound of Music*.

He smiled and couldn't seem to stop staring at me.

I blushed at his attention and looked away, embarrassed and thrilled. He confused me until I stuttered, "Hello, Nikolai."

"Hello." He flattened his hand over his heart. "I think day. I think night. I think about kissing you again and again. I dream about kisses. Memory is like wasp in my basket."

I had to think that one over. "Bee in your bonnet?"

"Yes, that. I think and think and you never leave my head."

I admit it had been the same for me, but telling him that would only encourage him, so I said nothing.

"You like, too?" he pressed. "You think of kiss?"

"Nikolai"—I grabbed my purse and books, avoiding eye contact—"we should get ready for class."

He handed me the loaf of bread. "For you."

"Thank you." I knew better than to refuse. To Nikolai, bread was everything. He'd admitted that he let the bread say what he couldn't with words. Him telling me that had been burned into my memory. Never had I heard anything more romantic or loving.

We walked toward the center when Nikolai reminded me, "You come have Ukrainian beer with me tonight?"

Even before I left the house I knew he'd remind me that I said I would. I intended to beg off, but at the warm look in his eyes I couldn't bear to disappoint him. I nodded. His smile was bigger than ever.

Class seemed to fly by, and before I knew it our time was up. My students left the room, chatting and talking to one another on the way out the door. As always, Nikolai was the last to go. "We meet same place?" he said.

I hesitated. "Nikolai, I don't know that—"

"We no need go to Milligan's. We go close. Walk from here, okay?"

Refusing him was almost impossible. I couldn't look into his deep, dark eyes so full of life and happiness and refuse him.

"Okay," I said.

He took my hand, curling his fingers around mine as we walked three blocks to an upscale tavern. It wasn't as busy or loud as Milligan's.

We were directed to a booth and Nikolai helped me take off my coat. As soon as we were seated he handed me a drink menu. Nikolai frowned with disappointment as he scanned the sheet. "They no have Ukrainian beer, so we must drink American beer. Not as good but okay."

I hid my smile. "I'd prefer a glass of wine, if you don't mind."

"No, no, I no mind. You have whatever you want. You hungry?"

I shook my head. "I ate before class."

The waiter came for our order and left, promptly returning with our drinks.

Nikolai waited until the other man had left before he spoke. "You worry?" he asked, his face full of concern. "I see it in you. You not smile as deep." He stretched his arm across the table and gripped hold of my hand. "Tell me. You can say everything to me."

I didn't realize I was so transparent. Although I'd had a couple days to mull over what to tell him, I found myself lost in him, lost in the love and warmth radiating from him.

"Is it about kisses?" he asked.

"I liked kissing you, Nikolai." It was important that I not offend him. The truth was that I'd enjoyed his kisses more than I dared admit. "You have to remember I was married for thirty-five years . . . I was faithful to my husband."

He studied me, not speaking, waiting with what looked like worried anticipation.

"I haven't . . ." I briefly closed my eyes, unsure how to explain what I felt. "I like you so much . . ."

His face exploded into a smile; the corners of his eyes crinkled with thin lines fanning out. I paused, thinking he might want to respond, but he didn't.

"You were the first man I've kissed since my divorce," I whispered, lowering my head. I sipped the wine, hoping it would lend me courage to say what needed to be said.

"That is great honor." His eyes sparkled with happiness. "And you like me. I like you, too. I not kiss lots of women since my wife die. My heart too sad until I meet you and then I say, Now is time. This is good woman. When I come to America I think it time. I think this is second chance for me. When I arrive, I have nothing but my two hands."

To make his point, he held up his hands.

"All I know is bread. Bread is life and I feel it my honor, my privilege, to bake my bread. Friends help me, friends from Ukraine help me, find me place to live. It's nice apartment, you come visit sometime, okay?"

I made a noncommittal gesture, but he didn't seem to notice, as he was busy talking.

"Friends introduce me to Mr. Koreski and I bake bread for him and he ask me to come work at deli. I happy. I think Magdalena help me from heaven. She tell me it time for me to start new life in America and let go of old life in Ukraine."

This was the first time he'd mentioned he was a widower. I'd suspected he'd been married, but he'd never said. "It's good that you have friends."

"I make more friends. From class. Good friends."

He continued to study me intently.

"Female friends, too," I said, feeling shy and a little embarrassed.

He hesitated. "Some."

I continued to press, hardly able to understand myself. "You've kissed other women since your wife died, right?"

He sobered and nodded. "I sorry. I not meet you yet."

"Nikolai, please don't apologize. That wasn't why I asked."

"No one else make me feel like you. When I with you I feel joy in my stomach, in my arms and legs. My head feel joy and I want to bake bread again, bread with my own hands, not bread from mixer like in deli."

I knew what I was about to tell him would wound him. Just knowing that hurt me. It was important that I not mislead him. This was all new to me and rather unexpected. "I need to see other men, Nikolai. You're the only man I've kissed since my husband, and I don't know what I'm feeling with you. It could be the simple fact that it's been a long time since I've felt a man's touch. I don't want to hurt you, but I don't want to lead you on, either."

The happiness drained out of him as he stared at me as if he was sure he'd heard me wrong. "You want to meet other men to kiss? How you meet these men?"

I swallowed and nodded. "I signed up with an online dating service."

He shook his head as if to say this was all wrong. He pulled his hand away from mine. His eyes grew intense, as if he were unable to understand what I'd told him. "What is this dating service?"

"It's a place where single men and women go to meet other people."

"You need to meet other people?" Again he shook his head. "You go to meet and kiss other men?"

"Maybe. I don't know yet."

"When you do this?"

I wasn't sure what to tell him. "I'm seeing someone Friday night. It's not a date. We're just meeting for coffee to see if we're compatible."

A frown darkened his face. "What this word *compatible*?"

"It means that we're meeting to see if we want to date, to continue spending time together."

Nikolai looked utterly dejected.

"Do you understand why I'm doing this?" I asked.

He shook his head. "No, I not understand why you want other man. Why you want to kiss other man you not even know."

"I won't be kissing him." I needed to clarify that, because the time might come when I would kiss Earl. "Not on Friday."

Relief showed in his eyes. "You no kiss this man?"

"We're only having coffee," I explained again, and glanced at my watch. "I need to get home. Thank you for the wine."

Nikolai left money for our drinks on the table and then helped me put on my coat. "I walk you to car."

"I'd like that."

He took my hand again and was quiet on the return trip. I knew he'd need time to absorb what I'd told him. When we reached the parking lot, I unlocked my car and he opened the door for me. He didn't kiss me and as I drove away I realized how disappointed I was that he hadn't.

By Friday I was an emotional mess. Thankfully, I had Kacey to talk me off the edge of the cliff. She stopped by the apartment and spent most of the afternoon offering me advice and encouragement.

"Just be yourself," my longtime friend said, as if this evening would be a breeze.

"I feel . . . I don't know . . . unnerved." I needed to remember this meeting hit two items on our list—number two and number three—**let go in order to receive** and **make new friends.**

Kacey thrust her fists against her hips. "Unnerved? Whatever for? It's coffee. What could possibly happen? He's vetted, you've vetted. Have fun. Live a little." She was full of advice. I wondered how she'd do in my situation. Silly question. Knowing Kacey, she'd sail through the entire meeting without so much as a hiccup.

I shook my head and didn't feel the least bit reassured. "Do you realize how long it's been since I've gone on a date . . . I know, I know, this isn't a date. We're just meeting for coffee."

"Have you and Earl spoken?"

"Just by email." Earl sounded pleasant enough. We were around the same age and both divorced. On paper we were a perfect match, or so the computer seemed to think. I liked that he was local. It seemed we had a lot in common. Like me, he enjoyed reading and puzzles. We shared the same political views and values. He believed in God and family the same as me and he attended church. I did as well.

Once I was dressed and ready to go, Kacey stepped back and wore a smug, satisfied smile. "You look great."

I should, after we'd spent the better part of three hours shuffling through every item of clothing in my closet. I'd tried on more outfits than a Macy's mannequin.

Nichole stopped by just minutes before I was set to leave the apartment. Kacey had returned home in order to get ready for some wine-tasting event at the country club with her husband, Bill.

"I wanted to wish you luck," Nichole said, hugging me.

"How do I look?" I asked, slowly twirling around.

"Stunning. You'll blow his mind. He's going to be overwhelmed by your charm and beauty. After an hour sipping coffee you're going to ruin him for any other woman."

I shook my head and laughed. I couldn't ask for a better cheering squad. "Jake's got Owen?" I asked.

"It's his weekend," she confirmed. "He picked him up from daycare this afternoon."

I knew Nichole was still raw from the divorce. I was proud of how hard she'd worked to move on. We both had. It didn't make it easy, but being close and being able to encourage each other was a big help.

Earl had suggested we meet for drinks, but I preferred Starbucks instead. I would need a clear head. I'd never been one to indulge in alcohol. A single glass of wine was my limit.

I walked to the Starbucks, which was in the neighborhood. The sound of my footsteps pounded like nails of fear in my head. I didn't have a good feeling about this and doubted I was ready. But then I doubted that I'd ever be ready.

As soon as I walked in the door I spotted Earl right away. He sat at one of the tables and I noticed that he'd already purchased two coffees. He sat so he could see the door, and when I came inside, he stood. I noticed he had a nice smile. As I approached, he extended his hand.

"You must be Leanne."

"And you must be Earl." I made a genuine effort to smile and appear relaxed and comfortable.

"I hope you don't mind, I took the liberty of buying your coffee."

"I don't mind at all." He pulled out my chair and I sat.

The conversation flowed easily for the next hour. Neither one of us brought up our exes, and I was grateful to leave Sean out of the conversation. I learned that Earl had been single for four years and worked for Intel. He had three children, all adults, and was a grandfather twice over. It didn't take me long to discover how likeable he was or what a great sense of humor he had. Like the computer predicted, we were a good match.

Which was exactly what I told Kacey when I phoned her later that evening. She'd made me promise to call as soon as I got home. If I didn't, she'd threatened to drive into the city and beat down my door.

"He sounds perfect," Kacey commented.

"But . . ."

"But, you mean there's a *but* in this?" she cried. "I don't want to hear it."

"This is my first almost date," I reminded her, pressing the phone to my ear as I walked the carpet barefoot, sinking my toes into the lush thickness.

"Tell me about the *but,* and hurry because we're supposed to leave in ten minutes."

"Okay, okay. On paper Earl and I look like we were made for each other, but, Kacey, there simply wasn't any spark. Nothing. I enjoyed him and Earl said the same about me, but there was no connection. Zilch. Nada. Nothing."

"It isn't always about physical chemistry," my friend reminded me.

"I know. But Earl didn't feel it, either. We hugged when we parted and wished each other good luck."

I could hear Kacey exhale a sigh. "Are you depressed?"

"Not at all. I had an enjoyable evening, and meeting Earl gives me hope. It was encouraging."

Kacey was far more disappointed than I was.

"Don't be discouraged. There's someone special waiting for you."

"I know," I returned, and I did.

By the time I was in bed, I was relaxed and tired. The day had been exhausting. I slept like a lamb and woke Saturday morning feeling refreshed and eager to tackle the day. Nichole and I were meeting later in the morning to shop at the farmers' market.

I had dressed in jeans and a sweater and a deep blue fleece jacket when the doorbell rang. I assumed it was Nichole and was surprised to find Nikolai.

The instant he saw me, he broke into a smile. I stepped aside so he could come into my apartment.

"Nikolai, what are you doing here?" I hadn't realized he knew my home address.

"I sorry. I know it not good thing I come, but I not sleep. I worry and then I have idea. Very good idea." He took hold of my shoulders with both hands and stared at me intently before he asked, "You meet other man for coffee?"

"Yes."

"You kiss other man?" He frowned, as if he found the question difficult to ask.

"Not really." I didn't consider Earl's kiss on my cheek at the end of the evening as a real kiss.

Nikolai's eyes darkened as he continued to intently study me. "What does 'not really' mean?"

"He kissed my cheek."

"That is good." His relief was obvious. "You say you need to meet other men. Kiss other men. At first I no understand why, then I realize you need this after so many years with one man. But I think maybe you need more."

"More?"

"Yes, yes. You need compare."

"Compare? How?" I wasn't following him.

"Like this." His large hands framed my face, his long fingers sliding into my hair as he lowered his mouth to mine. I hadn't felt any spark or chemistry with Earl. At all. If I was looking for sparks, then Nikolai's kiss gave an entire Fourth of July fireworks display.

Slowly, with reluctance, he released me. I stood with my eyes closed, savoring the kiss, unwilling to let go of the warmth that filled me.

"You date other man, then date me and compare. Okay?"

I remained dazed, unable to speak.

"You need more compare?" he asked, bringing me back into his arms.

I smiled softly and nodded.

# CHAPTER 13

# Nichole

Leanne and I were heading for the farmers' market, a favorite Saturday excursion for us. Since I was teaching full-time, if only temporarily, I'd cut back volunteering at Dress for Success to one Saturday a month so I had more free time.

Leanne and I usually met in the hallway outside our apartments, which were across the hall from each other. When she didn't show, I knocked on her door. A couple of minutes passed before she answered, and when she did her face was flushed and there was a man in her apartment. I instantly knew this had to be Nikolai. He had the look of someone from Eastern Europe, with a broad forehead, pronounced cheekbones, and thick, straight salt-and-pepper hair. Leanne had mentioned him several times.

When she saw it was me, Leanne looked flustered and blurted out, "Oh sorry, I . . . I didn't realize it was that time already." She grabbed her purse and then seemed to remember that she had company. She turned abruptly and thrust out her arm. "Nichole, this is Nikolai Janchenko, one of the students in my class. Nichole is my daughter."

I loved that she chose to introduce me as her daughter.

Nikolai hurried forward and took my hand in both of his large ones, shaking it enthusiastically. "It is great honor to meet daughter of my teacher."

I couldn't help smiling back at the warmth and affection he radiated. "You're the one who bakes her the bread, aren't you?"

He nodded. "Bread is life. Bread is love."

"Nichole and I are going to the market this morning," Leanne explained, clenching her purse like she was in danger of meeting a mugger. "I'll see you Monday night, Nikolai."

"Monday," he repeated as his gaze shifted to Leanne. The look he gave her told me everything. Nikolai loved Leanne. His feelings for her radiated off him like candlelight in a mirror. If the way she reacted was any indication, my wonderful mother-in-law had tender feelings for him, too.

We all rode down in the elevator together. Nikolai went in one direction and we went in the other.

We hadn't gone more than a few feet when Leanne said, "Go ahead and say it. I know you're dying to comment."

She knew me well. I was squirming inside, hardly able to hold back the words. "OMG, Leanne, Nikolai is a treasure. Did you see the way he looks at you? He thinks you can walk on water."

"I'm his teacher," she insisted. "That is all."

"Nothing else?" I finished for her. "Are you sure?"

"I . . . don't know."

I didn't want to embarrass her, so I didn't press further. "He adores you."

Leanne bit into her lower lip and whispered, "He kissed me."

She seemed so unsure and embarrassed, but I knew it was because she was unfamiliar with these emotions. She'd been married all those years, and while we'd never openly discussed it, I suspected there had been few private displays of affection between Leanne and Sean. Anything physical had been done for show. It might have been years since she'd last been kissed.

"Did you like it?" I asked, slipping my arm around hers.

"I did," she said, her voice gaining strength. She raised her hand to her face. "I really did, but, Nichole, I'm so confused. I have mixed feelings. I'm Nikolai's teacher and I'm not sure getting romantically involved with him is ethical."

"Phooey."

"I'm afraid what he really feels is gratitude."

I laughed. "Phooey squared. I saw the way he looked at you."

"He's so different from Sean."

"That's a bad thing?" I asked, and laughed. "And isn't that one of the items on our list? Loving ourselves? We have to love ourselves in order to love others."

"It's just that I don't know what I'm doing. These feelings are so unfamiliar. I'm all twisted up in knots. Yet when I'm with him this happiness comes over me and I can't stop smiling."

"Be happy, Leanne. Don't let anyone tell you what you should feel. Just be happy."

She grew quiet. "I don't know what I feel anymore. I met the guy from that online dating site and he was great, but we didn't click. We both knew almost right away that while we could easily be friends, there wasn't any romantic spark between us. I blame myself for that."

This was part of Leanne's problem. She took on far more responsibility than was warranted.

"Instead of enjoying the evening," she confessed, "all I could think about was Nikolai."

"We need to add another rule to the list. Number five: **Be open to new experiences. Don't let the past taint the future.**"

"That sounds like a good addition," she whispered.

We had a great time at the market; we always did. We returned to the apartment with our arms full of farm-fresh produce and eggs that had been laid that morning.

"Do you have plans this evening?" Leanne asked.

Actually, I'd been looking forward to seeing Rocco and Kaylene. "Yeah, I'm heading over to Rocco's to take a few photos of him and his daughter before the big father-daughter shindig."

"You like him, don't you?" Leanne pressed.

I did, and felt a little silly admitting it. "He's a friend." And he was. We'd talked a couple times since he'd dropped off the ice cream. Basically, he'd called to check up on me. He'd given me good advice about letting go of the past. He'd sent it in a text:

I know you're hurting, but this will pass. I promise you
in time your tears will dry and your heart will heal.

I'd written it down and set it on the desk in my bedroom with the promise I'd never let anyone know, especially his friends, that he was the author.

Leanne didn't insist on more information about my
friendship with Rocco, and I was grateful. I dropped
the veggies off at the apartment, and vacuumed and
cleaned the kitchen before I met Laurie, my BFF, for
lunch. The two of us had taken an extravagant trip to
an Arizona spa a couple of years back when I was
married to Jake. My husband had arranged everything. Now I suspected that he'd done it in order to
spend time with his girlfriend. In retrospect, I had to
wonder if that was the weekend when he'd gotten the
other woman pregnant.

After lunch and a long gab fest with Laurie I returned to the apartment and finished housework and
laundry. The weekends without Owen felt strange. I
missed my son. I'd need to get used to this alone time,
which felt uncomfortable and awkward. Silly mind
games filled my head of all the might-have-beens in
my marriage and my life. I never expected to raise my
son with a part-time father.

At five-thirty I grabbed my coat and headed out the
door to see Rocco and Kaylene.

When I arrived Kaylene answered the door and told
me that Rocco was still getting dressed. He showed
about five minutes after I arrived. "Wowza," said Kaylene, and I had to agree with his daughter's assess-

ment. I barely recognized Rocco as the tow truck driver I'd met all those weeks ago.

Gone were the grease-smeared coveralls and shirts. He actually wore a shirt and tie. His hair had been cut and he'd shaved, emphasizing a strong chin. I nearly did a double take.

"Well?" he said, directing the question to me.

"You clean up nice," I teased.

He rubbed his hand along the side of his clean-shaven face. "I'll take that as a compliment."

"I meant it as one." The difference in him was striking. He could be a business executive from the way he carried himself, well, other than the tattoos. It felt like he filled up the entire room, and for a couple awkward moments I couldn't take my eyes off him. Kaylene may have said it, but I was certainly thinking it. *Wowza.*

Kaylene and I had already decided on the best lighting for the photo, so I had the two of them stand in front of the fireplace. I snapped a number of photos, shifting my position a few times for a better angle. I could tell Rocco was growing impatient as I continued to take pictures.

"I can only hold this smile for so long," he muttered after about ten minutes.

"Okay, I've got more than enough pictures." I handed the camera back to Kaylene.

Seeing that my mission was accomplished, I reached for my purse and was ready to leave when Kaylene stopped me. "Nichole, would you help my dad?"

My gaze shot to Rocco, who'd stuffed his hands in his pants pockets.

"You need help?" I asked him.

Kaylene answered: "Dad's forgotten how to dance already."

Rocco frowned at his daughter. "Don't worry about it. I'll figure it out once we get there."

I set my purse down. "A refresher course can't hurt."

Kaylene grabbed her iPad and turned on some music. I held my arms out to Rocco and wiggled my fingers. "Come on, handsome, let's dance."

He didn't look happy about this.

"Dad has trouble with the slow dances," Kaylene explained. "He thinks he looks silly."

Seeing that he wasn't coming to me, I moved toward Rocco. "You're stressing over this way too much," I said. "The slower dances are easier than the fast ones. All you really need to do is hold me." I decided the best way to explain this was to loop my arms around his waist. "Now hold on to me," I told him.

Reluctantly, he did as I asked. He held himself stiff and his touch was light, as if he'd rather do just about anything else than this.

"Now what?" he muttered, sounding none too pleased.

"Close your eyes."

"Why?" The question was a challenge.

"Because I want you to feel the music."

Rocco muttered under his breath and then dropped his hands from my waist. "This is ridiculous."

"Dad," Kaylene cried, pleading with him.

"If you'd rather not hold my waist, then take my hands."

He groaned in protest, which did little to boost my ego. He couldn't have made it any more obvious that he'd rather not touch me.

"So did you meet Shawntelle?" I asked, thinking he could use a small distraction.

He nodded.

"What did you think?"

He shrugged and didn't answer the question. "Do I still need to close my eyes?"

"It'll help. Would you rather try this with Kaylene?"

"No," he whispered, and his eyes slammed shut.

I gave him time to listen, and after a few moments he seemed to get the gist of it. I felt him relax.

"Once you feel the music, just sway your body. You don't need to learn any fancy steps. This is about you and your partner; it isn't necessary to impress anyone with fancy footwork."

Kaylene's phone rang. "It's Maddy," she announced, as if the name had major significance. Whatever they needed to discuss was important enough for her to leave the room.

Rocco was doing great. His steps grew slow and confident. By all that was right we could have stopped then. The truth was I was enjoying dancing with him. I closed my own eyes, letting the music carry me away. It was a beautiful love song and I felt Rocco's arms tighten around me. I could feel his breath in my hair as he pressed his chin against the side of my head.

It'd been so long since I'd been held with such tenderness. I could hear his heart, which beat in unison with my own. Rocco locked his hands at the small of my back and gently rubbed the side of his head against mine.

*Oh my.*

I could feel myself sinking into the music, but more surprisingly, into Rocco. Just this morning I'd told Leanne what a good friend he was. But now, with his arms around me, I wasn't thinking *friendly* thoughts. It was as if my body had awakened to the fact that I was a woman and Rocco was a man—a virile, vibrant man.

My heart picked up the pace, beating strong and fast. I bit into my lip when I felt his kiss on the top of my head. Right then I should have broken away. I should have claimed he knew everything necessary for the dance and pretend nothing had changed. But it had. We had.

Big-time.

For the life of me I don't know how to explain what happened next. Tilting my head back ever so slightly, I brushed my lips against the underside of his jaw. He smelled so good. A combination of citrus and man that left me heady and filled with longing.

Rocco's steps stilled and he moved back just enough so that he could look down at me, his eyes narrowed and intense. I felt my cheeks redden under his scrutiny. I should have apologized and claimed I'd lost my head and that kissing him was a silly mistake. But it would have been a lie.

All at once his hands were in my hair and I knew he intended to kiss me. He paused as if waiting for me to break eye contact or pull away. I knew I should. I knew it was the right thing, but I couldn't make myself do it.

In a slow descent he lowered his mouth to mine and we kissed. When I say we kissed I mean *we kissed*. The world could have ended in that moment and I wouldn't have cared. My knees nearly buckled at the warm sensation that shot through me like lightning.

His kiss knocked me into the next county, involving our mouths and tongues and even our teeth. It was as if we were both starved and had stumbled upon a Texas barbecue. His hands cupped my face and we lost all pretense of dancing. Only when we heard Kaylene approach did we break apart.

I couldn't look at Rocco, and so I lowered my head as I frantically tried to regain my senses and still my racing heart. His hands on my shoulders held me steady and I was grateful.

"That was Maddy," Kaylene said again, and seemed unaware of what was going on between Rocco and me.

"So you said," Rocco murmured. He tucked his finger beneath my chin and raised my head so he could look at me. His eyes stared deeply into mine. He seemed confused and unsure, or it could have been my own reflection I saw.

"Dad? Is everything all right?"

"Perfect. Go get your coat. It's time for us to go." Although he spoke to his daughter, his hungry eyes refused to release me.

I knew I should probably say something, but I couldn't find any words. Rocco seemed to share my predicament.

Kaylene returned with her coat. "I thought you said it was time to go."

"It is."

Rocco took hold of my hand and raised it to his lips, kissing the back side. Then he smiled and whispered, "Wowza."

# CHAPTER 14

# Leanne

Tuesday night following dinner, I went on a second date arranged through the online dating service. It was another meet-and-greet at Starbucks. His name was Ron and at first glance he was enthusiastic and charming. Unfortunately, he reminded me too much of Sean: too polished and suave, taking pains to impress me. It felt as if he wanted to be sure I understood how successful and accomplished he was. I listened politely for nearly sixty minutes, thanked him, and stood to leave.

"How about dinner one night this weekend?" he asked as he reached for his coat.

I tossed my empty coffee container in the bin and looked back, surprised he hadn't read my body language. "Thanks, but I don't think so."

He frowned, as if my refusal had taken him by surprise. "What's wrong? I thought we hit it off. You're one of the more interesting women I've met. I'd like to get to know you better."

"Really? And what do you know about me that makes me interesting?" I asked. "Do you know I have a son and one grandchild? Do you know I was married for thirty-five years? Tell me what you know about me, because the entire time we've sat here you've talked about yourself nonstop."

He took a step back, as though the unexpected truth had shaken him.

"I don't need a man in my life, Ron. I'm not entirely sure why I signed up for this service. I appreciate your time and wish you the very best." From the shocked look he wore, I could tell that no one had bothered to mention how self-absorbed he was. "If you don't mind a suggestion, the next time you meet someone don't work so hard to impress them. Show interest in the other person. Ask questions and listen and you'll be surprised by how entertaining the other person will think *you* are." This was the most I'd said the entire hour we'd been together.

He appeared to be struck dumb. It took him several seconds before he nodded and said, "Thank you . . . I will."

"You're welcome."

He followed me outside. "I . . . no one has ever been so blunt with me before. Is this the reason only a couple of women have wanted to see me beyond the first meeting?"

"That would be my guess."

He rubbed his chin. "You sure you won't give me a second chance?"

His invitation gave me pause, and I seriously considered it, but I already knew we would both be wasting our time. "I'm not the woman for you. She's out there and you're perfect for her. Find her and don't waste your time on me."

His smile was genuine. "Will do."

I returned to the apartment and wasn't home five minutes before Nichole knocked. She had left her apartment door open in case Owen woke, so she could hear him. "How'd it go?" she asked.

"Don't ask."

"That bad?"

"No, not bad. I'm telling you, Nichole, I don't know why I signed up for this. I meet these men and they all seem wonderful on paper—well, on-screen—and then I realize something I read a long time ago: *It takes a hell of a man to replace no man.* The fact is I'm happy. I enjoy my life just the way it is. I'm not looking for love and am perfectly content being single."

"It's good to test the waters, don't you think?" my daughter-in-law asked. "I mean, this has helped you realize what you already know."

I brightened. "*Test the waters.* That's a great idiom for class tomorrow," I said, not that I was thinking about class as much as I was thinking of Nikolai. On Monday I'd mentioned I would be meeting Ron the following evening. I wasn't sure why I felt the need to tell him, and I immediately regretted it because I could see how distressed the news made him. Perhaps I was subconsciously seeking more of his comparison kisses. I didn't know any longer. More and more of my thoughts were taken up with the Ukrainian man who baked me the most delicious bread.

Bread. Because bread would say what he could not say with words. Even now, remembering that caused chills to run down my arms.

"Come over," Nichole said, breaking into my thoughts about Nikolai. She tilted her head toward her apartment. "Let's chat awhile."

It'd been far too long since we'd done exactly that. Naturally, living so close, we saw each other on a regular basis. I watched Owen as much as my schedule would allow. Now that Nichole taught at the high school and Owen was at the daycare center, she didn't need me as much as she had before.

I sank onto her sofa while Nichole brewed tea. "It seems we hardly have a chance to talk anymore. I know it's because of my job, but I miss you, miss our pep talks."

I missed our pep talks, too, and I had news. "I heard from Sean," I said. "He wants to stop by on Saturday for a few minutes." I'd seen or talked to him only a few times since the divorce, and to have him contact me twice within a few short weeks was unusual.

"Sean wants to see you?" Nichole asked as she carried in two mugs and sat beside me.

"He implied it had something to do with Jake, but I got the feeling it was more than that." Instinct told me he had something else on his mind and our son was only an excuse. I'd heard it in his voice. A tinge of worry, of doubt, and something that might have been fear. Of course, it could have been my imagination.

Nichole paused, studying me. "It must not be good news about Jake. I had a feeling something was wrong when I picked up Owen on Sunday. I couldn't put my finger on it, but I don't think it's woman troubles. Not this time, anyway."

If Jake was the concern Sean wanted to discuss, then it might have something to do with his job. I'd heard through Kacey that Jake had taken a lot of time off work since Nichole had moved out. "I'm upset with myself," I admitted.

Nichole raised her eyebrows in question.

"When Sean called he suggested we meet for lunch. I hesitated and then he laughed and said he'd let me fix him something." It was almost as if he was looking for an excuse to spend time with me, something he hadn't done in the last thirty years of our marriage, which naturally raised my suspicions.

"You didn't agree, did you?"

I raised both hands in a helpless gesture. "I did." Even now I wasn't sure why. It hadn't been what he'd said, it was the timbre of his voice, the underlying nuance that suggested something wasn't right. I shrugged off my suspicions and then tried to make a joke of it. "I know exactly how it'll go, too. Sean will arrive and make several flattering comments. He'll ask if I got a new hairstyle or if I lost weight and tell me how good I look."

Nichole laughed. "I hope you realize he wouldn't be exaggerating. You do look great and you have lost weight." She cocked her head to one side. "There's been such a change in you over the last couple of months."

"In me?" I pressed my hand to my chest, taken aback by her words. I couldn't imagine what she meant.

"You're radiant," Nichole went on to say. "I don't know any other way to put it. I look at you and I barely recognize you any longer."

"What you're seeing is happiness," I said, eager to explain away the compliment. I think I might have been blushing, which was ridiculous. If what she said was true, I had to believe it came from the satisfaction I found in all the changes I'd made in my life, like volunteering at the Community Center and . . . oh, how I hated to admit this . . . from Nikolai's kisses.

"Leanne," Nichole said, gripping both my hands in hers. "I've never seen you happier, and that gives me hope." Her eyes grew dark and serious. "Promise me you aren't going to let Sean back in your life."

Something wasn't right with Sean, that much I knew, but whatever it was, I could guarantee it had nothing to do with wanting me back in his life—not after everything I'd heard from Kacey about his carousing. My head came up. "What makes you think I would even consider that?"

Nichole's eyes widened. "Your soft heart."

I shook my head. "You have no worries." Not wanting to talk about myself, I asked, "Anything new with you?"

Nichole hesitated and immediately looked away.

Something was up. "Okay, what gives?"

Nichole tucked her feet under her and fussed a bit before getting comfortable. Even when she spoke she avoided eye contact. "I mentioned I'd be going over to Rocco's on Saturday, didn't I?"

"Yeah."

"After the photo shoot Kaylene decided Rocco needed a refresher lesson, so we danced. Then while Kaylene was out of the room we sort of kissed."

I wasn't up on the latest jargon when it came to relationships, so curiosity made me ask, "How do you *sort of kiss* someone?"

"Okay, we kissed, and when I say kissed I mean we

kissed like I've never been kissed before." She squeezed her eyes shut, as if reliving that moment. "Leanne," she whispered, "I felt that kiss like nothing else. It was all I could do not to melt at Rocco's feet. I haven't been able to stop thinking about him ever since. The only thing I can figure is that it's been so long since I've felt desire that intense that there must be something wrong with me. I . . . I haven't been with another man since I met Jake. Do you think what I feel for Rocco is real, or is it because I'm starved for affection and love?"

How I wish the answer were that simple. "I . . . don't know." The truth was I'd felt much the same when Nikolai kissed me, only it'd been much longer since I'd experienced anything close to desire. Although Sean and I were married, we hadn't slept together the last ten years of our marriage. Other than perfunctory kisses for appearance's sake, Sean and I hadn't kissed. Knowing what I did about my husband, I couldn't bear to have Sean touch me.

"It's humbling to admit that I practically melted in his arms." I could see that Nichole's response to Rocco deeply embarrassed her. She lowered her gaze. "He's reached out to me since but either I don't answer or I put him off because I don't know what to say."

"Do you like him?" I asked. "As a person?" Clearly his kiss had twisted her into tight knots.

"Very much. He's not like anyone I've ever known and he's a great father. Owen loves him."

That much I knew. My grandson was full of talk about Rocco and his trucks.

"If that's the case, what are you afraid of?" I asked.

Nichole's head shot up. "I'm not afraid," she argued. "I'm uncertain and frazzled."

It took some effort not to laugh. "Hey, you're the one who wanted to add trying new experiences to our guide. That can apply to people, too, you know. Don't be afraid of what you feel toward Rocco. Follow your gut."

"My gut," she repeated, and placed her hand over her stomach. "My gut tells me Rocco is really a great guy. Yes, he's a little rough around the edges, but he's wonderful."

"I think you have your answer."

Her shoulders relaxed as she sighed. "Yes, I think I do, but I've made a mess of this and I'm not sure how to move forward."

I thought of awkward situations that I'd faced in the past. Once I'd sat at the dinner table with a woman and her husband when I knew Sean was currently having an affair with her. I'd been forced to be polite and friendly when what I really wanted to do was rage at them both.

For far too many years I'd been sailing on the river called denial. "It gets harder the longer you put it off. Talk to him, explain. You said Rocco's a friend; treat him like one."

"I will," Nichole said, and gave my hand a squeeze as if to thank me. I could tell that she felt better already. Strangely enough, I did, too.

"We need to do this more often."

"I agree." I stood, ready to return to my own apartment. Nichole stood, too, and we hugged each other.

Wednesday night I was eager to get to class and left home early. Nikolai met me in the parking lot and had the same grave look as the one he'd left with on Monday evening.

"You meet this other man?" he asked me expectantly.

I nodded.

"You kiss him?" His gaze intently studied mine.

"No."

His shoulders relaxed. "You see him again?"

I pressed my hand to Nikolai's cheek, my gaze holding his. "No."

His eyes brightened and he twisted his head so that he could kiss the inside of my palm. "I happy now like cow skip over moon. I breathe again. I think maybe I teach you. You teach me and I teach you."

We started toward the center. "What would you like to teach me, Nikolai?"

He looked at me as if the answer should be obvious. "How to bake bread. Real bread. You make before?"

"I had a bread machine. You know, the kind where it mixes and bakes it all in one."

A horrified look came over him and he automatically shook his head. "Never again. Promise me you not do that with bread ever again."

I tried to suppress my smile, with little success. "I promise."

"You let me teach you?"

I agreed, but the truth was I would have agreed to just about anything he suggested, I was that eager to spend time with him.

Skydiving? Sure, why not. Rock climbing? Always wanted to try that. *Not.*

We arranged a time to meet Saturday afternoon. In retrospect, I wish I'd suggested Sunday instead. The timing was tricky. Sean was scheduled to stop by at around noon. I asked Nikolai to come at two, thinking that would give Sean plenty of time to say what he wanted, eat lunch, and be on his merry way.

On Saturday I had lunch ready before Sean arrived. He was late and kissed me on the cheek.

"You're more beautiful than ever."

I folded my arms over my chest. "Really? I haven't been feeling well and thought I looked deathly pale." No reaction. Nothing had changed. My ex hadn't listened to a single word. Ron, meet Sean.

"You've lost weight recently, haven't you?" he asked.

I smiled. It was just as I expected.

His gaze went to the table. "Is that sandwich ham salad? You remembered that it's my favorite."

I did remember; how could I not? We were married thirty-five years.

We ate lunch and chatted. Sean gave no hint of there being anything wrong, which left me wondering if I'd completely misread his call earlier. Between bites he chatted good-naturedly about friends from the club, and his score after golfing with Liam Belcher, a doctor friend.

What he had to tell me about Jake wasn't anything he couldn't have mentioned over the phone. Apparently, Jake had changed jobs, though whether this was his employer's choice or his own, I didn't know. To hear Sean tell it, Jake had been lured away by another wine company. My ex made it sound like Jake was sitting on top of the world. This wasn't news that required that the two of us meet. The fact was I already knew about the job change from Nichole.

"Sean," I said sternly, demanding his attention.

His eyes shot to me.

"What's wrong?"

"Nothing. What makes you think anything is wrong?"

Frowning, I studied him closely. He met my gaze and I couldn't see if anything was amiss.

"If anything is wrong," he said in that smooth, calculated way of his, "it's the fact I miss you."

The only appropriate response was to laugh. "Sure you do. Perhaps my ham-salad sandwiches more, though."

He studied me for half a second. "This is a new you, Leanne, and I have to say I like it. How about we do this more often?"

"Do what?"

"Have lunch. Spend time together."

"No thanks."

He looked completely crestfallen, which was a big act. "Oh, so strong. I love it."

My doorbell chimed and I saw it was fifteen minutes before Nikolai was set to arrive. I prayed it was a delivery or a friend. My hope died when I opened the door to find Nikolai standing there, his arms loaded down with bags of what I knew had to be ingredients for baking bread.

"Nikolai."

"I come early. It okay?"

"Of course." I stepped aside so he could come into the apartment.

I reached for one of the bags, but he shook his head. "No, no, I carry."

Sean stood and his gaze drifted from me to Nikolai and then back to me. Nikolai saw him, too, and stopped, nearly dropping one of the grocery sacks. He caught it in the nick of time.

"Nikolai, this is my ex-husband Sean." I placed heavy emphasis on the *ex* part.

"Sean, this is Nikolai Janchenko. He's one of my students in my English-as-a-second-language class."

The two men stared at each other. The air in the room grew thick and tense.

"Nikolai is teaching me how to bake bread," I explained.

"So that's what was different with lunch," Sean said. "It was the bread. I don't know when I've ever tasted better."

Nikolai's head swiveled toward me with a look of shock.

"Sean was just leaving," I said meaningfully.

My ex-husband smiled, kissed my cheek before I could stop him, and left the apartment.

Nikolai carefully placed the grocery bags on the kitchen counter. He kept his back to me.

"I apologize," I said, and meant it. "I didn't expect Sean to be here when you arrived." Naturally, my ex had been more than forty-five minutes late. I should have known better than to trust the time he told me.

When Nikolai turned to face me I was stunned by the hurt and anger I read in his eyes. "You give him bread I bake for you?" he demanded.

I didn't understand the problem. "Well, yes. You give me so much that I have no need to buy bread."

"This man . . . this Sean," he said, sneering his name, "his heart black like charcoal." He bit out the words. "And you feed him bread I make with my own hands for you. Bread from my heart. This is the bread you give to other man." His face was full of pain. He shook his head as if he couldn't believe what I'd done.

I moved closer to Nikolai, "I'm sorry . . . I didn't realize . . . I didn't think."

"You make chicken stock of me."

I had no idea what idiom he was confusing now, but whatever it was, he was deeply pained.

He stepped away from me as if it was all he could do to remain in the same room. "I go now."

"You're leaving?" It took a moment to realize he was serious. His reaction stunned me.

He made it to the door. "I go. I think hard before I say words I no mean."

He left everything he'd brought with him on the counter, and when the door shut, I closed my eyes and sank onto a chair, washed in guilt and regret.

# CHAPTER 15

# Nichole

This was the second weekend in a row that Jake had Owen. Last weekend he'd picked up our son at the daycare center on Friday afternoon and then dropped Owen off at his grandmother's.

Jake was avoiding me and that was fine. I knew about avoidance. I'd been avoiding Rocco all week. He'd phoned three times and left messages, which I hadn't returned. Once, when I inadvertently did answer, I'd quickly put him off, promising to call him back. I hadn't. The reason was I didn't know what to say. The kisses we'd shared had bewildered me. What I hadn't explained to Leanne was how shocking it was to feel anything sexual for another man. My divorce had been final only a couple weeks. Yes, it'd taken two years, and yes, this was what I knew had to happen. But it seemed I should be grieving more over the death of my marriage.

Saturday morning I arrived at Dress for Success and

was busy sorting through the donated items when Shawntelle arrived with her cousin.

"Hey, girl, what's up?" Shawntelle said as she sashayed her way into the shop. She looked good in tight jeans and an oversize shirt. "Meet Charise."

"Nichole," I answered, introducing myself.

"Charise just got her GED and is signing up for bookkeeping classes same as I did," Shawntelle said, nodding toward her cousin.

Charise rubbed her palms together in a nervous gesture. "I figured if my cuz could make a success of herself, then so could I."

"Hold on. You got a job?"

"Sure did. Thanks to you."

"Me?" This was a surprise. "What did I do?"

Her face broke into a smile, her teeth gleaming. "Rocco. He called and said he was looking for a new bookkeeper and asked if I wanted to apply for the job."

"Wait. When did that happen?"

"Last week."

"Last week," I repeated. "Why didn't you tell me?"

She shrugged. "I thought Rocco would."

That might have something to do with the number of phone calls from him.

"I thought he told you."

"Ah . . . I've been busy all week."

Shawntelle hugged me tight, nearly squeezing the breath out of me. "Working for Rocco is just the start I needed."

As much as I wanted to, I couldn't take credit. I'd mentioned Shawntelle to Rocco and her disappointment after missing out on the job at the car dealership. It'd been the same time I told him she was hot to meet him. When he asked for her contact information I'd assumed it was because he was interested in dating her.

Shawntelle straightened her shoulders and pride shone in her eyes. "As soon as I got the job, I applied with Habitat for Humanity. I'm looking to build a house. Now, ain't that something? Me! I figure once I've got six months and a little bit of money in savings I'll qualify. Now that I've got me a job I need a decent home for my children."

My heart filled with pride and I perked up. "My sister built a home through Habitat for her and her daughter."

"Get outta here," Shawntelle cried. "Your sister?"

"And she did it all within a year."

"Did she meet any handsome men? I have a weakness for beefy, muscular men."

I laughed because Cassie had met Steve while working on her home. "As a matter of fact, she did, and now they're about to be married."

"You have a weakness for men period," Charise pointed out, frowning.

"That's in the past," Shawntelle insisted. "I'm pickier now. I've got standards. Speaking of which, you talked to Rocco lately?" The pointed question was directed to me.

"Ah," I hedged. "Not recently."

"What's the matter with you, girl? He's been in a bear of a mood all week and I have a feeling it has to do with you. You need to appreciate what you got."

"Yes, well . . ." I didn't want to think about Rocco, let alone talk about him. In an effort to change the subject I looked to Charise. "Let me find you a dressing room to try on a few outfits."

"Speaking of you know who, look who pulled into the parking lot," Shawntelle said pointedly. Her hand was braced against her hip as she stared out the window.

I closed my eyes and groaned. There would be no escaping him now.

"Charise," Shawntelle called, "come look. This is going to be good."

Coward that I am, I hesitated and cast a pleading glance at Shawntelle. "Why don't you go find out what he wants?"

Shawntelle shook her head. "No way, sweetcakes, that man is all about you. He isn't here to talk to me. Now, I don't know what's happening with you two, but something is. Whatever it is, settle it, 'cause I'm not putting up with another day of his bull because of you."

"But Charise needs my help," I said, my heart in a panic. Flustered as I was, I desperately wanted a way out of a confrontation with Rocco.

"I know what she needs. Now go." Shawntelle practically tossed me out the door.

By the time I was outside, Rocco had parked the truck. He climbed out, and when he saw me he stopped. We stood across the parking lot from each other, staring. We must have resembled gunfighters facing off against each other.

His face was hard and anger radiated off him in waves. "You gonna run?" he asked as he walked toward me.

"No." I clenched my hands in front of me and

stepped off the curb into the parking lot. I didn't want Shawntelle and her cousin privy to our conversation.

Rocco didn't give me a chance to explain. His eyes narrowed as he spoke. "Listen, Nichole, I'm not into these games you're playing."

I did feel bad. "I'm sorry, I—"

He cut me off. "If you don't want to see me again, that's fine. I'll deal with it. But don't kiss me like I'm your last meal and then slam the door in my face."

I blinked repeatedly, embarrassed by my behavior and at a loss at how best to explain. "I didn't expect that to happen . . . I didn't know what to say or how to act," I stuttered. "How was I supposed to know what you were thinking or what I should think." The words tumbled out of me as I waited, hoping he would help me understand myself, which in retrospect was impossible. I should have been able to figure this out, but I hadn't. And the truth was I'd missed him this week. I missed talking to him and laughing with him. That was one thing I did most with Rocco—I laughed.

"Tell you what," he said, the anger more pronounced now than ever. "When you've got your head straight, let me know." That said, he headed back to his truck.

Right then I knew if I didn't do or say something I'd never see Rocco again. A hundred thoughts zoomed through my brain at laser speed. Letting him leave was probably for the best. Instantly, I was filled with the knowledge I would miss him terribly. I wasn't looking for a relationship, and heaven knew Rocco was unlike any other man I'd ever known. We were different, but I'd never been more comfortable with any man the way I was with him. Before I could debate the wisdom of what I should do, I raced after him.

"Rocco."

He stopped but he didn't turn around.

I moved so that I stood in front of him, but he refused to make eye contact. Even now I didn't know what to say. "I really am sorry," I blurted out, though I didn't think my apology carried much weight with him.

"I get it," he said, his hands knotted into fists at his sides. "You're way out of my league. You're not interested in a tow-truck driver. No problem. There's no need to apologize."

"That is so not true." I couldn't believe he'd even suggest such a thing. This had nothing to do with his occupation or anything else. This was about me and my insecurities.

"That's not the way I see it." He started to walk around me.

"Damn it, Rocco, you're really starting to piss me off."

He blinked and so did I. This wasn't language I normally used, but I was upset. "Give me a chance, will you? I don't know what I'm doing here. It's been two years for me and I was married five years before that and . . . and I met Jake while in college and we dated for two years." What this had to do with anything was beyond me, but I felt it was important that he know.

He crossed his arms and waited for me to finish. His gaze wasn't on me, but focused on some point in the distance.

"I like you . . . I'm strongly attracted to you," I continued. "I enjoy spending time with you and Kaylene.

When you kissed me . . ." Explaining this part was probably the most difficult of all. "Your kiss felt like a bomb going off in my head." And other places I was too embarrassed to mention. "The thing is I haven't a clue what any of this means. All I'm asking is that you give me a chance to figure it out."

My words were met with silence and then, "Okay."

Nothing had changed about his tight features. I was more confused than ever. "That's it? That's all you have to say?"

"What more do you want?"

I shrugged and tossed my hands around a bit. "I don't know." And I didn't. Well, other than how much I'd enjoyed feeling his arms around me. "Maybe you could hug me," I suggested, and opened my arms.

For the first time since he arrived, Rocco smiled and reached for me, wrapping me in a tight embrace. His nose was in my hair and it felt as if he was sniffing it, which was ridiculous. His embrace felt as warm and wonderful as I remembered.

"I swear, woman, you're driving me crazy." He buried his face in my neck and exhaled as if he'd been withholding oxygen from his lungs for the last seven days.

Stretching up on the tips of my toes, I slipped my arms around his neck and held on to him as he lifted me from the ground. For the longest moment all we did was cling to each other.

"I promised Kaylene I'd take her and four of her best friends to the movies tomorrow. Do you want to come and keep me company?"

I laid my head on his shoulder. "I'd like that more than you know."

Rocco kissed the top of my head. "I'll find out what time the movie is and text you."

"Okay, and Rocco, thank you for giving me another chance." The temptation was too much, and I kissed the underside of his jaw.

Rocco froze and it felt as if he'd stopped breathing. "Be careful, Nichole. The way I feel about you, kissing me like that is playing with fire."

I smiled, happier than I'd been all week.

He left then and I headed back to Dress for Success. Shawntelle and her cousin had come out of the store and stood on the sidewalk watching me. As I approached, they clapped and whistled and pounded me on the back.

It was almost four by the time I finished for the day. I should have been tired after working all week at the school and then spending Saturday volunteering. Instead I was jubilant, excited. Things were squared away with Rocco. I hadn't realized how heavily the uneasiness between us had been weighing on me.

Just as I was heading out of the shop my cell rang. Caller ID told me it was my sister Cassie. "Yo, Cassie, how's it going?" We'd had this "yo" thing going since we were kids.

"Hold on, I'm going to get Karen back on the line. I have news."

I could hear the excitement in her voice and suspected her reason for calling had to do with Steve. The two had been dating two years now. I loved seeing them together. My sister had been through hell and had fought her way back. She'd built a home with her own two hands and supported herself. I hoped she'd talk to Shawntelle at some point because I knew Cassie's story would encourage my friend.

"Karen? You there?" Cassie asked.

"I'm here," Karen confirmed. "Now, what's your big news, although I think I can guess?"

"It's taken me a while," my middle sister admitted, "but I believe I'm ready to spend the rest of my life with Steve. We've decided to set the date for our wedding."

Both Karen and I started talking at once, congratulating our sister. Karen was in the car on her way to Buddy's soccer game and had to hang up. I stayed on the line with Cassie.

Tears clogged my throat. "This is so great, Cassie."

She must have heard the emotion in my voice because she said, "Are you crying, Nichole?"

I sniffled. "Yes, I'm just so happy for you and Steve and Amiee. From the minute I met Steve I knew you two were meant to be together. It gives me hope, Cassie, that there's a happy ending for me, too."

"There is, Nichole," Cassie assured me, "but remember it doesn't always come easy."

"Nothing worthwhile ever does." I'd learned that the hard way.

"I want both you and Karen to be my bridesmaids. It's going to be a small wedding with just family and friends, but Steve wants to have a big reception and a dance. He's making all the arrangements, so mark down the date."

"Cassie," I whispered, tears brightening my eyes. "I wouldn't miss this for the world."

All in all, I couldn't have asked for a better day. First Rocco and I were back on track and then Cassie's good news. On the way to my apartment I decided to stop in and see how Leanne's visit had gone with Sean. I knew Nikolai planned to stop by later in the afternoon, and if I was lucky, Leanne might offer me a freshly baked loaf of bread.

When she answered the door I could see that she was upset. She held the door open, silently inviting me inside.

"Hey, Leanne. What's going on?"

She was pale and her shoulders slumped forward.

"Didn't things go well with Sean?"

"They went fine. I'm not even sure why he wanted to see me."

I sat down and she joined me. "That's good, right?"

She nodded blankly, as if her mind was somewhere in outer space. "Sean arrived late and he was still here when Nikolai stopped by."

That shouldn't be a problem. My thought was that it would do Sean good to learn this wonderful man was interested in Leanne.

"Nikolai was deeply offended that I would share the bread he'd baked for me with Sean. He could hardly bear to look at me and then he just left. From the way he acted, it was if I'd committed some grievous crime and had deeply insulted him."

It hurt me to see how upset Leanne was over this. I hoped to reassure her. "He'll get over it."

My mother-in-law shook her head. "Not this; it

seems what I did was unforgiveable. I don't know that I'll ever see him again."

"Oh Leanne, I'm sure that's not true."

"It's fine," she whispered.

I could see it was anything but.

"I've had all afternoon to think about it." She raised her hands to her face. "I don't know what I was thinking. A woman my age acting like a teenager in love for the first time. I should never have allowed myself to get involved with Nikolai."

"You don't mean that."

"I do," she insisted.

I didn't know that I'd ever seen Leanne like this. Even the day she told me she'd learned Jake had gotten another woman pregnant didn't match the hurt I read in her now. This was about more than what'd happened with Nikolai, though. It had to be.

Leaning forward, I reached for her hands. "Tell me what's really wrong."

She looked down and shook her head. It was a long time before she spoke, but I was patient, unwilling to leave her until I learned what tormented her so.

Minutes must have passed before she was ready, and even then it was a whisper so low I had to move closer in order to hear.

"When Nikolai kissed me . . ." She stopped and swallowed. "It'd been over ten years since a man had touched me. Sean and I basically lived separate lives. Any affection between us was for show. I cooked his meals, cleaned his home, managed the social elements of his career, but there was no love between us. That had died long ago. I was an accessory in his life as he was in mine. I'd dried up sexually . . . I didn't think I still had those feelings in me until Nikolai."

I'd suspected this might be the case but had never asked. It wasn't my place.

"I don't think I'm loveable, Nichole. I've held myself aloof all these years, living a pretend life. Nikolai is the first man since college to make me feel desire. It made me heady and happy and I blew it."

I pressed my head against hers. "If Nikolai is half the man I think he is, he'll get over this. Give him the weekend. Trust me, he'll show for class on Monday."

She shook her head. "If he does or doesn't, it doesn't matter. I learned something about myself today. I don't like being vulnerable. I prefer to think I'm strong and independent. I've had to be. I'm just not as smart as I want, but I'm learning. If Nikolai is in class on Monday, I'm going to tell him I don't want to see him again, and then I'm going to see if the school can find a replacement teacher."

My heart ached for Leanne and I released a heartfelt sigh. "Please think this over," I pleaded. "Don't make a rash decision."

"I have thought it over," she whispered. "I need to do this to protect me, to protect my heart."

# CHAPTER 16

# Leanne

I woke Sunday morning with the most insistent physical pain. My sleep had been intermittent at best. My head was full of what had happened with Nikolai and my decision not to see him again. By the time I went to bed I'd decided that to quit teaching was an overreaction. Every week I looked forward to spending time with my students. They were wonderful. As for Nikolai, I strongly suspected he wouldn't be coming to classes any longer. And if he did, well, I'd deal with him then.

By midmorning the pain in my back had gotten worse, more intense. It wasn't like I'd twisted it the wrong way. This was sharper, more pronounced, throbbing and unrelenting, a burning sensation. Checking my reflection in the mirror, I couldn't see a thing, which frustrated me. With this amount of pain there should be something visible. It felt as if someone had put a red-hot knife against my skin.

I waited until just before noon before I called Nichole. By then I could barely stand still. The pain was all-consuming. "Could you stop by for a minute?" I asked.

"Of course."

Nichole didn't wait for me to answer the door, but came straight into the apartment. "Is everything all right?" she asked.

She must have detected the agony in my voice because I heard the concern in hers. "Would you check my back? Something's wrong. I'm in awful pain."

I lifted up my shirt. It was crazy; even the cotton against my skin hurt. "Do you see anything?" I asked, twisting my head around, trying to look myself. Again, I was frustrated to see nothing.

Nichole studied the area intently and then shook her head. "I don't see anything."

She pressed her finger against the area that ached the worst and I cried out and then bit my lower lip.

"Oh my goodness," Nichole whispered. "You better get to the doctor."

I shook my head. "I'm sure whatever it is will be gone by tomorrow." That was my hope. I knew I wouldn't be able to stand more than a day of this agony.

Nichole looked skeptical. "Promise me that if you don't have relief in the morning, you'll make an appointment."

That was an easy promise to make.

"Do you want me to stay with you?" she asked. "I told Rocco I'd go to the movies with him and Kaylene, but I can call and explain."

"No," I insisted. "I'll be perfectly fine. Go with Rocco and have a good time."

Nichole protested, but in the end she left to join Rocco and his daughter. I didn't want her to cancel her fun because of me. At noontime, I tried to eat, but nothing appealed to me. Although I looked for something to distract me from the discomfort, nothing helped. Finally, when I couldn't stand it any longer, I got on the Internet and did a search on back pain. Nothing seemed to fit until I started to describe what I was feeling. That was when I got my answer.

*Shingles.*

I had shingles.

Nichole stopped to check on me late in the afternoon. I tried to put on a good face, but I fear I failed. She took one look at me and shook her head. "Something is drastically wrong."

"I think it's shingles," I said, not giving her a chance to say anything further.

She raised her hands to her mouth. "Oh no."

"I did an Internet search and that's the only thing I could find that explains this pain I'm feeling."

"Do you want me to take you to the ER?" she asked.

"No, no, I'll wait until tomorrow to see my doctor." In this amount of discomfort, the last thing I wanted was to sit for hours on end in a hospital waiting room.

"You're sure?"

"Positive." Wanting to change the subject, I asked about the movie with Rocco.

Nichole's face relaxed into a smile. "It was fun. Kaylene and four of her friends sat three rows in front of us. No way did they want to be associated with Rocco or me." Her eyes brightened with delight as she laughed. "Rocco didn't like being ignored, so he threw popcorn at them."

Although I didn't know Rocco well, I liked him just for the way he'd helped Nichole come out of her shell. He was great with Owen, too. Owen talked about him incessantly, which was nice. It worried me that my grandson had little to say about his own father.

Later I came to regret not accepting Nichole's offer to take me to the ER. I don't think I slept more than an hour the entire night, if that. The unrelenting pain made it impossible to fall asleep. By morning I could barely function. I got the earliest appointment possible with my doctor, which wasn't until midafternoon.

On her way to school and the daycare center, Nichole stopped by with Owen to check on me. She made me promise to text her as soon as I left the doctor's office. After seeing her I called the Community Center and explained that I'd be unable to teach that night and didn't know how long I'd be out. I hated doing this to them at the last minute, but they were kind and understood.

My doctor's appointment confirmed what I already knew. I was given a prescription for an antiviral drug and heavy painkillers. I swallowed both the minute I got home. Within hours I was zonked out, asleep on the sofa. When I woke it was close to five and I was sick to my stomach from the meds, dizzy and disoriented.

I vaguely remember Nichole checking on me again after school. She forced some soup into me and then put me to bed. I slept through the night and didn't wake until well into Tuesday morning.

Kacey phoned, suggesting we do lunch. I begged off.

"Okay, I'll let you off the hook this time, but we're setting a date to get together right now," she insisted. "It's been far too long since I saw you. I know you have a new life, but I'm still your friend."

"You'll always be my friend," I assured her. The truth was she was right. I had stepped away from her friendship mainly because every time I was with Kacey, she brought up Sean. I didn't want to discuss my ex-husband. I didn't care who he was involved with now or if and when he'd embarrassed himself at the club. The gossip concerning my ex-husband didn't interest me. No matter how many times I explained that to Kacey, she didn't listen.

Wednesday passed in a blur. I could function on the pain meds, but just barely. They made me sick to my stomach and sleepy. Nichole and Owen stopped by at least once or twice a day to be sure I was eating. They didn't stay long and frankly I was grateful. Owen didn't understand why I didn't read to him or tell him stories. His big round eyes looked at me and I could barely stand to disappoint him.

Thursday afternoon my doorbell rang and, suspecting it was Nichole, I called for her to come in. When the door opened, though, it wasn't Nichole. Instead, it was Nikolai.

He came into my apartment, stopped, and frowned when he saw me.

It took every shred of dignity I had not to cover my face and ask him to leave. I'd had a shower earlier in the day but hadn't styled my hair. Nor did I have any makeup on. I was in my robe and slippers and probably looked like an Ebola victim.

His eyes widened in alarm. "Leanne?" he whispered as if he wasn't completely sure it was me.

"Go away," I pleaded. "Please, please just leave."

He refused with a hard shake of his head. "The teacher no say why you not in class."

"It's obvious, isn't it? I'm . . . sick." I wasn't sure he even knew what shingles was and I didn't want to take time to explain. "Go away, you might catch this bug," I said. That was a blatant lie, but I was desperate.

"I won't leave." He was insistent.

"Please, Nikolai." I was close to tears. "Please just do as I ask."

He shook his head. I didn't know he could be so stubborn.

"You're angry with me, remember?"

"I was wrong." He remained standing just inside the apartment, refusing to budge.

"I served the bread you made for me to Sean." Perhaps if I reminded him of the terrible thing I'd done he'd leave.

He shook his head as if to say that no longer concerned him. "I was angry, but no more."

"You should be angry," I insisted. "You shouldn't be so willing to forgive me," I said, grasping at straws.

"I not leave you. Tell me this sickness and I cook for you."

I was too tired and beaten down to argue. Hanging my head I told him, "I have shingles."

His eyes widened and he started talking quickly and adamantly in his mother tongue.

"You know what shingles are?" I asked, surprised.

He nodded and his eyes filled with sympathy. "Oh my Leanne, my Leanne, I cannot bear for you to suffer this terrible pain."

His words and his look were so tender they brought tears to my eyes. I blinked and looked away, unable to meet his gaze.

Before I knew what he was doing, Nikolai tenderly took me in his arms and hugged me as if I were the most fragile of flowers. He kissed my forehead and then my cheeks, all while speaking softly in Ukrainian. Although I was unable to understand a single word he said, his gentle voice soothed me more than any prescription I might have been given.

Nikolai led me to the sofa and sat down next to me, gripping both my hands in his. He didn't say anything for the longest time, and I noticed his Adam's apple moving up and down in his throat as if he was struggling within himself.

"When you not come to class on Monday, I was glad. I still angry. I think you no respect me."

"Oh Nikolai, that's not true, I—"

He shushed me with his finger against my lips. "The teacher no say why you not come. I think, *Good;* I glad you not there. I think you feed that pimple-on-log ex-husband more of my bread and I bubble with anger."

"I didn't."

"I know. I make excuse to be angry; otherwise, I hurt too much."

I had no idea Nikolai would take what I'd done personally. It had been a matter of practicality to me and nothing more.

"On Wednesday I think and think. All day I think. I

miss you. I see sadness in your eyes when I leave you. I talk with friend at deli and he tell me I wrong. He tell me I am foolish man. I not want to hear that. I want to hear that you foolish one, not me. My friend say I act like jealous fool and he is right. He say I should tell you sorry . . . that is why I come."

I raised my hand to his cheek and cupped it, my heart melting at his apology. I'd been utterly miserable since we'd last talked, and that misery had little to do with the discomfort of shingles.

Nikolai raised my hands to his mouth and kissed my fingers one by one. "When you no come to class again I ask teacher and she say you must be sick, but she not know for sure. I think maybe you sick because of me, because of what I say, because I jealous. I no wait until next week. I can't wait. I come see you now."

"Nikolai," I whispered . . . but I was unable to say anything more than his name, for the knot blocking my throat.

He leaned forward and kissed me, his lips gentle and undemanding. He raised his head and then brushed my hair away from my face, looping it around my ears and holding my head between his hands.

Having him look at me when I was at my physical worst was almost more than I could bear. I lowered my eyes, knowing what he must see: a woman well past her prime with wrinkles around her mouth and eyes whose sight had dimmed. A woman unloved and discarded by her husband years before she had the courage and the strength to walk away.

"You so beautiful," he whispered. "So beautiful."

I shook my head, unwilling to hear or believe him.

His hands tightened. "You no believe you beautiful?"

"Nikolai, I don't have any makeup on, and my hair—"

"You no need makeup," he said cutting me off. "You no need hair."

I smiled.

"You beautiful person here," he said, pointing to my heart. "More beautiful there than beautiful outside. And outside so beautiful I look at you and forget to get air."

Tears pooled in my eyes.

"My heart pounding, and I think this woman is most beautiful woman I ever meet. I simple man. I not rich, but I work hard all my life. I marry young and hope for family, but no children come. I love my wife. I happy for long time, then Magdalena get sick and there are no doctors, no medicine. I do everything to help her. I go from city to city to find doctor to help my wife, but she get sicker and sicker. But to me she always beautiful. I see you and know you like my Magdalena. You beautiful person; you no need makeup, you no need hair; all I see is woman, good woman."

I bit into my bottom lip, not knowing what to say or if I should speak. His words watered my soul.

"First time I see you in classroom, I think this beautiful woman," he continued. "More times I see you, I learn better English. I learn more of you and every time I learn more of you my heart fills up until you are always with me. You are with me in my sleep; at my work you with me." He paused and placed his hand over his chest. "In my heart you with me."

He threaded his fingers through my hair, twisting my head up until I had no choice but to look at him. "When I see you on Saturday I think it easy to forget you. I put you out of my head. I think it easy, but now I know it not possible."

"It's been a long time since I felt loved or loveable," I whispered, wanting him to understand.

"This man you marry . . ."

"The pimple on a log," I added, smiling.

"Yes, this pimple-on-log man, he foolish more than me. He let you go; he no love you. I never stop, I can't. I know I will never be same man without my Leanne."

There was no holding back the tears now.

He held me close and I let him, despite the pain his embrace caused me. The ache was a small price to pay to be in Nikolai's arms.

# CHAPTER 17

# Nichole

When I arrived at school I found a long-stemmed red rose on my desk. The card attached had Rocco's name. This was a pleasant surprise. I didn't think Rocco was a flowers and chocolate kind of guy. Five minutes before class started I reached for my phone and sent him a text.

Me: Thanx for the rose.
Rocco: What rose?
Me: The long-stemmed red rose here on my desk.
Rocco: What are you talking about?
Me: You didn't give me a rose?

Maybe I had a secret admirer, but that didn't make sense. Why would a secret admirer sign Rocco's name to the card? I was beginning to get the picture, and it seemed Rocco was, too.

Rocco: Wait. K asked for $ this morn. Didn't say Y.
Me: Interesting.

My phone buzzed before I could type back a reply. "Hello?"

"It's me," Rocco returned. "I figured it was better to talk this out than do it by text."

"So you didn't send the rose?"

"Yes and no." He sounded amused. "Like I said, Kaylene asked me for a few bucks this morning, which isn't anything out of the ordinary. She's always needing money for one thing or another at school."

"I think the choir is doing a fundraiser," I said, remembering something I'd read in the teacher bulletin earlier in the week.

"Roses, right?"

"I think so. It was a nice gesture on her part, so thank you, even if you didn't intend for me to get the rose." I wasn't disappointed, and I certainly didn't want Rocco to think I was.

"The thing is . . ." He hesitated as if unsure how to continue.

"The thing is what?" I pressed.

"Kaylene's been giving me advice."

"Advice on what?"

"You know, on dating and such."

"You need advice?"

He hesitated. "According to her, I do."

If he hadn't been so serious, I would have laughed. "You realize you're getting advice from a fifteen-year-old?"

"You're right, it's ludicrous," he muttered.

"That's very sweet, Rocco." It said a lot about the way he felt about me, which made me want to kiss him again. I'd enjoyed the movie with him, although it'd been about a psycho killer. It'd terrified me to the point I slid so far down on the seat that I was in danger of slipping onto the floor. Rocco placed his arm around me and I hid my face in his jacket. For the rest of the movie he had his arm around me. I wasn't complaining.

"It's sweet?"

"Yeah, it is."

"I don't know, Nichole. First ice cream, now flowers. If my guy friends hear about this, there will be no end to the razzing."

"I have yet to meet any of your friends, male or otherwise," I reminded him.

"You sure you're up to that?" he asked, and hedged. "I don't exactly hang with men from the country club."

"Not a problem, Rocco. I'm into making new friends and having new experiences." I wasn't exactly hanging with my country-club friends. Most of my so-called friends had taken Jake's side. I understood. It would be difficult to be friends with us both, and he'd stayed in the community while I'd moved away. It'd hurt to be cut off from people I'd once considered close. It was a couples world and I was single now. The truth was those so-called friends really hadn't been.

"You're serious. You'd actually be willing to meet the guys I hang with?"

"Sure. Why not?" I found it a silly question.

"Okay, Saturday night, then."

"You're keeping your promise to Owen, aren't you?" Rocco had agreed to give Owen a ride in his tow truck on Saturday afternoon. Owen had talked of little else and even shared it with his preschool class. Owen's toy tow truck was his absolute favorite toy. My three-year-old was constantly on his hands and knees pushing that truck across the floor, making all kinds of noise in the process.

"I don't break my promises," Rocco reminded me.

I appreciated that he was a man of his word. "I'll need to find a babysitter for Saturday night; Leanne is still under the weather or I'd ask her."

"Kaylene can watch Owen."

"You'd better check with her before you commit her," I reminded him. Kaylene had a mind of her own and wouldn't appreciate her father volunteering her services.

"Will do," he said.

Students began filing into the classroom, and while I would have liked to continue our chat I couldn't. "I've got to go."

"Yeah, me, too. See you tomorrow."

"I'll call you once Owen is up from his nap."

"Bye. Enjoy that rose."

I was smiling when I disconnected.


Saturday afternoon I met Rocco in his company parking lot. He'd mentioned earlier that he was the sole owner of Potter Towing, but I hadn't a clue how large the business was. He had a fleet of about ten tow trucks in various sizes, and those were just the ones in the lot. More had to be out on jobs. Before he took us outside, Rocco gave Owen and me a tour of the garages and the office. I met a couple of his crew and I had to admit they were a tough-looking crowd. It wasn't until later that Rocco told me a few of the men he'd hired were on work release. They needed a second chance and he'd given it to them.

"Is this where Shawntelle sits?" I asked when I saw the glassed-in office.

"Yes." He frowned when I mentioned her name.

"Is there a problem with Shawntelle?" I hoped not, seeing how badly she needed the job.

"Not really. The woman seems to have an opinion on just about everything. She had a run-in with one of my drivers because he didn't hand over his time card. I heard her giving the poor guy hell the other day. It worked, though. Jerome gave it to her first thing this morning."

"In other words, she's doing a good job for you." I had known Shawntelle would and was grateful to hear it.

"Yes, and she's keeping the books balanced, too, which is a lot better than my previous bookkeeper."

Owen tugged at my leg, growing impatient. "I think Owen is ready for his ride," I said.

Rocco looked down at my son. "Well, first off, he needs a uniform."

"A uniform?" Rocco hadn't mentioned that earlier. If he had I would have seen to it before now.

"No worries, the shop provides those." He walked over to a locker and removed a sack. Inside was a striped coverall that zipped up the front in Owen's size.

I watched as my son's eyes rounded with delight. "Fo me?"

"Let's make sure it fits first," Rocco said. He got down on his knees next to Owen and unzipped the suit so my three-year-old could step into it, one foot at a time. The fit was perfect. Owen thrust his small chest out with pride and rubbed his hands down his front. He wore the biggest smile I could ever remember seeing.

"Wook, Mommy, wook," he said, twirling around.

"I see. You're a real tow-truck driver now. It's official."

"Official," Owen repeated.

"You ready to drive your rig?" Rocco asked.

Owen nodded eagerly.

"Follow me." He held out his hand and Owen placed his much smaller one in Rocco's huge one.

I traipsed along behind, excited for my son. Rocco lifted him up and set Owen inside the biggest tow truck on the lot. He'd explained earlier that this larger tow truck was used for hauling eighteen-wheelers. Rocco climbed in after him and then set Owen on his lap.

"Ready?" he asked Owen.

"Weady," Owen repeated.

"Turn the key to start the engine."

Owen leaned forward, stretching as far as his short arms would allow, and turned the ignition key. The truck roared to life and Owen squealed with delight. I stepped back and watched as Rocco drove with my son in his lap around the parking lot. Owen's small hands gripped the steering wheel along with Rocco's much larger ones. My son's eyes were bright and intense. I lost count of the number of circles they made before Rocco pulled the rig into the designated spot. Once the engine was turned off, Owen clapped with delight, happier than a pig in mud.

———

Later Saturday evening, Rocco was going to drop Kaylene off to watch Owen while the two of us went out. He hadn't mentioned where we were going, but he had said we'd be meeting a few of his friends. This seemed like a big deal to him, although I wasn't completely sure why. I had to believe this was more about him than me.

I dressed in my skinny jeans and a V-neck pink sweater with a white cowl and my cowboy boots. I'd spent two hundred and fifty dollars for those boots when Jake and I were married. I couldn't imagine spending that amount of money on any single clothing item now. One time, just before I learned Jake had been cheating on me, I bought a designer purse for seven hundred dollars. When I left Jake, I hadn't taken into account the consequences of my financial situation. I knew the divorce had hit Jake hard, too. In a petty way, that made me glad. Maybe he'd have less money to spend on other women.

I checked my reflection in the bedroom mirror and was satisfied. I could use a haircut, but that would need to wait until my next paycheck.

The doorbell chimed and Owen raced into the living room ahead of me. His face broke into a huge smile when he saw Kaylene and Rocco.

"How's it going, little man?" Rocco asked, bending down and extending his palm.

Owen's arm did a complete three-hundred-and-sixty-degree swing before he slapped his hand against Rocco's open palm.

"Thanks, Kaylene," I said. "Owen's had his dinner and there's ice cream for later, but only if he's good."

"I wike ice cream," Owen said.

"Me, too," Kaylene added.

"Tell her to wead me stories," Owen reminded me.

I looked to Kaylene. "Oh yes, there's a big stack of books. He likes to be read to at bedtime."

"Will do," the teenager promised.

I grabbed my coat and purse and we left within a few minutes of their arrival. Rocco seemed nervous. "You okay?" I asked, once outside the apartment.

"Sure."

"You're fidgeting."

"Am not," he argued.

"Listen, Rocco, if you'd rather I not meet your friends, it's fine."

He hesitated in front of the elevator. "I've never introduced them to a woman before. They might say something to embarrass you."

"Hey, I'm a big girl. I can handle myself, so quit worrying."

He studied me and then slowly nodded. "If you're sure, then okay. Let's do this, but don't say I didn't warn you."

He made it sound like we were about to cross into uncharted territory, and perhaps for him we were. I remembered him telling me that he'd never married Kaylene's mother and that he didn't do relationships. I wasn't sure if we were even in a relationship. We did things together and he'd been a good friend, but this was the first time we were going out just the two of us. Technically, this was our first date. I hadn't realized it until that moment. It felt like I'd known him forever, but all the time we'd spent together other people had been involved.

Once outside my apartment building, we walked to where Rocco had parked. He opened the door to his truck and helped me inside.

When he joined me I asked, "Is this a date?"

He placed his hands on the steering wheel and stared straight ahead. "I don't know. Is it?"

"It feels like one."

He leaned his head back and closed his eyes.

"What?" I asked, not understanding his strange behavior.

"I don't date."

I laughed, which was probably not the wisest response. "Okay. What would you like to call this, then?"

"Do we need to call it anything?"

*Good question.* "I suppose not. You're taking me to meet your friends and we'll leave it at that."

"Fair enough."

He was still nervous, though. I could see it in the way he gripped the steering wheel and how he bounced his knee when stopped at red lights. I was curious about his *I don't date* statement. "If you don't date, then what do you call it when you take out a woman?"

He ignored the question.

"Rocco?"

"I don't take women out."

Now I was confused. "But—"

"Leave it, Nichole," he barked, and then quickly apologized. "Sorry, I didn't mean to snap at you."

He really was nervous about this, which surprised me. I wasn't sure what to make of it, but decided I should be honored that he'd bent his self-imposed rule to "date" me.

We drove to a tavern that had a lot of motorcycles parked out front. Rocco helped me out of the truck and then, with his hand at the small of my back, he led me inside. As soon as we entered it seemed everyone in the entire room went silent and looked at us. Rocco stood with the tips of his fingers tucked into his back pockets.

"Hey. Everyone, this is Nichole."

Several of the guys lifted their beer mugs in greeting.

"Hi," I said, and, unsure what to do, I gave a small wave.

Rocco found us a table and ordered us each a beer, which was promptly delivered by a waitress in shorts and a halter top that exposed more skin than a bikini. I watched Rocco, but his eyes didn't follow the scantily clad woman, which pleased me.

I sat in a chair at the high-top and Rocco stood next to me in a protective stance. A couple guys drifted by and Rocco made small talk with them, including me in the conversation whenever possible. There didn't appear to be many women around, which garnered me a lot of attention.

"Where'd you two meet?" a guy named Sam asked.

I knew his name because it was labeled on his leather jacket. "He pulled me out of a ditch," I answered.

Sam chuckled. "I gotta get me one of those tow trucks so I can meet a pretty lady like you."

Rocco circled his arm around my waist as if claiming his territory. "Back off, Sam," Rocco said, but his eyes held a teasing light.

Sam raised both hands in surrender and winked at me. I liked him immediately. He was about Rocco's age, or maybe a bit older. "Rocco's a good guy. Not many of those around, so if I was you, I'd hold on to this one."

Rocco muttered something I couldn't hear.

"I think you're onto something," I told Sam.

Rocco looked to me, his eyes narrowed. "You mean that?"

My answer was to simply smile, which appeared to satisfy him.

He noticed that I hadn't drunk much of my beer. "I'd order you wine, but they don't serve it here."

"No wine?"

"Sorry, the guys who come here are a beer-drinking crowd."

"Don't worry about it." Beer wasn't my favorite drink, but I'd manage.

After we finished our beers, Rocco and I shot a game of pool. I was offered plenty of advice from his friends, who seemed more than willing to aid me. I could see Rocco didn't appreciate the attention I attracted, but he kept his cool. It was almost as if he wasn't sure how to act around me when he was with his friends.

After a second beer I relaxed and laughed, enjoying myself. I'll admit his friends were rough on the outside, but nothing like one would expect. First impressions could be misleading. It seemed a lot of them rode motorcycles and hung out together.

I played a second game of pool, but this time it was with Sam and a couple others while Rocco stood back and watched. When we won I slipped my arms around

Rocco and looked up at him, wearing a triumphant smile.

"Having fun?" he asked, grinning down on me.

"I am." I actually was enjoying myself. It'd been far too long since I'd been on a date, even if Rocco didn't want to call it that.

A huge man with bulging muscles, a beard, and a leather jacket joined us, along with a woman, also wearing a leather jacket, stating she was his property. Was she nuts? She had her arm around his middle. She smiled at Rocco and it seemed there might have been something between them at one time.

I stepped closer to him and tucked my finger in his belt loop and glared at the other woman.

The man looked at me and then at Rocco. "This your woman?"

Rocco looked to me as if unsure how to answer.

I smiled up at him.

"Yeah," he said, not breaking eye contact with me. "Nichole is my woman."

# CHAPTER 18

# Leanne

I met Kacey at Lloyd's Center. Jake and her son, Adam, who was two years older, used to ice-skate in the center rink. Jake was around ten at the time. The ice rink held a lot of fond memories for me. Kacey needed a mother-of-the-bride dress, as her daughter was getting married in the summer, and she'd decided to start the search early.

"I hate this!" Kacey declared, studying herself in the dressing room mirror, twisting around to study her backside. Her shoulders slumped forward. "I look like a dumpy middle-aged woman."

"You are a dumpy middle-aged woman," I reminded her, shaking my head. "We both are."

"No one needs a friend who speaks the truth," Kacey joked. "Come on, let's go have lunch. I need a break."

I was more than happy to agree. It took far more stamina than I realized to shop for a mother-of-the-bride dress. It'd been a long time since I'd spent two or three hours shopping for just the perfect outfit. Since the divorce I rarely went out and definitely had no need for formal attire. I didn't envy Kacey the search for the perfect dress.

"You feeling okay?" Kacey asked as we walked out of Nordstrom.

I still had shingles, but the antiviral medications had started to work and I was down to half a painkiller every few hours, which cut back on the nausea side effects and sleepiness. "I'm certainly better than I was last week."

We found a restaurant inside the mall and were seated right away. As soon as we ordered, Kacey leaned closer to me. "Guess who I saw last weekend?"

I didn't need to guess. "Sean."

"Yup, and he was full of questions about you."

I had no idea why Sean would ask about me, especially when we'd seen each other recently.

"Aren't you curious what he wanted to know?" Kacey asked. She seemed disappointed that I hadn't taken the bait.

I shook my head. "Not really. I can't imagine why he asked about me, and frankly, I don't care."

"Okay, to be accurate he wasn't as curious about you as he was about the man who brings you the bread. You know the one I mean? The guy we met that time at the deli."

My back stiffened. This definitely raised my curiosity. "What about Nikolai?"

"Sean was pretty sneaky about getting information out of me, but I was onto him right away."

"What do you mean?"

Kacey was in her element, using her hands expressively, eager to fill in the details. "Bill and I were having drinks at the club. You know how busy it gets on Saturday nights. We were at the bar waiting for a table when Sean sauntered in. Naturally, he had a woman with him."

Naturally. That was information I wasn't interested in hearing.

"When he saw us he left his flavor of the month and came to talk to me and Bill. He made small talk for a few minutes. He asked Bill about his golf game, mentioned they should get together soon, you know, that sort of thing."

I nodded, anxious for her to get to the part about Nikolai.

"Then Sean looked at me and said how lovely I looked, blah, blah, blah. It was all I could do not to roll my eyes and ask him what he wanted." She pursed her lips together.

"That is very Seanlike." I always knew when he complimented me that he needed something from me.

"He mentioned that he stopped by your apartment recently and met some foreigner. I knew right away he meant the man from the deli. I didn't know that you were seeing him outside the classroom."

"I don't think 'seeing him' is quite the right term," I said, downplaying our relationship.

"He was at your apartment, though. That's what Sean said."

"Yes, he was there . . . he's teaching me how to bake bread."

Kacey's eyes widened ever so slightly.

I wasn't giving her any additional information. Nor did I mention I'd be seeing Nikolai that very evening.

"Does he still bring you bread every class session?"

"I haven't been back to school since I got shingles." I avoided the question as best I could.

"But you are going back?"

"Yes." I planned to return the week before Halloween in order to give myself time to heal.

"Well, anyway," she continued, "Sean wanted to know what I could tell him about Nikolai."

I didn't like the sound of this. "And what did you tell him?"

"Not much. I mean, I didn't know a lot; for instance, I didn't realize he gave bread-making lessons. Does he do this often? If so, I'd sign up in a heartbeat. The bread is delicious, but then so is the teacher." She laughed and waved her hand in front of her face, indicating that she thought Nikolai was hot.

I wasn't amused. I'd never considered myself a jealous woman. Sean had cured me of that years earlier, or so I'd thought. I didn't care that Kacey was my best friend or that she was married. I resented her telling me she thought Nikolai was hot. "I can ask him if you want," I said, discounting my uneasiness. I didn't want Nikolai anywhere near Kacey and immediately felt silly because there was no way Nikolai would get involved with a married woman. Besides, I knew Kacey was only teasing me.

"Getting back to Sean," Kacey said. "He seemed concerned."

"Concerned?"

"He's afraid you're at a vulnerable point in your life and could easily be misled, especially by an immigrant. He came right out and said that he didn't trust the way Nikolai looked at you. He suggested Nikolai might be dangerous and then lowered his voice to warn me Nikolai could be part of the Russian Mafia."

"Oh please." I laughed out loud. That was insane.

"I know, I know," Kacey said, laughing lightly. "It isn't like you're involved with him." She hesitated and studied me closely. "Or are you?"

That was a question I was determined not to answer. I looked up, hoping the waiter was about to deliver our meals. Naturally, he was nowhere in sight.

"What else did Sean want to know?" I asked, avoiding a direct answer.

I should have known Kacey wouldn't be easily put off. "Are you two involved?" she pressed.

"Nikolai and I are *friends*."

"F-r-i-e-n-d-s?" She dragged out the word. "Close friends?" she added.

"What do you mean?"

"Friends with *benefits*?"

My mouth sagged open. "You know me better than that."

She laughed. "But there's something going on between you two." Kacey was almost giddy with excitement. "I knew it. Sweetie, if I was you I'd drag that man to bed so fast it'd make your head spin like that girl in the movie *The Exorcist*."

"Kacey," I snapped. "Please." She had me blushing. I'd never been one to treat sex casually, and I wasn't about to start at this point in my life.

"That man is gorgeous, and if he makes you happy, then so what?"

The waiter came with our salads and I was so glad to see him I was tempted to jump up and kiss him on both cheeks. This conversation had quickly grown uncomfortable.

Kacey reached for her fork and speared a fat shrimp. "I think Sean's jealous, and frankly, I couldn't be happier. After everything he put you through, it's time he got a taste of his own medicine."

"I was never jealous of Sean's women," I said, and I was being honest. Perhaps in the very beginning, the first or second time I'd discovered he was having an affair, but I soon learned jealousy was a useless emotion. I'd closed myself off from any feeling toward my husband for so long that nothing seemed to faze me.

"I'm happy for you, Leanne," Kacey said with all sincerity.

I looked over at my friend and told her what was most important for her to know. "I am happy, Kacey." And I was far happier than I had been in a very long while.

We parted ways after lunch and I returned to the apartment, exhausted. I took one of the pain meds and despite my best efforts I fell asleep, only to wake when the doorbell chimed.

It was Nikolai.

I hadn't meant to sleep nearly that long and immediately felt guilty. I'd wanted to refresh my makeup and fix my hair before he arrived.

Nikolai stood on the other side of the threshold with a large takeout bag in his hand and wearing a huge smile.

"I come too early?"

"No, no, it's fine." I ushered him inside and he set the bag on the kitchen countertop.

"I'm sorry. I was out this afternoon and then I fell

asleep." I felt the need to apologize for my appearance. But Nikolai had seen me when I was at my worst and it hadn't bothered him.

Nikolai brought me close and his large hands framed my face. He brushed the hair behind my ears and then slowly lowered his mouth to mine. The kiss was slow and deliberate, and I melted in his arms. Oh, the things this man made me feel. It was as if my insides turned to mush every time he touched me.

When the kiss ended, he pressed his forehead against mine. "All day I think about you. I think three hours then I see you. Then two hours, and then I think only one hour. The last hour take longer than all the other hours."

I leaned forward and kissed him, slipping my arms around his solid frame.

"You too good for me," he whispered. "I not know why you kiss me."

"Stop," I demanded, and pressed my fingertips over his lips. "Don't even think that."

Nikolai grinned and rubbed his nose against mine. "I kiss you like Eskimo," he whispered.

The doorbell rang, and when I opened it Nichole was there with Owen.

"Owen wanted to check to see if you're feeling better," Nichole explained.

I noticed that her attention went past me to Nikolai. She stepped forward and extended her hand. "I'm Nichole. We met a while back."

Nikolai smiled. "Yes, yes, I remember."

"I'm Owen," my grandson said proudly. "I dwive a tow twuck."

Getting down on one knee so that he was eye level

with Owen, Nikolai extended his hand. "You fine young man to be so smart to drive big truck."

Owen frowned and looked up at his mother. "He talks funny," he whispered, as if Nikolai couldn't hear him.

"I only learned English five years now. I am citizen."

"Am I citizen?" Owen asked me, pronouncing the word with the same voice inflection as Nikolai.

"Yes, you are," Nichole assured her son.

Owen had on his zippered one-piece outfit that Rocco had ordered for him. He'd worn it every day since Rocco had taken him for a ride. Nichole told me that she was hardly able to get him to take it off for bed, Owen was so proud and excited. I wished Jake showed as much interest in his son as Rocco did.

The time Jake spent with Owen had shortened every week he took him. In the beginning Jake would bring Owen home around seven on Sunday night. Last Sunday he had him back to Nichole around three. I could see this was becoming a pattern. It was almost as if having Owen over the entire weekend had become a nuisance.

Nichole and Owen left after a few minutes. Nikolai gripped hold of my hand. He tapped his finger in the space between my eyes. "You frown. You not like your grandson visit?"

"Oh no. I love Owen and Nichole. She's like a daughter to me. I was just thinking about Jake, Owen's father. I'm worried he isn't taking his responsibility toward his son seriously." Owen spoke frequently about Rocco and Kaylene and said little about his own father.

"You worry?"

"Yes, I worry, but there's nothing I can do about it."

"Come. You sit. I bring dinner so you not cook." He glanced toward the large bag he'd brought with him. "I no cook, either."

"From the deli?" I asked, as he led me to the small table I had in the kitchen area.

"No, from Sun Young. From class. He sorry when I tell him you have shingles. He say he cook for you."

"So it's Chinese food." One of my favorites.

"Special Chinese soup because you good teacher. Sun Young say no one else get this soup. He make for you . . . just you."

"And you," I added. I didn't want to eat alone. "Please stay, Nikolai, and join me."

He hesitated. "Sun Young cook for you."

"I couldn't possibly eat all that myself and I'd end up throwing the rest away. Please," I added again.

Nikolai exhaled a sigh. "I cannot tell you no. You ask and I have no heart to refuse."

"Good." I brought two bowls down from the cupboard and set them on the table. While I got out the silverware, Nikolai reached inside the bag and removed the container.

Before we ate, he gripped my hand and bowed his head in silent prayer. I was touched he would do that. I knew so little about him and I wanted to know more.

"What brought you to America?" I asked.

"Airplane."

I laughed, which confused him. "I meant, why did you come?"

"For opportunity. To bake my bread, to start new life. I am alone, but I have American friend in Ukraine. Like soldier but not in uniform. He help me, arrange for me to come to Oregon because I help him. Because I help him he able to help me."

"What did you do, Nikolai, to help this soldier?" I speculated this was some undercover operation. Oh heavens, I knew next to nothing of foreign intrigue.

"What I do?" he repeated and looked away. Slowly he shook his head, dilemma written in his face. "I promise not to say, not to anyone. I sorry, but I make promise, then I keep promise. I cannot tell, not even for you."

"I understand." A man who kept his word was an honorable man and I appreciated his integrity.

"I not talk about this, okay?"

"Of course." I wasn't sure I understood what role he might possibly have had. I decided it didn't matter how or why he came to America; I was simply grateful he was here. I dipped my spoon into the soup and looked down. Nikolai had mentioned his wife and that he'd been married. I wanted to know more about her, but felt funny asking. "Tell me more about Magdalena."

His eyes grew sad. "We meet at school. I sixteen, she fifteen. She come from poor family. We marry and live with my family. I bake bread and she help my mother at the house. She sad we have no children. She sick long time."

"When did she die?"

He reached for my hand. "Long time. Twenty years now. I alone twenty years. I love Magdalena. She only woman for me, I think. Then I meet you."

"I was alone thirty years," I whispered, my throat thickening. The emotion wasn't because of Sean or the sad state of my marriage. It was what Nikolai had said about meeting me.

He frowned, not understanding. "You married. How you be alone?"

"I was married, but I was alone. My husband didn't love me. He loved other women."

Nikolai scowled. "He fool, that man. I not understand how he not love you."

"Pimple on a log," I said, not wanting to belabor the point of my marriage. I'd started a new life now and didn't want to look back.

"You mentioned your mother. What about your family in Ukraine?"

He looked away and cast his eyes down. "My mother die long time. My brother die. He in Army and my sister angry; she move away and not speak to me for long time. Before I leave for America I call and tell her I go to Oregon and she cry. She sorry, but she bitter woman. She think our mother love Magdalena more than her, but she wrong."

"I'm so sorry."

"No, no. I not alone. I have friends. I have new life. I work for deli now, but I dream of baking bread for more than people who come to deli. I think and plan and work hard for this new life I plan. I tell you one day what I dream. Okay?"

"Okay." If he continued to look at me with those intense dark eyes I feared I would throw myself at him. Steeling myself against the strong attraction I felt for him, I said, "I have a new life, too."

Nikolai's grip on my hand tightened. "You alone no more, either. You have Nichole and me and class. First time I see you it like someone stick a fork in my heart. I can hardly find seat to sit in desk."

I remembered the first class with Nikolai. The entire class period he didn't speak. I was afraid he was so new to the country that he didn't know any English. He did, I learned later. In fact, his English was better than most everyone else's in the class. That first class, however, all he'd done was stare at me. It was after that night that he'd started to meet me in the parking lot and bring me bread.

He told me I was no longer alone and I believed him. Nikolai, for whatever reason, loved me. Me, who for far too many years had felt completely unlovable and unloved.

# CHAPTER 19

# Nichole

Rocco and I either talked or texted every day since our first official non-date when I'd met his friends. Unfortunately, due to our schedules, we hadn't been able to see each other. I hoped we'd be able to square things later this afternoon. He'd texted to ask for help with Kaylene's Halloween costume and I was happy to lend a hand, glad for the excuse to see him. Besides, there was something important I needed to set right with him.

Since my position as a substitute teacher was full-time and I volunteered one Saturday a month at Dress for Success, that gave me only one free weekend a month when Jake had Owen.

Kaylene had attempted to make her own rock-star costume with limited success. Her version and Rocco's version clashed, so I'd been called in as mediator.

Rocco had to work half a day Saturday, which was for the best. I figured the costume making would go better without him and agreed to drive over to his house. Rocco and I could talk later.

I didn't let Owen, who was with Jake, know, because he'd be disappointed not to see Rocco and Kaylene. He'd been reluctant to go with Jake as it was, and I didn't want a battle on my hands. I'd already called Jake twice to see how Owen was doing. Jake was polite, but I could tell he didn't appreciate the second call.

I arrived at Rocco's around ten on Saturday. Kaylene had the door open before I made it to the front porch. I liked the house. It was an older two-story, probably built around the early 1960s, with a big hedged-in porch and dormers. It reminded me of the house I'd grown up in in Spokane, minus the gazebo my father had built for my mom.

"My dad's impossible," Kaylene complained, even before I entered the house. "He refuses to let me wear the costume I made. He said I looked like . . . well, it's probably better I not say."

"Let me take a look at it and we'll see if we can re-shape it into something he finds presentable," I suggested. I shrugged off my coat and purse and brought out five gossip magazines I'd picked up at the store. I figured the photos would give us both ideas.

Sitting at the kitchen table with the magazines spilled across the top, Kaylene flipped through the pages. She found several dresses she thought would work and I did, too. We tore the pages out and set the magazines aside.

"You ready to shop?" I asked.

Her eyes widened. "Shop? My dad would never spring for a dress like that," she protested.

"We're not going to buy anything new," I told her. "We're headed to a few secondhand stores. I promise you, by the time we're finished Lady Gaga will envy your outfit."

Kaylene's eyes widened before she raced into the other room to grab her coat.

Rocco had been smart to seek my advice. Dressing others was something I loved, which was why I chose to volunteer at Dress for Success. We hit pay dirt at the first shop. The perfect dress was on display at Goodwill and we found complementary jewelry at St. Vincent de Paul. We splurged on a hat we found at an antiques store. The outfit was fantastic, if I did say so myself.

We arrived back at one just as Rocco pulled in to the driveway. Kaylene dashed across the yard and threw her arms around his neck, squeezing until he protested.

"Hey, hey, I thought you weren't speaking to me," he reminded his daughter. He made eye contact with me and grinned. Kaylene dragged him into the house and showed him our purchases and then modeled her outfit. As expected, he gave our choice his seal of approval.

"Thank you, Nichole," she said, hugging me, too. "You're the best ever."

That was high praise coming from a teenager.

"Can I go over to Dakota's?" she asked. "She's going to go c-r-a-z-y when she sees my costume."

"Be back by five-thirty," Rocco shouted as the teen raced out the door, packages in hand.

I'd been waiting to talk to Rocco. "Do you have time for a cup of coffee?" I asked.

He studied me apprehensively. Perhaps it was something in my voice.

"Yeah, sure," he said. "Something on your mind?"

I had to admit there was.

We moved into the kitchen and Rocco went about getting us each a cup of coffee. I pulled out a chair and sat down, hoping he wouldn't take this wrong. No matter; it needed to be said.

He handed me a mug and held his own, standing with his back against the kitchen counter, his ankles crossed. "What's the problem?" he asked, keeping his gaze steady on me.

I was surprised he was able to read me this easily. "It's about last week when I met your friends."

"What about it?" His mouth tightened slightly and he tried to hide it by taking a sip of his coffee.

"I need to tell you something first."

He gestured with his free hand for me to go ahead.

"I'm not much of a drinker. A glass of wine does it for me and I rarely drink beer. I had three that night with you."

"So?"

"So . . . three beers mess with my head." Rocco wasn't making this any easier. He kept his distance, I noticed, and his guard was up. I could almost feel the room growing chillier. "And then your friend asked if I was your woman. I could see you weren't sure how to answer. That woman was there with that ridiculous leather jacket that said she was his property. Really? Apparently, she hasn't heard about the Emancipation Proclamation."

"That's what you want to talk to me about?"

"No. Sorry, I didn't mean to get sidetracked. It's about what your friend asked . . . you know, if I was your woman."

"What about it?" He straightened and set the mug aside.

"You looked uncomfortable and hesitated, and I've never seen you hesitate about anything. But that's not the point. I smiled and you thought . . . I don't know what you thought, but then you told him I was . . . your woman."

"And you have a problem with that." His mouth got tighter and I could see that he'd clenched his jaw.

"I think we should talk about this first, because I didn't see us in a committed relationship. You wouldn't even call it a date."

"In other words that's a problem for you." Rocco pulled out a chair and sat down, crossing his arms. It took me a moment to tear my eyes away from his massive arms. One of these days I was going to ask him about his tattoos, which I'd never had a chance to study.

"Nichole! Answer me. You're saying you've got a problem with me saying you're my woman. Is that right?"

I didn't know how to answer. "I'm not sure." I was being as honest as I could.

He shrugged. "Okay."

That was all he had to say. Again? He'd said that before and I didn't have a clue what he was thinking. "That's it?" I challenged. "I really hate it when you do that, because I don't know what you mean."

"I mean I'm okay with you not wanting to be my woman."

"First off," I said, drawing in a deep breath as I thrust my index finger into the air, "I'm not a piece of property—yours or anyone else's."

"I agree."

"Stop being so accommodating. I'm serious."

"So am I."

I decided to ignore that. "And second"—up went a second finger—"if there is ever going to be a committed relationship between us, we need to come to an understanding first. It isn't something announced on the spur of the moment in a bar because neither one of us knows how to answer the question."

Rocco relaxed. "I couldn't have said it better myself."

I hadn't anticipated this. I wasn't sure how I'd expected him to respond, and I'd been prepared for an argument.

The silence stretched between us and I didn't know how to fill it.

"Listen, Nichole, I can see you're a little lost here, so let's clear the air."

"Yes, please." I was grateful he wanted to set the record straight, the same as I did.

He leaned forward, his elbows at the edge of the table as he straightened his arms. "I have a past and most of it isn't pretty. I made mistakes, got caught up in the wrong crowd. In my twenties I pretty much ran wild and got into a whole lot of shit that I'd like to forget ever happened. But it did and I paid the price. When I learned I had a daughter I figured it was time to get my life together, and by the grace of God I did.

"I took a job, worked hard, and was lucky enough to find a friend in old man Potter. It was something of a shock to realize I actually had a head for business. Potter Towing has doubled in size since I took over."

I hardly knew what to say. I held my breath and waited for him to continue.

"When you talk about a committed relationship I don't know what to tell you because I've never been in one. I barely knew Kaylene's mother's name the night I slept with her. I didn't claim Kaylene as my daughter until I had proof she actually was mine. That's the kind of life I used to lead."

"But you don't any longer," I added.

"No. I've got responsibilities and a kid to raise, and I'm working hard to make sure she doesn't make the same mistakes her mother and I did." His deep blue eyes held mine and grew more intense as he spoke.

"I know you're part of that highbrow country-club set. You've got a college education and speak French fluently. I speak pig latin and not that well. If your daddy knew you were seeing me he'd probably run me off with a shotgun, and I wouldn't blame him."

"You really speak pig latin?"

He didn't crack a smile. "Not fluently."

I wanted to smile, but I could see that Rocco was serious and he wasn't finished.

"The entire time I've known you I've been waiting for you to tell me to get lost because women like you don't mix with men like me. I'm everything your daddy warned you against and . . ."

"Stop," I said softly.

He blinked. "Stop?"

"I'm not going to sit here and listen to you tear

yourself down. You're a decent and honorable man who was willing to give Shawntelle a chance when no one else would. You're a loving, generous father, and you're kind to my son and more of a father figure to him than his own."

"You don't know me that well, and . . ."

"And I happen to like you." I said it with conviction. "In fact, I happen to really, really like you, and you're a good kisser. A damn good kisser." And although we hadn't done more than share a few kisses, I strongly suspected he was just as talented in other areas as well.

For the first time since we came into the kitchen, Rocco smiled.

"And furthermore, I like your friends." I added, "Sam's crazy funny." Although Sam had a really bad habit of using foul language.

He looked away. "They liked you, too, especially Sam. He called to ask about you and I told him hands off more than once and I didn't do it politely."

I held back a laugh. "The only reason he asked about me was because I'm a good pool player."

Rocco shook his head. "Not even close. Sam had other things in mind, things that would make your beautiful face blush. But before you put me on a pedestal, you should know I've had those same thoughts myself."

I stretched my arm across the table and grabbed hold of his hand. "It might surprise you to know I've thought about you in that way, too."

His eyes widened and the biggest grin I've ever seen slowly took shape. "Nice to know."

I sipped my coffee and he did, too.

"Like I said," Rocco continued, "I don't know anything about this committed-relationship thing. I've never been in one—hell, I've never even dated. Maybe it'd be best if you explained what you mean."

"Ah, sure. I mean I'm committed to you and won't be going out with other men and that the two of us are serious about each other."

"Hell, that's all it means? I was serious about you the minute I pulled you out of that ditch. The entire time I kept hoping to find a way to see you again. Then I found your phone and it was as if God had handed me a gift, because I had a legitimate excuse."

"Are you saying you'd like to be in a committed relationship with me?" I asked.

His eyes held mine. "Hell, yes . . . if that's what you want, too."

I wasn't sure how to answer. "I'm meeting Matthew Brown after school next week for coffee."

Rocco's face tightened, but his voice remained level. "You dating him?"

"No. He's another one of the English literature teachers and he asked me to have coffee with him."

"You going?" His gaze held me prisoner.

"I said I would."

He shrugged as if it was no big deal. "Then you aren't ready."

I studied Rocco for a long moment. He was open, honest, sincere, and responsible. He reminded me of Steve, my sister Cassie's fiancé. Steve was a little rough around the edges, too. Beyond a doubt, I knew Rocco wasn't a man who would cheat on his wife.

I looked down at his hand. I'd laced our fingers together. "I'm going to tell Matt I won't be able to have coffee with him after all."

"Why?"

"Because I'm seeing someone else and we've decided to only date each other. To have coffee with Matt would mislead him."

Rocco's fingers tightened around mine. "I'm going to need a bit of guidance now and then, so if I do something wrong let me know, okay?"

"You got it."

"You don't mind introducing me to your friends?" He asked this in a way that suggested I might have a problem with that.

"I'd like that, only I don't have as many friends as I once did . . . before the divorce."

"Then they weren't your friends," he told me, and he was right.

"There's a family wedding coming up in three weeks. Would you like to attend with me? I'd like you to meet my two sisters and their husbands and families."

He hesitated, as if this was a big step for him. "You sure you want me there?"

"Very sure. Kaylene, too."

His eyes softened and he released my hand, stood, and walked around to my side of the table. Slipping his arm around me, he brought me upright and then took my mouth in a kiss potent enough to make me dizzy and breathless. It'd been no exaggeration to tell him he was a good kisser, which naturally led me to anticipate other things he was good at. He saw me as a good girl, and I was, but I was a woman, too.

We continued kissing until I heard my phone buzz.

Rocco reluctantly broke off the kiss. "Is that your phone or mine?"

"Mine. I better check. Jake's got Owen this weekend." I didn't catch the phone in time and saw that the call had been from Jake. I called him right back.

"Is everything all right?" I asked. Owen had been cranky earlier and had a small tantrum when he'd left with Jake.

"What's this stupid jumpsuit Owen's wearing?" Jake demanded.

"Why?"

"He refuses to take it off. He keeps talking about driving a tow truck."

"Yes. Rocco took him out in the truck and bought him the uniform."

"And who exactly is Rocco?"

My eyes connected with Rocco's. "Rocco and I are dating. He owns a towing company."

"This is a joke, right? You're dating a guy who drives a tow truck?" He made it sound like it was some hilarious joke.

"Yeah, I'm dating a guy who drives a tow truck. If you were half the man he is, Jake, we'd still be married." And with that I disconnected the call.

# CHAPTER 20

# Leanne

I spent my Saturday morning on the Internet, poring over recipes from the Ukraine. I'd asked Nikolai to dinner, promising to cook for him, and hoped to surprise him.

My first thought was to cook borscht, a beetroot soup that was well known. The recipe looked easy enough. As for the main course, it was a toss-up between the potato-and-mushroom dumplings, the cabbage rolls in sour-cream sauce, or the kruchenyky, which, if I read the recipe correctly, was stuffed pork rolls. I had no problem deciding against fried liver in sour-cream sauce. It seemed Ukrainians were keen on sour cream and beets. In case I needed something else to go along with the dinner, I copied the recipe for horseradish-and-beet relish.

My next stop was the market. By the time I finished reading through all the recipes, I had a lengthy list of items I needed to purchase. Doing this for Nikolai as a surprise filled me with joyful excitement. On the way back to my apartment I heard myself humming. I couldn't remember the last time I sang or hummed. Nikolai had brought music into my heart, into my life. Memory escaped me when I'd felt this excited about doing something for someone else.

Once back in my apartment, I set about getting everything organized for this special dinner. Having never tackled dumplings before, I was surprised by how time-consuming they were. I had the borscht simmering on top of the stove, the dumplings resting on a lined cookie sheet, and the horseradish-beet relish in the refrigerator. I was working on the cabbage rolls when my doorbell chimed.

I glanced at the clock and saw that it was another hour before Nikolai was due. Wiping my hands on a kitchen towel, I headed for the door and was surprised to find it was him.

"You're early," I cried in dismay. I'd hoped to have everything prepared and ready before he arrived. Although time was fast slipping by, I'd wanted to change my clothes, too. As it was, the kitchen was a mess and I was sure I'd gotten flour down the front of my blouse and slacks.

Nikolai's face fell at my distress. "I come early to help. I go now, come back later."

"No . . . stay." I reached for his arm and half dragged him into the apartment. "I want you here."

"I am sorry."

"No, don't apologize." In an effort to show him how glad I was to see him, I leaned forward and kissed him. He moaned when our lips met, or maybe it was me. He tasted of mint and spice and everything that reminded me of Nikolai. Everything that filled me with happiness.

He smiled at me with a look of such tenderness it almost brought me to tears. He placed his hand over my chest. "My heart beat with your heart until we like one person. I feel it. You feel, too?"

I bit into my lower lip and nodded.

He raised his head and sniffed. "What I smell?"

"Dinner," I whispered.

"It smells like home." He walked past me and into the kitchen. When he saw what I'd done he whirled around. "You cook Ukrainian dishes?"

"I'm trying. It was supposed to be a surprise."

"I am surprised. I am happy, so happy." He came back to me and gripped hold of my upper arms and brought me close to kiss me again. "What you make?"

I pointed to the recipes I'd printed out. Most were wet and smudged from repeated readings, often with my wet or doughy hands.

Nikolai noticed the cabbage leaves soaking in the hot water. "Stuffed cabbage not easy."

"You're telling me."

"Yes, I tell you already." He shucked off his jacket and then rolled up his long sleeves. "I help. My mother teach me as boy."

I'd already prepared the pork mixture for the stuffing and had the baking pan ready to lay the rolls. The tomato-based sauce simmered on the back burner.

Before he dug in, Nikolai opened the drawer for a spoon and dipped it into the borscht. I held my breath as he tasted it. I'd sampled it earlier and it tasted fine to me, but I had no idea if it would meet his expectations. I watched him closely and saw the appreciation come over him as he closed his eyes and savored the soup.

"Perfect," he whispered, before setting the spoon in the sink.

"You're sure?" I knew recipes varied from region to region, and I'd hoped the borscht was close to the flavors most familiar to him.

"You most wonderful woman. I not know why I so lucky man."

I didn't contradict him, but I didn't think luck had anything to do with our meeting. I felt as if Nikolai was a special gift God had sent into my life.

I reached into the bottom drawer and brought out an apron and tied it around Nikolai's waist. He washed his hands and then drained the half-boiled cabbage leaves and flattened them out on the large cutting board.

"I show you," he said.

"Okay." I stood beside him and watched as he expertly filled the cabbage leaf and then folded it with such precision it didn't need anything to hold it together. He set the first roll in the prepared pan. "You try."

"All right."

Nikolai stood behind me, his hands resting on the curve of my shoulders. I flattened the cabbage leaf and was about to scoop the pork into the center when he leaned forward and kissed the side of my neck. The spoon splattered against the pan.

"Nikolai!"

"Sorry. I not able to stop. I am so happy. I'm with you, my Leanne. I smell food from my country and I think I not ever been this happy."

"I don't think I've ever been this happy, either," I whispered, abandoning all pretense of rolling the cabbage leaf. Twisting around, I pressed my head against his chest. I could have stood with Nikolai's arms around me for an eternity and been perfectly content for the rest of my life.

He kissed me and I kissed him, and all thought of the cabbage rolls was abandoned until I heard my doorbell.

Nikolai groaned as though resenting the intrusion.

I didn't appreciate the interruption. I sighed, not eager to leave Nikolai's arms. Worse, I had a premonition it was Sean.

I was right. My ex had called twice in the last week and I'd let the calls go to voice mail, unwilling to talk to him. The pain from the shingles still bothered me and I wasn't in the mood to deal with Sean. As far as I was concerned, we had nothing to discuss. I should have known better. Sean wasn't the kind of man who took kindly to being ignored.

When I opened the door, he was holding a large bouquet of flowers in front of his face. He peeked around the arrangement with a huge smile.

"Surprise," he said, as if I should be overwhelmed by his thoughtfulness.

"Hello, Sean," I said, with little enthusiasm.

He stared back at me with that hurt-little-boy look, as if shocked by my lack of welcome. "Can I come in?" he asked pointedly.

I stepped aside and he walked into my apartment. Nikolai came to stand behind me, hands on my shoulders. I noticed that he'd removed the apron and that he stared back hard at Sean.

Sean didn't take kindly to finding Nikolai with me, either. "This is that Russian *again*, isn't it?"

"Nikolai is from Ukraine," I corrected, when I felt Nikolai's fingers tighten on my shoulders. Ukrainians weren't Russians and didn't like to be referred to as such. "What do you want, Sean?" I asked, getting to the point.

"I heard you had shingles."

"I did two weeks ago. The pain is mostly gone now." It was worse at night, but I preferred to downplay any discomfort, especially to Sean.

"I brought you flowers." He lifted them slightly, in case I hadn't noticed them earlier.

"Yes, I see." Once Sean left, I'd give the arrangement to an elderly neighbor lady who would appreciate them far more than I would.

"You didn't answer my calls." His voice was full of accusation, as if he assumed I would fall all over myself to talk to him.

"I've been busy." Although Sean spoke to me, his gaze landed squarely on Nikolai, his eyes narrowed and wary.

"I wanted to ask about Nichole," Sean said.

Why he would come to me about Nichole was a mystery, and not one I was willing to solve. "She has her own cell. I'll give you her number if you'd like."

"I have it."

I knew he did. "Then I suggest you contact her yourself."

Sean shifted his feet. I hadn't invited him to sit down and I hoped he got the message that I'd rather he left. In the last few weeks he'd paid more attention to me than he had in the last two years of our marriage, and certainly since the divorce was final.

"I wanted to ask you about this man she's dating," Sean said, looking concerned. "That tow-truck driver."

"Rocco is none of your business."

"Rocco," he repeated, as if it was a swear word. "Jake tells me this . . . Rocco has a negative influence on Owen. As Owen's father, he's deeply concerned. I wanted to know if you've met him."

"I believe this is something you need to discuss with Nichole and not me."

"Have you met Rocco?" he said, a bit louder, more insistent.

"I have."

"What kind of name is Rocco, anyway?" He shook his head, as if he found it distasteful.

"Italian, I believe." I immediately regretted giving my ex any additional information. As far as I was concerned, this conversation had gone on long enough. "As you can see, Nikolai and I are busy. I don't mean to be rude, but it's time for you to go."

A hurt look came over Sean. He looked down and slowly exhaled. "I have something to tell you, Leanne, but I can see now isn't the time. Would it be possible to have a conversation later . . . just the two of us?"

Again Nikolai's fingers tightened, pinching my shoulders. "I'll call you when it's convenient," I said, and it would be a long time before I found it convenient.

Sean turned toward the door and then looked back. "You've changed, Leanne."

"Yes," I agreed. "I have."

He nodded, cast a frosty look toward Nikolai, and then left, closing the door behind him.

I released a deep breath, relieved he was gone. Nikolai dropped his hands from my shoulders. As soon as the door closed he started pacing my living room, his fists knotted at his sides. He spoke heatedly in his mother tongue and shook his head.

I watched for several moments before I spoke. "Nikolai."

He whirled around to face me and spat out, "I no like this Sean, this man who no love you. He no real man. He pretend man." Nikolai continued to pace. "I no like he come to you. He up to something."

I shook my head. "Are you jealous?" I asked him softly.

Nikolai didn't hesitate and quickly nodded. "I look at this man and I see blue."

"You see red," I corrected gently.

"That color, too. I not like him close to you. I want to be the one close to you."

"You are close to me," I assured him. No matter where this relationship led, I would always treasure Nikolai. He'd given me so much. When I'd separated from Sean I felt like a dried-up prune, useless, old, used up.

How thankful I was that my daughter-in-law had given me the courage to do what I should have done years earlier. And I was grateful for our guide, the list of things to help us adjust to our futures. Until Nichole, I'd been resigned to remaining in a loveless marriage, not realizing that year by year I was slowly dying.

Nikolai seemed to need an outlet to vent his anger,

and he continued pacing. I stood in front of him, blocking him.

"Stop," I said, planting my hands in the middle of his chest. "You have no reason to be jealous. Sean means nothing to me. Whatever love I felt for him died a long time ago."

Nikolai studied me as if to gauge the truth in my words. "I not know this jealous before. I had no reason to know this word. Magdalena only love me and I only love her. Sean not like me and I not like him."

He'd accurately stated the truth. I could see the dislike in Sean's face as he'd studied Nikolai. And Nikolai didn't bother to hide his disdain for my ex-husband. I could only imagine Nikolai's response if I were to mention that Sean thought he might be part of the Russian Mafia. To even suggest it was preposterous.

"I see him watch you," Nikolai whispered. "He see you happy and he jealous."

I couldn't keep from laughing. "You've got that all wrong. Sean has no feelings for me. Not love, not hate. We were married thirty-five years and after the first few years all there was between us was indifference."

"I don't know how you mean indifference," Nikolai said, frowning.

"It's not important. I don't want to spend the rest of our evening talking about Sean." I'd learned my lesson, though. The next time Sean called I'd answer no matter how I felt at the time. I didn't want any more of these unexpected visits.

As for his concern about Nichole seeing Rocco and the influence Rocco had on Owen, that had all been a convenient excuse. I didn't know what was up with my ex-husband, but clearly something was. Whatever it was, I didn't have time to think about it now.

Perhaps Nikolai had been right when he suggested that Sean didn't like the idea of seeing me happy. Sean's ego was too big to deal with that. When I left him, my husband assumed that I would fall apart; that I wouldn't be able to survive without him dictating my life, my friends, how I spent my time.

It embarrassed me to admit that I'd wanted the same for him. When I packed my bags to leave Sean, my head had been in a strange place. I desperately wanted Sean to miss me and the comforts of the home I'd meticulously maintained for him. I dreamed about him struggling to figure out how to wash his own clothes and cook his own meals. I wanted him to miss me to the point he would be willing to admit that the thirty-five years I'd dedicated to him and his career meant something.

It was ridiculous, of course. One of the first things Sean did after my departure was hire a housecleaning service. From what Kacey told me, he ate most of his meals at the club. As far as I could tell, he'd garnered the sympathy of our friends by telling everyone I'd walked out on him—leaving him, in his words, "high and dry."

The divorce had given him the opportunity to parade his "flavor of the month" around publicly. He was living the good life and doing it without me. That didn't bother me now. I'd found my own happiness.

The naked truth was Sean and I did much better apart than we ever did as a married couple.

# CHAPTER 21

# Nichole

My sister's wedding was set for the Saturday of Thanksgiving weekend. I was thrilled for Cassie and excited to be a part of her wedding.

I'd been angry and hurt when my eighteen-year-old sister had run away with Duke and not eager to forgive her when she returned all those years later with her daughter, Amiee. Cassie had been a stranger to me; I no longer knew her and I wasn't sure I wanted to. My judgmental attitude shocked me now. I was filled with regret at the way I'd been willing to write her off and keep her out of my life.

And yet Cassie had been the first one to reach out and support me when she'd learned about Jake. I'd gone to her often for advice. She'd been generous with her love and support. We were close now, closer even than we'd been as children. She knew about my relationship with Rocco and had invited him and Kaylene to attend the wedding with Owen and me.

I'd driven up to Seattle for a visit. My other sister,

Karen, had managed to get the weekend off as well. It would be the first time the three of us had gotten together since last August. We talked nearly every week, but it wasn't the same as being together.

We all crowded into the house Cassie had built through Habitat for Humanity. I'd missed seeing my sisters. Missed the camaraderie we shared and was so very grateful to have Cassie back in our lives.

I sat with my legs folded on the carpet in Cassie's living room with Owen tucked in front of me. I didn't expect him to stay content for long. He was still shy around Amiee, Cassie's teenage daughter. That wouldn't last long, though.

"I don't want you two to get stuck with dresses you'll never wear again," Cassie had insisted. "So wear whatever you want and it'll be fine."

That worked great for me. I had a number of fancy gowns that would be suitable to wear as a bridesmaid. Jake had always made sure I had the best for the annual Commander's Ball at the country club.

I'd decided to wear the midnight-blue one I'd worn the year before I got pregnant with Owen. I saw it in the back of my closet and tried it on for fun. I'd been surprised when it was a perfect fit again. The baby weight was gone. Guess that was what a long, drawn-out divorce will do for a woman.

Cassie turned to me with a regretful look. "Nichole, I think I made a big mistake."

"Really. How so?"

"When you mentioned you hadn't gotten the wedding invitation, I checked my address book. I think I might have mailed it to your old address in Lake Oswego."

"Don't worry. I know when the wedding is." Jake hadn't forwarded it on, which didn't surprise me. He'd been short-tempered and nasty to me ever since he learned about Rocco.

Fifteen-year-old Amiee sat down next to me and pretended not to notice Owen. My toddler covered his eyes and then cautiously peeked over at his cousin. Amiee reached for his toy tow truck, which got an immediate reaction from Owen.

"Mine."

"Oh, sorry," Amiee said, pretending she didn't know. "It's such a cool truck, I thought I'd like to see how it runs."

"I show you." Owen sprang out of my lap as if he'd been sitting inside a jack-in-the-box. The two of them went into the kitchen, where the floor made it easier to scoot the truck around.

"You doing okay?" Karen asked. She'd been worried about me since the divorce, and our regular long-distance conversations weren't enough to ease her mind. We were all busy, but Karen and Garth, her husband, had recently started their own business having to do with listing and selling commercial real estate and were busier than ever. Both Lily and Buddy had stayed in Spokane with their father for the weekend.

"Actually, I'm doing great." And it was the truth. I enjoyed teaching, and having a regular income had done a lot to help my budget. I was scheduled to fill in until the first of the year. I got along well with the staff and had learned that a full-time position was opening up in the spring for a French teacher. I planned to apply for it, as I was fluent in the language, and felt I'd have a good chance of getting hired.

"Rocco's coming to the wedding, right?" Cassie asked. "I'm anxious to meet him."

"He said he would." Which surprised and delighted me. I was eager for my sisters to meet Rocco. He was becoming an important part of my life. Although he had a rough and gruff exterior, he was thoughtful and smart and a good father. Owen loved him, and I found myself thinking about him more and more. We were very different people outwardly but we shared the same core values and beliefs.

Cassie, who sat on the carpet next to me, said, "After everything you've said, I'm really looking forward to meeting him."

I thought I should give my sisters fair warning. "He's not your typical guy. He's got tattoos and he's big and tall."

"But you like him."

"I do." I wasn't going to downplay how attracted I was to Rocco. Yes, he was handsome, but not in the same way Jake was. Rocco oozed masculinity, whereas Jake was suave and urbane. No two men could be more different.

"Is it serious?" Karen asked me.

I needed time to think about my answer. We'd agreed not to date others and to give our relationship a chance to grow. I wasn't sure if that meant we were serious. "Not yet. We're still getting to know each other, but it could be serious at some point. We both have a lot of stuff to work through. Two of my college friends rebounded from divorces with fast second marriages that lasted less than a year. I don't want to make that mistake."

"Steve is bringing dinner over later," Cassie said.

Amiee stuck her head out from the kitchen. "Is it KFC?"

"No," Cassie answered, laughing.

"Darn," Amiee muttered, and retreated back to the kitchen.

Karen, Cassie, and I spent the afternoon assembling wedding favors for the tabletops at the reception. We laughed and rolled through childhood memories, and cried when we talked about our parents, both of whom had died far too young.

Steve arrived with Chinese takeout and we sat around and ate with chopsticks and talked well into the night. Sunday morning, Cassie cooked us breakfast and Karen and I headed back to our respective homes.

When Owen and I stopped at a rest stop I called Rocco to tell him we were on our way back.

"Hey," I said when he answered.

"Hey."

The rough timbre of his voice gave me a warm, happy feeling.

"Did you have a good time with your sisters?"

"The best."

"How far out are you?"

I gave him my best guesstimate. "Maybe an hour or more."

He hesitated. "Can I see you when you're back?"

I looked down at the asphalt and kicked a small rock. I was hoping he'd suggest we get together. "I'd like that."

"Come to my place."

"Okay."

He hesitated, as if unsure whether he should say anything. "I missed you."

I closed my eyes. Rocco wasn't one to make flowery speeches or romantic declarations. His simple words had a strong impact on me. "I've missed you, too. My sisters are anxious to meet you."

Again, the hesitation. "You sure you want me with you at this wedding? I mean, it won't upset me if you'd rather I didn't come."

"Rocco, of course I want you at the wedding. Why would you think otherwise?"

He didn't answer.

"Rocco?"

"I'll tell you when you get here."

I'll admit he had me worried. All the times I'd talked about my sisters with Rocco, I knew he was looking forward to meeting them. He teased me that he was going to learn all the weird things I'd done as a kid from Karen and Cassie so he could taunt me.

Rocco had one sister who currently lived in Texas. Her husband was in the military and they moved around quite a bit. Although he hadn't said much, I got the idea that the two of them were close. His parents had moved to be near his sister, and his mother was in poor health.

Because I was curious about Rocco's concerns over the wedding, instead of returning to the apartment I drove directly to his house. He must have been watching for me, because as soon as I pulled up, he stepped out of the house. By the time I had the engine off, he'd opened the back door and was getting Owen out of his car seat.

"How're you doing, little man?" Rocco asked my son.

Owen laid his head on Rocco's shoulder and yawned. "Amiee liked my twuck."

Rocco looked to me. "His cousin?"

I nodded. "It took him a while to warm up to her, but they were best buds by the time we left."

Rocco led the way into the house, his hand at the small of my back. I followed him into the kitchen and he automatically brewed me a cup of coffee. Owen sat in my lap, asleep with his head against my shoulder. Kaylene was either in her bedroom or out with friends.

"You want to tell me what your hang-up is about the wedding?" I'd been stewing about this ever since he first mentioned it.

Rocco shrugged and looked uneasy. He expelled his breath and then said, "I've never been to a wedding before." He made it sound as if this was a major flaw in his character.

"Never?" I found that hard to believe.

"Not one that took place in an actual church," he elaborated. "A friend of mine knocked up a girl and they got married in a tavern. I sat at the bar, but that's as close to a formal wedding as I've come."

I wasn't sure what to say.

He tucked his hands into his back pockets and then promptly removed them. "I told you, Nichole, I'm no prize."

"Attending a church wedding isn't the criteria I consider necessary." Frankly, I was relieved. I thought he didn't want to go.

"Will I have to do anything special?" Leaning against the counter, he crossed his thick arms.

"Not a thing. I won't be sitting with you during the actual ceremony. I'll be standing next to my two sisters and Amiee at the altar. But as soon as the wedding is over I'll be with you."

He studied me for a long moment. "You sure you still want me attending this shindig?"

"More than ever," I assured him.

He shook his head. "Before I know it you'll have me sipping tea with my pinkie in the air."

I laughed and Rocco grinned. He had the most beautiful smile. I could drown in it, just the way it made me feel.

He momentarily looked away. "The thing is I'd be willing to do just about anything if it meant I could be with you."

Stunned, I leaned forward and stretched out my arm. "Come here so I can feel your forehead to see if you have a temperature. You okay?"

His head came back. "Yes, why?"

"That was the most romantic thing you've ever said to me."

"Don't get used to it," he teased.

The front door opened and Kaylene burst into the house, shouting, "Dad."

"In here."

"Where's Nichole? I saw her car parked outside."

"In here with your dad," I called back. By the time I finished, the teenager was in the kitchen.

"We're still going, aren't we?" Kaylene asked, looking from her dad to me and then back again.

"It seems we are," Rocco said, grinning over at me.

Kaylene gleamed with delight. "I've never been to a real wedding and Dad let me get a new dress and shoes and he even liked what Kelly and I picked out. Dad looks handsome in his suit, too."

I looked to Rocco. "I remember."

He shrugged and grinned. "Glad you think so."

"About Thanksgiving," I said, looking to the two of them. "We're all invited to Steve's house."

"All of us?" Kaylene said, eyes widening.

"Yes. Cassie and I are cooking all our family's favorite recipes. Steve's house is much bigger than Cassie's. The wedding is Saturday, so it makes sense for us to spend the holiday together."

"What about your older sister?" Rocco asked.

"Karen and her family are going to her in-laws' place. She'll arrive Friday."

"We're going to have a real Thanksgiving at a home and everything." Kaylene looked like she was going to clap her hands. "Dad and I usually have Thanksgiving at Denny's. You're going to cook a whole turkey and everything, like for real?"

"With stuffing and mashed potatoes and giblets gravy."

"I'm hungry already," Kaylene said.

"You'll like Amiee," I told her. "She's your age, maybe a few months older."

Rocco had been suspiciously quiet while the two of us chatted away, reviewing the menu Cassie and I had decided on. Kaylene hurried up to her bedroom to call her friends and tell them she'd been invited out for Thanksgiving dinner.

I looked to Rocco. "Something wrong?" I asked.

He frowned. "I hate to say anything, but Thanksgiving is a busy time for me. I need every truck and driver I can get. I can't be taking time off when I've got a business to run. It's going to be hard enough for me to take off for this wedding, let alone Thanksgiving Day."

Reality hit with a hard punch to the gut. "Rocco, I'm sorry. I shouldn't have said anything to Kaylene without talking to you first."

"I'll see what I can do, but no promises."

I understood. It'd been thoughtless of me. "If you can't get away, would it be all right if I brought Kaylene with me? I'd hate to disappoint her."

"Yeah, that'd work."

But that would leave Rocco to spend the holiday alone and I didn't want that.

"I have a better idea," I said, brightening. "I'll stay in Portland for Thanksgiving. I'll cook and all of us can be together."

Rocco immediately dismissed the idea. "I appreciate the thought, but no. You need to be with your family."

It was then that a realization hit me. I was already thinking of Rocco and Kaylene as part of my family.

# CHAPTER 22

# Leanne

I'd put off meeting Sean as long as I could. He'd insisted we have lunch together at the club. I refused. I couldn't imagine why Sean would think I'd willingly show my face there. I had no intention of dining with Sean at the club after he'd paraded a long line of other women in the same restaurant where everyone knew me.

The only reason I agreed to this meeting at all was because of Jake. I got a call from my son and he sounded worried. "Mom, you really need to talk to Dad. It's important."

"He can't tell me over the phone?"

"No," Jake insisted. "He needs to do this face-to-face, Mom. You need to do this."

I didn't like it, but I finally agreed. Immediately, Nikolai was suspicious. "I no trust that man."

"Nothing he has to say is going to change what's between us," I assured my Ukrainian sweetheart.

Still, Nikolai worried. As a compromise, I suggested

Sean and I meet at Koreski's. Sean didn't know Nikolai worked at the deli. Nikolai still wasn't comfortable, but he agreed that was the best solution.

Sean and I met in the small restaurant inside the deli on a Thursday afternoon a week before Thanksgiving. Sean had a table before I arrived, and I noticed right away that he'd lost weight. He stood as I approached and pulled out my chair for me. He'd always been the epitome of a gentleman. He thought nothing of lying and cheating on his wife, but he never missed opening a door or sliding out a chair. I made sure I sat where my chair faced the kitchen. I smiled to myself when I saw Nikolai looking out the small window. He was my protector.

"Thank you for meeting me," Sean said.

"Yes, well, you were persistent enough."

I took the paper napkin and unfolded it on my lap. The waitress came with waters and asked for our order.

"I'll have the soup of the day." It was a hearty white-bean-and-ham soup that came with a slice of Nikolai's bread. It was a way of keeping him close while I spoke to my ex.

"That's all?" Sean looked surprised.

My stomach was unsettled over this meeting and I didn't have much of an appetite. I suspected the day he'd come to the apartment that there'd been something on his mind. Whatever it was could be linked to our meeting today.

Sean ordered a salad and the waitress left.

As soon as she was out of earshot I asked, "Can you tell me what this is about?"

Sean looked down and I noticed that his hands were

shaking. "I've been experiencing some headaches lately and went to see Liam—Dr. Belcher."

"And?"

"At first we assumed it was stress. My blood pressure was slightly elevated and there'd been the emotional trauma of the divorce."

Liam was a friend. The two played golf together nearly every week. As for the emotional trauma he mentioned, it seemed he'd recovered quickly enough. I'd barely removed my clothes from the house when Sean had another woman move in. From what Kacey told me, his live-in *friend* hadn't lasted more than a few weeks. Apparently, she wasn't nearly as good at pressing his shirts and cooking his meals as she was in the bedroom.

"I did my best to put off going back to see Liam," Sean continued. "It's a hassle and I guess maybe I was afraid to learn the truth."

I sat up straighter. Of all the things I expected Sean to bring up, I didn't think it had to do with a medical issue. "But you did go back to see Liam?"

"I did, and after a short examination, he ordered a brain scan."

"And?" I held my breath.

Sean looked up and the worry and pain in his eyes cut straight through me. I'd assumed I had no feelings left for my ex-husband, but I did. "Sean, what is it?" I asked.

"I have a brain tumor."

I gasped and my hand automatically flew to my heart.

Sean lowered his head and exhaled slowly. "Liam

sent me to a surgeon specializing in this type of tumor."

"Will they do surgery?"

"Next week on Monday."

"Sean." I swallowed hard. "Is it cancer?"

He looked up and I could see the fear in his eyes. "We won't know until after the surgery. I'm prepared for the worst . . . I need to be."

"Jake knows about all this?"

Sean shook his head. "Not the full extent. The surgery is tricky and there are risks involved."

Our meals were delivered at what seemed to be the worst possible moment. What little appetite I had completely disappeared. I reached for the slice of bread as if reaching out to Nikolai. I was sure all the blood must have drained from my face, and when I looked up I saw that Nikolai was watching me closely. Once he saw me, he started out the door, but I gently shook my head and he paused.

"I wanted to tell you earlier, but you—"

"I thought you wanted to talk about Nichole and Rocco," I whispered, humbled now. I'd suspected something, but I didn't know what. He'd been acting strange for some time, seeking me out, which frankly wasn't like Sean, and hadn't been in a very long while.

"I understand why you want to avoid me, Leanne. I don't blame you. I was a rotten husband; you deserved better. I wish I'd been a different person for you."

I looked up and tears clouded my eyes. I never expected to hear those words from Sean.

"I don't have any right to ask you this, but . . . would you mind coming to the hospital on Monday for the surgery? I . . . I don't have anyone else."

"What about Jake? Won't he be able to be there for the surgery?"

Sean shook his head. "He started a new job and he can't take time off work. He feels bad about it, but I assured him I'd be fine." His eyes held mine. "I . . . I don't want to be alone."

The lump in my throat had grown to the point it was nearly impossible to swallow.

His eyes didn't leave mine. "You'll come?"

I nodded.

His relief was obvious. "Thank you."

I reached across the table and took hold of his hand. Sean had always been an arrogant, proud man. I barely recognized the man sitting across from me now. He was humble and apologetic. And, more than anything, he was afraid of what the future might hold.

"How long will you need to stay in the hospital?"

"Depending on the outcome, I'll only be there two nights."

"Only two nights?"

He gave a half-laugh. "Shocking how quickly they shift people out, isn't it?"

He didn't need to say it, but if Sean wasn't in the hospital that meant he'd be going back to an empty house. I think that unnerved him as much as the surgery itself.

Sean tightened the grip on my hand, as if I was the only solid thing in a world that had gotten kicked off its axis.

"Thank you, Leanne," he said. "You don't have any legal obligation to be at the hospital, but I want you to know how very grateful I am."

"Of course I'll be there."

Neither one of us touched our lunches. Sean gave me the necessary details of the hospital, the surgeon's name, and the time slotted for the surgery before he paid the tab and left.

I needed a few extra minutes to absorb what he'd told me and remained sitting at the table. As soon as Sean was out of sight, Nikolai came out of the kitchen and joined me.

"What this no-man want?" he asked, sitting in the chair closest to me. He reached for my hand, holding it between his own two.

"Sean has a brain tumor," I whispered. Even as I spoke the words I had a hard time believing this was happening to my ex.

Nikolai responded, speaking in Ukrainian. He didn't seem to realize he'd switched languages until I looked up at him blankly. Then he sighed and patted my hand. "I sorry for him."

"He's having surgery Monday morning. The surgeon is going to do his best to remove it if possible. It might be cancer."

"That would be bad."

"Yes, very bad. We won't know if it's cancerous until the test results come back."

Nikolai nodded.

He noticed the wetness that coated my face and leaned forward to brush the tears from my cheeks. "You cry for him?"

I looked away, a little surprised at myself.

"Why you cry? You love him still?"

That was a difficult question to answer. "I didn't expect to feel anything for Sean. I assumed whatever love I had for him had died a long time ago."

Nikolai looked stricken and tried to pull his hand away. I wouldn't let him and held on tightly.

"Do you love Magdalena?" I asked.

"Of course, she my wife."

"Do you love her any less since we met?"

His eyes widened and he slowly shook his head.

"I was married to Sean for thirty-five years. I spent the majority of my life with him, and while I'm surprised, I realize I still do have feelings for him. He was my husband. He was my first love."

Nikolai's shoulders relaxed as the anger left him. "I go with you to hospital. I sit with you."

"No." I immediately rejected his offer. "The deli depends on you, and it wouldn't be right for you to be there."

"I no mind missing work. I do anything for you, my Leanne."

"I know and I'm grateful, but it isn't necessary."

"You come see me after the surgery? You tell me what doctor say?"

"Of course. First thing."

He leaned forward and pressed his forehead against mine. "I worry all morning. I not like you eat lunch with your ex-husband. I afraid I lose you. I am Mr. Jealousy."

I pressed my hand to the back of his head. "You have no need to be jealous. Not now, not ever."

He straightened and his face brightened with a smile. "Your words are song to my ears."

My hands cupped his beautiful face.

"You wait here? I almost finish work."

"Of course I'll wait." In many ways I felt like I'd been waiting my entire adult life for Nikolai.

"I not be long," he promised.

Nikolai was back in less than fifteen minutes. He'd changed out of his white uniform and was dressed as I knew him best, in slacks and a sweater. He had his coat over his arm as he reached for my hand and raised it to his lips. He set his coat over the back of the chair and helped me put mine on. I collected my purse and gloves while he slipped into his own coat.

Once we were ready to go, he took hold of my hand.

"Where are we going?" I asked.

"You see. Not far. You okay to walk?"

"Sure."

Once outside, he tucked my hand into the curve of his elbow and matched his pace to mine. We'd gone about four blocks when I asked, "Nikolai, where are you taking me?"

"You see soon."

We rounded the next street and I knew. I saw the dome of the church and recognized it as Russian Orthodox.

"You're taking me to church?" I asked.

Nikolai nodded. "We light candle for Sean. We knee together and say prayer to God to make him well again."

I stopped; my feet refused to move as overwhelming emotion took hold, clenching at my throat and tightening my chest.

"I pray each day ask God to heal Magdalena. Now we pray for Sean. You pray. I pray. God hear two prayers. God listen."

At his words, I bit into my lip.

Nikolai turned to me, his face worried and sad. "You no want to pray?"

Tears rained down my cheeks. I could no more control the emotion than I could the weather.

"My Leanne, what I say? What I do? Why you cry like this?"

He hauled me into his arms and held me so tightly that I found it even harder to breathe than it already was.

"Tell me, please," he begged. "Whatever it is, I make right. I no bear to see you cry. You better stick knife in my heart. Tell me please why I make you sad like this."

I snorted a series of undignified sniffles in an effort to hold back the tsunami of tears.

"It Sean and his sickness?" Nikolai asked.

I shook my head and wrapped my arms around Nikolai's neck, hiding my face in the collar of his thick coat. His fingers tangled in my hair as he spread small kisses down the side of my face.

"Nikolai," I sobbed.

"Yes, my Leanne."

"I. Am. So. In. Love. With. You."

His fingers stilled. His whole body froze and it seemed he stopped breathing as well. "What you say?"

"I said"—I paused to sob again—"I'm so in love with you . . . You are a wonderful man and I love you."

Slowly he released me and his hands cupped my face. His eyes searched mine as if to gauge the sincerity of my words. He must have read what was in my heart, because I watched as tears gathered and pooled in his own eyes. After a long moment he smiled as if he was the happiest man on the face of the earth. Then he leaned down and kissed me full on the mouth in the middle of the sidewalk in front of the Russian Orthodox church.

"My heart belong to you a long time. I wait and wait for you to give me your heart. Now I know why God bring me to America. You best gift God ever give me."

# CHAPTER 23

# Nichole

I pulled into the Potter Towing complex around four on Saturday afternoon. Owen was with his father and I'd worked at Dress for Success most of the day. Rocco had to work. I hadn't seen him all week, although we talked every day. He hadn't been successful in finding anyone to take over for him on Thanksgiving. I understood, but I couldn't help being disappointed. As Rocco explained, no one works harder than the owner of the company. I knew he was right.

All the trucks were out, so I knew Rocco wasn't at the office. Taking a chance, I climbed out of my car and checked the office door and found it unlocked.

"Anyone here?" I called out.

"Who's there?" a woman shouted from farther back in the complex.

I'd recognize that voice anywhere. "Shawntelle?"

"Nichole." Within seconds I was wrapped in a huge bear hug from my friend. "It's been a month of Sundays, girl. Where you been?"

"Around," I told her. "Working, mostly. I'm teaching at the high school. Do you know when Rocco is due back?"

"He should be here anytime. You two still an item? I'd ask him, but he don't tell me a thing. That man should work for the CIA; he isn't talkin'." She paused and then lowered her voice. "But I will tell you that from the scuttlebutt going around the office something has happened to that man. The guys tell me Rocco's smiling and whistling and happy, and that just ain't Rocco. I know what's gotten into him—you. Rocco's got himself a woman and that woman is you." Her knowing grin was bigger than that of the Cheshire cat.

My heart did a little flip-flop of joy. Shawntelle looked more than pleased with herself. She crossed her arms. "And you aren't the only one who's got herself a man."

"Oh?"

"No. Did ya hear?" she asked, looking pleased with herself. "I found me a man right here: a driver, name of Jerome. At first we fought like wild alley cats, but then he came around. He's a good man, and honey, I got to tell you he's real sweet on me. Can hardly keep his hands to himself." She placed her fist on her ample hip. "I ain't giving him nothing yet and he wants me bad. I learned my lesson. Men will say whatever they think a woman wants to hear until they get what they want. And once they do they backtrack so fast they spit gravel."

"Good for you." I was proud of Shawntelle. "By the way, Rocco says you're doing a great job with the bookkeeping."

Shawntelle nodded. "He gave me a chance when no one else would. He's done that for Jerome and Buck, too. Buck's got a record and no one would hire him. He's our dispatcher."

I'd met a couple of the guys when Rocco brought Owen and me to the complex a few weeks back. Owen still talked about driving the tow truck.

"You and Rocco got something going tonight?"

We'd been seeing each other for three months now, and to this point we'd been out together, just the two of us, only a few times. We saw each other as often as we could, but it was almost always with Kaylene and/ or Owen. We'd had little time to ourselves.

A truck pulled into the yard and Rocco jumped down and started toward the building. A smile instantly lit up his face when he saw me talking to Shawntelle.

"You got a visitor," Shawntelle told him, unnecessarily.

Just the way his eyes roved over me made my insides quiver. He looked around. "Where's Owen?"

"With his dad. Where's Kaylene?"

"Spending the night with a friend." As soon as he said the words we both seemed to realize at the same moment we were each without responsibilities for the evening.

A slow, easy smile came over Rocco. "Give me a chance to clean up and I'll meet you at your place in an hour."

"You got it." My heart was pounding with anticipation. I started out the door and was halfway to the car when I heard Rocco call my name.

I turned back and looked up at him expectantly.

He exhaled and then reached for me, dragging me close to him as he lowered his mouth to mine, kissing me with a hunger that nearly had me pooling at his feet.

I kept my eyes closed when he lifted his head.

"I should have waited," he whispered, "but I've been starving for a taste of you."

"Was it worth the wait?"

"Baby, you have no idea."

I left and hurried back to the apartment, showered and changed clothes. I'd just put the finishing touches on my makeup when the doorbell sounded. Rocco stood on the other side, wearing clean jeans and a shirt, and a leather jacket with several patches on the front and sleeves. He looked yummy enough to eat.

He stared at me as if seeing me for the first time. It made me wonder if I had lipstick on my teeth. "Is something wrong?" I asked, wishing there was a mirror close at hand.

He shook his head as though coming out of a trance. "Every time I see you I'm struck with how lovely you are."

I hardly knew how to respond. Men had told me before that I was attractive, but it'd sounded practiced and insincere. It didn't with Rocco. He couldn't seem to take his eyes off me, and frankly, I felt the same way about him.

"I shouldn't kiss you, I really shouldn't," he said, as if talking to himself. "If I do I'm afraid we'll never leave this apartment." Even as he spoke he leaned closer to me. It seemed he had every intention of kissing me, but instead he hugged me. A deep sigh rumbled through him as he held me in his embrace. "I want to make love to you so bad it hurts. I know that probably shocks a good girl like you."

"I'm not as good as you think," I whispered, kissing the underside of his chin, running my tongue over his fresh shave, loving the taste of him. I knew we were tempting fate, but it felt so good and so right to be in his arms. We'd done little more than share a few passionate kisses, and I was ready to take this to a deeper level and I knew he was, too.

He growled as if in pain. "Nichole, please, don't make this any more difficult than it is. I want to do everything right by you. You deserve that." He released me by inches, as if it demanded every ounce of self-restraint he possessed to let me go.

"Where are we going?" I asked, once I'd collected myself and could think clearly.

"I thought I'd take you to dinner. You okay with that?"

"Anything." All I really cared about was being with Rocco.

He traced his finger down the side of my face. "My aunt owns a small Italian restaurant. I'd like you to meet her. You're the first girl I've ever introduced to my relatives, so they might make a bunch of embarrassing comments."

"Forewarned is forearmed," I said, smiling up at him.

"I called and she's got a table for us. I know it's a little early for dinner, but they pack out the place every night."

"I'm starved. I didn't have lunch."

"Me neither."

A half-hour later we were seated at a table for two

with a red checkered tablecloth in a dimly lit restaurant that had only about ten tables. We had barely sat down when Rocco's aunt arrived with fresh bread and cheese. She kissed Rocco on both cheeks and he introduced me.

"Aunt Maria, this is Nichole."

The woman was barely five feet tall and smelled of garlic and Italian herbs. She looked at me and nodded approvingly. "It's about time Rocco got himself a wife. You going to marry my nephew?" she demanded. "Kaylene needs a woman's influence."

"What did I tell you?" Rocco mumbled under his breath. "Aunt Maria, you're embarrassing my girl."

She laughed and I laughed with her.

His aunt disappeared, but shortly afterward a steady flow of food began to arrive. We never saw a menu, not that we needed one. The bread and cheese were followed by a plate of pickled vegetables and sliced meats, then soup. When I was convinced I couldn't eat another bite, a huge plate of pasta with red sauce came. By then I was so full I couldn't stuff down another forkful.

"Please, tell me this is the end of it."

Rocco grinned. "We haven't gotten to the main course yet."

With my hands pressed against my stomach, I looked across the table at him, appalled. "Rocco. Please, I can't do it. I don't want to insult your family; the food is delicious, but I simply can't."

"No worries."

I leaned back in my chair and dragged in several deep breaths in an effort to relieve the pressure on my stomach. Everything I'd tasted had been worthy of a

five-star restaurant. Rocco spoke to his aunt Maria
and she nodded understandingly.

"Next time you save room for more food," Maria
told me.

Rocco, however, finished off a full plate of some
chicken dish. He told me the name of it, but it was in
Italian and it quickly slipped my mind. It looked
amazing, with lemon slices and capers over thin slices
of chicken.

Rocco was talking to his aunt about dessert when
my phone rang. I grabbed my cell out of my purse and
saw that it was Jake. I didn't want to talk to him, but
seeing that he had Owen, I had no choice but to answer.

"Hello."

"Owen's being fussy," he snapped, as if I was the
cause.

Most three-year-old boys tended to be like that
from time to time. "What's wrong?"

"If I knew that, do you think I'd be phoning you?"
Jake continued in the same accusatory voice.

I arched my brows. "Is he sick?"

"How am I supposed to know that? All he does is
cry and say he wants to go home. He needs to learn
that this is his home and I'm his father. Furthermore,
if I hear Rocco's name one more time I swear to you,
Nichole—"

"Find out if he has a fever," I interrupted, hoping he
heard the frustration and anger in my voice.

"How am I supposed to do that? I'm no nurse."

"You take his temperature," I said as calmly as I
could.

Jake was having none of it.

"Feel his forehead and tell me if it's warm," I suggested. I heard him walk into another room. Owen's hiccupping sobs sounded over the phone and I felt terrible for my son.

Rocco's eyes met mine. "Owen?" he mouthed.

I nodded.

Jake came back and he seemed more reasonable when he said, "He feels warm."

"Let me talk to him," I suggested.

"Okay." I heard Jake tell Owen that I was on the phone.

"Mommy?" Owen's sad voice called out to me.

"You feeling okay, buddy?" I asked.

"I want to go home."

"It's your daddy's weekend," I said as gently as I could.

"I want to go home," Owen insisted. "Daddy took my twuck and his friend is mean."

I could only assume Jake's friend was female.

Jake grabbed the phone back and I could hear Owen wail in the background that he wanted me.

"You've spoiled him," Jake shouted. "You've turned my son into a snot-nosed brat."

Rocco clearly heard Jake and rushed to his feet. "Let's pick him up right now."

I couldn't agree with him more. "I'm on my way. I should be there in less than half an hour."

Jake didn't bother to respond. All I heard was the phone click.

We thanked Rocco's aunt for the incredible dinner and hurriedly left the restaurant. Rocco's hand was at my elbow, guiding me through the parking lot to where he'd parked his truck. He seemed to be in even more of a rush than I was.

"Owen doesn't cry like that unless something's wrong," I said, worried about my son.

"It doesn't sound like Jake's comfortable caring for him."

"He isn't." I'd seen evidence of that myself and it worried me. I'd hoped that with time Jake would learn to be more patient with Owen. From what I'd been able to glean from my son, he spent the weekends with his father mostly with babysitters.

We drove in silence to Lake Oswego. My fingers were tight as I clung to my purse strap, my heart thumping impatiently, wanting to get to Owen as quickly as possible.

When we arrived the porch light was on and I noticed the draperies fall back in place as soon as we pulled into the driveway.

"You get Owen and I'll collect his things," Rocco suggested.

I nodded, eager to get this over with.

I could hear Owen crying even before I reached the front door. It felt odd to ring the doorbell to the very home in which I'd once lived. This wasn't the first time.

Jake yanked the door open and glared at me. "It took you long enough."

"We came right away."

It was as if Jake hadn't seen Rocco, who stood directly next to me. " 'We'?" He took one look at Rocco and burst out laughing, as if this was the biggest joke he'd ever heard. "You're kidding me, right? This is the guy you're dating? This . . . Neanderthal."

I ignored the comment, and thankfully so did Rocco. "Where's Owen?"

"No, no, I want to meet this Rocco fellow. I don't get it, Nichole. I always thought you were a classy woman. You're really scraping the bottom of the barrel with this one."

Rocco took one step forward but then stopped. It went without saying that one punch from him would flatten Jake. Maybe that was what my ex wanted, so he could press assault charges against Rocco.

I heard a woman's screech come from down the hallway. "The little shit just threw up on me," she screamed. Her outrage was followed by a string of swear words.

"Speaking of classy women," Rocco muttered.

I wasn't waiting while these two played chicken. I scooted around Jake and hurried down the hall to collect Owen, ignoring the woman who stood frozen in the bathroom. The minute my son saw me, he burst into tears. "Mommy, Mommy, I got sick."

"So I see." I grabbed a washcloth in the bathroom and wet it down.

The woman seemed to think it was for her and made a huffing sound when I wiped Owen's mouth and hands. I picked him up, grabbed his backpack and coat, and carried him and everything else into the living room.

Rocco and Jake were standing chest to chest, only Jake was about five inches shorter than Rocco, which made for a comical sight. If I'd been in a laughing mood I would have said something.

"Rocco." Owen stretched his arms out to Rocco, wanting to go to him.

Jake blinked and stepped back. I saw the disappointment in his eyes as Owen leaned forward and Rocco
took him from me. Jake watched me slip past him and
follow Rocco out to the truck. Owen had his small
arms wrapped around Rocco's neck and his head on
the big man's shoulder. In every way it seemed Jake's
affair had cost him more than just me and our marriage. It looked as if he'd lost his son as well.

# CHAPTER 24

# Leanne

I arrived at the hospital at seven in the morning in order to see Sean before he headed into surgery. The attendant at the surgery desk checked the chart, running her finger down the list of names on the schedule, and then asked, "What is your relationship to the patient?"

Fearing I would be denied access if I admitted that I was his ex-wife, I murmured, "Wife."

She made a check on the sheet and said, "Follow me."

I was led down a long corridor to the room where Sean was. He was reclined on the bed, in a hospital gown with a number of IVs hooked to his arm. A monitor registered his heart rate and blood pressure every few minutes. His head had been shaved; he looked deathly pale and terribly frightened.

"You came." He stretched out his free arm and took hold of my hand in a death grip, squeezing my fingers to the point of pain. "I wasn't sure I'd see you before the surgery. Thank you." He had tears in his eyes, which I'm sure embarrassed him, because he turned his head and looked away.

Standing at his bedside, I gently placed my hand on his shoulder and gave it a squeeze. "Of course I'm here," I assured him. "I wouldn't want to be anyplace else."

He expelled a wobbly breath. "I don't mind telling you I've never been more terrified in my life."

"Anyone would be." I noticed that his blood pressure was elevated and his pulse rate was above normal. The proud, arrogant man I'd spent the majority of my life married to was reduced to a frightened child needing reassurance. "It's going to be fine, Sean. Take one day at a time and don't worry about anything more than that."

He nodded. "You're right."

"I prayed for you this morning," I told him. "You're in God's hands now."

Knowing that I'd prayed didn't appear to comfort him.

After a few minutes the surgeon came into the room, dressed in blue hospital garb with a blue cap on his head. A displaced face mask hung around his neck.

"Hello," he said, looking to me and extending his hand. "I'm Dr. Allgood."

We exchanged handshakes. "Leanne."

"This is my wife," Sean said.

I wanted to correct him, but I'd basically said the same thing to the attendant. It seemed easier that way, although it made me slightly uncomfortable.

The surgeon went over the surgical procedure with us both and explained what was about to happen. He told me the surgery could take as long as four or five hours. It was delicate, to say the least.

I listened and nodded at the appropriate times, but the medical terms and a lot of what he said went over my head. It wasn't important that I understand as much as it was for Sean to know I was there to lend him emotional support.

When it came time for Sean to be wheeled into surgery, I walked alongside the gurney and held his hand. The fear in his eyes ate at me. He held my gaze as long as possible, until he went through the doors to surgery. I waited there in the middle of the hallway until the automatic door closed.

A nurses' aide took me to the surgery waiting area, where a volunteer sat behind a desk. "There's no need for you to stay here, seeing that the procedure will take several hours," the volunteer told me. "If you'll give me your cell-phone number I can call you if there are any updates. The doctor will want to talk to you following surgery. As long as you're back between ten and noon you'll be able to chat with him."

I'd assumed I'd just sit in the waiting area, but the volunteer was right. I could be out and about doing something constructive in that amount of time. I left her my cell number and headed toward the parking lot, wondering what I would do. Kacey would love a visit, I knew, but it was still early and I didn't want to appear on her doorstep before eight in the morning.

It came to me that perhaps I should check the house to make sure everything was in order for when Sean returned from the hospital. I no longer had a key, but I knew where the spare was kept.

I hadn't been to the house since the divorce had

been finalized and I'd removed my personal items. We'd built this custom home twenty years into our marriage. It'd been our dream home, situated next to the golf course, with a beautiful view of the clubhouse in the distance. When we first moved in, I had taken great care and pride in decorating each room.

Sure enough, the spare key was in the fake rock in the flower beds. Sean had hired a lawn service, and while the yard was maintained, I could see that the flower beds were in bad shape. I'd always been the one to see to the care of the flowers. I found it disheartening to see how neglected they were. Not my problem, though.

I unlocked the door and walked into the home that had once been my pride. I knew Sean had a cleaning service come in once a week. My sense of self-importance had been stung by how easily I had been replaced in his life. A lawn-maintenance company and a cleaning service were all it took. To my shock, the house was an utter mess.

The kitchen counters were littered with mail, newspapers, empty glasses, and cartons of takeout food. I started there, ready to fill the dishwasher, until I realized it was full of clean dishes. I spent nearly an hour in the kitchen before I was satisfied.

The bedroom wasn't much better. Sean had discarded clothes on the floor. He'd always been meticulous when it came to hanging up his clothes. I found the hamper full of dirty laundry and ran a load of whites through the washer and dryer while I stripped the sheets and remade his bed.

The bathroom and living room were also a mess. I found a pair of women's black lace underwear under the sofa cushion and rolled my eyes. Taking a pair of tongs from the kitchen, I removed them. They were the skimpiest pair I'd ever laid eyes on and probably cost a fortune. I suspected whoever owned them was upset that they'd turned up missing.

It took three and a half hours to clean the house. I left in a rush and hurried back to the hospital, afraid I might miss talking to the surgeon. I hadn't gotten a call, so I had to assume everything was on schedule.

As it turned out, I needn't have worried. It was a full hour after my return before the surgeon came to talk with me. I stood as he stepped into the room. He drew me into the hallway outside, where we had a bit more privacy.

"Your husband came through the surgery without a problem."

My shoulders relaxed with relief. "Were you able to get all of the tumor?"

"Not all of it. What I was able to extract is being tested. We should have the results in a couple of days."

"And if it's cancer . . ." I could barely get the question out.

"If it's cancer we'll do everything we possibly can. But there's no need to concern yourself with that now." I noticed that he didn't quite meet my eyes as he spoke. It didn't sound good, but I could be wrong. I hoped I was.

"Your husband is in recovery now. I'll have the nurse come and get you so you can see him before you go."

"Thank you," I whispered, feeling uneasy about the white lie.

He patted my shoulder and turned away.

I wasn't in the mood for company, so I didn't call

Kacey the way I'd originally planned. Instead I wandered down to the cafeteria for a bowl of soup. I knew Jake would be wondering about his father, so I contacted him.

"How's Dad?" Jake asked as soon as he picked up, his concern obvious.

"He's out of surgery and doing the best that can be expected."

"Was the tumor cancerous?"

This, of course, was on all our minds. I knew Jake hated not knowing as much as I did. "We have to wait for the test results. The doctor said it would take a couple of days."

"I feel bad I couldn't be there for Dad. I know he appreciates you going to the hospital."

"It's fine, honey. I don't hold any ill will toward your father." I was sure he knew that, but a reminder wouldn't hurt.

Jake went silent, and when he spoke again his voice was full of pain. "Mom . . ."

"Jake," I whispered, "you don't need to worry. Your father takes care of himself physically. He's going to be fine." I tried to sound confident and reassuring.

"I know, I know. This weekend . . . Listen, Mom, I met Rocco. Is Nichole serious about this guy? Because I have to tell you, he looks like he's part of a motorcycle gang or something."

My son wanted to use me to find out information about his ex-wife. I was having none of it. As much as possible, I tried to remain neutral when it came to matters between Jake and Nichole. "The person you need to ask is Nichole, not me."

"But the two of you are close."

"Yes, we are," I agreed. Jake had already used me once to influence Nichole, and I wouldn't allow myself to be manipulated again.

"Nichole can't be serious about him, she just can't. That kind of guy is a bad influence on Owen. I don't want my son hanging around a man like that. Is she desperate? Is that it?"

Knowing some of the women my son had brought into the house, gossip Kacey had been far too eager to share, I found it interesting that he was asking me these questions. "Nichole isn't desperate," I said, doing my best to keep the irritation out of my voice. "Furthermore, I don't believe you have a say in who Nichole sees or doesn't see, Jake." I tried to be as nonjudgmental as possible. Unfortunately, I hadn't been able to bridle my tongue.

"It about killed me to see her with that guy," Jake admitted, his voice stiff and angry.

The double standards of my ex-husband and son astonished me. I found myself lashing back, despite my best intentions. "Did you think it was any easier for Nichole to learn you were cheating on her? Or to hear about the parade of women you've brought into the home that had once been hers?" I asked.

He sucked in a breath. "That was low, Mom."

I should have kept my opinion to myself. Jake was angry now; I could hear it in his breathing. His voice was hard when he spoke next. "Let me know what you hear about Dad."

"I will," I promised.

Jake ended the call before I had a chance to say anything more. It gave me no pleasure to know my son was suffering because of the end of his marriage. Like his father, he'd brought this on himself, but he didn't seem to recognize or accept his part in the divorce.

By the time I returned, Sean was out of recovery and had been taken down to his room. I sat at his bedside and read a magazine until he woke. He rolled his head and smiled when he saw me.

"I knew you'd be here," he whispered, his eyes shining with gratitude. "How long was I in surgery?"

I told him. "I didn't wait at the hospital. I went over to the house and got it ready for when you're able to go home."

Regret flashed in his eyes. "The housekeeper didn't work out. It was a mess, wasn't it?"

I didn't confirm or deny what he already knew. "Would you like me to hire someone for you?"

"Please." He found it difficult to speak, and I reached for the water cup and put the straw in his mouth. He drank thirstily.

When he finished I withdrew the straw and set the cup back on the side table. "I should leave now. I'm teaching this evening."

I could see by his look that he wanted me to stay.

"I'll be by tomorrow," I reassured him. "You might have the test results back by then."

He shut his eyes and whispered, his voice emotional, "Thank you, Leanne. I don't think I could have made it through this without you."

I bent forward and kissed his forehead. As I left the hospital, my cell rang. Caller ID told me it was Nikolai.

"Hello," I said.

"How is Sean?" he asked, concerned and caring. "I

pray this morning. I light more candles and ask God to be merciful."

"Thank you." My heart swelled with love, knowing he'd prayed for my ex-husband. "Sean came through the surgery fine. He's pretty much out of it just yet, which is what I expected."

"And cancer? You no have answer?"

"Not yet but soon."

Nikolai hesitated, as if he wasn't sure he should ask. "I see you before school?"

After the day I'd had, I was eager to see Nikolai. "I'd like that."

"I like, too. We meet for dinner before class, okay?"

"Okay."

We set a time and decided on a small restaurant not far from the Community Center.

By the time I arrived a few hours later, Nikolai was outside waiting. As soon as he saw me, he walked toward me and hugged me close. His eyes held mine and his look was dark and intense.

"Is something wrong?" I asked as we entered the restaurant.

He didn't get a chance to answer before we were led to a table and handed menus.

"Nikolai?" I asked again.

He read the menu. "I embarrassed to tell you."

"What is it?"

He waited a couple of long moments before he answered. "Mr. Jealousy stayed with me all day." He planted his hand on his chest. "You in my heart all day I think of you. I know you with Sean and he need you and I feel like I have no compassion. I tell myself I need to be bigger man."

"Nikolai," I said, stretching my arm across the table and taking hold of his hand. "You were in my heart all day, too. You."

"But you were with Sean."

"Actually, I wasn't. He was in surgery for several hours, so I drove over to the house. I wanted to be sure it was clean for when he got out of the hospital." I knew I was chattering, but I couldn't seem to stop. "It was a good thing I did, because the house was a dreadful mess. Apparently, his housekeeper didn't work out. He asked me to hire someone for him."

Nikolai jerked his hand away and his face tightened. "You clean for him?"

"Yes. The house was in terrible shape. I couldn't let Sean come home from the hospital to that filth."

Nikolai scooted back his chair and started pacing next to the table, his mood brooding and dark. He yanked his splayed fingers through his salt-and-pepper hair and mumbled in his native tongue.

"Nikolai, what is it?" I asked, watching him.

He leaned forward and braced his hands against the back of the chair, his fingers curving around the wood. "This not right. You clean for him is wrong."

I wouldn't have done it if I didn't think it was necessary for Sean's well-being. I didn't dare let Nikolai know that I'd told the hospital that I was Sean's wife in order to see him before his surgery. If Nikolai found out about that, he'd blow a gasket.

"Nikolai, please don't be upset with me."

He sat down and covered his face with both hands. I could see he was working hard to hold himself together.

Apparently, what I'd done was akin to serving Sean the bread Nikolai had baked for me.

The waitress chose that moment to come to the table for our order. I hadn't even looked at the menu yet.

"I no eat," Nikolai muttered.

The truth was I wasn't hungry, either.

The woman left and Nikolai stood. "It not good that I be here right now," he said as he reached for his coat on the chair next to mine. "I need to think."

I felt dreadful. "I'm sorry," I whispered. I didn't consider helping Sean by cleaning his house would be a cause for concern, but clearly it was. "Will I see you at school?" I asked.

Nikolai hesitated and then nodded. "I see you then and try to forget you like maid for this man who no loves you."

# CHAPTER 25

# Nichole

Thanksgiving Day was a blast. I arrived at Cassie and Steve's late Wednesday afternoon with Owen and Kaylene. I really hated leaving Rocco behind, but he'd be joining us Saturday morning in time for the wedding later that afternoon. I felt mildly guilty about him spending the holiday working and alone, but he insisted. We texted back and forth all day.

Me: Miss you.
Rocco: A man's got to do what a man's got to do.
Me: Turkey is yummy, best stuffing ever.
Rocco: UR an evil woman.
Me: Take that back. I saved you some.
Rocco: Got anything else for me?
Me: Pecan pie?
Rocco: I was thinking of something more personal.
Me: Like?
Rocco: Better delivered in person than texted.

Me: Can hardly wait.
Rocco: Grrrrrr.

Smiling to myself, I tucked my phone back inside my apron pocket and brought down the dishes to set the table with the help of Kaylene and Amiee. The girls were getting along great. I could hear them chattering away; they'd been up half the night talking. Cassie and I were in the kitchen cooking at eight Thanksgiving morning and dinner was on the table by three.

My parents died within a short time of each other. Basically, Mom was lost without my father and didn't feel she had anything to live for any longer. It was hard to lose them both so quickly.

Although it'd been several years now that they were gone, it seemed they were with us this Thanksgiving. It was the first one I'd spent with Cassie since I was thirteen. Together we cooked the recipes from our childhood, ones handed down from our mother and grandmothers.

After the meal we leaned back in our chairs, stuffed and happy. When we were children we would go around the table, each one mentioning something we were most grateful for that year. It was so nice to do that again, especially when we had all been so blessed.

It'd been a hard year for me with the divorce and all. I'd learned a lot about myself. I was much stronger emotionally than I realized. Of course I'd had help, mainly Leanne and the guide we'd created. As the youngest in my family, I'd been spoiled, and after I'd married Jake he'd pampered me. This was the year I'd learned to pull myself up and wear my big-girl panties. It hadn't been easy. I hadn't quite decided which one thing I was most grateful for when it became Kaylene's turn.

"I'm most grateful for Nichole," she said, surprising me. "And not because she helped me buy a dress and gave my dad dancing lessons, although that was way cool. I'm grateful to her because she makes my dad happy. He whistles now and he never used to." She blushed and looked over to Amiee.

Amiee looked around the table as a slow grin came into play. "I'm grateful for Kentucky Fried Chicken."

"Amiee," Cassie protested.

"Just kidding, Mom," she said, giggling. "I'm grateful for my cousins and for new friends." She looked at Kaylene. "Just think, if your dad marries my aunt Nichole, we would be cousins."

"Cool," Kaylene whispered.

"Nichole," Cassie said, looking at me. She sat next to Steve and the two held hands. I watched as Steve brought her hand to his lips for a kiss.

"My turn," I said. "I'm grateful to be surrounded by the people I love, who have encouraged and supported me through this last year. I am blessed."

"And loved," Cassie added.


We all helped with the cleanup. The girls cleared off the table and Cassie put away the leftovers while I stacked the dishes in the dishwasher. Owen tried to help, but he removed the silverware from the dishwasher as fast as I could place it inside. Steve shooed everyone out and washed the serving dishes by hand.

Once cleanup was finished we collapsed in front of

the television. The kids were in another room watching a movie. Owen went with the girls, who thought he was adorable. Steve wanted to catch a football game, and that was fine with Cassie and me. Cassie was more interested in taking a nap, and I wouldn't have minded that myself. Steve took the recliner and Cassie was at one end of the sofa and I was at the other. We used to share a sofa like this when we were kids.

My phone pinged and I looked to find a text from Rocco.

Rocco: Kaylene said dinner was great and she enjoyed the sharing time.

Me: Do I make you happy?

Rocco: Is that what she said?

Me: Yup. Do I?

Rocco: More than you know.

Me: You make me happy, too.

Rocco: Good to know.

Me: I so wish you were here.

Rocco: Me, too, baby. Me, too.

Friday was a blur as Cassie and I got ready for the rehearsal dinner. Karen and her family arrived mid-afternoon and the rest of the day was spent with kids running wild in happy chaos. The dinner went off beautifully at a hole-in-the-wall Mexican restaurant in downtown Kent that was Cassie and Steve's favorite. They rented out the entire place to the wedding party and friends. The margaritas flowed freely and there was music, singing, laughter, and good-natured razzing. The owners joined in. By the time the evening was over I was more than a little tipsy.

As soon as I got to the house I texted Rocco, who was leaving first thing in the morning.

Me: heLLo.
Rocco: Dinner party over?
Me: YuP n bed R now.
Rocco: How many margaritas did U have?
Me: dONT now.
Me: NOW.
Me: Know. Friggin spell check.
Rocco: You're killing me, babe.
Me: ?
Rocco: Will be there in the morning.
Me: Hurry.
Rocco: Damn. Wish I was there now. Hate to miss seeing you tipsy.
Me: WiLL REpete 4 U.

Saturday morning, I woke slightly hungover but happy. By ten Karen, Cassie, Kaylene, Amiee, and I headed to the hair salon where Cassie worked as a stylist. The girls in the shop had basically closed it down for the day in order to get us ready for the wedding. Our hair was washed, dried, and whipped into shape. We got manicures and pedicures and facials. By the time we got out of the salon we'd been poked, plucked, and painted. I'd never laughed so hard in my life as I did with Cassie's coworkers, who were thoroughly delightful. They would attend the wedding, too.

I was anxious to get back to Steve's house because I'd gotten a text that told me Rocco had arrived. Steve had entertained him while we were away. When we burst in the door, Steve and Rocco were sitting in front of the television, drinking beer and watching yet another football game. Steve appeared relaxed and at ease, and so did Rocco.

As soon as the door opened, Rocco twisted around, and when he saw me, he set aside his beer bottle. He came out of the chair and walked toward me, wrapping his arm around my waist. Then he nearly bent me in half backward with his kiss. It was hungry, demanding, and told me exactly how much he'd missed me.

When he lifted his head, I gasped for air. If he'd hadn't kept his arm about me I was convinced I'd have dropped unceremoniously onto the carpet.

"Damn," Steve said, saluting Rocco with his beer bottle. "You could get a woman pregnant with a kiss like that."

Rocco chuckled. "Maybe so, but I prefer the old-fashioned way."

Steve laughed.

With Rocco's help I straightened and drew in a stabilizing breath. "I see you and Steve are bonding."

"Yeah. He found the dinner plate you'd put aside for me. Like you promised, best stuffing ever."

"I'll make it for Christmas," I said, and then frowned. "Please don't tell me you have to work Christmas?"

He shrugged. "It's negotiable."

Other than that brief five minutes, I didn't see Rocco again until I walked down the church aisle. Rocco stood at the end of a pew, dressed in his suit and tie. I have to say he looked hot enough to set the building on fire. I nearly stumbled when I saw him. His eyes were intense as his gaze met mine. I walked past him and stood at the altar with my sister, and Amiee served as the maid of honor.

Cassie was a gorgeous bride. I'd never seen her look more beautiful. I had felt Mom and Dad's presence on Thanksgiving Day, but I felt them even stronger here in the church as Cassie pledged her life to Steve. My sister wore the beautiful cameo that had once belonged to our grandmother.

Dad had always intended for her to have it and it was understood she would wear it on her wedding day. When she'd run away and married Duke, we didn't hear from her for years, never knowing where she was. We assumed she wanted nothing more to do with our family. Years later Dad gave me the cameo, but in my heart it had always belonged to Cassie.

When we reconnected I saw how difficult her life had been with Duke. I realized what grit and courage it'd taken for Cassie to find her way home. I didn't feel I could keep the cameo, and I returned it to her. I know Dad would have been proud to see her wear it on the day she married Steve.

As Steve and Cassie exchanged their vows, I had the almost irrepressible urge to turn and look at Rocco. Steve's voice rang strong and clear with no hesitation, full of love. Cassie answered with the same heartfelt conviction. These were two people, deeply in love, pledging to cherish and honor each other for the rest of their lives.

The church held fewer than fifty people, as Cassie

and Steve wanted only their closest friends and family for the actual ceremony.

The dinner and reception that followed were a completely different story. The reception was held in a hotel ballroom. Steve had spared no expense. The men and women who worked for Steve were there, along with large numbers of close friends from Habitat for Humanity. It was through this organization that Cassie had met Steve.

I knew Cassie had made a number of good friends through Habitat. I could see how deeply my sister was loved and admired. I admired her, too, and realized my middle sister had more gumption and courage than anyone I would ever know. Mom and Dad would have been so proud of her.

Karen must have been thinking the same thing, because our eyes met and I noticed hers, like mine, were shining with unshed tears. I struggled to hold back the emotion.

Rocco sat next to me at dinner, and Kaylene and Owen were on the other side of me. Rocco reached for my hand, gently wrapping his fingers around mine.

"That was the most beautiful wedding I've ever been to," he said.

I leaned toward him and whispered back, "As I recall, this is the only wedding you've ever been to."

"I'm not going to another."

My face fell with disappointment. "You're not?"

"I don't think he should, either," Kaylene said from the other side of me.

"Kaylene," Rocco warned, glaring at his daughter.

"He cried like a baby," Kaylene told me, lowering

her voice. "It was awful to see my dad sobbing through the wedding."

"I was not sobbing," Rocco insisted righteously. "I teared up. Nothing more. Just a little emotional is all."

I squeezed Rocco's hand. We intertwined our fingers and held on to each other through the entire meal. When the dancing started I looked over at him, hoping he'd take the hint.

"You going to dance with Nichole?" Kaylene asked her dad.

Rocco looked uncomfortable. "If I don't have a choice."

"Dad. That was a terrible thing to say."

"If you recall," I took delight in reminding him, "the first time we kissed was when we were dancing."

His eyes brightened and he scooted back his chair. "All right, let's shake some booty."

I didn't bother to hide my amusement. By the time we reached the dance floor the area was crowded and it was easy to blend in with the others. Rocco tucked his arms around me, knitting his hands at the small of my back, and I placed mine around his neck. I loved being this close to him.

"Have I told you how beautiful you look?" he asked me softly, his eyes full of warmth.

I smiled. "About a dozen times, but don't worry, I won't grow tired of you saying it." He looked mighty fine himself. I saw a number of women looking at me with envy. What I loved, what made me want to kiss this man senseless, was that he didn't notice a single one of them. He had eyes only for me. Every other woman at this party faded into the background. He didn't even seem to notice. Just knowing that made me want to spend the rest of my life with him.

I was about to tell him he looked dashing and debonair when I heard my name. I twisted my head around, and to my horror, I saw it was Jake. My ex-husband had shown up at my sister's wedding. Jake had his hand on Rocco's much larger shoulder.

"That's my wife you're dancing with and I'm cutting in," he said loudly, garnering the attention of those around us.

"I am not your wife," I insisted, mortified that Jake would make a scene.

"Let me handle this," Rocco answered softly. He removed Jake's hand from his shoulder. "You're drunk."

"So what? I don't want a grease monkey dancing with my wife. You're a lowlife and a . . ." Apparently, he couldn't think of a suitable word.

"Nichole," Jake cried, pleading with me. "Don't do this to us. You're my wife."

Steve appeared. "Why don't we take this outside?" he suggested.

"Go back to your wife," Rocco insisted. "I'll escort Jake outside."

"I have an invitation," Jake insisted. "You can't throw me out."

"I believe we can," Steve said calmly. He looked to Rocco. "Don't deprive me of the pleasure. I was never keen on this jerk. I couldn't understand what Nichole saw in him."

Steve and Rocco, standing on either side of Jake, each took an arm and lifted Jake three inches off the floor. By the time they got to the exit, hotel security was there to escort Jake off the premises.

I was embarrassed and pressed my hands to my mouth until Steve and Rocco returned.

"Steve, I am so sorry," I whispered.

"No problem, Nichole. Fact is, I rather enjoyed that."

Rocco wrapped his arm around me again and brought me close. "Now, what was it you were saying about the first time we danced? As I recall, you were overwhelmed by the sheer force of my masculinity and couldn't keep your hands off me."

I smiled up at him. "Yes, it was something like that."

He brought his mouth down to mine. "That's what I thought," he said, before he stole a kiss.

# CHAPTER 26

# Leanne

Nikolai wasn't happy with me. During our classes on Monday and Wednesday, he sat silent. Before, he'd been an enthusiastic contributor to our discussions. He didn't seem to understand that while I was no longer married to Sean, I felt a certain obligation to help him through this medical crisis.

Sean ended up needing to stay in the hospital an extra day and was released Thanksgiving morning. The timing couldn't have been worse.

"I can't get ahold of Jake," Sean called to tell me. "There's no one who can drive me to the house. I hate to ask you, Leanne, but I don't have any choice."

Nikolai and I had plans to share dinner with friends from class. One of my students, Jakob Cirafesi, had invited us to join him and his wife for Thanksgiving. Those attending were to bring a dish from their native country. Sun Young had promised to cook a pot of the same wonderful soup he'd made for me during my shingles episode, and three others were eager to bring food as well. Nikolai and I had planned to attend, and naturally he promised to bring his bread.

"I'll see what I can do." I'd assumed Jake would be there for his father. I hadn't spoken to my son since our last conversation, when I refused to discuss Nichole's relationship with Rocco. Jake had been short-tempered with me, just short of belligerent.

"I need to know soon," Sean said. He sounded more like a child than the confident businessman I knew him to be.

"I'll contact Nikolai now." I dreaded making the call. Nikolai and I weren't back on solid ground yet, and this latest request from Sean was sure to complicate matters even more.

Being put in this position wasn't convenient. I knew what Sean was saying, though. It was Thanksgiving and our friends, or those who had once been our friends, were involved with their own families or were out of town. Our son had disappointed us both. I disconnected with Sean and called Nikolai.

He answered right away, his voice cheerful and happy. "Yes, my Leanne."

"Happy Thanksgiving, Nikolai."

He paused and I swore he knew.

"I got a call from Sean this morning," I said, striving to sound as upbeat and positive as possible. "He's being released today. Unfortunately, he can't reach Jake and he needs someone to drive him home from the hospital. He didn't want to ask me, but he didn't have any choice."

"Today?"

"Yes, today."

"And he ask you?"

"Like I said, there's no one else." I silently pleaded for understanding.

Nikolai said nothing.

"It shouldn't take long. I'll collect Sean, get him to the house, and get him settled. Then I'll meet you at the Cirafesis' house." It seemed the perfect solution. I'd be as quick as possible.

"No," Nikolai said.

"No?" I repeated, hardly able to believe what I was hearing.

"I come with you. You no meet me later, because I know this man. I know he keep you. He no want you with me. I burst his basketballs," he said.

I held back a laugh. "You mean you want to burst his bubble."

"Yes, that is what I mean."

And that was how Nikolai came to join me when we went to collect Sean following his release.

As soon as Sean saw Nikolai I could see he wasn't happy. Nikolai could very well have been right. Sean would use any excuse he could think up to delay me and keep me away from this dinner party. "You remember Nikolai, don't you?" I said, coming into Sean's hospital room.

The two men glared at each other like boxers before a match. One looking to intimidate the other.

"I remember," Sean said, his voice low and tight.

Nikolai nodded sternly, his eyes as hard as I had ever seen them. "I remember, too."

The aide came to collect Sean with the wheelchair. I stayed with him while Nikolai left to get the car and drive it around to the front of the hospital, where patients were released. The nurse followed with a list of instructions and his medications. I listened intently, although everything had been written down. Sean was the one who needed to remember, not me.

My ex-husband looked nothing like himself with his shaved and bandaged head. He was thinner than I could remember him being. I could tell he was weak. He hadn't mentioned the test results and I was afraid to ask. My guess was if he had information he'd let me know. At least I hoped he would.

Finally I couldn't stand not knowing. "Any word?" I asked, when the aide was out of the room, picking up his discharge papers.

"None," he said, frustrated and irritated both at once. "Doc said it was because of the holiday. I'll know first thing Monday morning."

"That long. Oh Sean, it must be tearing you apart not knowing." I gave his shoulder a gentle squeeze. He reached up and grabbed hold of my hand and held on to it on the ride down the elevator. As soon as we were on the main floor, I pulled my hand free, not wanting Nikolai to see.

Nikolai had the car parked and the passenger door open by the time we made it outside. The aide helped Sean into the car and handed me the bag of medications.

"Your wife has the medications," she told Sean.

Nikolai bristled and said with gritted teeth, "She not his wife."

The aide looked at the paperwork. "I'm sorry, but that's what it says here. You are Leanne Patterson, aren't you?"

"Yes," I answered, not looking at Nikolai. "I'm Leanne, but I'm Sean's ex-wife."

"I'm sorry." The aide sent me an apologetic look.

"It's a simple misunderstanding," I said, eager to leave the hospital.

The tension in the car was thicker than the Great Wall of China as Nikolai drove to the house. The only words spoken were by me as I gave Nikolai directions. I could see when we pulled into the driveway that Nikolai was taken aback by the splendor of our custom-built country-club home.

We helped Sean out of the car and into the house. I set him up in his favorite chair in the family room.

"We go now," Nikolai said as soon as Sean was settled.

"Just a minute." I didn't want to rush away until I was sure Sean had what he needed. I checked the refrigerator and realized the shelves were mostly bare. Nikolai saw it, too. "Sean could use a few groceries," I said, leaving the decision in Nikolai's hands.

His frustration was clear. He waited an uncomfortable moment and then nodded. We left Sean and drove in silence to the first open grocery store we could find. I grabbed a few essentials: bread, milk, orange juice, and bananas, along with several cans of soup and a jar of peanut butter. Because it was Thanksgiving, I also tucked a package of sliced turkey breast in the stack. All in all, it took less than fifteen minutes to gather the supplies for Sean.

Nikolai insisted I remain in the car while he took in the groceries to Sean. I don't know what the two said, but it took far longer than necessary.

When he returned his face was red and he didn't look happy.

"Thank you for doing this," I said as soon as he

climbed into the car. I knew Nikolai was right. If I'd gone alone, Sean would have found an excuse for me to stay. I would have completely missed our Thanksgiving celebration.

Nikolai's hands clenched the steering wheel. "I do not like this man. I pray for him, but he need more than prayer. His heart is dark."

I didn't exactly need a reminder.

"Please don't be upset," I said, my voice low and trembling.

At my words Nikolai pulled over to the side of the road and parked the car. Turning, he cupped my face with his hands and looked deep into my eyes. "Upset with you, my Leanne? Never. You too much in my heart. If I upset, it is with that man who not love you. He is fool and I not like fools. He use you and make you feel bad for him. You are too kind. Too caring."

I smiled up at him and he kissed me ever-so-sweetly.

"I do not like you be maid to him. You promise me you not do that again."

"I promise."

"If he need soup, I cook. I take to him. He not use you. I tell him so. I tell him you in my heart now. He is fool to lose you."

So that was what took Nikolai so long. "You told Sean that?"

"Yes and more. I say he have son to help. I say he have girlfriend. I say he leave my Leanne with me. My job is care for you. My job now to love you. Not his job," he said, struggling with his English. "It my joy to care for you." His hands continued to hold my face. I watched as his eyes grew troubled.

"Nikolai?"

"I never buy you house like that one. I never give you many pretty things. I not rich man like Sean. I poor, but I am rich with love."

I'll never know what I did to have found a man as wonderful as Nikolai. "Don't you know I had all that before and willingly gave it up? None of what I once shared with Sean was worth what it cost my soul. I would rather spend five minutes with you than a hundred years with Sean."

For the first time that day, I saw Nikolai relax his shoulders and smile. "I am luckiest man in America," he said, and then chuckled. "Luckiest man in world to love you."

Funny, I was thinking I was the lucky one.


Our Thanksgiving feast was truly wonderful. We shared traditional Thai dishes and Sun Young's delicious soup with Nikolai's bread. I brought candied yams and fruit salad and the Cirafesis' brought out a pork roast and some kind of stuffed dumplings that were delicious.

After we ate we gathered around and watched a football game. My immigrant friends had no understanding or appreciation of the sport, so I explained as best I could. My dad and brother had both been big fans, so I had a better grasp of the game.

At the end of the day, I got my coat and purse and brought out my cell phone to text Jake. I didn't know what his problem was but he needed to get over it.

You need to check on your father.

His response came back quickly.

I'm with him now. Not cool what you did.

What I did? I'd taken time out of my Thanksgiving celebration to pick up Sean and take him home because my ex-husband had been unable to reach our son. Before I could reply, another text from Jake flashed on my screen.

No need to rub Dad's face in the mud with your immigrant boyfriend. You're as bad as Nichole. That was beneath you, Mom. Loosing respect for you and my EX.

I suspected Jake had been drinking, so I ignored the texts. It wouldn't do any good to argue with him, and in fact it might do more harm than good.


Sunday afternoon Nichole and Owen returned from her sister's wedding. I'd cooked dinner for them and was eager to hear the details of the long weekend. We ate together in my apartment as Nichole inquired about my Thanksgiving.

"I had a good day with Nikolai and friends from the class." I didn't mention the incident with Sean or the text from Jake. "The wedding went well?" I'd much rather hear about her time with her sisters and Rocco.

A dreamy look came over Nichole. "Oh Leanne, the wedding was beautiful. I've never seen my sister look happier or more radiant. She told me she and Steve would like to start a family right away." I knew my daughter-in-law didn't want Owen to be an only child. I knew she would want more children if she did decide to remarry. If that was the case, I fully intended to be their grandmother.

Nichole shifted in her seat and looked away. "Jake showed up drunk at the reception."

My heart sank. I didn't know what was wrong with my son. He knew better than that. "Oh Nichole, I'm so sorry. Did he cause a scene?"

She shrugged. "It wasn't too bad. A few people noticed, but it didn't stop the festivities. Rocco and Steve escorted Jake out of the ballroom and then security took over."

"I believe he was drunk when he sent me a text on Thanksgiving." I was worried about my son. This wasn't typical behavior from him. I would need to talk to Sean and see if he knew something I didn't.

"Speaking of Sean, how is he?" Nichole seemed eager to change the subject, and I didn't blame her.

"Sean's good. I've only talked to him once since he's been home from the hospital."

"Any word on the test results?"

I shook my head. "The holiday messed up the timing with the labs. He won't know until tomorrow."

"That's awful."

I agreed with her. I knew he was anxious—who wouldn't be?—but he hid it well. I wasn't privy to all the information because of the HIPAA laws. I prayed my ex-husband would be spared having to deal with cancer.

———

Monday midafternoon Sean called, and when I saw his name on caller ID I knew he'd gotten word from the doctor.

"Sean, you heard?" I asked, eager to hear his news.

"Yes, I just finished talking to the doctor." His voice was bleak, frightened, and in that moment I knew.

"It's cancer, isn't it?"

"Yes."

I expelled a sigh. "Oh Sean, I am so sorry." I was no longer his wife. The only connection we had was Jake. We'd had a terrible marriage, but I didn't wish this on Sean.

"I know; I'm sorry, too." He went silent, as if struggling within himself. "I had to make a choice and it was difficult. I hope you'll support me in this."

Chills went up my spine. "What is it?"

"I talked with the oncologist, who recommended radiation and chemotherapy, but I've decided against it."

I sucked in my breath. "Sean, why would you do that?"

"At best I have six months to a year." He went on to explain the cancer was an aggressive form and there was little hope.

"No." I was shocked.

"If I only have that short amount of time left, I don't want to waste it undergoing painful treatments."

"Oh Sean." I had a hard time wrapping my mind around what he was telling me.

"Please don't try to talk me out of this. I've already made my decision."

My throat was thick with unshed tears. "Okay."

"I know this new man in your life doesn't want you

seeing me. He made that clear on Thanksgiving. I only ask one thing of you and then I won't trouble you again."

"Yes, of course. What is it?"

Sean sounded as if he were close to breaking down. "I know it's a lot to ask, but there's no one else I would trust."

"Sean, what is it?"

"Will you help me pick out my casket?"

# CHAPTER 27

# Nichole

"I like your sister and her husband," Rocco mentioned Friday night a week after Thanksgiving. I hadn't seen him all week and I'd missed him. Really missed him. He was beginning to feel like an important part of my life. His work kept him busy and it was a treat when we were able to be together.

I suggested we have dinner at the tavern where he'd taken me the one time, knowing Rocco enjoyed it there. It was important for him to know that I was comfortable in his world. His friends were my friends.

We sat in a booth and ordered beer and chicken wings, Rocco's favorite food. The music was loud and the crowd boisterous. It seemed to be a biker hangout or at least for wannabe club members. I did my best to dress accordingly. I had on tight jeans and a red v-neck sweater along with my knee-high boots. I had a holly pin on my sweater. It was the holiday season, after all. Despite that I seemed to be the only one not dressed completely in black. Johnny Cash would have fit right in. Me, not so much, although I tried.

"Karen and Garth are a great couple," I agreed, a little surprised because I didn't see Rocco talking to them as much.

"I was talking about Cassie and Steve."

"Of course." I'd lived the majority of my adult life without Cassie. It was only natural to assume Rocco meant Karen and Garth. "I'm so glad you came to the wedding with me."

"I am, too." Rocco reached for another chicken wing. He'd eaten three to my one, which I ate with a knife and fork, much to Rocco's amusement. Truth was, they were a tad too spicy for me. I liked my wings hot, too, but not to the point that it required a fire hose to quell the burning in my mouth.

Rocco licked his fingers and didn't look at me. "Jake come for Owen?"

I knew the two men basically hated each other. Their animosity shimmered off them at the wedding reception.

"He picked up Owen at daycare, so I didn't need to talk to him." Or see him, either.

Looking up, Rocco pinned me with his gaze. "Have you talked to him since the wedding?"

"Talk to Jake?" I had, and it'd been less than comfortable. Jake had ranted on for several uncomfortable minutes about his objections to me dating Rocco. He'd had a lot to say about Rocco being a negative influence on our son.

"You're avoiding the question." Rocco's eyes hardened. "He giving you a bad time again?"

I shrugged, not wanting to discuss my ex-husband.

"It's fine, Rocco." I didn't want to waste our evening discussing Jake.

"You need me to have a man-to-man chat with him?"

"No!" That was the last thing I wanted. I couldn't see any good coming from it.

"I'd be more than happy to set him straight."

I was sure he would, and I didn't think there'd be a whole lot of talking involved. "Let me handle Jake," I insisted. Even talking about my ex-husband upset me, and I ordered a second beer. Rocco eyed me suspiciously.

"You sure you want that?"

"Yup." Jake was driving me to drink.

Rocco grew silent. "I hate the thought of Jake upsetting you."

"It's fine," I promised, and it was. My ex would soon learn that he had no control over whom I dated.

Rocco intently studied me and grew silent.

"What?" I asked, laughing at how intense he'd gotten.

He offered me a weak smile. "I want to do everything right by you, Nichole. You tell me to back off Jake and I will. I don't like it, but if that's what you want, that's what I'll do." He glanced down for a moment and then up again. "I've never been in a relationship like this one. I don't know what love is between a man and a woman . . . the emotional aspect. The physical I've got, but this gut-wrenching *I would die for you* feeling is beyond anything I've ever experienced."

All I could do was stare at Rocco. For a man who

claimed he was poor with words, poor with express-
ing himself, he was doing a beautiful job.

"Every time we're together you show me what it
means to care about someone in a way that's rich and
deep and powerful. I want that for us. I know you're
not ready for that yet . . ."

Rocco paused when Sam, his friend, wandered over
to our booth. I could tell Sam had been drinking for a
while.

Sam set his hands against the edge of the table,
leaning toward me, grinning, as if he knew something
I didn't. "See you're still hanging with this motherf—"

"Sam!" Rocco snapped, cutting him off. "Nichole
isn't used to that language, so watch your mouth."

"Rocco," I whispered. "Don't worry about it."

"No," he countered swiftly. "I'm not having anyone
use that kind of language in front of you."

Sam's head came back as if Rocco had assaulted
him. "You gotta be kidding me, Rocco. What's the
matter? You turning into a pussy?"

"I want you to respect my woman," Rocco said.
"You're a friend, Sam, a good one, and I'd like to keep
it that way. Nichole's special and I won't have you disrespecting her. Got it?"

Sam's eyes bulged. "So says the man who had a one-
night policy."

"A what?" I asked, confused.

Sam looked to me. "Bet she don't know about that."

Rocco ignored him and looked at me. "I don't think
coming here was such a good idea."

"I'd say you're right," Sam said, laughing. "She
don't fit in here, and from the sounds of it you don't,

either. Not anymore." He made a huffing sound and left.

Rocco looked decidedly uncomfortable.

"What did he mean by a one-night policy?" I asked, curious now.

"It was a long time ago," he said, and shook his head. "I haven't been that person since I got custody of Kaylene."

"Rocco, tell me." I figured I had a right to know.

He exhaled and looked past me. "All right," he said forcefully. "I told you before I had a past and that I'd been pretty wild back in the day. You might as well hear the worst of it. My one-night policy meant that I only slept with a woman once and when I finished getting what I wanted I shoved her out of my life. No repeats."

My eyes widened and a chill went down my spine. Rocco had always been open and honest with me. To the best of my knowledge, he'd never lied to me.

"I'm not that person any longer, Nichole," he reiterated. "I haven't been that man in a lot of years."

"I know."

"It was a mistake to bring you here." He reached for the check and set some bills on the table. "Let's go."

"Okay." The evening that had started out so beautifully had taken a sharp turn south.

Rocco helped me put my coat on and then reached for my hand. Once outside, he released me and stuffed his hands in his back jean pockets. "I apologize for Sam. He's had a little too much to drink. He's usually not like that. He knows how I feel about you."

"It's all right," I assured him. Rocco seemed to forget that I taught at a high school and heard kids swear on a regular basis. I didn't like it and certainly hadn't been raised in that environment. My father used to say that someone who used foul language was someone who needed to study vocabulary because there were more civilized ways to get one's point across.

I wrapped my arm around Rocco's elbow. "Where would you like to go now?" I asked.

Rocco was deep in thought and I wasn't sure he'd heard me.

"How about my apartment?" I suggested. "We'll cuddle on the sofa and watch a movie. I've got popcorn."

He looked at me as if I'd suggested he jump over Multnomah Falls.

"What?" I asked. Personally, I thought it was a great idea.

Rocco simply shook his head. "No way."

"Why not?"

"Get a grip, Nichole. I have a hard enough time keeping my hands off you as it is. Besides, you've had two beers."

"So what? And who said I wanted you to keep your hands off me?" I demanded.

He glared at me. "Don't say things you don't mean."

"Do I look like I'm kidding?" I planted my hand on my hip. As for the beers, all they'd done was loosen me up a little.

His eyes didn't leave mine. "You need to understand something. We start this and there's no going back."

I wasn't sure what that entailed. "What do you mean?"

He exhaled and grabbed hold of my hand. "That's what I thought."

"What?" I asked, nearly stumbling along in order to keep up with him. The boots looked great, but they weren't the best for walking fast. I slid once and would have taken a tumble if Rocco hadn't caught me.

"Where are you taking me?" I asked.

"Not to your apartment."

"You aren't?" I didn't bother to hide my disappointment. "We going to your house?" I asked.

"Kaylene's there."

"Oh."

"I'm taking you to the movies."

"The movies?" I cried, disappointed. "You're joking."

"No." He tilted his head back and looked up at the sky. "I wish I was. God knows I wish I was."

"All right, if going to the movies is what you want." I was disappointed and hurt.

"I'll buy you popcorn," he said, in an effort to lighten my mood.

"With butter?"

"With butter."

He let me choose and I opted for a chick flick. Halfway through, Rocco fell asleep. I had to wake him and he yawned and then drove me home. He kissed me outside the elevator and didn't take me to my apartment the way he'd always done.

"Will I see you soon?" I asked.

"Of course, baby," he assured me.

My thoughts were muddled as I walked into the apartment. It was still early and I couldn't help but wonder about Rocco's mood. I wasn't sure what to think. Everything had been good between us, I thought.

My sister's wedding had been a week ago and we'd danced almost every dance. Rocco had been wonderful and my family had really liked him, especially Steve. The two had connected on several levels. Both were men who owned their own businesses. They each enjoyed talking sports and drinking beer. Although no one had mentioned it, I instinctively knew these were men who loved deeply and devotedly.

By the time I was inside my apartment I could feel my spirits sinking. Impulsively, I decided to pay Leanne a visit. I hadn't talked to her since she'd gotten the bad news about Sean. I knew learning he had cancer had deeply distressed her.

Leanne felt terrible for her ex-husband. I understood. After spending most of her life with Sean, she continued to have feelings for him. It would be impossible not to. It might not be the love she'd once felt, but she still cared. She was that kind of person.

I tentatively knocked on her door. Nikolai might be visiting. She hadn't mentioned if they were doing anything when we'd last talked that morning.

Leanne answered the door and I felt her welcome. "I thought you and Rocco were going out tonight?" she said, bringing me inside. I followed her into the kitchen and saw that she had a salad on the kitchen countertop. It looked like she hadn't eaten. It was late for her to be having dinner.

"I interrupted your meal," I said, feeling guilty. "Were you out for the evening?"

Leanne shook her head. "No, I didn't have much of an appetite and thought I might feel hungry a bit later, but I don't."

It didn't look like she'd taken more than a bite or two. "You feeling okay?" I asked.

"I'm fine. This whole thing with Sean has depressed me. I can't stop thinking that he has as little as six months to live."

"Did you tell Nikolai?"

"Not yet. I promised him that I wouldn't be what he calls 'Sean's maid,' but he's going to need help."

"Hire someone," I suggested. It made sense. No doubt Sean was going to need someone to look after and care for him, especially as he grew progressively weaker, but that didn't mean Leanne should be the one to shoulder the burden. I sided with Nikolai in that instance.

"That's a good idea."

"Let Jake take on that task. He needs to show some responsibility for helping his father." It irritated me that he hadn't taken time off work to be with his family when Sean had gone in for surgery.

At my suggestion, Leanne rolled her eyes and I nearly laughed. Her look said it all. Jake wasn't a responsible son any more than he'd been a responsible husband.

"Point taken." I sat down at the counter and pressed my elbows against the bar top. Knowing me, Leanne automatically brewed me a cup of coffee.

"So what's the deal with Rocco?" she asked as she set the cup in front of me.

"I don't know. We went to one of his favorite places. It's a tavern where his friends hang. Sam and Rocco have been friends for years. I'd met him before and we'd played pool together. He's an okay guy, but pretty rough around the edges. He tosses out four-letter words like Mardi Gras beads."

Leanne nodded as if she knew exactly the kind of person I was talking about. "In other words, he's like Rocco but harder, with a mouth his mother should have washed out with soap."

"Exactly. He came over to where Rocco and I were sitting and started in. Right away Rocco took offense at Sam's language. The thing is, Sam used the same swear words when we were playing pool and Rocco didn't object then."

"There was probably a reason he didn't."

I couldn't imagine what it would be.

Leanne answered, as if she'd heard my unspoken question. "Rocco might have been waiting to see your reaction," she offered, "or . . ." She paused and a smile grew until it looked as if she was at the point of laughing.

"What?" I pressed, wanting to know.

"Or it could be that he cares for you more now than he did earlier."

I smiled, hoping that was the case. I didn't mention what else Sam had said about how Rocco treated relationships with women. Like Rocco told me, that was years ago. I knew that Kaylene had been the result of one of those one-night stands.

"What happened next?" Leanne asked, drawing me back to the present.

"Sam and Rocco exchanged words and I could see Rocco was angry." I admired the way he'd held himself together, not only with Sam but with Jake, too. He wasn't easily manipulated into a fight.

"We left and went to a movie and he fell asleep. So much for my hot date."

I was disappointed he hadn't come up to the apartment with me. I didn't want to be treated like a fragile piece of porcelain.

I waited until I was back in my apartment before I sent Rocco a text.

Me: You home?
Rocco: Yeah.
Me: Why didn't you come up to the apartment?
Rocco: You know why.
Me: I wish you had.

I waited and there wasn't any response for several minutes.

Rocco: UR not ready. Soon, baby, soon, and next time no beer.
Me: Next time no popcorn and no excuses.
Rocco: My pleasure and hopefully yours.

# CHAPTER 28

# Leanne

I made an excuse to stop by Jake's house on Sunday afternoon. I called ahead and offered to pick up Owen. Jake readily agreed, and I suspected he was looking to avoid Nichole, especially after he'd made such an ass of himself at Cassie and Steve's wedding reception.

When I arrived I found Owen sitting in front of the television, watching a movie. Happy to see me, my grandson leaped up and ran around the living room in his bare feet before racing into my arms.

"Where's Mommy?"

"She's at home," I told him as I lifted him up and rested him on my hip. It wouldn't be much longer that he'd let me do that. Owen liked to think of himself as a big boy, especially now that he attended preschool.

"Did you have a good time with your daddy?" I asked him.

Owen nodded. "He took me to see Santa and he let me dwive the golf cart."

I made eye contact with my son and gave him a thumbs-up sign. More often than not, Owen mentioned the sitters who looked after him on the weekends he was with his father. It worried me that Jake didn't spend quality time with his son.

"Can I get you anything, Mom?" Jake asked.

"Water," I said, although I wasn't thirsty. I followed him into the kitchen and Owen returned to watching his SpongeBob movie, which I swear he should know by heart by this time. The toddler sat cross-legged in front of the television with his play tow truck at his side.

Jake took two bottles of water out of the refrigerator and handed me one. His look was mildly defiant. "I suppose you're here to lecture me about last weekend. If so, don't bother."

"That wasn't my intention."

"Good."

"I'm here to talk about your father."

Jake opened his water and took a swig. "What about Dad?"

It occurred to me that Sean might not have told Jake his news. Seeing how close the two were, I found that hard to believe. "I'm worried about him."

"We all are, but there's nothing more we can do."

I could hardly believe our son's flippant reaction to the fact that his father was dying. "I think we should both do whatever we can to help him through the next six months," I said pointedly.

"What can I do?" Jake asked, stretching out his arms palms up in question. "First off, I've got my own life. I work fifty hours a week and then I've got Owen every other weekend. I don't have time for myself as it is. I'll do what I can, Mom, you know that, but there really isn't much I can do other than check up on him."

"I was hoping you'd be able to look into finding a caregiver for him."

"What?" Jake demanded. "Dad would hate that."

I knew Jake was right. Sean would intensely dislike having someone wash and feed him. "Not right away, but, you know, later."

Jake shrugged. "Let Barbara handle that."

Barbara. I didn't know any Barbara.

He must have read the question on my face, because he added, "She's one of Dad's *special* friends."

He didn't need to elaborate; I knew what he meant. I wouldn't say it, but I strongly suspected that once Sean's health deteriorated to the point he needed a caregiver, Barbara would be long gone.

"Have you seen the house?" I asked. "He definitely needs a housekeeper."

"Then let him hire one. I'm not his babysitter." He rolled his eyes and reached for the water bottle, taking another long drink. "Mom, I don't mean to sound callous, but the fact is I've got my own life and my own problems. It hasn't exactly been easy for me. I'll do what I can for Dad, you know I will."

This conversation was an eye-opener for me. I hadn't realized how self-centered and self-absorbed my son was. In many ways Jake was indeed his father's son. "Maybe hiring a housekeeper is something else I should leave to Barbara," I suggested with a hint of a smile.

"Not a bad idea," Jake said, grinning. "But you should know that woman is a slob."

That helped explain why the house was such a disaster. "I cleaned the house for him when he was in the hospital. The skimpy underwear I found in the sofa cushion must belong to her."

"Or Candace or Susan."

*Oh.* I held up my hand. I didn't need to listen to a litany of names. I decided it was time to get serious. "Your dad asked me to help him select a casket."

"What?" Jake nearly spewed the water from his mouth. "That's a bit macabre, isn't it?"

"Perhaps," I said. I had trouble wrapping my mind around the fact that Sean had cancer. "It might seem premature, but he asked me to help and I didn't feel I could refuse."

Jake rolled his eyes. "Dad always has been something of a drama queen." He hesitated, then added, "I guess in his case it would be drama king."

"I promised I'd go with him." It was plain now that Jake was in denial and couldn't accept that his father had only six months to live.

My son slouched down on a kitchen chair. "Have you told Nikolai about this?"

I hadn't. "Not yet."

He screwed the cap back on the water bottle. "I heard about him and Dad squaring off. Dad said Nikolai made it clear he was *your man* now and that Dad had had his chance. Apparently, he told Dad that he was a fool." Jake snickered. "I thought that was low, seeing how weak Dad was, just home from the hospital."

"I don't know what they said. Nikolai asked me to wait in the car."

Jake kept his head lowered. "Seems you're not the only one who's moved on. Nichole certainly has."

"It looks that way," I said.

Jake ran his hand down his face. "It was stupid of me to make a scene at Cassie's wedding," he murmured, and sounded genuinely regretful.

I purposely didn't respond. He didn't need me to confirm what he already knew.

"I don't like this man she's seeing," he said, and his jaw tightened.

I had the feeling Jake would feel that way about any man who was interested in Nichole. "Rocco's a good guy."

"He isn't, Mom." He looked up and his eyes were intense. "How well do either of you know him?"

"Only what Nichole has told me." It wasn't like I'd paid for a background search on him. "I know he's a single father. He owns Potter Towing and works long hours."

"Were you aware he's got a record for assault and avoiding arrest? Plus, there's a bunch of other issues with him that are a matter of public record." Jake said it as if he was proud of it. "That isn't the kind of man I want hanging around my son."

"How long ago was that?" I asked, because that didn't sound like the Rocco I knew.

"A few years, but it's on his record. If he didn't own that company of his he probably wouldn't be able to get a job. Not with an assault conviction and jail time."

"Owen loves him." The minute the words were out I knew it was the wrong thing to say.

"That's another thing," Jake flared, angry now. "All

Owen talks about is Rocco this and Rocco that. How
do you think that makes me feel? I'm Owen's father."
His voice rose with each word until he was close to
shouting. "It's like Rocco is stealing my son away from
me. I was out in my golf cart driving around in the
friggin' cold and rain this morning because I felt the
need to compete with a jailbird. There's something
wrong with this picture."

"Owen loves you."

"Sure he does, but I had to tell Nichole to leave that
stupid jumpsuit at the house because that was the
only thing Owen wanted to wear. Not only that, it's
the friggin' tow truck he plays with constantly. I buy
the kid an iPad mini and instead he plays with this
plastic truck."

I knew the coveralls Rocco got him had been a
source of contention as well. It was a battle every
other weekend for Nichole to keep them at the apartment, for fear Jake would make them disappear.

"Owen is going through a truck phase. Don't worry,
he'll grow out of it."

"I'm not letting that man steal my wife and my son
away from me. I'm telling you right now, it ain't happening."

I didn't argue with him. It wouldn't do any good
and it might well put an additional strain on our already rocky relationship.

The rest of our conversation went fairly well, although Jake's cavalier attitude toward his father's
cancer disturbed me. Jake had yet to accept that this
was real and that his father was dying.

In many ways Sean and Jake were a lot alike, certainly in temperament. When they were on the outs

I'd always been the one to smooth over their differences. Mostly I was gone from the picture now and they'd been left to their own devices, which led me to think there might be a misunderstanding brewing between them.

"Everything okay between you and your dad?" I asked, on the off chance I was right.

Jake shrugged. "We're fine. Don't worry about it, Mom."

But I did worry, despite the fact that I was no longer married to Sean and my relationship with my son was on shaky ground.


Monday afternoon I stopped by the deli at about the time that I knew Nikolai would finish his shift. As soon as he saw me, his face lit up with happy anticipation. I'd never had this sort of loving reaction from a man before and found it addictive.

"My Leanne." I loved the sound of my name in his strong accent. Sometimes, when Nikolai wasn't around and I found myself missing him, I'd close my eyes and hear the echo of him saying my name in my mind.

Nikolai grabbed hold of my hands and gave them a gentle squeeze before he leaned forward and kissed my cheek. "I am happy you here."

"Do you have a few minutes?" I asked.

"For you all time every day, always." He wrapped his arm around my waist and led me out of the deli. "What you need tell me? You be at school tonight, yes?"

"Yes."

"This not wait until class?"

"I thought it best for us to talk before class."

"What is this about?" he asked, and then he stiffened, as if he'd guessed the subject. "This have to do with that man who not love you, right?"

"Sean called me last Monday . . ."

He released me and took a step back. "You wait a whole week to tell me?"

I could see he was upset. "Nikolai, I have no obligation to tell you who I talk to and who I don't. If you think I do, then we need to have a serious discussion."

I could tell he didn't like it, but he slowly nodded and admitted, "You right about that. All I want is to protect you."

I wrapped my arm around his elbow as we continued walking, no real destination in mind. "I heard you told Sean that I'm your woman now."

Nikolai exhaled harshly. "That make you want to have serious discussion with me, too?"

"No." Knowing he felt that way made me want to kiss him senseless. "I'm rather happy you told him."

His smile was as wide as the Columbia River, but then he sobered. "Why Sean call you now? He want you clean for him again? I put my nose down if he ask you that. No way my woman clean for that man."

"Sean is dying, Nikolai. He has cancer." I didn't feel the need to soften the truth.

Nikolai stopped walking. "Cancer?"

"The doctor set him up with a regimen of chemotherapy and radiation that they hope would prolong his life."

"I am so sorry, my Leanne. So sorry." He hugged me close, as if to absorb the shock of this. I felt warm and safe in his arms. Eventually we broke apart and continued our stroll.

"I'm sorry for him, too. Sean called to tell me that he's decided against receiving any of the treatment."

"Why would he do that?"

I had the very same question. "The chemo and radiation would only prolong his life. It won't cure the cancer. His doctor told him he has six months to live without treatment and a year with treatment. Sean chose to live the last months of his life to the fullest."

"He live only six months?"

"I promised you that I wouldn't cook or clean for Sean."

"No way. I don't care if you be mad. You have serious discussion and it not change my mind."

Oh, how I loved Nikolai. He made me so happy that it was hard not to love him. "I talked to my son yesterday about his father. Something is going on between the two of them, but I don't know what it is. Jake is angry with his father, but he is refusing to discuss it with me." It hurt me that Jake felt the way he did.

"I am sorry to hear," Nikolai whispered.

"This morning I talked to Sean and asked if he'd like me to hire a cleaning service for him. He said he would greatly appreciate if I would."

"You not clean?" he clarified.

"No, but I'll find a company who can come in and see to it."

"Sean not able to do this on his own?"

The truth was Sean could, but he hadn't to this point. Rather than admit that, I subtly changed the subject. "He's returning to work in a few days and he asked that I not let anyone in the office know the diagnosis."

"If it happen to me I not want people to know," Nikolai agreed.

I was grateful for his understanding.

We walked a short distance before he asked, "That all you do, right? Find cleaning person?"

"Later I might need to hire a caregiver." I didn't trust that task to Jake or to the elusive Barbara.

"When the time comes, I help. Okay?"

"Okay."

My arm tightened around Nikolai's. "There's one last thing Sean asked me to do for him this week."

"Whatever it is I go with you."

"Not this time, Nikolai. This is something Sean and I need to do alone."

"Whatever it is he ask you I not like." He narrowed his eyes. "What it is he want you for now?"

"Sean wants me to help plan his funeral and pick out his casket."

Nikolai went still and quiet. "I not like. I not trust this man, but if you feel you need to do this, then okay. I not keep you from your promise."

"Thank you, Nikolai."

"He not love you."

"I know."

"I am the one who love you."

"And I'm the one who loves you."

Nikolai beamed me another one of his beautiful smiles and then walked me to my car. I would see him later that evening and I looked forward to it.

# CHAPTER 29

# Nichole

Jake asked to see me on Tuesday afternoon and I agreed. We hadn't spoken since Cassie's wedding and I assumed he wanted to apologize. His behavior at the reception was completely out of character for him. I knew, given time, he'd regret making a scene.

We met at a Starbucks close to the high school. He was waiting for me by the time I arrived and was sitting at a table in the corner by the window. I saw that he'd bought me a drink. He stood as I approached, his eyes dark and serious.

"You look"—he paused and cleared his throat—"beautiful, as always."

"Thank you." I saw the regret in his eyes as I took a seat. How different our lives might have been if he'd taken into consideration the consequences of his cheating.

"I got you a skinny mocha latte," he said, scooting the drink a little closer to my side of the table.

He remembered that was my favorite. "That was

thoughtful." It would forever remain a mystery how my ex-husband could be considerate and kind about the small details of life and disregard the most basic.

Jake sipped his coffee. "I thought it was time we talked."

"I agree."

"First off, I'm sorry about showing up at Cassie's wedding. That was stupid of me."

"I agree," I said, echoing my earlier comment. "I appreciate the apology, Jake. I don't want us to be enemies. We're Owen's parents and it's important that we treat each other with respect."

"I want that, too." He shifted and leaned slightly forward. "There's another reason I asked you to meet me this afternoon."

"Okay." With Christmas approaching, there could be any number of details we needed to sort through. We had our parenting plan in place and this was his year to have Owen for Christmas Day. I didn't like to think of not having my son with me, but I was a fair person.

"I'm not doing this to start a legal war between us, Nichole. I want you to know that."

"A legal war?" I repeated, both flustered and alert at once. "What do you mean?"

"The bottom line is I don't feel good about you dating Rocco. I don't know how involved you are with him or if you're sleeping with him—"

I cut him off. "What's between Rocco and me is none of your business." I could feel my anger rising and struggled to hold on to my temper. My hand tightened around my latte. I didn't care if Jake liked Rocco or not. Jake had no say in who I dated.

"The man has a police record."

"I know that." Jake wasn't telling me anything I didn't already know. From the beginning, Rocco had been honest with me.

"He's spent time in jail."

"I know all that," I repeated, a bit more forcefully this time. "He paid for his crime and has moved on. He learned his lesson. Rocco isn't the same man he was fifteen years ago."

Jake's gaze narrowed and his face was full of accusation. "I knew you were going to defend him. You're in love with him, aren't you?"

"That's not your concern."

"And that's where you're wrong. It is very much my concern."

"I think we're finished talking here." I started to get up, but Jake firmly grabbed hold of my wrist.

I wanted to jerk free, and I would have if not for the unyielding hard look in his eyes. "Sit down, Nichole. We need to finish this conversation. Otherwise I'll have my attorney do it for me."

My heart was pounding erratically and my breathing had gone shallow as I sat back down. Jake released my wrist and I sipped the latte because my mouth had gone surprisingly dry.

"Who you date is very much my concern, because of Owen. I don't want my son associating with a man who has a criminal record. If that makes me a bad guy, then so be it."

All at once I knew where this was coming from. Jake was afraid Rocco was stealing Owen away from him. "You're jealous because Owen loves Rocco," I said, hoping to reason with him, "but Jake, our son loves you, too. Owen is only three. The capacity of his heart is huge."

Jake shook his head, refusing to listen. "Rocco is a negative influence."

"How can you say that? Rocco has been great with Owen from the moment we met."

"It's more than that," Jake insisted.

"What do you mean?"

"Okay, fine, if you must know, I want our son to have bigger aspirations than driving a truck," he said, and shook his head as though disgusted by the thought.

It probably wasn't a good idea to laugh, but I couldn't help myself. "Owen is three years old," I reminded him. "He's going through a stage where he loves big trucks. I think it's a little premature to worry about his career choice now."

"You think this is funny?" Jake demanded, his voice as hard as nails.

"Frankly, yes."

"Trust me, it's not, Nichole. You have an option here, and if you think this is a bluff then you're dead wrong. I'm as serious as I've ever been in my life."

"What is it you want from me?" I asked, finding this entire conversation preposterous. I could only hope that, given time, Jake would realize how ridiculous he sounded.

"I want you to stop seeing Rocco."

I was stunned. "No way. I refuse to let you dictate my relationship with Rocco or any other man just because you don't happen to like the fact he drives a tow truck."

"It's a lot more than his occupation, Nichole. It's his past."

I refused to hold Rocco's past against him. "Everything you mentioned happened years ago."

"I don't care. Either you break it off with Rocco or I'm going to file for full custody of Owen."

Unable to speak, for one wild moment all I could do was stare at my ex-husband. Anger gripped me, followed by shock. I'd stood up to Jake from the moment I'd learned he'd cheated. I'd been strong, but when it came to my son and the possibility of losing him, I was immediately filled with terror. Jake knew Owen was my weakness. I couldn't lose Owen. I couldn't let Jake take my son away from me.

"As soon as I present the courts with the evidence of Rocco's past you won't have a leg to stand on. Sorry to use the cliché, but you know what I mean."

"Are you serious, Jake?" I was light-headed from the shock of it. No way on earth could I afford the attorney fees to fight Jake. All at once I felt sick to my stomach.

"I had the papers drawn up already." He pulled them out of his inside jacket pocket and handed them to me. I unfolded the sheets and read the contents. This wasn't a threat or a joke—Jake was serious. My head was reeling; I was unable to believe my ex would follow through with his threat.

"Will you do it, Nichole, or do you want this to get ugly?"

I stared back at him for a long time, taking into consideration what it would mean to get caught up in a legal battle.

"If you think I'm doing this for selfish reasons, you

should know I've met someone, too. Carlie's a good person; we met at work, and she'd make Owen a wonderful stepmother. This isn't a bluff, Nichole. I don't want to file, but I will."

Jake was serious.

"Either you break it off with Rocco or we're going to court. I won't have my son spending time with a felon. And it isn't just Rocco, it's the men he hires who are on work release. It isn't safe for you or our son to be around this man. What are you thinking, Nichole? Don't you understand the risk you're taking with Owen?"

I closed my eyes, battling down my outrage. "I . . . I won't let you manipulate me with threats."

"Fine, then. I'm filing the petition." He stood and I knew he wasn't bluffing.

"Okay, okay," I said in a panic, unable to breathe. "I'll do it." I was sick to my stomach and my head was throbbing. Everything Jake said about Rocco was true. He did have a record; he hired men on work release. I knew how all that would look before a court of law. I'd always been strong, standing up to Jake. I'd made difficult decisions before. Owen made me vulnerable, and Jake knew that. My son was everything to me. As much as I cared about Rocco, I wouldn't risk losing custody of Owen.

"I want to be sure we're clear," he said. "You are agreeing to sever your relationship with Rocco?"

My heart was in my throat and I nodded.

"Say it."

"I won't be seeing Rocco again."

"Thank you," Jake said, his voice softening. "I know you think I'm doing this for my own selfish reasons, but I'm not. I'm doing this for the sake of my son."

I sat in my car and phoned Leanne to ask her to pick Owen up from daycare for me. Something in my voice must have alerted her to the fact that I was terribly upset.

"What's happened?" she asked.

"I . . . I need to talk to Rocco." I still hadn't completely wrapped my head around Jake's ultimatum. One thing was certain: I needed to end it with him. My stomach was in knots, and the sooner I severed our ties the better. If I thought about it too much I might be tempted to stand up to Jake and take him on. I would if it was anything but custody of my son. The risk was too great.

I drove to Potter Towing and sat in the car for several minutes, wondering what I could say, how I would find a way to do this. Rocco had always been honest with me, never hiding his past. From the first he'd been completely open. It killed me to know I was going to hurt this man who'd only been decent and kind to Owen and me.

He deserved the truth, but I didn't dare tell him, for fear of how he'd react. I was afraid Rocco would confront Jake and it would be a standoff much like there'd been the night I picked up Owen when he was sick. Jake would look for a way to taunt Rocco into a fight and then have him arrested for assault. I could see it as clearly as an Oscar-winning movie.

The crux of Jake's demands wasn't his fear of Rocco corrupting Owen or me. Jake was jealous and he couldn't bear the thought of me loving another man. Nor could his ego take the fact that Owen looked up to and admired Rocco.

Once the trembling had subsided I climbed out of my car and went into the office. The minute Shawntelle saw me, she left her desk and hurried out of the glassed-in area. "You okay, girlfriend?" she asked. "You're pale as a ghost."

I tried to smile. "Rocco around?"

"He's out on a run, but he should be back in the next thirty minutes. Come sit down. I'll get you some water or coffee or whatever you need."

"Water," I said, more to hold on to something than because of thirst.

Shawntelle brought me into her office and sat me down in the chair across from her desk. Rocco had been good enough to give her a chance, and I loved him for his willingness to hire her.

Shawntelle brought me a bottle of water and handed it to me. I sipped from it.

"You feel better now?"

*Did I? Doubtful.* "Yes, thanks."

"You look like someone died," she said, and then slapped her hand over her mouth. "Did you lose someone, sweetie? Me and my big mouth. I can't seem to keep my foot out of it. I'm sorry."

"No one died." Something had, though. It was my heart. I had to remind myself the sole function of my heart was to pump blood, not to become emotionally involved. Especially if that meant I was going to be hurt or hurt someone else.

"I'm still seeing Jerome," Shawntelle said, blushing a little, "and I haven't let him talk me into going to bed with him, either." She laughed and sounded a little giddy. "Not that I haven't been tempted. I'm telling you right now that man could get a gold star for the way he kisses. I swear his kisses are strong enough to melt the panties right off me."

I knew exactly how she felt. Rocco's kisses did the same for me. A stab of pain went through me at the thought of never being in his arms again.

"I'm thinking of introducing him to my kids. The way I figure it, if he still wants me after meeting all five of them, then he's worth keeping around. If he runs as far away from me as he can, I'll know all he wants is mattress time, and I ain't putting up with that."

"Smart girl."

Shawntelle rose from behind her desk. "I think that's Rocco rolling in now."

"Thanks," I said, and finished off the water. I tossed the plastic bottle into the recycling container and walked out of the office and into the parking lot.

Rocco must have had a premonition, because he didn't smile when he saw me. He climbed out of the tow truck and walked toward me. The wind was cold, but the chill I felt had nothing to do with the weather.

"Nichole?"

"Do you have a minute?"

"Sure." He started toward the office, expecting me to follow.

"It would be best if we could do this privately," I said, and already my voice had started to tremble.

"All right."

I felt him distancing himself from me emotionally and I had yet to tell him the reason why I was here. Looking around the yard, I bit down on my lower lip.

I'd lost count of the number of times Rocco had taken Owen out driving trucks. Owen sat on Rocco's lap and Rocco let my son steer while Rocco discreetly kept his hands low on the wheel. Owen was going to miss Rocco as much as I would.

Rocco led me into one of the empty garage bays.

"What's up?" His eyes bored into mine.

I couldn't look at him, so I focused on the concrete floor. "I've been doing a lot of thinking lately and I feel it might be a good idea if we didn't see each other for a while."

My words were met with silence until I couldn't bear it any longer and looked up. Rocco didn't show any emotion one way or another. He didn't try to argue with me, didn't ask questions. He seemed completely accepting of my decision. In fact, he said nothing.

The silence between us was terrible. "I'm sorry," I whispered, not knowing what else to say.

"Basically you're saying you want to take a break."

I nodded.

"No."

"No?" I asked, and blinked.

"We're done."

The complete lack of emotion on his part shook me. I was stunned with disbelief. "That's all you have to say?"

"Did you want me to beg you to reconsider? Is that what you want?" His eyes were hard and cold.

"No," I whispered, hardly able to get the word out.

"Do you think this surprises me?"

I didn't know how to answer.

"I have been more or less waiting for you to break it off from the beginning, but especially after last Friday."

He thought this had to do with what I'd learned about him: his one-woman, one-night policy. That so wasn't the case, but I couldn't tell him otherwise.

I fought back the urge to argue, but he apparently didn't want to hear it anyway.

"You said what you came to say. Now go. Get out of here."

All I could do was stare at him.

"Leave," he said, forcefully.

The anger in him caused me to take two steps in retreat.

"Get the hell out of my life," he blared.

I blinked. "Go," he demanded. "Just go."

I walked over to my car and stood there feeling bewildered, bereft, and alone. Five minutes must have passed before I found the strength to open my car door.

A terrible commotion took place behind me. I knew it had to be Rocco. He had remained in the garage. I flinched as I heard something crash. The sound was followed by another and then another. Each discordant crash made me jerk.

As I drove away the sense of loss was nearly overwhelming. Numbness had settled into my bones. I don't know how I got through the heavy traffic of Portland's downtown area or even how I managed to drive home. The next thing I knew I was in my parking space at the apartment complex with no memory of how I'd gotten there.

Again I sat in my car for several minutes while the dead feeling in my heart kept me immobile. I hadn't known what to expect from Rocco, but it hadn't been that cold, hard resolve of acceptance, as if not seeing me again was of little consequence.

CHAPTER 30

# Leanne

Nichole told me about her meeting with Jake and I had to say I was furious. I should have guessed he was hiding something when I'd talked to him last Sunday. He knew Rocco was no threat to Nichole or Owen. To suggest otherwise was a new low for my son. I needed to cool off before I talked to Jake, but when I did, he was going to hear my opinion loud and clear. I'd done my best to stay out of affairs between the two, but this time I couldn't keep quiet.

My bigger concern was Nichole. She was heartsick, and frankly, I was worried about her. It was as if she were living in a fog. When she'd first learned about Jake's infidelity she'd been angry and smart. One of the first things she did was call a college friend who was an attorney. She found out exactly what she needed to do to protect herself financially. I admired how she'd taken control of the situation and how she'd handled herself. I'd witnessed plenty of emotion in her then. She'd been crushed, but she knew how to take care of herself.

Not so now. It was as if she was wandering waist-deep in regret. How she managed to teach and maintain her daily schedule was beyond me. I tried to talk to her several times, but she just stared into the distance. I sincerely doubted she even heard me.

Sean and I had set up a visit to the funeral home on Friday afternoon to make the arrangements for his burial. Apparently, it wasn't as simple a process as Sean had made it sound. Most likely he didn't understand everything himself.

Nikolai was still not happy about me doing this, but I promised I'd connect with him as soon as we were finished.

I called him before I headed to Lake Oswego.

"You call as soon you finish, okay?" Nikolai asked.

"I will."

"You remember you with me now."

"I remember," I said, hoping that would be enough to reassure him.

"I wait to breathe till you call."

I couldn't imagine what he thought might happen. It wasn't like I would be so overwhelmed by Sean's sad news that I'd agree to marry him again. That was so unlikely that I nearly laughed out loud.

I met Sean at the house. He'd only been back to work that week and wasn't working full days. From what he said, it was unlikely he'd ever return full-time. Sean wanted to work long enough to get his accounts in order before he handed them off to the new person assuming his position. I knew it was hard for him to talk about his lack of a future, so I avoided the subject.

Sean answered the door and I could see that the house was in disarray *again*. I'd talked to a cleaning service that came with excellent recommendations and sent them out to clean.

"Thank you for this," he said, sounding more reserved than I could ever remember. "I can't tell you how much I appreciate you going with me, Leanne. I don't know that I could ever have managed it alone."

I looked around the house. "The cleaning service didn't work out?"

"No, unfortunately."

"What happened?"

He shrugged and looked chagrined with himself. "I was having a bad day. One of the workers broke my favorite coffee cup and in a fit of anger I fired them." He looked away, as if embarrassed. "It was stupid of me. I regretted it almost right away and called the service back and apologized."

"What did they say?"

"Just that it didn't look like I was a good fit for them. Can't say I blame them; I behaved badly."

He impressed me with his willingness to admit he'd been wrong and the fact that he'd regretted blowing up at the work crew. I'd done my best for him. I wasn't going to look for another cleaning service. As Nikolai was quick to remind me, Sean was fully capable of finding one on his own.

"You could always ask Barbara to tidy up for you," I teased.

A stricken look came over Sean. "You know about Barbara?"

"And Candace and Susan. Jake mentioned them."

His face fell and he looked away. "As soon as Barbara heard about the cancer she quit taking my calls. Guess she isn't interested in dating a dying man."

That said a lot about the women my ex chose to associate with. "I'm sorry to hear that." I deserved a reward for not reminding him about the other women he'd paraded through his life before and after the divorce.

When it was time to go, Sean set the security code and we walked to the car. It was best that I drive. As soon as we were seated and comfortable, I asked him, "Everything okay between you and Jake?"

Once again he looked uncomfortable. "Mostly."

"I think he's in denial about your cancer."

Sean agreed, his eyes sad. "I got that impression. He hardly checks in on me these days. If he doesn't see or talk to me, then he won't need to face the fact that I won't be around much longer."

I suspected Sean was right. Avoidance was something Jake had inherited from his father.

Sean had chosen a funeral home several miles from Lake Oswego. I assumed he'd want one closer to the area in which he lived. He gave me directions and explained.

"I looked at several cemeteries online and chose this one because it has a beautiful view of the water."

I frowned, wondering why he would consider that an important criterion. To remind him he wouldn't be able to enjoy that view would have been unkind, so I didn't, although I was tempted.

We arrived in plenty of time for the appointment. The funeral director met us and led us both into his office. As we sat there discussing the details of Sean's funeral and burial I felt myself starting to get emotional. It was like the reality of it all hit me in the face. This was no joke; Sean was dying.

This man I had once loved with all my heart would soon be gone from my life in a way that brought me pain, an emotion I hadn't expected. Oh, we had our issues and had for years. I'd divorced him. I hadn't lived with him in more than two years, but I'd never wished this on him.

What surprised me most was how accepting Sean was of his demise. He chose a particular financial plan that was a little above the average, but not much. When we finished going over a number of options, flowers, music, and a dozen other minute details I'd never considered, we were led into a room where the caskets were displayed.

Sean ran his hand over the mahogany one and I noted that all the blood had drained from his face. For a moment I thought he might faint. I wrapped my arm around him and he thanked me with a weak smile. "This one is fine," he whispered.

"Would it be all right if we finished this up at a later date?" I said. "My husband is weak. I need to get him home."

"Of course, of course. Call when you can and we'll schedule another appointment."

"Thank you." I led Sean out to the car and helped him inside.

He waited until I was sitting beside him before he spoke. He reached for my hand and clenched it to the point of pain. "Thank you," he whispered brokenly, and I knew he was thanking me for more than helping him this afternoon.

"I never deserved you," he added, and I swear I could hear tears in his voice.

I started back to Lake Oswego and I kept a close watch on Sean. He leaned his head against the passenger window and closed his eyes. "You called me your husband," he whispered.

"You were for thirty-five years."

"Thirty-four."

I found it amazing he would remember such a small detail. "All right, thirty-four years and seven months."

When we reached the house, I helped Sean inside. He leaned heavily on me and I was afraid to leave him alone. "Can I get you anything?" I asked.

"I'm cold," he whispered.

"I'll get you an afghan," I said, until I remembered that I had taken the best one with me when we divorced. Sean was so rarely home he'd never used it. I found another in the hall closet. Unfolding it, I spread it over him and tucked it around his shoulders. "Better?" I asked.

He smiled and thanked me.

"When was the last time you ate?" I asked.

He looked terribly tired. "This morning."

I was afraid of that. I went to the refrigerator and brought out the eggs I'd purchased Thanksgiving Day, along with bread and butter. I had the pan on the stove when Sean stopped me.

"Please don't."

"You haven't eaten, Sean. You need something in your stomach. It isn't any wonder you're weak and pale."

"Nikolai . . . he wouldn't want you to do this."

The reminder caught me up short. I'd promised Nikolai that I wouldn't cook or clean for Sean again, but these were extenuating circumstances.

"He'll just have to deal with it," I said, cracking the eggs against the side of the bowl.

"I don't want to cause trouble between you two."

"You won't." And he wouldn't. I'd make sure of that.

I fixed Sean an omelet and set it on a tray in front of his recliner, along with a glass of orange juice and two slices of buttered toast. Sean ate as if he was ravenous. When he finished I washed the dishes I'd used. It seemed a little ridiculous to ignore everything else in the sink.

By the time I finished loading the dishwasher there was a full load. I started it and washed by hand the pans that didn't fit inside, and then wiped down the kitchen countertops.

When I looked over at Sean he was sound asleep. I imagined his body needed the rest. I didn't want to disturb him. I knew it might be a while before he would eat again. One of his favorite meals, beef Stroganoff, was cooked in the Crock-Pot. Checking the freezer, I saw that he had the meat and I found the other ingredients in the cupboard. I assembled everything and set the Crock-Pot on low. Sean would be able to make several dinners out of this and it had been nothing for me to get it going for him.

I was about to sneak out and let him sleep when I saw that the living room wasn't so much a mess as I'd first thought. Newspapers and mail were carelessly set about, but that was mostly it. I took care of the papers and then fluffed up the pillows. Once I got started it seemed silly to stop. By the time I left the house I'd changed his sheets and cleaned the bathroom, too.

Not until I started back to Portland did I remember that I'd promised to call Nikolai. I knew he would be upset with me, but I didn't dare use my cell while driving. I'd waited this long, a few more minutes wouldn't matter.

When I arrived at my apartment building, I was shocked to see Nikolai pacing the foyer.

"Nikolai, what are you doing here?" I asked, hardly knowing what to think.

"We talk serious," he said, his eyes dark and brooding. We rode the elevator up together. As soon as we entered my apartment, he turned to me. His eyes were like a laser beam focused directly on me. "Why you not answer your phone? I call and call and you no answer."

I grabbed the phone out of my purse and remembered I'd put it on silent when we'd gone in to talk to the funeral director. "I'm so sorry," I said and explained.

"What take you so long? You say two hours, maybe three. You gone almost seven."

Had it really been that long? Apparently so. "Sean was tired and hadn't eaten, so I made him an omelet . . ."

"You cook for him?" Nikolai's eyes widened. "You promise you not do that again."

"I know, but Nikolai . . ."

"It not take so many hours for you to cook eggs." He grabbed hold of my hands and looked down at them. His eyes widened. "You clean, too. You become maid to this man when you promise me you not do this."

He was right. I knew he was right. "Have a little compassion, Nikolai," I said, not wanting to argue with him. "Sean is sick. He's growing weaker by the day."

He glared at me as if seeing me for the first time, taking in the pleading look in my eyes. I don't know what he saw that made him retreat a step. A stricken look came over him. He opened his mouth to speak and then closed it again. It took a second attempt before he was able to utter the words. "You still love him."

His words shook me and I swallowed hard while I processed the emotions racing through me. Nikolai was right. I did love Sean. The shock of it hit me. I assumed all I'd felt was sympathy, compassion, but it was more. I still cared for Sean, despite the fact that we were divorced. He continued to hold a place in my heart. "We were married . . ." Sitting in the funeral director's office, I'd been overwhelmed by the sense of loss, knowing the man I had divorced would soon be gone from this world.

"This different," Nikolai said. "You tell me one time you love memory. You love the man from when you first married, but that love dried up and died. What was left not like young love. It something else."

I remembered well the conversation. "You loved Magdalena."

"She loved me. This man, he not love you. He use you. He treat you like tissue. He blow his nose on you and then throw you away."

"You're wrong, Nikolai," I argued. "This is different. Sean is different." I remembered the way my ex-husband had clenched my hand earlier, as if holding on to me was all that kept him going.

"No," Nikolai said loudly, startling me. "No, he not different. The one who is different is you."

I sagged onto the sofa and covered my face with my hands. A chill went down my back. In that moment I knew Nikolai was right. All those years I'd craved my husband's love, needed it, and now he was dying and desperately needed me. I couldn't say for sure if Sean had changed, but I knew I had. No matter how hard this would be and regardless of my feelings for Nikolai, helping Sean was something I had to do. For Sean, certainly, but also for myself.

"What you say?" Nikolai demanded. "Tell me what you say?"

I shook my head. I had nothing to tell him.

"That is what I think," he whispered. "I not fight dying man. I not win. I leave you now. I not bake bread for you again."

I wanted to call out and stop him, but I knew he was right. The door clicked gently and all I seemed capable of doing was staring at it. Nikolai had left me. He was gone, and instinctively I knew he wasn't coming back.

I barely slept or ate all weekend. Sean called me twice, needing my help, and despite everything I went to him, cooked and cleaned for him. He was grateful to the point of tears. I couldn't abandon him.

Monday night when I arrived for class Nikolai wasn't in the parking lot waiting for me. Once inside I was handed a notice that told me Nikolai Janchenko had withdrawn from the class.

# CHAPTER 31

# Nichole

Teaching classes was torture for me. It didn't help that the kids' heads were wrapped around Christmas and the upcoming winter break. I somehow made it from day to day for the next two weeks. Every class taxed me to the limit. All I wanted to do was curl into a tight ball and hibernate, but that was impossible.

If Jake had been looking for a way to punish me for having the gall to divorce him, then he'd found the perfect torture. To my dying day I would always remember the look of pain that flashed ever so briefly in Rocco's eyes before he closed himself off from me. Rocco had been nothing but wonderful to me and I missed him.

Owen asked daily when he would see Rocco and Kaylene again. I put him off until he had a crying fit. After the first week I'd been forced to tell my son that we probably wouldn't be able to see Rocco again. It was then that I felt the first cloud of emotion break through my fog of pain and loss.

Friday afternoon I caught sight of Kaylene in the hallway. Students were moving up and down the crowded aisle, rushing between classes. I froze and she did, too. Her eyes held mine prisoner and then narrowed. The two of us had always had a great relationship. My heart immediately filled with questions. I wanted to know how Rocco was. Knowing I'd hurt him was a constant pain I carried with me. I was hurting, too, far more than I ever thought I would.

Kaylene's gaze speared me with what could be described only as hate before she whirled around and marched off in the opposite direction. For the rest of the day I couldn't get her look out of my head. After school I sat in my classroom and propped my elbows on my desk. I needed help. I couldn't do this any longer. I couldn't face another day of this.

I had no options; my back was to the wall. Jake had threatened to challenge me for custody of my son. Deep down I knew he didn't want Owen with him. Having to care for a three-year-old would put a damper on his lifestyle. What he wanted was to hurt me and hurt Rocco, and he'd succeeded, and I'd let him do this to us.

To this point I hadn't talked to anyone about this except Leanne. She'd been furious with Jake and promised to talk to him. It hadn't happened. Sean seemed to be slipping downhill a little each day and she'd spent a lot of time with him. Besides, she was dealing with her own heartache. I wasn't sure what had happened between her and Nikolai, but I knew they were no longer seeing each other.

Owen was going with his father for the weekend and Jake picked him up at the daycare center. I preferred it that way, and I knew he did, too. I hadn't been sleeping well and was grateful on Saturday that I was scheduled to work at Dress for Success. It gave me something to do rather than remain at home and stew. Our Christmas tree wasn't up yet, nor any of the decorations. I wasn't in the Christmas spirit.

I hadn't been in the shop more than a half-hour when Shawntelle came bursting in the door, opening it so hard it was a wonder the glass didn't shatter. She stood just inside the store, hands on her ample hips, searching the area until she saw me.

This woman was a force to be reckoned with when she was angry. Seeing her now was downright scary. She pointed her index finger at me and shouted, "You and me, sister, are going to have a come-to-Jesus talk."

A couple women had stopped in to do some Christmas shopping. They took one look at Shawntelle and headed for the door as if their lives were in danger. As for me, I was rooted in one spot, unable to move. Shawntelle didn't need to explain why she wanted to talk to me. I already knew.

She marched over to me as if she was related to Attila the Hun. "You better have a damn good reason for what you did to Rocco," she demanded.

I took one look at her and tried to smile. "How is he?" I asked, desperate for news of Rocco.

"How do you expect? That man is hurting. No one's ever seen him like this. He nearly destroyed the garage, tossing around every tool he could find; he punched his fist through the wall, and now he's in such a bear of a mood no one dares talk to him."

I closed my eyes, afraid if I murmured a single word I wouldn't be able to hold back the tears.

"What's with you, girl? You got yourself a good man and then you treat him like this?" Her eyes were full of disgust. "You're not half the woman I thought you were."

She was right and I knew it.

"Jerome sat Rocco down with a six-pack and you know what Rocco said? He said he always wanted to know what loving a woman heart and soul felt like. Now he knows and all he can say is it's a bitch."

I covered my mouth with my hand. It felt as if my legs were about to fold on me. Reaching out, I grabbed hold of a display rack for fear I was about to crumble to the floor.

"What kind of woman are you?" Shawntelle spat. "Why would you do that to a man for no good reason?"

"For my son," I whispered.

"You're not making any sense. Don't matter, 'cause you ain't no friend of mine. Not anymore. I thought you were different. Rocco did, too, but you proved to us both exactly the kind of person you are. I don't want anything more to do with you." Having said her piece, she stalked out of the shop with her head in the air, as if an entire marching band was directly behind her.

For several seconds there was dead silence in the shop. It took that long for me to breathe again.

Once home, I reached for my cell and stared at it for a long time. I needed someone to talk to, someone who would help me see my way through this emotional minefield. My sister Cassie had been through much worse, and while I hated to burden her with my troubles, I was fast growing desperate.

We connected right away. "Hey, Nichole. How's it going?" she asked, cheerful and happy, and she had every right to be.

"Okay. Just checking in on the newlyweds. How's married life?" I did my best to sound upbeat.

"We're loving it. Steve and I are spending the day getting my house ready to put up for sale."

"Great."

"How's Owen?"

"Good." I swallowed tightly.

"Rocco?"

I heard a slight hesitation in her voice, as if she'd caught on to the fact that there was something amiss with me. It was then that I lost it. The tears seemed to burst out of me in a storm of emotion and I blurted out the whole dreadful story, starting with Jake's and my meeting at Starbucks and ending up with Shawntelle's visit that morning.

"Nichole, Nichole," Cassie said, stopping me. "I can't understand you when you're crying so hard."

"What part didn't you get?" I asked between sobs.

"Okay, let me see if I've got this straight. You are no longer seeing Rocco because Jake threatened to take you to court for custody of Owen?"

"Yes," I answered, with a hiccupping sob.

"And Shawn hates you?"

"Shawntelle . . . she works for Rocco and is my friend. Or used to be. Now she hates me, too, and I don't blame her." At this point I didn't feel like I had a friend left in the world.

"And you're sobbing your heart out because you love Rocco?"

"Yes. And I hurt him so badly."

Cassie released a deep sigh. "You called me because you're miserable and you don't know what to do?"

"I didn't know who else to talk to," I said, doing my best to stop crying.

Cassie muttered something under her breath that I wasn't able to make out. Then she started into a tirade that lasted a good ten minutes. "Are you telling me that you're going to let Jake manipulate you like this? Come on, Nichole, you're a better woman than that. You've been strong and fearless to this point—"

"But this is my son," I cried, cutting her off.

"He's bluffing. You know Jake. Do you honestly think he's serious? And so what if he is? No judge in his right mind would give Owen to his father when the boy clearly is better off with his mother."

"Yes, but—"

"What is wrong with you, little sister? Come on, girl, show a little backbone."

*Me?* I didn't get it.

"Don't you dare let Jake make this kind of demand," she continued. "That weasel has no more interest in getting custody of Owen than some stranger off the street. He knows you love Rocco and he has a convenient excuse to make both of your lives miserable. And fool that you are, you let him."

"But I can't risk losing my son, and he knows I can't afford to pay for an attorney to fight him," I wailed.

"Of course you can't. But he can't, either, so call his crazy bluff."

"Call his bluff," I said, sobbing.

"You heard me. Just do it. He'll back down so fast your head will be left spinning."

I wondered if that could possibly be true. So much was at stake I feared what would happen if I did challenge Jake.

"You hear me?" Cassie said.

"Yes, only—"

"Only nothing. You stand up to Jake."

"Okay." I was willing to do just about anything to make this pain in my heart go away.

"Now that we've got that settled, let's get back to Rocco."

"Please." I knew he was angry with me, and getting him to trust me again wouldn't be easy.

"Steve and Rocco hit it off. Those two bonded so fast you'd think they were brothers. Rocco told Steve he'd never loved a woman until he'd met you and that you'd turned his world around. He's crazy about you and I swear if you don't find a way to make things right between you two Steve might not ever be able to forgive you."

"What do I do?" I pleaded.

"First off, apologize and then explain. If you'd told him the truth up front, you could have avoided all this. Don't be a schmuck, Nichole. You're smarter than this."

"What if Rocco won't have anything to do with me?" And, frankly, I wouldn't blame him if he turned his back on me, which I suspected he would.

"Be patient. He loves you. Keep remembering that, no matter how stubborn he is."

"I will," I promised. Already I felt worlds better.

"You finished crying your eyes out?" Cassie asked.

"Yes," I said, smiling for the first time in nearly two weeks.

"Then go out there, little sister, and kick some butt."

I laughed softly. "Thank you, Cassie."

"Hey, what are sisters for, anyway? Love you, Nichole."

"Love you."

We disconnected and I immediately contacted Jake. He answered, short-tempered and waspish. "What?" he demanded, as if it'd been a real inconvenience to hear my voice.

"I have two words for you, Jake. Just two words. *Lawyer up.*" With that, I ended the call. Dear, sweet heaven that felt good. I pumped my fist in the air, grabbed my coat, and headed out the door.

It went without saying that if I were to call Rocco he wouldn't answer. I needed to be smart about this, so I called Kaylene. I needed to find Rocco. I sat in my car and punched out her number.

Her attitude wasn't any better than Jake's when she answered. "What do you want?"

"Where's your father?"

"What makes you think I'd tell you? You're the last person he wants to see."

I knew she was right. "Because I love him."

"Not funny."

"Kaylene, please, I need to talk to your dad. Is he at the house or is he working?"

She hesitated, as if unsure what to tell me. "You hurt him. He loved you."

"I know and I'm sorry."

"It's too late. He doesn't want to see you."

"I know." God willing, I hoped to change his mind.

"He broke a bunch of stuff because of you."

Shawntelle had already told me he'd gone on a rampage. "I'll do everything within my power to make it up to you both."

Kaylene remained uncertain; I could hear it in her voice. "My dad really cared about you."

"Please," I whispered, closing my eyes and hoping with everything in me that she would help me.

"You promise not to tell him I gave you the information?" I could feel her wavering.

"I promise."

"Unless it turns out really well. Then you can tell him, okay?"

"I'll do whatever you want; just let me know where I can find him."

Kaylene paused. "The only reason I'm telling you is because he's been in a wicked mood ever since you two split. This better help, because if it gets any worse, I'm moving out."

"You can live with me," I promised. If she didn't tell me soon, I was going to scream.

"Dad went out to have a beer."

I inwardly groaned because I knew exactly where Rocco had gone. I thanked Kaylene, inserted my key in the ignition, and headed out. I was a woman on a mission and I refused to be thwarted. The weather was foul, with an ice storm threatening. I didn't care if there was a tornado warning blaring; I was going to find Rocco.

I drove to the tavern, parked, and squared my shoulders. I was ready to face the beast. I walked inside and it took a minute for my eyes to adjust to the dim lighting. It seemed the entire place went still. I saw Rocco sitting at the bar with his back to me, his shoulders hunched, discouraging conversation. He must have noticed the change in the atmosphere, because he glanced over his shoulder. His gaze landed on me, but I saw no sign of recognition. His expression remained blank as he turned back to drinking his beer.

I sauntered up to the bar like I did this every day of the week and took a seat two stools down from Rocco. The bartender looked at me and then at Rocco.

"What can I get you?" he asked.

"Give me a shot of fireball whiskey," I said, looking for liquid courage. I'd never had a straight shot in my life. Sam had ordered it the night we'd played pool. The bartender set the glass down in front of me. I took my first sip and thankfully didn't choke, although my eyes started to water. I swear it made my teeth go soft.

I didn't look at Rocco and he didn't look at me.

Five minutes passed before Sam came and sat on the other side of me, leaving the two empty spots between me and Rocco open.

"How's it going?" he asked.

I shrugged. "Not so well lately." I chanced a look in Rocco's direction. He gave no indication he'd heard me, not that I expected he would. "I made a stupid mistake," I added, watching Rocco out of the corner of my eye.

Nothing.

"What kind of mistake?" Sam asked.

Before I could answer, Rocco slid off the stool, slapped some cash down on the counter, and reached for his coat.

I was not letting him go until I'd had a chance to talk to him. Grabbing my purse, I set money on the counter and followed Rocco outside. He started walking away at a clipped pace.

As best as I could, I kept up with him until he finally whirled around and faced me, his eyes as hard as the threatening ice storm.

"What?" The lone word was shot at me with the strength and speed of a bullet.

For one crazy minute all I could do was stare at him. It took every ounce of restraint I possessed not to launch myself into his arms. When I spoke, it was directly from my heart. All I could do was pray he saw that and knew I was sincere.

"I love you, Rocco."

He shook his head. "Not good enough." He turned and started to walk away.

Well, that hadn't gone the way I'd hoped. I raced after him, my boots slipping and sliding on the slick sidewalk. "It damn well better be good enough," I shouted.

He increased his pace.

"I just put Owen's and my entire future on the line for you."

Nothing. He showed absolutely no response.

"Did you hear me?" I shouted.

Nothing.

He rounded the corner and I saw his truck parked three spaces down. He had his keys in his hands. He flicked a button and I heard the car beep, indicating it was unlocked. He walked around to the driver's side and opened the door.

I was growing desperate. He had to listen. He had to understand.

"Jake was going to fight me for custody—" I didn't get any further when my feet flew out from under me and I lost my balance. My arms flailed in a whirlwind motion before I went crashing down on the sidewalk. I landed on my side, hitting my shoulder hard. For a minute I was too stunned to move or speak or even breathe.

Rocco was already seated in his truck. He had the engine running. For the longest moment neither one of us moved.

I tried to get up and failed, sliding to my butt. I could feel the cold and ice seep into my jeans, but still I couldn't move. My heart ached in equal parts with my shoulder and hip. All I could do was stare at Rocco, sitting in his truck, glaring at me.

Rocco climbed out of the truck and came to stand on the curb. "You hurt?" he asked, his voice devoid of sympathy.

"I could use a hand up." I stretched out my arm. My entire body throbbed, but it was nothing compared to the pain in my heart.

Rocco helped me to my feet as his gaze assessed me. "You sure you're not hurt?"

I nodded, although I wasn't sure of anything at the moment. We stood on the sidewalk doing nothing more than staring at each other. I tried to speak and couldn't. Tears fell down my face, but I refused to look away.

I could see Rocco fighting within himself. He stepped back and I was convinced he was going to leave me. "I told you we're done."

In response, all I could manage was to shake my head.

He turned away.

I couldn't bear it. I couldn't watch. Looking down, I closed my eyes. Tears dripped off the end of my nose, falling onto the sidewalk, freezing instantly. That's what Rocco's heart was doing. He was freezing me out.

"Is that what you want?" I asked, stopping him. The door to his truck was open.

He stood still with his back to me.

"You said . . . you didn't know what it was to love someone to the point you'd be willing to die for them."

He didn't move.

"I love you enough to risk losing custody of my son. If that's not good enough for you, Rocco, then nothing ever will be. Go ahead, turn me away . . ." I had to stop because my voice wobbled terribly. "But if you do . . . if you do . . ." I couldn't say anything more.

Then, with a groan, Rocco turned back to me and within seconds his arms wrapped around my waist. He held me against him as if the world was about to come to an end, his grip so tight I couldn't breathe. Sobbing, I buried my face in his neck.

I don't know how long we stood like that. I didn't care if we ever moved. After what seemed like an eternity Rocco released a shuddering breath and eased his hold on me, letting my feet settle back down on the sidewalk.

"Please," I whispered. "Please love me enough to give us a chance."

He closed his eyes as if still fighting within himself.

"Rocco, please," I whispered again.

He exhaled, squeezing his eyes shut, as if getting the words out brought him horrible pain. "God help me, I do love you."

"I was afraid and I was stupid. I'm fighting Jake . . . I don't care how much it costs. I can't lose you."

His grip on me tightened as his hands bunched up my coat. I sobbed once and clung to him. He kissed me then, his lips punishing, but I didn't care. Just being in his arms was like heaven; it felt like I was coming home.

He broke off the kiss and his eyes held mine steady. "Jake threatened to take Owen away from you?"

My hands framed his face. "He's going to file for custody. I've decided to fight him." If what Cassie said was true, Jake would back down. Either way, I wasn't going to let my ex-husband manipulate me.

Rocco kissed me again. "That's why . . ."

I nodded. I couldn't stop looking at him even when my eyes blurred with tears.

"Let me deal with Jake," Rocco said gently, and his kiss was a promise.

I couldn't let him do that. "This is my battle."

"No," he insisted. "It's ours together."

We started to leave and when I took my first step pain shot up my leg and I nearly collapsed. Thankfully, Rocco had his arm around me and caught me before I fell again.

"You're hurt." His concern was immediate.

"No," I countered. "I've never felt better in my life." Ten broken bones would have been worth it if that fall brought Rocco back to me.

# CHAPTER 32

# Leanne

It shocked me how quickly Sean's health declined. Other than that one week in which he worked part-time, he never returned to the office. He worked from home for another week and then gave it up entirely.

As we headed into Christmas I found myself spending more and more time with him until it became far more convenient for me to stay at the house full-time. I worried when I left Sean at night, fearing that if he fell he wouldn't have the strength to get up off the floor. What shocked me was how few real friends he had. I knew if our situations were reversed I could always count on Kacey. A couple of the guys from the club came to see him, but that was it and they only stopped by the one time. Even people he'd worked with for years made only token visits.

As best I could I tried not to think about Nikolai. I wondered if he thought of me or if he'd put me out of his heart as effectively as he'd put me out of his life. A hundred times, perhaps more, I was tempted to reach out to him and call or text him. Then I realized I couldn't, not when Sean needed my full attention.

The Friday before Christmas Jake stopped by to see his father. Sean sat in his recliner, an afghan covering his legs. No matter how high I turned up the furnace, Sean couldn't seem to get warm. He'd lost almost fifteen pounds by this time, as his appetite was practically nonexistent. I did my best to coax him to eat, often without success.

"How you feeling, Dad?" Jake asked, scooting an ottoman next to the recliner and leaning forward.

"Better today, I think." Sean offered his son a weak smile.

I knew that wasn't the case. The doctor had just upped his pain medication, which he hated because he swore it made him sick to his stomach, and the nausea meds didn't seem to have an effect. The drugs were responsible for how sleepy he was. Sean slept several hours every afternoon and was often ready for bed by seven at night.

"Funny how life boils down to the news, the weather, and daytime television," Sean said, making an effort to joke.

He looked to me and his eyes grew warm with love and appreciation. I'd never thought to see that in the man I'd divorced.

"Don't know that I'd make it another day if not for your mother," he told Jake. "She's a good woman."

Jake looked at me and nodded. "She is."

"I never appreciated her the way I should have, and it cost me."

"And me," Jake whispered.

I wasn't sure Sean heard him as he drifted off to

sleep shortly afterward. Jake was referring to the fact that his own marriage had failed as he'd followed in his father's footsteps.

Our son joined me in the kitchen and I could tell he had something on his mind. "You got a minute, Mom?"

"Sure. What's up?" I asked. I was busy getting everything together to make homemade soup for Sean that evening. Because my freezer was full of Nikolai's bread, I'd brought a loaf of it from the apartment. If Nikolai knew I was serving my ex-husband his wonderful bread I was sure he'd be deeply offended. But I didn't need to worry about that any longer. I hadn't heard from Nikolai since our last heart-wrenching conversation.

Jake pulled a stool up to the kitchen counter. "I had a visit from Rocco Nyquist."

I stopped chopping an onion and set my knife aside. This was serious. Pulling out a stool, I sat down across from my son. I hadn't made a secret of how I felt about him suing for custody of Owen. As far as I knew, Jake hadn't followed through with his threat. If he had, I was sure Nichole would have mentioned it before now.

"What did he say?" I asked, working hard to remain outwardly calm.

Jake looked down at his hands. "As you can imagine, I wasn't happy to see him. To his credit, Rocco was polite. He asked if we could talk man to man about Nichole and Owen."

Confronting my son must have been uncomfortable for Rocco and equally so for Jake. "What did you say?"

My son looked almost amused. "I started off by telling him exactly what I thought of him, and I didn't hold back. I threw out the fact that I knew he'd been incarcerated. I let him know I thought he was a negative influence on Nichole and especially on my son. I wasn't polite about it, either. I gave it to him with both barrels."

I could well imagine.

The same amused look remained on Jake's face as he continued. "Frankly, I expected to rile him. I even thought he might take a swing at me. I sort of hoped he would, but he didn't.

"The truth is if I'd been on the receiving end of a tirade like that I probably would have lost my cool. Rocco didn't. He sat and listened and didn't interrupt. When I wound down he simply asked if I was ready for us to figure things out. It surprised me, you know."

"So what did he have to say?"

"Mainly, that he knew I loved Nichole and Owen, and he was sorry our marriage hadn't worked out. I wasn't sure I bought that, but I didn't argue the point. Bottom line, he feels the same way about them. He loves Nichole and he loves Owen, but he made it clear that he has no intention of taking Owen away from me."

Rocco impressed me. Naturally I knew Rocco and Nichole were back together and I was glad to hear it. They were good for each other. I liked Rocco and appreciated the way he treated her and Owen.

"Then he asked me about my threat to file for custody. Rocco said he hoped I'd change my mind, but if I did go ahead with the suit that I'd lose in the end." Jake paused and exhaled, as if this part was harder to explain. "He said that it would tear apart whatever relationship I hoped to have with Nichole and Owen. He felt certain a long, involved lawsuit would bankrupt us both and lead to bitterness and hostility, especially once attorneys got involved."

"He's right," I added, although I wasn't sure Jake appreciated my commentary.

"Looking at it from that point of view, I was forced to agree," Jake said, surprising me.

My son had a lot of emotional baggage he was dealing with in a short amount of time. The divorce, a change in jobs, his father's cancer, and now this. Deep down, I think he believed he would be able to fool Nichole into believing he was a changed man. He hoped he could talk her into reuniting and forget about the divorce. His plan failed; she'd seen through him. What my son hadn't expected was that Nichole would move on with her life. Move on and meet someone else, especially a blue-collar man like Rocco.

"Rocco loves and appreciates Nichole far more than I ever did," Jake whispered. "That isn't easy to admit. He loves her enough to seek me out and do what he could to save us both from a long court battle in which the only loser would be me. I have to say I respect that. It couldn't have been easy for him to let down his guard enough to confront me."

I'll admit my own respect for Rocco rose several notches.

"I don't expect us to be bosom buddies anytime soon," he added, "but it's good to know that we understand each other. As Rocco pointed out, we both love Owen, and working together instead of against each other is a win-win."

My son had shown more maturity in the last hour than he had in years, and I was proud of him.

A deep sadness settled over Jake as he glanced at his father. "You know, Mom, I blew it with Nichole. Dad . . . he always seemed to have it together. Outwardly he had the perfect life. He had you and money and a little fun on the side. You never said anything and looked the other way. I thought that was what all wives did."

It killed me to hear my son say that, because in essence he was telling me that by not standing up to my husband and fighting for my marriage I had approved of Sean's infidelity.

"I assumed Nichole would do the same," Jake said. "I knew if she ever found out she wouldn't like it, but that didn't stop me. I was stupid enough to think I could have it both ways."

I swallowed tightly.

"The other night I stopped off to check on Dad. You'd gone back to your apartment to collect a few things."

I remembered because I'd called Jake and asked him to sit with his father while I was away.

"Dad and I had a long talk. Seeing the two of you now and how close you are is an eye-opener, and I think Dad feels it, too. He told me he realized far too late how much he loved you. He might not be able to say it now, but he's sorry for the way he cheated on you. He told me that with tears in his eyes. He said you were worth ten of any of the other women he's ever known."

*Known* most likely in the biblical sense, I mused, holding back a smile.

"Dad doesn't ~~know~~ where he'd be now if it wasn't for you caring for him. I couldn't do what you're doing. Most likely he'd be in some nursing home and at the mercy of strangers."

My attention remained focused on Sean, and when I spoke it was from the heart. "I've always loved your father, Jake. For a long time I buried that love beneath my resentment."

"Dad didn't understand until you left him how large a part of his life you were. He didn't realize how much he loves you. He's dying and he knows it. He accepts that he only has a few months left, and you know what he said? Dad told me it was worth getting that tumor because it showed him what he should have realized long ago. He had a wonderful, giving, loving wife."

That did it; I bit into my lower lip in an effort to hold back tears.

Jake continued, "Dad gripped hold of my hand and pleaded with me not to make the same stupid mistakes he has. I told him it was too late, I'd already lost Nichole, but he wouldn't take that as an answer. He wanted to know if I'd learned anything from my divorce."

From the evidence I'd seen, Jake hadn't. According to Kacey, there'd been women in and out of the house, some staying weeks at a time. None that lasted long, though. From the first I'd been concerned about Jake's parenting of Owen. He'd been far too willing to shuffle his son off to sitters while he spent his weekends playing golf and socializing.

"Dad's question hung over me all last week, and as painful as it was to admit, I don't think I had learned anything from the divorce until recently. When Nichole first left, I was confident I could win her back. I figured I would use my persuasive powers to woo her into giving me another chance. But even then I was going out behind her back, dating other women. It infuriated me when she refused to give me a second chance.

"After the divorce was final I made a real ass of myself, dating women left and right, sleeping around, having casual hook-ups. The bottom line is I was miserable and I blamed her."

It did my heart good to hear the honesty in my son.

"By the time Rocco came to the house for our man-to-man chat, I'd pretty much decided I wouldn't have a foot to stand on when it came to getting custody of Owen. All Nichole would have to do was show evidence of the way I'd been living my life since the divorce. No judge in the land would give me custody of my son, and rightly so. Not that I would have let that stop me."

Reaching across the counter, I hugged Jake. It was a bit awkward, but I was proud of him, proud of the way he'd cut through all the bull he'd been feeding himself. For the first time in years I had hope that he would turn into a responsible adult.

Jake returned my hug and then smiled for the first time since we'd begun our conversation. "I met someone awhile back. Her name is Carlie Olsson and she works in my office. She's beautiful and smart as a whip. She didn't have a high opinion of me and she let me know she wasn't interested in dating me. I asked her out five times before she agreed to see me." His smile widened. "That first night we talked for five hours. The crazy part is I've seen her every night since and we haven't gone to bed together yet."

Holding up my hand, I smiled and said, "TMI."

Jake laughed. "Sorry. It's just that in the last couple of years that's something of a record. If things work out the way I hope they do, I'd like to marry her one day. Don't worry, Mom, if I cheat on this woman she wouldn't think twice about severing my dick."

Despite myself, I laughed. "Sounds like she's exactly the kind of woman you need."

Jake agreed. "I have Owen Christmas morning, and I thought I'd come by and spend part of the day with you and Dad, if that's all right?"

"Of course."

"I want Owen to have as many memories of his grandfather as he can."

"It'll be good for them both." I wanted to warn Jake how quickly his father tired out, but decided against it. "I'll make us a special dinner."

"Could you make that pasta dish I like so much? You remember, the one with the clams in it? Owen likes pasta and I wanted to share it with him."

"Of course." I'd need to dig through my recipes and make sure I had all the ingredients. It'd been several years since I'd last cooked it.

"We won't stay too long, I promise," Jake said, glancing toward his father again.

"Don't worry, son. It will do your father good to see Owen."

"I have him starting tomorrow. Do you think it would be too much to have him visit Dad then?"

"Not at all."

"I'd like you to meet Carlie, too."

He said this as if he wasn't sure I would want to, seeing how close Nichole and I were. "I'd like to meet her, Jake. And I don't think you need to worry about Nichole, either. She's moved on. I know she wants you to do the same."

He exhaled as though relieved. "I hope that we can be cordial to each other."

"Dropping the threat of suing for custody of Owen will go a long way toward seeing to that."

Jake grinned and looked almost boyish. "You should have heard what Carlie had to say when I told her what I'd threatened. She about chewed my ear off, giving me her opinion."

"In other words, you'd more or less changed your mind before you talked to Rocco."

"No, not really. Even though I knew I'd probably lose, I wanted to fight her. After talking to Rocco I realize how screwed-up my thinking was. Besides, if I'm going to have a serious relationship with Carlie, I was going to need an attitude adjustment."

"Looks like you're making progress."

"That's for sure. It's been an eye-opening month for me."

I was grateful for everything that had opened my son's eyes.

"What about you, Mom? How are you holding up?"

My thoughts instantly went to Nikolai and I felt the weight of regret settle over me. "Okay."

"I realize looking after Dad is taking up all your time now. What about those classes you were teaching?"

"The session ended and I didn't renew my contract." The last few classes had been torture for me without Nikolai. Seeing his empty space in the front of the classroom made my heart ache. Even if I'd wanted to continue teaching, I wouldn't have the time now. Sean needed me.

Jake left soon afterward and Sean woke. I helped him to the bathroom and convinced him to eat some soup and bread. He made the effort, and that pleased me. I know the only reason he ate was because he wanted to show me he appreciated that I'd cooked for him.

In the evening, I sat by his side and he reached for my hand. He'd done that several times now. Frankly, I couldn't remember the last time my husband had wanted to hold my hand. I think it was shortly after Jake had been born.

I knew Sean had regrets and I was grateful that he spoke to Jake about them. Our son needed to hear it and I was pleased Jake had chosen to share some of their conversation with me. In retrospect, I believe Sean counted on that. For Sean to tell me these things would have been too hard emotionally. The words weren't important. I already knew Sean realized all the years he'd wasted. It was better we not discuss it. We would spend his remaining months free of misgivings and tension.

After Sean was down for the night, I cleaned the kitchen and put away the leftovers. My gaze rested on the bread, my only contact with Nikolai at this point. I swallowed down the sense of loss and returned to the task at hand.

# CHAPTER 33

# Nichole

Christmas day without Owen was going to be difficult. I'd had him for Thanksgiving and it was only fair that Jake get to have our son for Christmas. Jake picked up Owen late Friday afternoon. Leanne had called previously to let me know Jake had been by to visit his dad and it had gone well.

I was a little nervous about seeing Jake. We hadn't really talked since our last short conversation, when I'd told him I'd decided to fight him if he sued for custody of our son. I'd already made an appointment with my divorce attorney for after the first of the year.

He stood outside my apartment and I invited him in while Owen ran to collect his backpack. "How's your dad?" I asked, making conversation.

A look of sadness came over him and I realized I should have chosen a different topic.

"Not so good."

"I'm sorry, Jake."

"Yeah, it sucks. Listen," he said, glancing down at

the floor, "you can forget what I said about taking you to court. You're a good mother and I was out of line."

This was a major surprise.

"Owen needs you."

"He needs you, too." Just not the majority of the time. In the years to come that might change, I realized, although I didn't want to think about that now.

"I haven't done a good job to this point, but I want you to know, Nichole, I intend to be a better father from now on."

For one wild moment I was too stunned to speak. "What changed your mind?"

"A lot of things. My talk with Rocco, mostly."

"Rocco?" My head started spinning. Rocco hadn't said anything about this. He'd mentioned he wanted to talk to Jake, but I'd heard nothing since.

Jake glanced up and shocked me even more when he added, "Rocco's an all-right guy. If I'd loved you half as much we wouldn't be trading our son off on holidays and weekends. Like I told my mom, Rocco and I aren't ever going to be good friends, but I trust him to do right by you and by Owen."

Leanne knew about this conversation and hadn't said anything about it to me. I didn't know how many shocks my brain could absorb. Perhaps she assumed I already knew, I reasoned.

Before I could question him further, Owen flew into the living room. "I'm weady, Daddy. Santa's coming and I get to open my gifts, wight?"

"That's right, big man." Jake lifted Owen into his arms and hugged him until my toddler squirmed and wanted down. "Come on, Dad, let's boogie outta hewe."

I had to smile because that was something Rocco said. Under normal circumstances I think Jake might have objected, but not now. Instead he laughed and took hold of Owen's hand.

As soon as my ex and son were out the door I grabbed my phone.

Me: Hey, what's the deal? U and Jake?
Rocco: On my way. Bring out the mistletoe and pucker up. I'm dying for a taste of U.
Me: Not until you tell me about what happened between U and Jake.
Rocco: Kisses first.
Me: We'll see.

That was one argument I was happy to lose.

Christmas Day was spent with Rocco and Kaylene at their house. Since a fair number of Rocco's employees were ex-cons, many of them didn't have family connections, so Rocco put out a spread for them. Otherwise they would end up spending the day alone.

When I volunteered to help with the buffet, Rocco was more than happy to have me there. A good portion of the morning and early afternoon was spent with the two of us in the kitchen, cooking up spaghetti sauce, along with garlic rolls and a tossed green salad.

I was busy cutting up lettuce for the salad when I whirled around and nearly bumped into Rocco. He caught me by the shoulders and paused, smiling down on me. The look in his eyes was enough to make my toes curl. Before I knew it we were in each other's arms. After only the slightest of hesitations, he kissed me. It was the kind of kiss that, in the words of Shawntelle, had the power to melt the panties right off a girl.

"Dad," Kaylene cried in complete disgust. "Don't you two have more important things to do than stand in the middle of the kitchen making out?"

Rocco's eyes connected and held mine like a vise. "Can't say that I do."

"You're embarrassing."

"Get used to it," Rocco told his daughter as he kissed me again, practically bending me in half over his arm.

"Dad, I'm serious."

Rocco reluctantly broke off the kiss. "I am, too," he whispered, looking deep into my eyes. "Very serious."

The teenager made a huffing sound and returned to the other room.

Despite all the pauses in the meal preparation, Rocco and I managed to get everything on the table in time. I'd brought homemade cookies and candies made from the very recipes my mother had once used. It was fun to learn that Karen and Cassie had baked many of the same recipes I had. Each one of us had happy memories of the goodies our mother had once lovingly prepared.

The first person to arrive was Shawntelle, along with Jerome. I hadn't seen her since our come-to-Jesus talk. The minute she walked in the house, she threw her arms in the air and headed straight for me.

"I knew you weren't as dumb as you look," she cried, wrapping me in a bear hug strong enough to lift me two feet off the floor. "You aren't no fool. You know a good man when you find one, same as me." She set me back down and grabbed hold of Jerome's hand, bringing him forward to meet me. "This is Jerome. He met my kids, all five of them, and he's still with me," she boasted.

Jerome was tall and thin and about as opposite of Shawntelle as a man could get. I doubted he could get a word in with that woman around, but it was clear from the way he looked at her that she was everything to him.

"Hi, Jerome," I said, grinning at them both. "Speaking of the kids, where are they?"

"With my cousin. Remember Charise? I had to bribe her to watch them for a couple of hours, but Jerome needed a break."

"You needed the break," Jerome countered.

Rocco joined us and slipped his arm around my waist. "What's this I overheard?" he asked, studying me. "You and Shawntelle had a long talk?"

Shawntelle piped up, eager to tell the story. "You bet we did. I gave this woman a piece of my mind because it was clear she was missing parts of her brain and needed my help." She had her hand on her hip as she spoke. "Got to say it's a good thing she listened, too."

"Good thing is right," Rocco agreed, and tightened his hold on me to the point that I was plastered to his side. This was Rocco's way of saying he wasn't going to let me go ever again. Not that I would argue. I liked being exactly where I was.

Within the next hour the house was full of employees and friends. Sam and a few other guys from the tavern that I'd met stopped by, too. Both Rocco and I were busy with our duty as hosts.

Everyone seemed to know who I was, although I hadn't met more than a couple of his employees previously. My guess was that Shawntelle had more to do with this than Rocco. By the end of the day I knew all their names and felt like I had learned a little about each of them.

Rocco had taken a chance on each one and none had failed him. He explained that he was a good judge of character and it didn't take him long to determine who would last and who wouldn't. It was clear to me that every man and woman would have gladly sung Rocco's praises. He was more than their employer. He was their friend, and for a couple perhaps the first person willing to look beyond their mistakes and give them a second chance at being independent.

By the time the last stragglers had left we were all exhausted. The only one who showed any real life left in her was Kaylene.

"Best Christmas ever," the teenager boasted.

"Better than last year?" Rocco asked, and then whispered in my ear, "She got an iPad, which was at the top of her list, *and* a cell phone."

"Yup, even better than last year."

"Why's that?" her father asked.

Kaylene flopped down on the sofa next to where Rocco and I had crashed. "Because I've never seen my dad so happy," she said. Her eyes lit up as she looked to me. "Thanks, Nichole."

"You could be jealous, you know." I'd heard plenty of stories where the daughter of a single father resented the dad's love interest.

"I could be, I guess," Kaylene said, weighing my words.

"Don't give her any ideas," Rocco whispered, and then nibbled on my earlobe, sending chills racing down my spine.

"It isn't only that you're good for my dad," Kaylene said, growing thoughtful. "You're good for me, too. You're teaching me how to be a woman."

"I am?"

"She eats her pizza with a fork now," Rocco muttered, and he didn't look happy about it.

"And you know about fashion," Kaylene continued, "and makeup and all the things a woman my age needs to learn."

"*Woman?*" Rocco repeated, lifting his brows with the question.

"I am a woman, Dad," Kaylene insisted, and then as quickly asked, "Can I watch TV? There's a movie on Hallmark I want to see."

"By all means," Rocco told her.

Kaylene jumped off the couch and headed into the other room.

Rocco had his arm around me. My tired feet were tucked alongside me on the sofa and my head rested against his shoulder.

"Didn't you love seeing Shawntelle with Jerome?" Rocco asked me.

The memory of the two brought a smile. "They're certainly an odd couple."

"So are we," he suggested.

"No, we aren't," I argued, lifting my head from his shoulder.

It seemed like he was too exhausted to disagree.

"Did you notice the way Jerome looked at her? It was as if that woman could do no wrong."

I had noticed and been touched by the tender looks Jerome gave Shawntelle.

"I recognized it because that's the way I look at you," Rocco whispered, nuzzling his nose in my hair. "Have I ever mentioned how much I love the way you smell? It's like nothing I could name—a combination of roses and almonds." He paused and then groaned. "Don't go mentioning that to my friends, or they'll think I've turned into a woman."

"My lips are sealed."

He grumbled about something else, but I didn't catch it. I closed my eyes. I could fall asleep right here with Rocco's arms around me.

"I love you, Rocco," I said on the tail end of a yawn.

He went still and quiet, and for a moment I was afraid I'd said the wrong thing. I knew some men freak out when women profess their feelings. This wasn't the first time, either. I'd said it that day just before I fell on the sidewalk.

A number of people had mentioned to me that Rocco loved me, so I wasn't expecting it would upset him if I said what was in my heart.

"I love you, too," he whispered, after what seemed like an eternity. "When you told me you wanted to stop seeing me it felt as if my entire world had imploded. I half expected you'd want to break it off with me at some point, but when it actually happened it was so much worse than I imagined. The only point lower was when I was tossed into a jail cell."

"It was a low point for me, too," I told him. "I wasn't even half alive afterward. Ask Leanne. It was worse even than the day I found out that Jake had been cheating on me. When I learned my husband had gotten another woman pregnant I was filled with righteous anger. When I broke up with you all I felt was this horrible sense of grief. The only thing I can compare it to was the feelings I had when my parents died."

"You should have been honest with me."

In retrospect, he was right; I should have told Rocco about Jake's threat right away. It would have saved us both a lot of unnecessary suffering. Still, I believe everything worked out the way it was meant to. In other circumstances, Rocco might have talked to Jake with a lot of anger and resentment clouding his head.

"Leanne met Carlie, the woman Jake's currently seeing," I told Rocco, "and she thinks this is exactly the kind of woman her son needs."

"You're exactly the kind of woman this man needs," Rocco returned. "And I need you bad."

How I loved hearing the things this man said.

"How long do you think it's going to take me to convince you to marry me?" he asked.

That was a heady question. "We haven't been seeing each other that long," I reminded him. "We should give it at least another six months, and a year would probably be better."

"It's hard for me to wait another six minutes," he grumbled. "You'll move in with me, won't you?"

"No." Although I had to admit the offer was tempting.

"I had a feeling you were going to say that."

"Let's give it a year before we make a serious commitment."

"A year," he groaned, as if I was being utterly unrealistic. "You want me to wait that long? Woman, be reasonable. This man loves you and you love me."

"I do," I said, kissing him with all the stored-up love I had in my heart.

"Then why make me suffer like this? I need you. Kaylene needs you."

"I want to be sure, Rocco."

"What do I have to do to prove to you no one will ever love you more than me?"

I hugged him close, savoring everything about this man who had proved himself over and over. "I don't know . . . possibly wait a year so we can both be sure of our feelings. For all you know I might have disgusting habits you can't live with."

"You mean other than eating pizza with a fork? Or slicing a friggin' expensive piece of chocolate into four sections before you eat it?" he muttered, and rolled his eyes.

I elbowed him in the ribs, which of course didn't faze him. "Something like that," I muttered.

"A year," he grumbled.

"I promise you it will be worth the wait."

"I can't convince you otherwise?" he asked, nibbling on my ear again.

"Well, maybe . . ."

"Let's negotiate," he whispered, turning me into his arms, and then he went about convincing me in the best possible way.

# CHAPTER 34

# Leanne

Sean died February 15, the day after Valentine's Day. By this time he was in hospice care, as I was no longer able to look after his needs on my own.

Both Jake and I were with him when he passed. We sat on each side of his bed, holding his hands. I prayed as my husband breathed his last while Jake stared stoically into space, grieving in his own way. Sean and I had already made his funeral arrangements, and I was grateful not to have to make those decisions now. We'd purchased his grave site and bought the marker.

The funeral was much larger than I anticipated. I was humbled at the friends who turned out to pay their respects. The church I'd attended was full and the pastor gave a wonderful message even though he'd come to know Sean only in his final weeks. I was comfortable knowing that my husband was at peace at last.

When we came to the burial, I looked out over the landscape and was glad he had chosen a cemetery with a view. It'd seemed silly at the time, but I realized the view wasn't for him so much as for me.

Nichole attended the services with Rocco. The two stood side by side at the grave site in front of Sean's casket with Jake and Carlie. Owen stood between the two couples, one hand holding his mother's hand and the other holding on to his father's. He was four now, and I wasn't sure he fully understood what was happening or why. Jake had wanted him there.

Sean had come to deeply love his grandson in his final weeks. The last picture I have of my husband is with Owen sprawled across his chest, his small arms locked around his grandfather's neck. Owen's sweet head rested against Sean's shoulder while they were both sound asleep. I'm saving it for Owen when he's older, in memory of the grandfather he barely got to know.

My marriage hadn't been a happy one, especially the last ten years. We were divorced, but Sean remained my husband in my mind these last three months. Those weeks I'd spent with him helped me remember why I'd fallen in love with him as a young woman. Although he was sick and often in pain, he never let on, and rarely complained. I admired his courage as he faced death, his acceptance and, in the end, his faith.

When he died I grieved for all the years we'd wasted and thanked God for the opportunity to love him again. He never let me forget how grateful he was for my care or how sorry he was for hurting me. I believe that he came to realize that the one he'd punished was himself for all the closeness and intimacy we might have had if he'd been faithful.

After we'd finished with the burial, Jake remained at the grave site, looking down at the casket in the ground. I saw Nichole and Rocco talking to Carlie. I walked over to my son and put my hand on his shoulder. Jake's shoulders shook with heart-wrenching sobs. It was the first time I'd seen my son weep since his father's death.

Carlie came to stand with him and her hand brushed mine as she placed her arm around him. I'd met her a few times now and liked her a great deal. She was a no-nonsense kind of woman and I thought the two were well suited. I didn't know what the future held for them, but Jake seemed to be serious about her. I was glad to see it. He needed a woman who would ground him.

After I left Jake with Carlie, Nichole came to me and slipped her arm around my waist.

"You doing okay?" she asked.

Her gentle care was a soothing balm to me. Nichole was as close to me as if I'd given birth to her myself. I rested my head against her shoulder. "I've been better."

"No doubt."

"Are you up for the wake?" she asked.

I assured her I was. The reception was held at the country club. Jake and I mingled with the crowd, thanking our friends for their condolences. In lieu of flowers Sean asked that donations be made to the American Cancer Society. I'd already heard that several hundred dollars had been given in his name. So few people had come to visit Sean while he was sick, it surprised me how well attended his funeral was. Of course, this included Jake's coworkers and friends along with my friends, too.

At the end of the reception I was exhausted and ready to unwind and be alone. I returned to the house. It would go up for sale now. Sean had changed his will when we divorced and I assumed the majority of his estate would go to Jake and Owen or perhaps to charity. Over the last two and a half months we'd talked about almost everything, but this was one subject Sean and I had never discussed. The divorce settlement left me in fine shape financially. I didn't need anything more from him and he knew that.

It wasn't until a week after the funeral that I learned that Sean had changed his will and he'd left me the house. Almost everything else went to Jake, with a college fund set up for Owen. When Sean's attorney notified me that I'd inherited the house, I was stunned. Other than the time I'd spent there while caring for Sean, I no longer considered it my home. I'd moved on. My apartment was plenty big and I fully intended to continue living in the heart of downtown Portland. I loved city life.

Now that Nichole and Rocco were seriously involved, I intended to buy a condo, hoping to find one in the same neighborhood in which I now lived. I was in no rush, however.

Because my time and energy had been taken up caring for Sean, I feared I would be at loose ends once I returned to life in my apartment. I wasn't. I found that I was emotionally and physically exhausted. My days were taken up with long delayed projects that kept me at home. I read one book after another, immersing myself in fiction. In the mornings I worked the newspaper's crossword puzzle and book upon book of Sudoku. I napped every afternoon, sometimes for as long as two hours. My body demanded it.

Before I knew it, March had slipped past. One morning I woke with the compelling urge to bake bread. I'd promised Nikolai I would never use a bread machine again, and I kept my word. I remembered everything he'd told me about mixing the flour and the water with the yeast. I found kneading the dough to be therapeutic. My first loaf turned out heavenly. I shared it with Nichole and Owen.

Nichole gave me high marks. "This is some of the best homemade bread I've ever tasted. Well, other than . . ." She didn't need to say it. I knew she was about to mention Nikolai and stopped herself in the nick of time.

Spurred on by her encouragement, I continued baking: bread, cinnamon rolls, dinner rolls, everything that took my fancy, and I fancied a lot. I loved every minute of it.

Every day I felt myself come more alive. The grief that consumed me left slowly, in degrees. Soon I found I could smile again, laugh again. I started taking long walks in the afternoons, replacing my naptime with exercise. I returned to the apartment feeling refreshed and exhilarated.

The more I baked, the more my thoughts drifted to Nikolai. I hadn't heard from him in all these months and I expected he'd moved on. On impulse one afternoon I walked to Koreski's Deli. I had a loaf of bread for Nikolai and hoped to say with bread what I couldn't with words. I chose a time when I knew the deli wouldn't be extra-busy.

Mr. Koreski was behind the counter when I approached. He looked up and had an odd look, as if he wasn't sure he remembered who I was.

"Mr. Koreski, I'm Leanne Patterson."

Recognition flashed into his eyes. "Ah, yes, I remember now. You're Nikolai's friend."

"Yes." I sincerely hoped that after all this time Nikolai still considered me a friend and hopefully a great deal more.

"I have something for him, if you wouldn't mind giving it to him for me."

The deli owner's face fell. "Nikolai doesn't work here any longer. I miss him every day."

My heart slammed against my ribs with shock. I'd never imagined he would leave a job he loved. "Oh," I managed after an awkward moment. I set the bread on the counter. "Then please accept this and enjoy." I didn't give him the opportunity to respond before I abruptly turned and left.

I was afraid that Nikolai had gone from more than his job at the deli. It felt as if he'd closed the door on me as well. Returning to my apartment, I felt empty inside, lost and alone. Worse, I felt old and used up, much the way I had when I'd first left Sean.

The next day Kacey phoned with the offer to take me to lunch. Refusing would do me little good. Kacey was determined not to take no for an answer, and not having an excuse she would accept, I gave in. She'd been after me for weeks now and it was time I broke out of my protective shell. I'd tried earlier with Nikolai, only to quickly retreat back to where I felt secure.

As always, Kacey was upbeat and lively, entertaining me with tales of life at the club. She'd been a rock while Sean had been ill, the one constant I could rely on. She sat with Sean on occasion, giving me a much-needed break. Although she wasn't much of a cook, she made the effort to bring us casseroles and other dishes, relieving me to concentrate on caring for Sean. I would always treasure her friendship—now more than ever.

I admit I did feel better after our lunch. It was later than usual when I took my walk. The weather in the Pacific Northwest in April was often unpredictable, so I grabbed my waterproof jacket. The skies were overcast and my phone app predicted rain later in the afternoon. Just in case, I brought along my umbrella.

My route took me past a park and I was thinking about my conversation with Kacey when I felt someone step up and walk beside me. Looking over, I saw Nikolai. My heart zoomed up into my throat and I froze, utterly speechless.

His smile was warm and bright. "Hello, my Leanne."

"Nikolai." I couldn't believe it was really him. I reached up and touched his cheek just to be sure he wasn't part of my imagination.

He took hold of my wrist and brought my palm to his lips, kissing the sensitive skin there.

"You baked me bread," he said, as if I had gifted him with the Hope Diamond.

"How . . . How did you know?"

"My friend tell me. He say you come to deli with bread."

"Mr. Koreski said you no longer work there."

"No, I leave and start my own business."

"You did?" I had no idea this was in the works for him.

"Yes. I now bake bread for restaurants. I rent kitchen."

I couldn't stop staring at him and hardly knew where to begin. All I could do was look at him. When I could finally speak, my words were thick with emotion, wobbling from my lips as tears filled my eyes. "I don't think I can survive another minute without you."

His smile was huge as he hauled me into his arms. He spoke in Ukrainian, his own voice filled with emotion. Although I didn't understand a word, I knew exactly what he said. He told me he loved me and that he'd missed me. Then he was kissing me, his rough hands cupping my face as he spread kisses from my forehead to my chin. It seemed to take him forever to get to my lips. I melted into his embrace, relishing the care and love I felt being in his arms.

We walked back to my apartment, our arms around each other. We kissed in the elevator and missed my floor and had to ride back down. Then we laughed at how silly we'd been. Once inside my apartment we kissed again and again. Tears shone in his eyes as he held my face and stared down at me as if even now he couldn't believe I was his. And yet for the entire time I'd been with Sean my heart was with Nikolai. I never understood how it was possible to love two men at the same time. I did now.

"Sean?" Nikolai asked.

"He died in February."

Nikolai hugged me close, as if to absorb my loss and pain. "I am sorry."

"I know." Of all those who'd offered condolences, I knew he was sincere. He'd buried his wife; he understood better than many of my friends did.

"You grieve long months."

"Yes. I'm better now." A thousand times better with Nikolai back in my life.

"I give you year to grieve," he whispered, and then changed his mind. "No, six months. Sorry, I cannot wait longer."

"Wait longer, Nikolai? For what?"

His eyes widened with surprise. "To make you my wife. You *my* Leanne now." He placed his hand over his heart. "You here from first moment I see you. I look at you and I know right then that this is woman for me."

"But you left me," I whispered.

He shook his head, denying what had happened between us. "No, my love, you left me. You go to Sean; he need you more than me. I never leave you, never forget. Always you right here in my heart. I know you come back one day. I wait. I pray. I trust God to bring you back. God hear my prayer and He send you to me."

I could feel myself weakening as I studied Nikolai. His heart was in his eyes as he spoke.

"You bake me bread," he continued. "You say with bread what too hard to say with words, same as me. Minute I hear about bread my heart sing and I know you not forget me."

"Never," I whispered. "I could never forget you."

"I know. Deep down I know. I wait, but waiting is hard. Every day I light candle."

"For Sean?"

"No, for you. I pray because I know you. I pray you remember me. Mostly I pray you feel my love."

"I do . . . I did."

"Six months is all I can give you. You need more, too bad." His smile nearly blinded me.

"Do you have any idea how much I love you?" I asked him.

He shook his head. "No, but I let you show me."

"I will show you," I promised.

"I show you, too. Every day for the rest of our lives."

That was good enough for me.

I never expected to find love like this. How blessed I was to have found the courage to move on.

# EPILOGUE

# Nichole

*Three Years Later*

My friends and fellow teachers from Portland High threw me a surprise baby shower a month before Rocco's and my baby boy was due to be born. They had plenty of help from Kaylene and Shawntelle.

Rocco got me out of the house early on a Saturday afternoon, insisting he wanted to buy a new family car. Being the good wife, I agreed to accompany him, although I had no interest in car shopping. The problem was my dear, loving husband refused to let me out of his sight. From the way he acted, one would think I was the only woman on earth who would ever give birth to a child.

When I complained, Rocco replied, "Argue all you want, but you're the only woman on earth who's giving birth to my son."

From the minute the test strip turned blue Rocco had hovered over me. He attended every doctor visit, and went to birthing classes and everything else. He couldn't seem to do enough for me. He loved me before I became pregnant, but I swear his love increased tenfold after he found out we were having a baby.

Many a morning I'd wake up with his hand over my protruding tummy and hear him talking softly to his son.

The only thing we disagreed on was the name. I wanted to name him Jaxon Rocco Nyquist and Rocco wanted a more traditional name: Matthew Saul Nyquist. He'd had an uncle Saul he'd been close to as a kid who died when Rocco was ten. No way was I naming our son Saul, and I definitely wanted him to be named after his father.

When we returned from our car-hunting expedition, I noticed all the cars parked down the street.

"Neighbors must be having a party," Rocco suggested.

"And they didn't invite us," I joked.

When we walked in the front door the first two people I saw were my sisters, Karen and Cassie. The room exploded with cries of: *Surprise!* Cassie had her two-year-old son, Myles, with her and was pregnant with a little girl.

I looked to Rocco, accusing him with my eyes. "You knew about this?"

He smiled and shrugged. "I did, but if I said anything I don't think I'd live long."

"No, he wouldn't," Shawntelle insisted. "That baby best be born soon, because I don't think one of us at the office can stand to be around him much longer. Every time the phone rings he is ready to head to the hospital, and the phone rings a lot at a towing company."

Leanne and Nikolai were there, and I could see that they'd provided a huge batch of yummy cinnamon rolls. The two worked together now, baking bread and rolls for area restaurants. They had become so successful that they'd hired two additional bakers. Leanne had been happily married to Nikolai for two and a half years now. No one could look at them and not see the love flowing effortlessly between them.

I was happy, too, happier than I ever imagined possible. I remembered how heartsick both Leanne and I had been when we'd left our husbands. We'd never believed a failed marriage would happen to us. We left defeated, depressed, convinced we were unloved and unlovable. Rocco and Nikolai had shown us otherwise.

"Mommy, can I help you open the presents?" Owen asked.

"Of course," I assured him. At seven, he was a big helper. Rocco and Jake were strong father figures to my son, and I appreciated how they worked together. It helped that Jake was with Carlie. The other woman brought balance into his life. I doubted he'd be able to get away with the same thing with her that he had with me. I didn't know Carlie well, but I appreciated that she was a good stepmother to Owen.

Everyone gathered around as I reached for the first gift and handed it to Owen, who sat cross-legged in front of me. He tore off the card and handed it to me to read.

I glanced up and saw Rocco standing on the other side of the room, talking to Nikolai. Our eyes met and

I remembered the day I'd backed my car into the ditch. At the time I'd been furious with myself, never realizing that was perhaps the luckiest day of my life.

When Leanne and I created our list for moving on, I never dreamed where it would lead me. The list had helped pave the way, leading us to healing and love.

To Rocco and Nikolai.

Read on for a sneak peek at the next
wonderful novel from #1 *New York Times*
bestselling author Debbie Macomber

# If Not For You

# PROLOGUE

It really was a shame. No, not a shame . . . a disappointment, Beth Prudhomme mused as she sat at the intersection, waiting on the red light. She glanced out the car window at the man her friend had invited her to meet over dinner. Sam Carney was stopped in the lane next to her, waiting on the light. Again she felt a twinge of regret, knowing nothing would ever come of their evening together.

It'd been silly to put any hope into this evening. One look at Sam and it was clear they weren't a good mix. Beth could just imagine what her parents would say if they were ever to meet Sam. The thought was enough to make her smile. Her mother would have a fit of hysterics. In her mother's eyes, she would view Sam as uncouth, vulgar, and a bane to society. All this because his hair was long and he had a beard. His tattoos would likely send her over the edge. But then her mother had high expectations when it came to the man Beth would one day marry.

It didn't take her long to realize Sam felt the same way about her. His eyes had widened briefly before he could disguise his reaction when they were first introduced. He probably saw her as prim and pristine and oh-so-proper, which she was, thanks to her mother. Beth suspected Sam hadn't been keen on this dinner date and briefly wondered what had led him into agreeing to meet her. She knew she'd been a big disappointment and felt badly about that. The truth was, she'd liked Sam. Although they hadn't spoken much she felt drawn to the unconventional attitude, which was unlike her own structured life. It'd been hard to get a read on him, other than when they were first introduced. Beth couldn't help wonder what he was thinking; he gave away little of his thoughts other than the fact that he was more than anxious for the evening to be over. Beth didn't blame him.

Beth had to admit Sam was handsome, definitely rough around the edges, but Nichole had warned her about that. His shoulder-length hair was tucked into a ponytail, tied at the base of his neck. He had nice dark eyes, she'd say that. The color reminded her of dark chocolate. He was tall; she estimated he must be six-two, which was a foot taller than her own petite frame. And he must outweigh her by a good seventy or more pounds. Her friend's description of Sam had given her pause, but her aunt Sunshine had persuaded her to give it a shot.

"Why not? What's it going to hurt?"

True enough, it hadn't hurt, but still the taste of disappointment settled over her.

Sitting in the tall cab of his truck, Sam must have noticed her scrutiny because he turned his head, looking down at her as they waited for the light to change. My goodness, the truck was so high up she'd need a step stool just to climb into the seat.

The turn signal turned green, and offering Sam a brief smile, she stepped onto the accelerator and moved forward into the intersection preparing to make the turn. That was when she noticed the car coming directly toward her, racing through the red light.

In that split second her eyes caught those of the teenaged driver in the other car. She had her cellphone in her hand; her face twisted in a look of surprised horror. From that moment forward everything seemed to happen in slow motion. The girl's mouth opened in a scream. She braced her hands against the steering wheel and slammed on the brakes, but it was too late.

Much too late to avoid a collision.

Knowing what was coming, Beth braced herself, too, but nothing could have prepared her for the impact of the other vehicle slamming into the driver's-side door. The explosive noise of steel crashing against steel was loud enough to burst Beth's eardrums. Despite her death grip on the steering wheel, her arms were jerked free, tossed above her head like string as the other car plowed directly into her, spinning Beth and her car around and around.

She opened her mouth to scream, but all that escaped was a gasp of sheer terror and pain, horrific pain.

And then. . . . then there was nothing until she heard someone calling her name.

When she managed to force her eyes open all she could see was Sam.

# CHAPTER 1

# Beth

*The Friday before the accident*

"Give Mozart a chance," Beth Prudhomme pleaded with the teenaged boy who stared doggedly down at the classroom floor. "Once you listen to his music you'll feel differently, I promise."

The youth continued to avoid eye contact. "The only reason I signed up for this class is because Bailey did and now we're not together. I like music, but I'm not into that classical stuff."

"But you might be," Beth said in what she hoped was an encouraging voice. Johnny Folgate sat through the entire class period with his arms folded and his head bent over his desk. She doubted that he'd heard a single word of her lecture despite her enthusiasm. At one point she was convinced she heard him snoring.

"Can I go now?" he asked.

"Will you give it a week?" She gave it one more try.

Despite everything she'd said, Johnny didn't look convinced. "Do I have to?"

"No."

"Then I'd rather drop out."

"You said you enjoy music though, right?"

"Yeah, a lot. I play trumpet, but that classical stuff isn't me."

"You might surprise yourself." She really hated to see him drop out of the class. Although she'd only been teaching five years, Beth had seen several students have a change of heart when it came to learning about the great composers and listening to their music.

"A week?"

"A week," Beth repeated, feeling a twinge of hope. Johnny was exactly the kind of student she enjoyed most. By his own admission he was fond of music and was a band member, but he had no understanding or appreciation of the depth and beauty of the great compositions. If she could only light the spark in him and gently fan it into a gentle flame his eyes would open and his love for music would explode. The challenge, of course, was to keep him from dropping out of class.

"All right, but I'm only giving it this week."

"Fair enough."

He offered her a tentative smile.

"Thank you, Johnny."

He nodded and left the classroom.

Feeling like she'd made headway, Beth straightened her desk. It was Friday at the end of a long week of classes and she was more than ready for the weekend, not that she had any big plans. She was a recent transplant from Chicago, and the only person Beth knew, well other than a few teachers, was her aunt Sunshine. Just thinking about her eccentric, fun-loving aunt produced a smile. She didn't know what she would do without Sunshine. Her aunt had given her the courage and the encouragement to break away from the dictates of her family. Beth loved her parents, but they had definite ideas about who she should marry, her career, her friends, and just about everything else. Even now her mother bought her clothes, not trusting Beth to choose her own wardrobe. Without realizing what they were doing, her parents, her mother in particular, were strangling her. Either she broke away now or she'd suffocate. Sunshine was the one who'd invited Beth to move to Portland, Oregon. She'd helped her find an apartment and was a constant source of encouragement. To put it mildly Sunshine and Beth's mother didn't get along.

Beth collected her books and purse and was heading down the hallway when she heard her name.

"Beth." Nichole Nyquist called out from behind her.

"Hey," Beth said, smiling as she turned around, happy to run into her friend. It'd been a couple of weeks since they'd last connected, just before the start of the last semester. She'd met Nichole the first day of classes, and the two had immediately struck up a friendship. Nichole had given up her full-time position and currently worked as a substitute teacher after the birth of her son, Matthew. Seeing Nichole was a treat. "Good to see you."

"You, too. Do you have a minute?"

"Of course."

"I wanted to invite you to dinner tomorrow night."

"Oh." The invitation came as something of a surprise. She'd been to Nicole's house once, shortly after the baby was born, to bring her a gift, but that was it. They ate lunch together in the teachers' lounge when they could, but now that Nichole only worked intermittently, those times were rare.

"I know its last minute. I hoped to connect with you earlier and didn't, and the next thing I knew it was Friday. I've been thinking about this a while, and I do hope you can come."

"I don't have any plans," Beth said a bit wary of this sudden bout of chattiness from Nichole. "You've been thinking about what?" Nichole had left that part suspiciously blank.

"Ah . . ."

"Is there something you aren't telling me?"

Nichole scratched her ear and then let out a long sigh. "Actually there is. Rocco is inviting his best friend, Sam Carney, to dinner. I wanted the two of you to meet."

Beth held the textbook closer to her chest. So that was it. Nichole planned on setting her up with Rocco's friend. Normally that wouldn't be a problem. Nichole, however, seemed hesitant. Beth wondered what that was about. "Tell me a little about Sam."

Nichole paused as if she wasn't sure where to start. "He's a great guy and not bad looking either."

"Divorced? Single?"

"Single. Never been married. He's a mechanic, and from what Rocco tells me, he's one of the best in the city. What I do know is that he can fix just about anything. He's great with Matthew. I've never seen a man take to a baby the way he has. He's perfectly content to hold him, and he isn't averse to changing a diaper, either."

If nothing else Beth would know where to go if she experienced car trouble. Still she sensed there was something Nichole wasn't telling her. "And . . ." she prompted.

"And, well, Sam probably isn't like any other guy you've ever dated."

Seeing as her dating experience had been limited to an approved list from her mother, that wouldn't be difficult. Still, she felt obliged to ask, "Different in what way?"

Nichole glanced down the hall as if looking for someone. "It's hard to explain."

Beth waited, giving Nichole time to collect her thoughts.

Nichole sucked in a deep breath. "When I first met Sam, he was . . . I'm not sure how to explain it. Let's just say he was a bit unconventional . . . still is, for that matter."

That was a curious way of putting it. "How so?"

"He swore a lot."

"Not good."

"It's better now," she was quick to add. "Owen makes Sam pay him a dollar for every swear word he uses." She struggled to hold back a smile. "The first few months I was convinced he was going to pay for my son's college education."

Owen was Nichole's son from her first marriage. "Good for Owen."

"I can't say what Sam's language is like now, but

when he's around the house, his descriptive phrasing isn't as picturesque as it once was. Rocco and I don't get out as much as we once did so we don't see Sam socially much anymore. He stops by the house a couple of times a week, though. He's crazy about Matthew."

So he liked babies. That was a good sign. The swearing was troublesome though. Sure as anything her parents would cringe at the thought of her dating a mechanic, but then she'd specifically moved from Chicago to get out from under their thumb.

Ellie Prudhomme had definite ideas when it came to the man Beth would marry. Beth never doubted her parents' love. They set their standards high and expected her to exceed their expectations, and for most of her life, Beth had.

"Anything else you care to tell me about Sam?" she asked, undecided. Frankly this dinner didn't sound promising and could well be a waste of time on the part of everyone.

Nichole held her gaze. "Actually, I think it would be best if you made up your own mind about Sam. All I can tell you is that he's a really great guy. I had my doubts when I first met him, and you might, too. All I ask is that you give him a chance, okay?"

Beth nibbled on her lower lip. "Let me think about it. I'll get back to you either tonight or first thing tomorrow morning."

"I know it's a last-minute invite . . ."

"It's fine, Nichole. Thanks for thinking of me. I'll connect with you soon. Promise."

———

They left the building together, and by the time Beth reached her aunt Sunshine's studio, she'd decided against meeting Sam. It would be a waste of time on both their parts. From what little Nichole had said, it didn't appear they had anything in common. The music teacher and the mechanic.

Not a good match.

Not a good idea.

Sunshine was busy painting, her long, thick, salt-and-pepper hair hanging straight and loose, reaching all the way down to the middle of her back. Beth couldn't ever remember seeing her aunt in anything other than long skirts and Birkenstocks. She'd remained a flower child who never outgrew the 1960s. Concentrating on her work, Sunshine apparently didn't hear Beth enter her studio.

Standing back Beth waited and watched. Her aunt was a talented artist. Her work was highly desirable and hung in galleries all across the Pacific Northwest. What fascinated Beth was the prices she got for a few squiggly lines. It was between those lines that Sunshine's talent came to life. In that space was intricate artwork, cleverly hidden so that it became a part of a greater picture. It often took Beth several minutes to see the full picture.

This current project displayed rows upon rows of blooming poppies, their color vibrant against a backdrop of what appeared to be random strokes of black paint. She stared at it several minutes until she saw it. A school of fish. Unbelievable. Beth couldn't help being mesmerized.

Her aunt released a deep breath as if she'd been

holding it in and then relaxed, stepped back to consider her work, and nearly tripped over Beth.

"My love, how long have you been here?" she asked, setting down her paintbrush.

"Not long."

Sunshine apparently followed Beth's eyes and cocked her head to one side. "You like?"

"It's brilliant." As far as Beth was concerned there was no other word for it.

Sunshine tossed back her head and laughed, the sound bubbling up from her like champagne fizz. Beth loved hearing her aunt's laugher. It had a magical quality that never ceased to amuse her. Just listening to it made her want to laugh, too. She resisted the urge to close her eyes and store it in her memory bank for times when she was low and struggled with worry or frustration.

"You say that every time, you know?"

"Because it's true."

Sunshine walked over to the tiny refrigerator, similar to the one in Beth's college dorm room, opened it, and took out a bottle of water. Handing one to Beth, she grabbed another for herself. "To what do I owe this pleasure?"

Beth felt a little silly turning to her aunt for advice. "I have a question for you."

"Fire away." Stretching out her arm, Sunshine saluted her with the water bottle.

"A friend asked me to dinner tomorrow night and . . ."

"Male or female?"

"Female, but it's a set up. She wants me to meet a friend of her husband's; technically he's her friend, too, I guess." Beth felt a little funny talking about this but the fact was she was rather naïve when it came to men and relationships.

"And the problem is?"

Beth leaned her backside against the edge of the table and waved her hand back and forth, unsure how to explain. "To hear Nichole tell it, he's a bit coarse, what my mother would term as uncivilized."

"You've mentioned Nichole before haven't you?"

Beth took a sip of water and nodded. "Yes, she was one of the first teachers to welcome me at the high school. She's friendly and kind. I have her stepdaughter in one of my classes."

"Again, my dear, the problem is?"

"Sunshine," Beth cried, "I can only imagine what my mother would say if she heard I'd agreed to have dinner with a mechanic."

Sunshine set her water bottle aside and cupped Beth's face with both hands, staring deeply into her dark eyes. "My dear girl, that is your problem in a nutshell. You are living your life to please your mother. This man . . ."

"His name is Sam."

"Sam could be the most wonderful man you're likely to meet. You haven't even met him, and you're already judging him, deciding he is undesirable. My dear girl, take a chance." She lowered her hands and gave an expressive sigh. "I knew a Sam once, and fell instantly in love with him. He was another artist, unconventional, crazy talented, married, but I didn't learn that until much later when it was too late and he'd stolen my heart."

"Oh no." Beth had never heard her aunt talk about

anyone named Sam. But then there'd always been men in and out of Sunshine's life.

"I have no complaints. When we were together it was glorious; a time I will always treasure. We were so alike, so in tune with one another. It was as if we were made for each other." A wistful look and a smile stole over her as if caught up in the memory of her love affair.

"Is he the reason you never married?" Beth hadn't dared to ask the question before.

"Because of Sam?" she repeated and shook her head. "Oh dear, not at all. He was one of my many lovers. It was a good thing he was married, otherwise we would have grown to hate each other—we were far too alike. But while it lasted . . . it was heaven."

"Do you really think I should agree to this blind date?"

"Beth, my beautiful, beautiful child, of course you should. Let go of your inhibitions, live free, fall in love; make the most of this opportunity. Who knows, this Sam could end up being the man of your dreams."

Beth managed to suppress a giggle. "Do you really think that's possible?"

"Why not? You'll never know if you decide not to go. Be positive; throw away your doubts and pretend you're meeting a prince."

From the meager description Nichole had given her Sam sounded nothing like royalty. Still, her aunt was right. She needed to give meeting him a shot. No harm, no foul.

Beth kissed her aunt's cheek and left wearing a smile. Fact was, she couldn't ever remember leaving Sunshine without smiling.

As soon as she was home Beth sent Nichole a text.

**Count me in.**

Not more than a minute passed when she got a return text.

**Great. C U at six.**


Beth knew it was a mistake to feel the least bit optimistic about this blind date. She'd heard about blind dates from her friends often enough to know they rarely worked out.

Even with all her doubts, she spent Saturday morning filled with happy anticipation, a sense of excitement. She had two piano students in the morning, which left her afternoon free.

When the time came to get ready it took her nearly two hours to decide what to wear. She didn't want to appear too formal in a dress or skirt nor would she be comfortable dressed casually in jeans and a sweater.

Before long she had nearly her entire closet laid across the top of her bed. In the end, five minutes before she was scheduled to leave, she decided on black leggings and a white linen top. Instead of heels she wore ballet slippers. Giving herself one final inspection, she drew in a deep breath, gazed at herself in the full-length mirror in her hallway, and decided this was about as good as it got. She looked a little like Audrey Hepburn in *Breakfast at Tiffany's,* although she wasn't nearly as beautiful as the iconic actor.

As she left her apartment complex Sunshine's words rang in her head.

*This could be the man of your dreams.*

At twenty-five, with twenty-six fast approaching,

Beth hoped that was true. Making her own way in life was the very reason she'd left Chicago. She was her own woman, living as she pleased, making her own decisions, and as Sunshine would say, living free.

And Beth was ready.

So very ready.

# Join DEBBIE MACOMBER
## on social media!

Facebook.com/debbiemacomberworld

@debbiemacomber

Pinterest.com/macomberbooks

Instagram.com/debbiemacomber

Visit DebbieMacomber.com
and sign up for Debbie's e-newsletter!